FORTUNE'S KISS

FORTUNE'S KISS

AMBER CLEMENT

UNION
SQUARE
& CO.

NEW YORK

UNION SQUARE & CO.

NEW YORK

ISBN 978-1-4549-5021-9 (hardcover)
ISBN 978-1-4549-5022-6 (e-book)
ISBN 978-1-4549-5023-3 (paperback)

Library of Congress Cataloging-in-Publication Data

Names: Clement, Amber, author.
Title: Fortune's kiss / by Amber Clement.
Description: New York : Union Square, 2024. | Audience: Ages 14 and up. | Summary: "Two best friends enter into a magical gambling den and wager their lives in exchange for their wildest dreams"— Provided by publisher.
Identifiers: LCCN 2024005968 (print) | LCCN 2024005969 (ebook) | ISBN 9781454950219 (hardcover) | ISBN 9781454950233 (paperback) | ISBN 9781454950226 (epub)
Subjects: CYAC: Magic—Fiction. | Gambling—Fiction. | Best friends— Fiction. | Friendship—Fiction. | Fantasy. | BISAC: YOUNG ADULT FICTION / Fantasy / Dark Fantasy | YOUNG ADULT FICTION / Fantasy / Historical | LCGFT: Fantasy fiction. | Novels.
Classification: LCC PZ7.1.C594756 Fo 2024 (print) | LCC PZ7.1.C594756 (ebook) | DDC [Fic]—dc23
LC record available at https://lccn.loc.gov/2024005968
LC ebook record available at https://lccn.loc.gov/2024005969

For information about custom editions, special sales, and premium purchases, please contact specialsales@unionsquareandco.com.

Printed in the United States of America

2 4 6 8 10 9 7 5 3 1

unionsquareandco.com

Created in association with Electric Postcard Entertainment, Inc.

Cover and interior design by Marcie Lawrence
Cover art by Jorge Mascarenhas
Interior image credits: Shutterstock.com: Irina-PITTORE: 250 (old paper); Ivchenko Evgeniya: 6 (skulls); Vecster.com: 6 (pinned note); Vector Tradition: throughout (flowers)

To my grandma Teresa. There was no magic or fortune to help you, but you've done so much for your family. Thank you for believing in me and my dreams.

It is here.
The legendary:
~EL BESO DE LA FORTUNA~

FORTUNE'S KISS

Try your luck to make your
greatest desires manifest.
If you dare . . .
Will fortune spare you a kiss?

ONE

Mayté

Three silver coins stood between Mayté Robles and her dreams. *Three.*

"You *must* pay off your bill before you can make any more purchases."

Mayté scowled at the buffoon of a new shopkeeper. "*No,* señor. I don't," she hissed between gritted teeth and pressed her fingers against the paint jar she needed to purchase. The glass was smooth and sturdy; it didn't threaten to shatter into a thousand sharp pieces. Like she did. "The other owner always allowed me to keep a tab. It's always been that way." She nudged the jar forward, trying her best to smooth down the cracks in her demeanor. "My bill really isn't that high. Only two silver coins. Then another silver coin for this purchase. I need this to finish a big commission."

Not *just* a big commission. Her once-in-a-lifetime opportunity: a painting for Señora Castro. If she could pull this off, the noble woman would become her patron for life.

The commission itself was simple. A garden portrait of Señora Castro's beloved pack of Xoloitzcuintlis. Mayté didn't care much for the hairless dogs, all wiry, wrinkly, and flimsy. With ears thinner than tortillas and tails that belonged on rats.

It was beyond her why the Castros pampered the Xolos as if they were royalty, but the handsome payment offered was enough to silence her disdain. Mayté would paint ugly dogs for the rest of her life if it meant no more scrounging and worrying.

She hadn't slept for almost two days, but she never felt more alive than she did with a paintbrush in hand. Mixing vivid colors into the perfect concoction and layering them onto a crisp white canvas, she had absolute control over the outcome. She was the goddess of the canvas, creating everything in her own image.

Outside of the canvas, though, it was a different story.

Nothing would have stopped a goddess, yet here she was, begging for a jar of azure paint. It was needed for the garden's signature morning glories and the cloudless sky of a lazy day. "I'll pay off my debt after I turn in the commission, and you will always have a loyal customer." She smiled, smooth and perfect like porcelain.

The shopkeeper stroked his goatee, which was graying and pointy. His golden-brown forehead wrinkled as his dark gaze flitted over her, razor-sharp. Mayté stiffened, fingers tightening around her rebozo. She wasn't some item needing to be appraised. *She* was the one who would soon put coins in *his* pocket. Why did anything else about her matter?

She pressed her lips tight. *Just endure a little more.*

The shopkeeper adjusted his straw hat and pursed his chapped lips. Mayté unfortunately was all too familiar with the malice oozing from such a face, like garish paint through thin parchment.

"You're a Robles, no?"

She should have anticipated this, yet her insides still iced over.

The rest of the shop's clientele slowed what they were doing, casting sideways glances. The air shifted as their whispers pierced the air.

"*Of course a Robles would hold up the line.*"

"*That entire family is full of trouble.*"

Her skin prickled and the hairs on her arm stood up. If she had been trapped in a painting, she would have titled it *La hija de la desgracia*. The Daughter of Misfortune. "Why does that matter?" Mayté croaked.

"How do I know your earnings won't just up and float away to the heavens?" The shopkeeper's mustache curled as he sneered. "If there even is a commission in the first place."

Snickers joined the hushed choir of gossip.

"There is," Mayté gasped, heat flushing her cheeks and surely lighting them up like roses—a flower she hated sketching, but enjoyed painting lovely shades of red. Her bronze skin had a reddish undertone. The kind that always gave her away whenever she felt the least bit angry or embarrassed, and right now she was *both*.

"Then where would you get the money to pay me back, hmm?" he continued as if she hadn't said a thing. "Your family barely has a coin to their name."

"I've always been able to pay back my—"

"Enough." The shopkeeper raised a hand, skin perfectly smooth. He didn't have the faded stains of paint on his nails or the calluses that came with being an artist. Of course he wouldn't understand . . . "Why do you think the last owner sold his shop to me? Too much debt from people not paying their bills. This is my business now, and this is the way it will be. Come back when you can afford the supplies."

Mayté's nostrils flared. The robust odor of paint dizzied her—paint she needed but couldn't have.

All because of this bullheaded oaf.

Fire consumed her, burning away all thoughts of reason. "Fine!" She snatched the pot of paint off the counter.

The owner's eyes widened, and his mouth gaped open. *Thief!* he likely wanted to shriek, but Mayté was no criminal. She wouldn't stoop *that* low. With a thin smile, she let the pot slip from her fingers. Azure paint spurted up like a triumphant fountain as the glass shattered into thousands of shards. Destroyed. Just like her plans to finish her commission. She turned on her heels and stomped away, passing stunned customers. Now they would have something meaningful to whisper about for once—and, even better, the shopkeeper couldn't make even a coin on the paint.

"Get back here, girl!" the owner roared. Mayté picked up her pace. Past the swatches of parchment in a variety of colors—lively teal like the ocean, a deep sunset orange, and rich cactus green. No one tried to stop her. Those cowards wouldn't. She stepped outside. The summer breeze carried freedom along with the scent of the distant ocean and fried tortillas. She pulled her rebozo over her head before completing her escape into the crowded street mercado.

The market was the heart of Milagro. Always packed during the summer and located between the pueblo district—with its homes stacked atop each other and ladders used to reach the higher levels—and the cathedrals all competing for the holy attention of Dios and Los Santos Sagrados. Every morning, vendors set up their stalls and tents on the dusty streets and stayed until sundown. Their quirky assortment of wares added a welcome burst of color against the surrounding stucco buildings, all dull shades of sand and cream with matching orange rooftops.

Mayté pushed her way through a family clad in brightly patterned skirts and rebozos. No one could catch her now.

Paint wasn't her only errand of the day; she could only hope
the next one would yield much better results. Clutching her
satchel close, she journeyed deeper through the mercado. She
passed stands selling fresh plantains, limes, and mangoes along
with finely ground pungent spices. Vibrantly patterned serapes
for sale dangled from wires above. The curandera sat in the next
stall over, preparing her healing herbs. Nearby, a man was
offering his nosy mules to the highest bidder. He screamed and
cursed as one of the mules floated away. A group of snickering
kids scurried off. One of them tossed an empty potion bottle
onto the street.

Mayté frowned. Children so young shouldn't have been
allowed to play with potions. One of these days, an accident was
sure to happen. A guard clad in a green-and-red uniform stood
idly nearby, his golden helmet reflecting the harsh sunlight. He
barely blinked at the unfolding chaos. Guards like him only
cared about keeping President Juan Manuel Hernández happy.
Likewise, the corrupt president only cared about being in good
standing with the wealthiest nobles and most influential clergy.
A couple of street kids flirting with danger were of no concern
to any of them.

Mayté passed a religious stand selling rosary beads, prayer
candles, and blessed charms dedicated to Los Santos. They
always stocked up on ones for San Amor, San Fortuno, and Santa
Prosperidad. The neighboring stand belonged to the bruja. She
was clad in a white dress with red and blue patterns, offering
encantos and tarot readings.

A horse-drawn carriage sped by, almost trampling a man
crossing the street. The man cursed, which in turn agitated a

group of men eating street tacos. Mayté got out of the way just as a fistfight broke out. Fried corn tortillas, soft lengua, and reddish al pastor meat dropped to the ground. What a waste. At least the seagulls would get a feast. Already a group of the white birds had landed and begun to devour the tacos.

Just another day in Milagro.

With a squawk, the seagulls flew off toward the distant mountains.

Some people wished they could turn into a bird and fly away from their problems, but Mayté wished for the seagulls to carry away her problems instead.

She rounded the corner, and the sizzling scent of elote hit her nose. Señor Vásquez must have just started a fresh batch. Her heart pounded in anticipation as she approached the stall. Señor Vásquez swayed over the steaming corncobs, sprinkling chile and cotija cheese on top. As he spun, he skillfully squirted fresh lime over everything. A true artist. Everything about the stout man sparked with joy. His big curly head of hair and bigger grin. His round face, rich and dark with ruddy undertones, beamed as bright as the sun. His teeth may have been yellowing, and deep furrows hung around his eyes, but these just added to his lively air. Joy like that couldn't be contained. Despite everything that had happened at the shop, Mayté couldn't stop grinning.

"Buenos días. I have something for you." Gingerly she reached into her satchel and pulled out a wooden sign. Bright-green painted letters read: FRESH ELOTES 3 BRONZE COINS. Below the letters she had painted a corncob. It had been quite fun sprinkling on red paint to represent the chile. She had tweaked it for hours, until looking at it made her stomach tingle with hunger. Only then did she know it was ready.

"Oh. How wonderful!" Señor Vásquez leaned over the counter to study the sign. "Thank you, thank you!"

"Of course!" This project may have been small fish compared to the commission, but maybe the payment would be enough to buy paint from one of the stalls. They weren't as good quality as the ones sold in the shop, and it was always a toss-up on which colors would be in stock that day, but she would make it work.

"Well, you see, I won't be able to pay you in coins this time."

Oh.

"I still owe you, of course." With a sheepish smile, Señor Vásquez took the sign and set it on the counter.

Everything inside her deflated, but she tried not to let it show on her face. It would be hypocritical to get upset. "Ay, this sign will bring you more business and you'll be able to pay me in no time!"

"Sí, sí!" Señor Vásquez brightened. "But in the meantime, I'll give you this. Elote on me and"—he ducked down, disappearing under the counter—"a potion. My sister-in-law brewed it just last night, and she really knows her stuff, you know? Why, last month she made a love potion for our cousin, and now the lucky fellow is getting married!"

"Really?" There were always several vendors in the mercado selling potions for cheap and promising miracles, but it was a gamble whether they truly worked. As they said, "You get what you pay for," and only the wealthy had access to the reliable stuff.

"Here."

Mayté took the bottle and turned it in her hands. It was made of clay—no way to tell what was inside. "What kind is it?" she asked. Icy-blue No Más Tristeza elixir would brighten her mood. Dame Energía looked rather unpleasant with its bouncing chartreuse slime, but it would give her the boost she needed to keep going for the rest of the day. Really, she would take almost any kind of potion except for Joven Para Siempre. That stuff made her squirm since it was thick and deep crimson, like blood.

"This"—Señor Vásquez rubbed the palms of his beefy hands—"is Una Pizca de Suerte."

A pinch of luck was something she could use. "Thank you." Mayté uncorked the bottle and guzzled the potion as Señor Vásquez prepared elote for her. Fizzy and sweet with a metallic aftertaste, it stung her throat on the way down. She put the empty bottle in her satchel as he handed over a cob on a stick.

Wasting no time, she took a big bite, not bothering to wipe the juice running down her chin. Sweet corn, spicy chile, salty cheese, and sour lime had to be the most irresistible combination.

A spark of gratitude tickled her insides. Elote was always a comfort—a welcome treat on the bad days or a relief from hunger when there wasn't enough food at home. Her five brothers always had to eat before her—the unspoken law of the Robles family. Which made that new shopkeeper's assumptions even more infuriating. She couldn't depend on her family. Never had. Never would. It wasn't fair to lump her with them, not when she was the one fending for herself.

She took another big bite, throat burning. Whether it was from her lingering fury or the spicy chiles was debatable. Elote might briefly fix some problems, but not this one. Mayté didn't want to go home and face the unfinished canvas. *Or* deal with her family. Her father always left as soon as he woke up, while her mother cooked and tended to her younger brothers. Maybe in a normal family she would have been able to cry about her woes to her mother, but no, all the sympathy had been wrung out of the woman years ago. Now she was dry and brittle. She wouldn't bat an eye or offer a hug. Instead, she would just say "Así es la vida." But that wasn't the life Mayté wanted. She refused to accept it.

"It's back! It's back in Milagro," a man yelled as he ran down the street.

Mayté turned. Carriages stopped. Shop owners stepped away from their stalls. Everyone spoke all at once.

"Appeared at midnight."

"Could it be real?"

"It must be. Don't you remember what happened ten years ago?"

Ten years ago.

"Well, then. The rumors must be true," Señor Vásquez muttered to himself. He rubbed his chin. "This could change everything."

Mayté's pulse quickened. Could it be? She rushed through the crowd, her plaited hair bouncing against her back. Her rebozo flew in the breeze like wings wanting to take flight. All around, everyone spoke of it. The rumors swirled in the thick humid air.

"They say it will be even grander than last time."

"Ay, son solo encantos y trucos. ¡Nada más!"

"No, no, you know what happens to those who win!"

"And what of those who lose?"

"They wander aimless like ghosts. Worse off than street beggars."

"But the risk more than makes up for the reward."

Mayté's ears pounded, making it even harder to hear.

Then she saw it.

Plastered on the smooth adobe walls of the grand cathedral like a divine blasphemy, a poster, black as ink. An ornate calavera contrasted with the dark background, outlined in shimmering amber as if penned with pure magic. Big white teeth, the *only* white on the entire page, grinned at her, as wide flowery eyes stared into her soul. She ran a finger over the skull's swirly floral pattern.

The rest of the poster's text was that same magical amber. In the harsh sunlight, it twinkled like the stars at night. IT IS HERE. THE LEGENDARY EL BESO DE LA FORTUNA.

"Fortune's Kiss," Mayté choked out, then slapped a hand over her mouth. As if saying it out loud would chase away the mirage. But no. This was real. It was happening. *Finally.*

Twice a year, during the summer and winter solstices, Fortune's Kiss was said to appear in a random city without warning, sometimes seemingly swallowing up whole buildings. But once it was there, it opened its doors for those brave enough to gamble. Those willing to accept the high stakes.

Now Fortune's Kiss had chosen Milagro once again.

A tiny lizard darted along the wall but kept away from the poster, as if the paper were cursed. But it was just the opposite. *This* was the biggest blessing.

Try your luck to make your greatest desires manifest, Mayté read. She let out a breath. Her greatest desires... To make a name for herself as a painter with enough money and commissions to support herself.

To be free from the weight of her family's name.

If you dare...

Yes, yes, she did. She would do anything to make her dream come true.

Mayté ripped the poster off the wall and held it against her chest. In her other hand, she squeezed the empty bottle of Una Pizca de Suerte. Señor Vásquez's sister-in-law was really onto something. Most potions only had temporary effects—it made the business more lucrative—but something told Mayté that her luck wouldn't run out anytime soon.

Her father claimed that the family fortune had floated away. All the way up to the sun, where it had melted into starlight, but no one believed him. Mayté heard enough whispers to form her own conclusion. Gambling. He had gambled it all away like a fool after Abuelita passed on. And to further ruin everything he became a drunkard, refusing to work and speaking barely a syllable to anyone. Their family had once been highly regarded. They had been members of Las Cinco Familias, representing everything the country of San Solera stood for. Still, the Robles's powerful bloodline couldn't make up for the damage her father had done, and soon Las Cinco became Las Cuatro. All because of him.

But now it was Mayté's turn to gamble. She wouldn't lose like her father. No, she would succeed, rise above everyone else, and forsake them for what they'd done to her.

Father, for not picking up the pieces of his life and running away from his problems.

Mother, for putting everything into her brothers and neglecting her.

Her brothers, for taking all that was left without leaving Mayté even the smallest of scraps. The list was endless . . .

The rest of Las Cuatro for shunning her.

The girls who stopped inviting her to parties.

The boys who suddenly forgot she existed.

She wouldn't need Señora Castro's commission, or that greedy shopkeeper's business either. Like imperfections on the canvas, she would paint over them until her life was pristine, flawless. She would blot out every last person—

Except for Lo. Her best friend.

They had a pact, the two of them. One that Mayté could never forget.

She studied her left palm. The thin straight scar cut straight through the middle. When she closed her eyes, she saw Lo's round cherub face and wild curls. Felt the misty breeze that cooled their skin. The dusty dirt under their knees. Tiny fingers trembling as they cut into each other's palms, then warm and sticky red hands clasping together. A pact by blood.

Still clutching the poster, she ran as fast as she could. She needed to tell Lo.

"If Fortune's Kiss returns to Milagro, we're entering. No matter what."

Mayté still heard Lo's words all these years later.

"No matter what," she whispered back.

TWO

Lo

Every girl dreamed of her wedding day. Fantasized about the suitors competing for her hand. Relished the doting attention, beautiful gowns, and anticipation of what was to come.

But Lorena de León did not.

Surrounded by bustling maids clad in black dresses and white shawls, she was dressed like a princess. Her custom gown, cream-colored with cheerful yellow vertical stripes, flattered her figure. Fitted from torso to hips, the gown flared into ruffles below. A white rose sat on her right shoulder with delicate fabric raining down like a cape. But a true princess wouldn't feel so suffocated. So desperate to be anywhere but here. She winced as Talia, the maid, yanked her hair into submission. It was always a long and arduous process to imprison, or rather *tame*, her curls into a proper bun. Her tender scalp screamed, and it took everything inside her to keep from yelping.

"Oh, don't make that dreadful face," her younger sister, Sera, scolded from a nearby love seat. "Stop being so dramatic. It doesn't even hurt." She scowled, making the mole resting above her lip bounce. The expression on her face was much too serious for a girl her age. At only fourteen, she acted more like an adult. Looked the part too, always wearing her dark brown waves in a tight bun and her perfect bronze skin dusted in gold. Today she wore a white lace blouse and a fitted black skirt with azure patterns. The only facet of her appearance that gave away her age was her figure. Slender with barely any curves. It was the only way in which she was a late bloomer.

"Oh, hush." Lo glared at Sera through the mirror. The room's soft cream walls only served to accentuate the eclectic items inside it: the ornate rug, red as freshly mined rubies; the colorful vases all imported from far-off countries. Yet what caught Lo's attention the most wasn't something bought—it was the cloudless blue sky visible through the doorways. A soft breeze cut through the parlor, teasing her.

"You look beautiful, though." Sera's sharp expression softened with a dreamy sigh. "Once it's my turn, I want a purple gown. A pink one, too."

Lo laughed. Sera had been looking forward to her debut since she was five, always talking about it and planning how she would handle her suitors. Lo had never felt like that. Instead, as the years flew by, a knot of dread formed in her chest that grew bigger and bigger. Now at seventeen, less than a year away from marriage age, the knot tangled all the way up to her throat, threatening to choke her. Was there anything about reaching courting age that she looked forward to? She had never given herself the chance to decide.

Just as Talia finished pinning Lo's hair, another maid rushed into the room. Lo smiled. Carmen, her favorite.

"El Señor regresa," Carmen whispered. Beads of sweat glistened on her forehead and a deep flush colored her pale brown cheeks. She must have run all the way here to warn them. Carmen's urgent eyes stared straight at Lo. The message was clear. The warning wasn't for the maids.

This was the exact reason Lo favored her. She would never forget the muggy afternoon many years ago when she carelessly played around in this very room despite Mamá's warnings. Of course, she had spun herself dizzy and clumsily stumbled into the shelf, knocking over a crystalline vase. Carmen, who had been dusting, witnessed everything. And when Lo's father came around huffing and puffing, Carmen quickly took the blame.

But now it seemed that even Carmen couldn't save her. Lo's stomach churned, and the other maids broke into worried whispers. "Go find Sofía and start on your studies," Lo told her sister.

"But I—" Sera began to argue.

"Go!" Lo pointed to the hallway.

"Fine." Sera stomped off.

She didn't understand, and Lo would see to it that she never did.

"Welcome back, señor." The maids spoke in unison and bowed.

Salvador de León strode into the parlor, his clean-shaven face the color of copper and his expression cold as steel. With his tall, broad stature and long black sideburns, many found him handsome, yet the maids always seemed much more nervous than enamored.

"We just finished up the fitting," Talia said. Her eyes wouldn't quite meet Lo's father's hard gaze.

"I see," he mused, his expression still unreadable. "You may leave." He waved the maids away. One by one they obeyed, though Carmen looked back, round eyes extra wide. Lo wished she could leave with her. But that wasn't how it worked. Soon it was just Lo and her father.

"Lorena."

"Papá." Ignoring her pounding heart, she straightened her shoulders and clasped her hands together like a proper young woman. "What do you think?"

He stared with narrowed eyes. His eyes were always like that, and his lips seemed stuck in a half smirk. At least, when he wasn't snarling.

Lo tried not to fidget. She could never tell what he was thinking at moments like this. Still silence before an earthquake. She tried her best to sense any tremors.

"I suppose," he grunted, "your suitors will find it favorable."

She exhaled. Prickles spread across her achy scalp.

"I've whittled down your choices. Only the finest families will be considered. I must keep our legacy strong."

Not "you" or even "we." Just *him*. Lo had no say in the matter.

"Oh, Papá," she cooed, hugging his arm. "But what about you? What do *you* think of my gown?" She stepped back and gave a twirl. She caught her face in the mirror, her beguiling smile slipping away and hardening. The older Lo grew, the more she detested dancing. Her feet grew weary from standing too long. Yet this song and dance had gone on for years. She couldn't take it much longer. She put her face back together as she turned to her father. Just in time for him to grab her chin and roughly tilt her head toward him.

"You look just like *her*." His eyes narrowed into slits. "With each passing day, you remind me more and more of your mother."

From any other father, this would have been a compliment. The highest compliment, in fact. But from Lo's father, it was a curse. Unlike her sisters, Lo's thick, curly hair was a lighter brown, especially this time of year when the sun embraced her strands. Her brown eyes drooped and her features were soft and rounded, yet striking all the same. Just like Mamá.

Her father hated it.

He never admitted it, let alone explained why, but Lo *knew*. Ten years ago, Mamá had fled. Never to return, and never to be found. But oh, did her father try to find her. Lo still remembered his barking demands as the search parties came back empty-handed. Without a doubt, if the man could have turned back time, he would have done anything in his power to keep Mamá from leaving. Even if it meant chaining her up. Unfortunately for him, time manipulation was a concept out of reach for even the most powerful of brujas.

He made up for this by exerting his dominance over Lo. Ruling her life, dictating her future. *Imprisoning her.* A beautiful cage with golden bars wrapped in delicate lace was still a cage. And she had no hope for escape.

His fingers dug into her cheeks. Hard. Rough nails bit into her skin. She tried not to wince.

"Don't ever betray me like she did," he hissed.

"Never ever." Lo stared intently into her father's eyes, numb to the lies escaping her lips.

"Promise me," he demanded.

Never ever will I be true to you.

"I promise." She sweetly smiled. *Agree and smile. Smile and agree.* That was one of the first lessons she had learned during her childhood.

Satisfied, her father released her. She caught her reflection. Pink marks from her father's nails marred her lower cheeks. If a maid had been there, she would have dabbed them with healing elixir, one of the most expensive potions. The concoction, shining like a star, erased bruises, scrapes, and other signs of her father's . . . temper. Yet it never chased away the dark thoughts blotting Lo's mind.

Just once, she wanted to make that man feel what he did to her. To squeeze his arm until purple bruises formed. To speak to him as though his thoughts were worthless. She would have loved to snatch his hand away from her face. *Never touch me like that again!* she wanted to yell.

"Serafina's almost of courting age. I hope she's been keeping up with her lessons."

Lo snapped out of her thoughts. "Sera's been doing very well, especially with her needlework." She was genuinely perfect. Too perfect. At her age, she should have been allowed to be messy and make mistakes.

"I already have some prospects for her. If all goes according to plan, she can marry a Las Cuatro boy as well. Sofía too. No more spending all her days in the stables. She must start acting like a proper young woman, or else no man will want her."

Sofía was only eleven. *A child.*

Did he even think of them as daughters, or solely as pawns to be traded? Assets used in the competition for control of Las Cuatro? With that kind of power, he would have more influence than even the president.

"I would much rather die than see you or your sisters wed below your potential."

Then maybe you should die.

Her own thought startled her. She turned back to the mirror just in time to see someone rush into the parlor. It wasn't either of her sisters, or a servant. "Mayté?"

Panting, Mayté hunched over. Her rebozo slid off her arms and tiny baby hairs stuck up from her braid. Her brown face was slick with a sheen of sweat, and her rosy cheeks bloomed bright red.

"María Teresa." Lo's father turned away and rubbed his mouth, clearly frustrated. He hated being interrupted. Good. Served him right. After composing himself, he scowled at Mayté. Lo hated the way he looked at her best friend. As if she were even lower than the servants. Yet, years ago, he would go carousing with Mayté's father, back when the Robles family had money to their name. Now it was as if that friendship had never existed. *Disgusting.*

"What brings *you* here?" Lo's father asked coldly.

"Papá, please," Lo sweetly scolded, ignoring the look of contempt her father flashed her. Surely, he would punish her later. He always demanded that she spend more time with the girls in their social circle. But Mayté was her best friend and the one part of her life she refused to include in this charade. She really didn't give a damn if something so trivial ruined her reputation.

"Buen día, señor. I'm doing well today, in case you were curious." Mayté lifted her chin. "I came to see Lo." No matter how many times Lo's father tried to chase her away, Mayté was like a mosquito. Either she would get her feast of blood or she would die trying.

Lo absolutely loved her for it.

"Welcome, welcome!" Lo waltzed over and kissed Mayté's right cheek before dragging her to the mirror. "Do you like my new gown?" She twirled once again.

"It's very nice. The yellow suits you."

"Oh, really? It's becoming my favorite color, you know."

"Is that so?" Mayté fidgeted, clutching the paper in her hands.

Lo studied her father through the glass. He impatiently tugged at the sleeve of his dress shirt. *Waiting.* Of course he was. Always around when he wasn't needed. The butler, Alfredo, strode in and spoke to him in a hushed voice, then helped him into his suit jacket, brown and embroidered with gold.

"Lorena," her father gruffed. "I have some business to attend to."

Business. He always spoke of his business, trading and selling land, yet Lo wasn't convinced that that was the full story. Some nights he returned in the wee hours of the morning, suit coat wide open and shirt ruffled, with a stupid smile on his face. Lo wasn't all that old when she overheard whispers about her father's mistresses. Mamá had been sitting nearby watering her potted plants and hadn't even batted an eye.

"Once you are done here, you are to tutor your sisters and continue your needlework until tonight's dinner banquet, where you will sing." Her father put on his hat and waited expectantly for her response.

A banquet and singing. On such short notice! To some, it might appear that her father was simply keeping her on her toes, but she knew without a doubt that he did it to torture her. These so-called banquets were all the same. Suitors would arrive, teeth gleaming, ready to spend the meal sucking up to her father while she and her sisters performed and sat quietly unless spoken to. A dreadfully boring affair.

"Yes, Papá." Lo obediently lowered her head like the dutiful daughter she never was.

She perked back up once he left. Mayté collapsed onto a chair, fanning her cheeks. By now, her entire face was flushed, almost as red as the flowers on her long, billowing skirt. "I thought he'd never leave."

Lo burst out laughing. "At least *you* don't have to live with him." Ever so carefully, so as not to upset her already achy scalp, she undid her bun and shook out her hair. Her thick curls sprang back to life, happy and free.

"Hmph. My father's never home," Mayté teased. "Trust me, it doesn't help."

The two had perhaps the worst fathers in all of Milagro, and they had been together for it all. Lo hid out with Mayté whenever her father was in one of his moods, breaking vases and raising his voice, while Lo lent Mayté dresses and coins whenever her family had to sell off their stuff to make up for her drunkard father's shenanigans. Both girls understood that the other was in a terrible situation, but it was never a competition to see who had it worse. That was why Mayté was one of the only people Lo could trust. Even more so than her own sisters.

"Ay, you look horrible." Lo sat across from her best friend and scrutinized her. The dark circles under her eyes looked like black petals from a cursed rose. All the wrinkles in her short-sleeved top gave away that she likely hadn't changed clothes in at least a day. Black paint stained her nailbeds, and there were flakes of green in her left eyebrow. Lo bit back a laugh. "Were you up all night painting again?" She took the opportunity to snatch Mayté's rebozo, tan and dull, and set it aside. Lo had never liked the dreadful things. They weren't very flattering and seemed like a hassle to carry around.

"Two nights." Mayté proudly grinned, but then let out a sound somewhere between a huff and a yawn. "But that's a story for another time. Look!" She handed the paper to Lo.

"Hmm?" Lo smoothed it out on her lap. A poster of a calavera. She ran her fingers across the parchment, dark as night, and the lettering winked in the sunlight. She skimmed the text, though she didn't get very far before gasping. "Fortune's Kiss?" Her mind raced, but everything was a blur. Like fiesta lights in the distance. They swirled into something beautiful, yet terrifying. "Mayté." Lo looked over her shoulder to make sure they were alone. "Is this real?"

It couldn't be. But what if it was?

Her pulse quickened and a flush crept up the back of her neck. Ten years ago, when Mamá ran away, her destination had been Fortune's Kiss. Loretta de León was supposed to return with a fortune big enough to set herself and her daughters free.

She had promised.

"Yes!" Mayté scooted to the edge of her seat and took Lo's hands, giving them a squeeze. "Think of all the duos that have won. The Lucky Angels, and weren't there those lovers from Milagro a long time ago?"

Lo remembered the legend of the Lucky Angels. Everyone did. Twin brothers named after archangels who stuck together and emerged from the game victorious. Their lives became heaven on earth. She couldn't quite remember what happened to the lovers. "What did they win again?"

Mayté shrugged. "More than we can imagine. The point is, that could be *us*."

It was true. The story was that every time Fortune's Kiss appeared, there emerged a winner or two who left with a huge fortune and their wildest dreams fulfilled. But still—

"It's risky," Lo whispered. Those who returned from the game as losers were a mess. Not only broke and humiliated, but barely uttering more than a few words and never leaving their homes.

Many didn't return from the game at all.

Like Mamá . . .

Whispers floated around that Mamá simply ran away. Some were certain she fled with another man, while others thought she was dead. But Lo knew better. Mamá definitely went to Fortune's Kiss and must have gambled and lost. Surely, she was stuck repaying her debts. Returning empty-handed wouldn't have helped anyone . . .

"Well, I for one am willing to risk it," Mayté said. "I'm tired of the way things are, and I know you are too. Those people who came back with nothing weren't thinking things through. If we lose, we can stay and spend a few years paying off our debts. In the meantime, the house will travel the world and we'll be along for the journey! I know it's not perfect, but isn't it better than what we have now?" She smirked, and all the exhaustion smeared on her face seemed to magically fade. "Remember our pact?"

Instinctively, Lo touched the scar on her right palm. How could she forget? She used to watch Mayté draw pictures in the dirt, imagining how Fortune's Kiss looked: a castle made of clouds and rainbows. The perfect fairy-tale escape for two little girls. But that was all it had been, a fantasy.

Now it was real. Risk. Reward. Everything.

Lo shuddered and rubbed her arms. Back then, their dreams had been much simpler. To live like princesses without any burdens or responsibility.

That was before Mamá left.

Before Mayté's family fell from grace.

"This might be our only chance," Mayté continued, her dark eyes full of fire. "Don't you want to gamble?"

Did she? Lo's heart skipped a beat. She looked between the poster and her best friend. Her fingers trembled. Mamá must have been desperate to risk it all. Was Lo that desperate? Did she want to follow in Mamá's footsteps? She would have to leave her sisters behind with their father. *Did* she want to gamble?

If she won, she and her sisters could escape from him forever. And maybe, just maybe, she could get Mamá back.

The realization made her dizzy. *Yes, yes, yes.* "Let's do it." Even if she lost everything, her best friend would be by her side. She would follow Mayté to El Infierno if she had to.

"Then let's throw our rebozos into the ring." Mayté flung out her arm.

Lo snorted. "I'll toss something much more fashionable, thank you."

"Oh, hush, you." Grinning widely, Mayté pointed at the bottom of the poster. "It says it's at Centro Street. We should investigate that. Maybe we can get more information about getting in."

It was so like Mayté to gather all the facts.

Despite the risk and everything that could go wrong, Lo's heart drummed with excitement. At Fortune's Kiss, there was so much more that could go *right*. And it would. *It had to.*

THREE

Mayté

The de León hacienda may have been the most lavish in all of Milagro with sprawling acres of lush land, hallways lined with painted portraits of family ancestors, chambers furnished with glittering treasures from around the world, and larger-than-life suites for each of the de León girls. But an uncomfortable tension always clouded the air. A five-minute visit had the same effect on Mayté's body as if she had spent five hours hunched over a canvas.

She always left drained and in need of a stretch. Especially when Lo's father was around. Always scowling, voice booming through the halls. As a child, Mayté was terrified of him. As much as she hated to admit it, she still kind of was . . .

Even after Mayté's family moved to an area full of crime and squalor, Lo still insisted on visiting their tiny shack instead of staying comfortable in her own palace of a home. More and more Mayté understood why.

Lo pressed against a pillar and peeked outside—cautious and swift like a mouse. She shouldn't have had to be a mouse in her own home, Mayté thought as she peeked out too.

Not a soul in sight. Lo grabbed her hand. "Hurry."

The two hustled through the huge paradise of a garden. Past the fountain and tall palms, between the potted dahlias and perfectly trimmed bushes. Lo must have had this escape route memorized. The gate was not too far off now. Leafy vines slithered down the orange walls lining the perimeter. Lo yanked Mayté behind a tall bush. Her golden-brown eyes bulged, and she smashed a finger to her lips.

What? Mayté mouthed.

Giggles filled the air as Lo's sister walked down the path. Little Sofía skipped around Serafina, who was carrying a stack of work booklets. The de Leóns all had the same smooth and beautiful faces the color of faded terra-cotta. It was the kind of skin that turned bronzy from the summer sun and faded to the color of pale sand during the gray winter.

"That's enough!" Serafina snatched Sofía's hand. "We must finish our studies before dinner. No more goofing off."

"Hmph." Sofía pouted. Dark brown curls sprayed out from her bun like little horns, and her chubby cheeks bounced with every stomping step.

Once they were out of earshot, Lo sighed and fell against the bush. The thick leaves kept her upright. "I didn't want them to see us and have to lie for me," she whispered.

Mayté remembered how Lo always used to have to lie for her mother. Lo had never liked doing it.

"Come on," Lo said. "Let's get out of here."

Centro Street was packed. Even busier than the mercado. A mob of bodies blocked the storefronts. Not even those on horseback or in carriages could get through. The flood of colorful dresses and ponchos reminded Mayté of an abstract painting. Several guards half-heartedly tried to keep everyone under control, but they seemed just as curious as everyone else.

As Mayté navigated the crowd, she couldn't ignore the way people stared. Heat crept up her neck. Whispers filled the air, buzzing fast like a swarm of wasps. She should have been used to it. Ever since her family was expelled from Las Cinco, they had become a fodder for gossips, and the whispers only intensified whenever she was spotted with Lo.

Lo stared straight ahead, seemingly oblivious. At moments like this, Mayté could never tell what she was thinking.

She stood on her tiptoes to try to catch a glimpse of something, anything, past the sea of hats and heads. Finally, she saw it. A building, standing in the distance. The shape reminded her of a circus tent with a pointed tip spreading down into a dome. But she had never seen a circus tent this grand. It dwarfed the rest of the surrounding buildings, not only in size, but with its bright colors—pure blue, crimson, and amber swirling into flowery Talavera patterns. Just like the painted ceramics sold at the street mercado.

"That must be it," Lo breathed.

Nothing that their childish imaginations could have conjured would have been as magical as this. It made their fantasies about golden castles with rooftops formed of clouds and starlight feel mundane in comparison. Beautiful yet baffling. To think it appeared in a snap, overnight. Not even ten thousand workers could have built it in that time. It was magic, plain and simple, and not the kind tied to potions or prayers. The sky around it seemed to shimmer as if encantos leaked out from the inside. Orchids and passionflowers bloomed on the nearby trees, dreamy and bright. Had they always been there? The grandeur of it all made her forget.

"It's amazing!" Lo clung to Mayté's shoulder. "I wish we could see more."

"We'll just have to push our way through." They had come this far; Mayté wasn't going to let anything stop her. They managed to squeeze in closer, but the crowd grew even thicker. Someone elbowed Mayté in the ribs, and she almost tripped over someone else's foot.

"Lorena, over here!"

Mayté's insides prickled.

A teenage boy pushed through a gap in the crowd. His crisp morning suit marked him as a young noble. Likely one of Lo's many suitors. Then another popped out. And another and another until five noble boys appeared.

"Oh! It's Lorena."

"What a sight you are today."

"You look beautiful."

"I'm so happy to see you."

All of them appeared so handsome and hopeful. Their faces were like a patchwork quilt of browns: some rich and earthy, others lighter shades of tan. Each one wore fanciful cravats—colorful silk neckerchiefs—like a flock of strutting peacocks. All of them spoke over each other, as if being the loudest would make the other suitors somehow disappear.

Ha! If that was the case, Mayté would have screamed at the top of her lungs.

"How wonderful," Lo grumbled, then took a deep breath. She batted her eyes and her downturned mouth softened. "I ran straight here from a gown fitting. Do you like it, by the way?" She gave them a twirl.

With a single spin, Lorena de León could bring the world to its knees. The boys clapped and cooed, unbothered by the way everyone stared at them. They would make spectacles of themselves if it meant winning Lo's favor.

"Magnífica."

"You look just like an angel."

"You are the most beautiful girl in all of San Solera!"

Lo put her hands on her cheeks and looked bashful. "How sweet. Thank you!"

Mayté hadn't realized she was grinding her teeth until her jaw ached. She loved Lo, she really did, but moments like this made it difficult. Mayté felt invisible watching this spectacle unfold. It wasn't that the boys refused to look at her; no, they looked *through* her. She was nothing to them. It was a fact she should have been used to. Everyone she grew up with stopped acknowledging her existence the moment her father's scandal came to light. She still remembered the day she told Lo and the other girls about what happened. Her skin still chilled at the memory of the way everyone but Lo stopped looking her in the eye from that point on.

She should have been numb to it.

But it still burned.

Mayté never received any love letters or requests to be escorted home by a chivalrous fellow. No boys approached her father asking permission to court her. None looked at her with half as much adoration as the suitors staring at Lo. Surely it was due to her family's fall from grace. No one wanted to get dragged down with her. But at moments like this, she wondered if there was *more* to it than that.

It was all horribly pathetic. Mayté reached for her rebozo, seeking its comfort, but it was missing from her shoulders. She had forgotten to grab it at Lo's hacienda. *Damn it, Lo.*

But as quickly as anger and resentment swelled up, guilt chased them away. None of this was Lo's fault. So, as always when these feelings came to the surface, Mayté covered them.

She layered other emotions over her upset, like paint on a canvas—defiance, anger, but also hope. Fortune's Kiss would fix all of this.

A gleaming white carriage led by an even whiter horse careened through the crowd. Mayté stumbled back along with the rest of the suitors as the carriage narrowly missed them. She caught a glimpse of the pair in the back seat. A teenage girl shaded her milky complexion and wheat-colored hair with a parasol. Next to her was a boy, leaning out the side of the carriage and laughing. His pointy chin and nose were a much healthier tan, his hair the color of burnt wheat.

"Montoyas," a suitor growled.

"Damn el orden antiguo," another spat.

Mayté could never forget how everyone in her former social circle despised el orden antiguo. It was perhaps the only thing everyone could agree on. Those families, who mostly descended from Hispana, much preferred how life had been when their king governed San Solera from his throne overseas.

The Montoyas were perhaps the most infamous of La Orden, proudly claiming to be direct descendants of the cruelest of conquistadors. They siphoned resources from Milagro, earning the nickname Los Vampiros.

"They best not be considering gambling in Fortune's Kiss," a suitor growled.

Mayté's stomach flip-flopped. According to legend, las grandes familias had come into power after one of their predecessors won Fortune's Kiss. The details were foggy from years and years of embellishments. No one knew for sure from which family the lucky one had come, but the result was as clear as day. More whispers floated around about nobles plotting to send their sons to gamble in Fortune's Kiss. What was there to lose? If they returned home a bit depressed, they still had their own wealth to fall back on.

What if Lo's suitors were planning on entering? Everywhere Mayté looked, there was potential competition. Anyone could easily take her and Lo's spot in the game.

"So, is it all true?" Lo asked, clearly bored of the Montoyas. "Has Fortune's Kiss really returned?" She was a master at feigning ignorance. Her performances were always flawless.

"Yes, it has." Juan Felipe Garcia swooped in to answer. He was tall and handsome with a narrow face, square jaw, and deep brown skin. His long, thin frame reminded Mayté of a cactus. "Can you see the gambling salon from here?" He put his arm around Lo as he pointed it out.

Mayté bit back a scoff both at the domineering gesture and his words. *Yes, because Lo hadn't thought to look for herself.*

"Oh, my! It's so beautiful—and probably even more wonderful inside," Lo cooed. "Are you going to gamble?"

"Why should I? I already have everything I need." Juan Felipe laughed, showing his teeth, perfectly straight with slightly pointy canines. None of the other suitors spoke up. *Good.* All these boys had more money and power than they knew what to do with. Let them stay home.

"Mm. I wonder how many people they let gamble at once," Lo mused.

"They're choosing ten entrants, my lady," Ernesto Alvarez proudly blurted. He was much shorter than Juan Felipe but made up for it with his muscular build. His full lips twisted into a grin, and he ran a hand through his luscious brown waves when Lo turned to him. "Might I add that you look even more beautiful than that silly tent? The crowd here should be gathered for you and you alone."

"Only ten?" Lo asked, ignoring that last bit.

Ten. Mayté scanned the crowd. There had to be hundreds of people here. Not the best odds.

Lo tapped her cheek. "I wonder when they'll choose these ten people."

"Doors open tomorrow at dusk! Everyone is to form a line and they will make a selection," Juan Felipe exclaimed. "That's what some workers at the salon said. They were quite eager to tell me. They must be hoping I'll gamble."

That soon? Mayté's pulse quickened, but her mind raced even faster. Tomorrow. That was when everything would change.

"You spoke with them? People from inside Fortune's Kiss?" Lo whirled around to face him. "How interesting."

Ernesto huffed and tugged at his suit coat.

Mayté rolled her eyes.

"Yes." Juan Felipe smiled, smoothly pulling Lo closer. "I'm sure it'll be an even bigger spectacle than today. If you want to watch it all unfold, perhaps I can escort y—"

"Did they say how exactly they are choosing the ten?" Lo interrupted. "Is it first come, first served? Is there a price for entry?"

Juan Felipe fell silent. Ernesto's eyes darted.

"You didn't think to ask?" Lo frowned.

Juan Felipe slowly shook his head.

Lo bit her lip. "Ay, I would have really liked to know. That's going to bother me until I find out. Mayté, maybe we should find someone who knows."

One by one, the suitors' eyes widened. Their shoulders sagged in despair.

"Uh, yeah. Let's go," Mayté said, stilted and awkward. Putting on a show was not her forte. They had only taken a step when— "Hello there!" Dominic Castro jogged over. A servant followed closely, walking four Xolo dogs on leashes. "Are you here to gawk at Fortune's Kiss too?"

Mayté's chest tightened for a multitude of reasons. Her patron, Señora Castro, was Dominic's mother.

Not only that: as an heir to Las Cuatro, Dominic had once been her potential suitor.

She would be lying if she said he hadn't been her favorite, with his long eyelashes and strong jawline, his dark eyes shining like the starlit sky. His cheeks were always a bit flushed and the skin under his eyes always puffed up when he smiled. To most it was a flaw, but Mayté found it quite charming. Just a look from him used to make her heart jump. Maybe it still did.

"Isn't this an exciting time?" He sounded breathless. "I just overheard someone say that a woman from a far-off land won and used her wish to heal her dying mother of an incurable disease. Isn't that amazing? Anything can happen!"

"Señor, please slow down." The servant rushed after Dominic.

"Perritos!" Lo squealed and dropped to her knees, letting Dominic's skinny gray dogs flop all over her and give her licks. Each one of those sorry excuses for canines only reminded Mayté of the hours she toiled getting their odd proportions right.

Lo kissed the dog's pointed muzzles one by one. "Did you happen to hear what the price of entry is?" she asked Dominic.

"Not exactly." He flashed a lopsided grin. "No one knows for sure, but there are rumors and theories. Some say since the prize is so wonderful, the cost must be huge! Like a large sum in golden coins. Others claim they'll only accept your most prized treasure. One of them might be right, no?"

"Maybe." Lo grinned, but Mayté felt sick. Golden coins? Her most prized treasure? She hadn't thought there might be a price for entry. How was someone who couldn't even afford a measly jar of paint going to get in?

"Well, *I've* heard that the payment is blood," Ernesto yelled as Juan Felipe shoved him out of the way.

"Yes, yes, but noble blood is worth more. Someone like María Teresa would likely get bled dry before she could pay the price." He smirked and the other suitors snickered.

Mayté's cheeks flushed with warmth. She caught Dominic staring and looked away. Of course, *now* the boys would notice her.

"Enough," Lo said, voice suddenly firm. "If you think that about my best friend, then you should find someone else to court."

Juan Felipe jolted as if Lo had kicked him in the stomach. He probably had never heard her speak like that. The other suitors looked just as shocked.

Dominic burst out laughing at his rival. He laughed so hard, it turned into a coughing fit. One of the dogs whined and the servant looked panic-stricken, but Dominic waved him off. "Sorry. That was . . . rude of me." He gasped for air, a wide grin still plastered on his face.

Mayté pressed her lips together. At least someone else was being laughed at for a change.

Lo turned away. The hunger and curiosity in her eyes had faded. Clearly, she had gotten everything she needed. "Oh, my, I think I've lost track of the time. I should go before my father gets worried."

"Wait!" Juan Felipe snatched her arm. His huge smile clashed with the growl in his voice. "I can escort you—"

The way he grabbed at her as if she were his possession. Mayté's blood boiled.

Lo made a strange face as she looked down at her arm and back up again at Juan Felipe.

"No, I can," Ernesto interrupted. "Let me walk you, my beautiful lady."

"I need to take the dogs home," Dominic said, hitching his thumb back. "It's on the way if you want to talk more about Fortune's Kiss."

Lo shook free from Juan Felipe and before any of those idiotas could get any closer, Mayté hooked arms with her.

"Sorry." Lo shrugged. "Let's talk more next time, okay?"

Mayté grinned. If the two of them played their cards right, there wouldn't be a next time. Ever.

Somewhere, somehow, people got it into their heads that home was where the heart was. But if Mayté *had* to choose, her heart's true home would be at the Fountain Garden.

Tucked away from the city's bustle, bathed in mist from myriad waterspouts, and guarded by cacti of all shapes and sizes, sat her and Lo's secret garden. Maybe *secret* wasn't the right word. *Overlooked? Underappreciated?* Not many people walked through here, and they were missing out.

Abuelita had introduced her and Lo to this magical place. It was her refuge from her husband and children, and it became the same for Mayté. Whenever her mother was too nagging, or her brothers too loud and brutish, or her father's absence too overwhelming to handle, she came here for peace and quiet.

As children, Mayté and Lo had spent many an afternoon splashing around in the fountains, bestowing names on the different cacti. Stuff like Verde and Flor. To this day, Señor Conejito was her favorite. Short and round, it sprouted two heads that looked like rabbit's ears.

"Good day to you, señor." Lo sat at the base of the fountain next to the bunny cactus. She took off her shoes and dipped her toes in the fountain's water. Some things never changed. "Do you think any of your brothers would be interested in Fortune's Kiss?"

"Hmm." Mayté plopped next to her and thought about it. The twins, Benito and Pablito, were still toddlers. Manuel had just turned nine, but Mateo was fifteen. Still, he was much too consumed with girls to care about wealth. Carlos was eighteen, but, according to their mother, his duty was to marry a respectable woman, winning the *favor* and *support* that would come from such a match. He didn't need Fortune's Kiss. Not like Mayté did. "None of them have the drive. Anyway, you only ask about my brothers when you can't think of what else to say."

"Ay, you caught me. It's just . . ." Lo swirled her toe through the water, fracturing the reflection like mosaic glass. "I wasn't expecting the doors to open so soon, you know? Tomorrow night is going to be here before we know it. And they're only accepting ten entrants!"

The spraying mist was usually refreshing, especially on sweltering summer days, but right now it chilled Mayté. Would they be able to get in? What if they couldn't? The thought of continuing like this, dirt poor, with a muddied family reputation, at the mercy of patrons and shopkeepers: she couldn't bear it. The two fell silent until the spurting, babbling waters became deafening.

At times like this, there was only one thing to do. Mayté went over to a sage bush. She pushed past the purply flowers and pulled out a pouch of old paint supplies. Her secret stash. It may not have been the safest place to keep her stuff, but the odds were much better here, away from the twins' grubby little fingers.

"Oooh. What are you going to paint?" Lo asked.

"Who else but you? You are my muse, Lorena de León." Mayté deepened her voice, impersonating a suitor. "With my art skills, I'll prove that I'm the best man for you, my lady."

"Oh, hush!" Lo splashed at her.

With a laugh, Mayté sat in the dirt and crossed her legs. Truth was, painting calmed her. The messier the effort, the clearer her mind became. She pulled out a small oval-shaped canvas and began outlining Lo's face and hair with graphite. Real cameos with engraving and glass were much too expensive, so she painted her own. Lo's curls were always so fun to draw. "Let's talk through what we know, and then make a plan. The doors open tomorrow at dusk and they're only accepting ten entrants. Also, the price of entry may be steep."

"The winner, or winners, are the last ones standing after everyone else folds," Lo said.

"Mm." Mayté nodded. "The winning pairs had to be on to something. Working together will increase the odds in our favor." She paused to quickly sketch out Lo's bemused expression. *Perfect.* "What do you think it's like inside the salon?"

Winners described it as a beautiful dream, full of luxuries, riches, and magic they could barely comprehend. The losers babbled about giving anything for a second chance to return.

A picture was worth a thousand words, yet no one had replicated it in a painting yet. And if the outside was so incredible, then the inside had to be absolutely stellar. A thrill shivered up Mayté's spine.

"Fortune's . . . Kiss . . ." Lo propped her head in her hand. "It sounds like something romantic and decadent. Like everything will be made of pure gold and like—" She smirked. "Lips and bosoms everywhere. Statues of lovers passionately all over each other," she drawled, eyes aglow with mischief.

"Please, no!" Mayté wrinkled her nose.

"But really, who cares what it looks like, so long as the prize is enough." Lo sat up, frowning hard as a marble sculpture. "Enough to live happily and never have to rely on a man ever again."

"It *will* be enough." Mayté layered golden brown paints for Lo's face and hair. "Every winner is happy. They come back with life-changing fortunes *and* their most desperate wishes granted. Kings have ascended to their throne not by blood, but from winning. People recover from diseases; even the dead have been brought back to life, and we all know the rumors about our"—she cleared her throat, correcting herself—"*las* grandes familias." Ever since they were little girls, they heard versions of the tale of triumph. "Hey! Do you remember the stories about the last winner from Milagro? Edmund Benedict III?"

"He won the round during winter solstice, right?"

Mayté nodded as she replicated the shine of Lo's luscious curls on the palette. "With his winnings, he moved himself and his entire family to a secluded island and turned it into his own personal kingdom. Every palm tree gilded in gold. Every meal an imported delicacy from nearby countries. An entourage of

elephants to ride as transport. Just imagine what we could do."
The endless possibilities tantalized her. More than anything, she
wanted this. "I'll use my fortune to become a famous painter.
Mayté, they'll call me. Not María Teresa Robles, just *Mayté*."
She admired the cameo. There was something alluring about
half-finished work. So much mystery. Less overwhelming than
a blank canvas. Too far in to give up.

"And your family, you'll really leave them all behind?" Lo
asked softly.

"Why shouldn't I?" Mayté replied without a thought. "They
only see me as a glorified babysitter. The boys are getting older,
and Carlos will take care of things. Plus, it'll be one less mouth
to feed. Once I'm free, I'll buy myself a big house by the sea."

"You better not forget about me when you go."

"Never." Mayté grinned. "You and your sisters could live
with me if you'd like. We'd make our own family."

Lo frowned.

"What's wrong?"

"It's just, I've been thinking." Lo twirled a curl around her
finger. "My mother could still be in Fortune's Kiss. Maybe that's
why she hasn't returned. We could bring her back."

Mayté's stomach lurched. All these years, Lo had clung to
the hope that one day her mother would come back home. She
was certain she had fled to Fortune's Kiss. Everyone else thought
she had simply run off. Mayté wasn't sure what she believed, but
whenever the topic came up, her gut twisted with dread. Deep
in her heart, she felt that Lo's mother would never return. Yet
she never had the heart to admit that to her best friend; so, like
always, she forced a smile. "Then if she's in there, we'll bring her
back too." And she truly meant it.

Seemingly satisfied, Lo turned away, gazing at the fountain's water. "But what if we lose?"

"We won't," Mayté assured her. "But even if we did, we'll have time to think of a plan while we work off our debts. Together, we'll come up with something."

"We're really going to do this, aren't we?" Lo whispered, just as the exact same thought crossed Mayté's mind. They were both on the same page. Always had been.

And that was why they would win.

"First, we have to get in." Mayté wet her lips. "And I'm worried about the cost," she admitted.

"Oh, don't worry about that." Lo stood and brushed off her gown. "If it's money, I'll handle it. We should also bring our most prized possession. Just in case."

Leave it to Lo to make problems just—*poof*—disappear! Mayté set aside her painting supplies and stood. "All right. Then let's meet at Centro Street tomorrow night, right after sunset."

"Deal." Lo held out her hand.

Mayté shook it. "Also, bring back my rebozo. That's my most prized possession," she teased.

They both burst out laughing. Mayté's heart pounded.

Their childhood pact started full of hopes, dreams, and fantasies. Promised with blood. Solidified with a handshake.

And now, they would fulfill it.

"Mayté!" Her older brother rushed over, out of breath.

She clicked her tongue in irritation. "What is it, Carlos?" Only ten months older than her, a lot of people confused them for twins. Out of all six Robles kids, they looked the most alike. They even had the same full upper lips that straightened out whenever they grinned, along with the tiny cleft in their chins. Though Carlos was taller, they were even built similarly—much to Mayté's chagrin. He was the only other person who knew about their secret spot, and he always had a knack for interrupting at the worst moments.

Water splashed as Lo nearly lost her balance and slipped into the fountain. She barely caught herself with her hand, instead soaking her sleeve.

"Are you okay?" Mayté and Carlos blurted in unison.

"I should be getting home." Lo abruptly stood, shook at her dripping sleeve, and avoided looking at Carlos.

"Are you sure?" Mayté asked.

"I need some rest." Lo smiled. "But I'll see you tomorrow evening, yes?"

"Yes." The excitement of Fortune's Kiss filled Mayté's head once again.

Carlos looked like he wanted to say something, but Lo quickly turned on her heels and rushed off. He stared at her retreating figure.

When their family had still been part of Las Cinco, everyone thought that Carlos would marry Lo. Then she and Mayté would have been sisters officially—bound by marriage. Lo and Carlos said they had feelings for each other back then. Mayté sometimes wondered if they still did. She always used to tease her brother about Lo. He would get so mad, yelling and huffing, but his reddening ears always told a different story. Not long after their father's fall from grace, she had once teased him out of habit. But that time there was no yelling or arguing. Just red ears and sad eyes.

"Was there something you wanted?" Mayté folded her arms.

Carlos jolted as if a trance had broken. "Ma sent me to find Father. He's been gone since yesterday."

"Of course he has." And *of course* Carlos couldn't find him on his own. He always had to involve Mayté. "All right. Let's find him."

As the two searched, the sun sank below the horizon. And dusk brought danger. Abuelita used to say that spirits roamed the street at night. Blending in with the gleaming fireflies, lights the color of peridots dipped in gold, the spirits' wills wisped about. But it wasn't just a pretty story, it came with a warning: hay que tenerle miedo a los vivos, no a los muertos—and she was right. It wasn't the dead they had to worry about.

Even with Carlos at her side, it wasn't safe. Drunks lumbered about, cursing anyone who would listen, and pickpockets grew bolder in the cover of dark. Not to mention the sneering men who would eye a girl as if she were freshly cut meat being sold at the mercado.

The warm wind picked up, taking with it a flock of bubbles. The bubbles were soapy and yellowing, like parchment left too long in the sun. The result of spiking alcohol with a bubbly Ni Una Preocupación potion. Mayté stopped. The bubbles wafted out from the windows of Cantina Esperanza, along with yells, laughter, and lively wails of the accordion. The trashiest cantina in Milagro was also one of the most popular. The small shack, its adobe walls stained with urine, vomit, and possibly blood, was always packed full. Even if she were old enough to consume alcohol, Mayté wouldn't want to set foot in there. After Carlos once had come back from the place with a black eye and all his coins gone, she knew it was nothing but trouble.

Carlos winced as if the sight of the building brought on those unpleasant memories.

The swinging doors flew open, and a rough-looking group of men threw another man out. Bubbles flew from the man's mouth as he landed in the mud. "Come back once you can pay your tab." The group of men blocked the door, jeering. Smoke from their cigars mingled into a thick smog.

"He comes in here acting like he's still part of Las Cinco. Pathetic."

"Don't let your coins fly away this time, hmm?" The men burst out laughing as they bustled back into the cantina.

José Robles sat up and wiped the mud off his face. His tattered poncho and patched-up pants were absolutely filthy. He seemed worn-down as usual, with his furrowed brow, the premature wrinkles on his brown face, and his graying hair—a shell of his former aristocratic self. But now, he looked absolutely trashed, bloodshot eyes wide as he slurred something. More bubbles flew from his mouth, even dirtier than before.

Those damn bubbles. Her father began guzzling drinks laced with euphoria potions around the time he lost the family's fortune. It got to the point where he became known in Milagro as El Desgraciado, always with a bubbling drink in hand. He must have enjoyed the hallucinating effect the potion gave him, helping him forget about all his horrendous mistakes. Whenever their mother saw the bubbles, she sent one of the kids— usually Mayté—to see if they were from her father, and if so, what trouble he had gotten himself into.

At least this time Carlos was here to help. "Well, here he is." Mayté pointed to her father, who still lay in the mud like a pig.

Carlos cleared his throat. "Let's get him back home."

"Right." Mayté nodded. Prickly shame danced across her back as she followed Carlos. Good thing Lo had left, otherwise Mayté would have been mortified. The two siblings went over to either side of their father and hoisted him up by the arms. Mud soiled Mayté's blouse and neck, but it couldn't be helped. She made sure his arm was on her shoulder before wrapping her arm around his waist. Carlos did the same. Sadly, this was second nature. Their father dragged his boots, leaving Mayté and Carlos to do all the work.

As they walked, it grew darker. The large buildings and cathedrals—pristine and light with their grand towers, arched doorways, and spired roofs—gave way to smaller shacks, all built too close together. Endless lines of laundry hung on flimsy wire and children darted about, avoiding the glowering men who smoked on street corners. Trash and debris littered the ground, and the smell of stale filth filled the air.

Soon, they came to their street. No matter how much Mayté wished it wasn't.

"They didn't hurt you back there, did they?" Carlos asked their father with a frown.

Their father hiccupped, unleashing a big bubble. "Just bruises," he slurred.

Mayté clicked her tongue. "They shouldn't be so rough with you." As much as she resented her father, she could never bring herself to wish him ill. "Those people are scum," she grumbled.

Mayté was grateful that by now the burping and bubbles had calmed down, and it seemed their father was half asleep, heavier than ever.

She could just make out the tattered curtains in the house's windows as they billowed in the breeze. The wood splintered off the roof—still not fixed after the big storm last year—looking as if it could fly off at any moment, impaling someone unfortunate enough to be in the way.

"¿Qué demonios?" Carlos stopped walking.

A group of men blocked the door. One wore a sombrero, and another had on a vaquero hat while the others wore serapes and bandanna scarves, covering the lower half of their faces. Thugs.

Mayté's mother stood at the doorway, dark face pinched and red. Manuel hid behind her skirts. They both trembled.

"Ma!" Carlos darted ahead, leaving Mayté to keep herself and her father upright. She struggled against his weight.

"Oh, there he is," one of the men gruffed and the group turned around. Their eyes burned like hot coals.

"Robles, we're here for the money."

"It's time to pay up."

They had no respect for her father even though he was quite a bit older than them. Mayté tensed. Her father had to borrow money, but he didn't have a way to pay it back. Now only shady people lent to him. The sort who didn't take too kindly to getting stiffed.

"Mmm? Oh!" Her father jolted and squirmed free from Mayté's grip. "Ay, I'll have it . . . later," he slurred and crumpled to the ground.

"Pathetic." One of the thugs spat on him.

"We gave you plenty of time, Robles. Plenty of warnings too. But did you listen? NO!" The man kicked him. Hard. He rolled over with a groan. Another bubble floated from his mouth, only to instantly pop. The group surrounded him, laughing as they kicked and cursed at him.

Carlos stood in front of their mother. He would always protect her over their father no matter what. One of the reasons why he was her favorite.

Which left Mayté to do the dirty work like always. "Hey, stop!" She rushed over to the man wearing a vaquero hat. He whirled around and grabbed her, holding her tight against him.

"Oh, look what we have here. This is your daughter, Robles? She's a pretty little thing." He played with her braid, twirling it in his grimy fingers. Clearly younger than the rest, he could have been considered handsome if he wasn't so vile. A scar sloped down his white cheek, through his scruffy shadow of facial hair, to his lips. His breath reeked of tobacco and booze. He took a whiff of her braid.

"Stop!" Mayté screamed. Her skin crawled. "Let me g—"

Another thug roughly grabbed her face, pinching her cheeks together. "If you can't pay us in coins, maybe this one will do instead. We can put her to work."

The other men leered at her, eyes gleaming with greed, cruelty, and—*Dios*—Mayté didn't want to think about it. No matter how much she struggled, the man held her still. Tears stung her eyes.

Her mother softly wept and held Manuel close. Carlos stood frozen as if San Desgraciado cursed him. Neither of them made a move to save her.

And then her father . . .

He stared straight at her, still and quiet. The look in his eyes made her stomach churn. Empty and lifeless. If it came down to it, he would let them take her, wouldn't he?

She had always known the truth, but she had pushed it away. Now she couldn't ignore it. She was on her own. No one would save her.

Dios, please . . .

A knee slammed against her back and her knees and palms hit the ground. A cloud of dust and dirt bloomed around her. She scrambled to her feet, ignoring the burning pain.

"Think about it, Robles," the vaquero spat. "We'll be back soon and next time, we won't leave empty-handed." Snickering, the thugs left, tossing their cigarettes and empty glass bottles aside.

Then there was silence. No talking. No breathing. And certainly, no bubbles.

Until her mother whimpered, "Hija, are you okay?" She dabbed her eyes with her frayed shawl and turned to Carlos. "You too, mijo?" As if *he* was the one who almost got taken by disgusting men.

It wasn't always like this. A lifetime ago, back when her mother wore beautiful silk gowns, she prided herself on every one of her children. But clearly that was only a luxury. Once they lost everything, she put her all into Carlos. If Carlos found a wife with a decent status, that could change everything for her. He was her savior, and if he failed, there was always Mateo. Or Manuel. Or even one of the twins once they grew up.

Never Mayté.

"Let's get you cleaned up and then I'll boil some café." Her mother ambled back inside and Carlos helped their father up. Mayté stormed into the house behind them.

"Can I have some too?" Manuel bounced around his mother, clearly unbothered by the altercation. "Please, please, please?" He cupped his hands together, but almost tripped over a chair. The tiny main room was a mishmash between a kitchen, dining area, and sitting room. There was barely space for a few people, let alone all eight of them. A turquoise cross hanging on the stained concrete walls was the only splash of color in the dingy house.

Mayté's room was even tinier with only a moth-eaten curtain dividing it from the area her brothers shared, but at least it was her own. The one perk of being the only girl. All it could fit was her bed along with some canvas and other painting supplies. Two heads full of black hair bounced in front of her half-painted canvas.

"What are you doing?" she shrieked at the sight of fingerprints and graphite scribbles on her commission. *No, no, no, no!*

The twin toddlers, Pablito and Benito, turned around with no remorse on their chubby brown faces. They pushed through the curtain, giggling.

"I can't believe this!"

The older Robles kids had learned their manners, but after they moved here, it was like her mother forgot how to parent. The twins and Manuel did what they wanted without even the tiniest smack on the wrist. Meanwhile, Mayté had vivid memories of her mother whapping her with shoes, wooden spoons, and even a cross once when she'd stepped out of line. It wasn't fair. Nothing was fair. She swiped at her eyes, failing to catch the falling tears.

"Mayté?" Carlos peeked in from behind the curtain.

"What do you want?" She turned away, wiping her face even harder. No matter how hard she rubbed, her eyes wouldn't stop burning.

"I just wanted to see if you were okay," he said but didn't offer anything else. Didn't tell her everything was going to be all right. Because it wasn't. Didn't tell her they were going to think of a way to protect her from those men. Because they wouldn't.

He was useless.

All she had left was Fortune's Kiss. The hot tears on her cheeks cooled. Fortune's Kiss was her only choice. Her only option.

Her only chance.

And if she couldn't get in—

No. She *could*. She *would*. *She had to.*

"Carlos."

"Hmm?"

"Take care of everyone," she croaked, her voice broken.

He wrinkled his eyebrows and gripped the curtain. "What do you—?"

"Marry someone with money. Ma's counting on you." Even if her family didn't value her, she wanted the best for them. If anyone could pull them out of their financial troubles, it was Carlos.

"But what about you?" He frowned. The look in his eyes pricked her heart. In many ways, they had only each other. The eldest children, old enough to understand the consequences of their ruined name. Forced to bear the burden of their younger siblings.

Carlos had the advantage. Yet he never could admit it.

That was the part that hurt the most.

Mayté let out a strangled laugh that burned her throat. "Does it really matter? None of you care." She went over to her painting supplies. Thankfully the twins hadn't torn into her stack of old drawings and paintings. This was where her heart was and surely among these was her most prized possession. Quite possibly her only way into Fortune's Kiss.

"That's not true," Carlos said, but his voice sounded weak. "There has to be something I can do."

It was far too late for that. "It's okay, Carlos, it really is." Her voice cracked. He was her older brother. He should have been there to help and protect her. He wasn't a drunkard like their father or near empty like their mother. What excuse did he have?

And yet, despite it all, she could never truly hate him. There was too much between them.

She set down the different pages. Some colored, others simple graphite sketches. "Just make sure they don't miss me too much. Tell them I'll be okay."

"What are you saying, Mayté?" Panic laced Carlos's words, yet they both knew he wouldn't do anything to stop her. "You're not going to do something crazy, are you?"

Going to Fortune's Kiss would be the craziest thing she had ever done, but now there was no going back. She couldn't stay here. Not anymore.

"I'll be okay," she told him. She had fended for herself most of her life, after all. "I'll make sure of it."

FOUR

Lo

Lo took the long way home. Different thoughts rippled through her mind like the whirling skirts of a hundred dancers. Fortune's Kiss was here. It was her chance to get Mamá back, and yet . . .

Mayté's face flashed through her head. The look when Lo brought up Mamá. Her smile, much too big. The flicker of panic in her dark eyes. Like everyone else, Mayté didn't believe she was in there. Unlike everyone else, though, she was too kind to admit it.

Lo would just have to prove them all wrong. But to do that, she would have to get into Fortune's Kiss. There was a lot to prepare for.

By the time she returned home, the stars above flickered like magic in a sea of soft violet and darkest blue. The shining moon was just a sliver away from being full. Her mind replayed the day's events. There was so much, and so little, they knew now about Fortune's Kiss.

She snuck in through the parlor and almost made it up the stairs when Sera jumped out from behind the corner.

"Where have you been?" Sera hissed, grabbing her arm. "Papá's furious."

Lo's heart skipped a beat. Those two words alone could cause a lifetime's worth of dread. "Wait. Why?"

"What do you mean *why*? Dinner was supposed to start almost an hour ago. You were supposed to sing too, remember?"

"Mierda." How could she have forgotten? A chill crept through her, but as Sera scowled, as if to blame Lo for their father's anger, her blood blazed.

"It's too late for singing. The meal will be ready at any moment. What will Juan Felipe think?"

"Well, sorry." Lo snatched her arm away. "It doesn't matter. Juan Felipe's already enamored with me and Father's the only person in Milagro who's hung up on punctuality. He shouldn't be so angry. After all, didn't he spend most of the day with one of his mistresses?"

"Don't you dare say that," Sera growled. The girl acted so grown up yet still believed their father's lies.

"Whatever you say." Lo stomped toward the dining room. In a way, she was glad she'd missed the singing. At one time she'd looked forward to her singing lessons and loved performing the new songs she learned for Mamá. That was so long ago, it felt more like a dream than anything, but at some point, like always, her father found a way to use her talent as a tool to benefit himself. Sing to impress his friends. Sing to attract suitors. Sing as an excuse for a lavish banquet. Each time she sang, she wanted to scream.

She lingered behind a pillar instead of making her presence known. The room was warm and extravagant with earthy orange walls that matched the patterned rug underfoot. A small chandelier glowed above, lighting up the medley of red-curtained windows. The centerpiece was the large table, carved from the most luxurious of dark woods and glossed until one could see their reflection on the tabletop.

Juan Felipe and Sofía were the only ones seated.

Lo's lips curled, and she dug her fingers into the hard marble of the pillar until they throbbed. Of course, it had to be *him*. He was the one she hated the most. While the rest would be dreadfully boring and controlling husbands, Juan Felipe would be absolutely brutish, not unlike her father.

Sofía's tight black curls bounced as she giggled and tried to grab Juan Felipe's deep brown fingers, but he kept playfully pulling away.

Charming as cursed gold, Mamá would say. He had certainly shown his true colors earlier today. Lo rubbed her wrist, which still ached from when he grabbed her, but it was his words about Mayté that burrowed under her skin like barbed hooks.

"If I was old enough . . ." Sera's whisper startled Lo. Her younger sister stood behind her, hugging herself. "I would be happy to marry Juan Felipe. Look at him. He's so kind and handsome."

No one else saw him for what he truly was. Lo gritted her teeth. "You don't understand."

A rough hand grabbed her wrist and whirled her around.

With a severe glare, her father pulled her into the hallway. He was in rare form tonight. He ground his teeth together, and his fingers threatened to rip her hand off.

"Did I not tell you to be here for dinner?" he snarled.

"I'm sorry, Papá." Lo winced, wanting so badly to wretch away. "It must have slipped my thoughts, but I'm sure dear Juan Felipe doesn't mind the wai—"

"Did. I. Not. Tell. You?" Her father leaned so close they were nose to nose. He didn't yell, only because Juan Felipe was in the other room, but Lo wished he would. This quiet, seething anger made him even more terrifying. "You know what else I've told you to do? To stop spending your time with that disgrace of a Robles girl."

"I don't care." The words came out before Lo could stop herself, but as soon as her father's eyes widened, she knew she couldn't take them back.

His hand crashed into her cheek. A yelp filled her ears. It was her own voice. Detached from her body. A stinging warmth raced across her face, and her heartbeat quickened as everything sank in. Her father had backhanded her.

"Don't you dare talk back to me." He yanked her shoulders, shaking her. She wanted to scream at him.

Wanted to slap him and shake him and—and—

"Apologize. Now." His fingers dug into her flesh.

Her? Apologize? Lo wanted to laugh but all she could do was glare at the disgusting roach that was her father.

"I said apologize, you ungrateful little—"

"Papá," Sera interrupted. If she saw the slap, it didn't show on her face. "The servants are setting the table."

He released Lo with a grunt. "Take care of your sister's face."

"Yes, Papá," Sera said, unaffected by the bruise surely blooming on Lo's cheek like a purpling rose.

Her father tugged roughly at his silver-trimmed jacket. A vulture preening after a slaughter. "And, Lorena?"

Lo closed her eyes. "Yes?" she managed.

"Do not embarrass me during this meal, and I'll forgive your disobedience."

"Yes, Papá." *But I'll never forgive how you struck me.* Her throat burned and all she could do was stand there until Sera came back with a washcloth and a bottle of Piel Perfecta. Sera soaked the cloth in the shimmering liquid, before dabbing Lo's face.

The cool sensation bit into her cheek, numbing the rest of the pain. It did nothing for the storm raging inside. Pain, terror, and anger swirled and mixed into a concoction of pure hatred.

Her father had most certainly spent thousands of gold coins to ensure he always had the strong potion on hand. The thought enraged her. Her fingers trembled, and her breaths came out in shaky puffs.

Sera wouldn't look her in the eye. Her dark eyebrows knit together, and she chewed her lips as if this were a delicate procedure that took all the concentration in the world. "You know, if you would just behave, then Father wouldn't—"

"Don't." Lo jolted away as if she had been slapped a second time. No, Sera's words hurt even worse than that. They dug into her skin like splinters and burrowed to the depths of her heart.

"But I—"

"Just *don't*." Lo pushed past her and made her way to the dining room. She didn't need a mirror to know the elixir had already worked its magic. For years, Mamá had used it, not only on Lo's cuts and scrapes from playing, but also on her own body. As a young child, Lo thought maybe Mamá secretly played outside at night.

But after Mamá left, the source of all the bruises reared his ugly head.

Mamá . . .

If everything went according to plan, in less than a day this would all end. For that exact reason, she put on her most contagious smile as she entered the dining room. This was her final performance, and she would make it the grand finale. "Oh! Juan Felipe! I hope I didn't keep you waiting too long."

"Ah, Lorena." Juan Felipe made a big show of standing up and kissing her cheek. The kiss was sloppy and much too close to the corner of her mouth. "I could never be upset with you."

Sure, because his outburst on Centro Street certainly *wasn't* anger.

"It's such an honor to see your beautiful face twice in one day."

"You saw her earlier?" Her father sat at the head of the table, smiling. The malicious monster from just minutes ago was nowhere to be seen. As much as Lo hated to admit it, she had inherited her acting skills from him.

"We crossed paths this afternoon." Juan Felipe helped Lo into the seat next to him. The servants came around, giving each of them a bowl of watery soup along with spiced rice. "Everyone sure is excited about Fortune's Kiss."

"Fortune's Kiss?" Lo's father raised an eyebrow. "You went to see it?"

Lo's heart skipped a beat and a mouthful of rice got stuck in her throat. She managed to swallow it down, keeping her composure. If her father found out about her plan, he would never let her leave. "Yes, Mayté wanted to see it. Right?" She locked eyes with Juan Felipe.

"Yes! Yes, it's no surprise someone like María Teresa would be interested in Fortune's Kiss, hmm?" Juan Felipe spoke the part, probably expecting a reward, but Lo would be long gone before he would get one.

"It was so enchanting, but there were too many people to get a good look." She pouted. "We saw a lot of nobles there. Everyone must be very curious."

"I see," her father simply said, between bites. She couldn't tell if the growl in his voice was because he was on to her, or because he didn't want to hear about Mayté. Maybe he just wanted to get on with the meal. Lo was beginning to sweat. She fought the urge to fan herself with a napkin. She glanced at her sisters. Sera was always the first to catch on, but she seemed too occupied with shushing Sofía, who played with her soup, swirling her spoon around and around.

Soon, the servants brought in the main course, filete chemita, seared steak with mashed potatoes. The head of the table was always the first to taste the main dish. Everyone watched as Lo's father cut into the steaming steak. The center was a lovely soft pink. A few of the servants lingered nervously. If her father didn't like it, they would have to remake the dish.

He chewed for several moments, then sputtered into a coughing fit.

Would he choke, done in by a piece of expensive meat for all his sins? Or even better, what if one of the servants had poisoned him?

Lo wondered: Was it wrong that she hoped so?

She looked down before anyone could catch the anticipation written all over her face.

"Are you okay, señor?" Juan Felipe asked.

"Papá." Sera rushed to him, holding her glass of water. "Drink this."

Her father swatted her away, splashing the water both on the table and on Sera. "Now look what you've done." He snatched the cup and took a big swig. A few coughs later and he was okay. Still breathing. Still alive.

Lo dabbed her mouth with a napkin to hide her disappointment.

Sera still stood at his side, gently patting his back. "Are you okay?"

"Enough," her father growled. "Sit back down."

Sera backed away, eyes watering. She put on a small smile before saying, "Yes, Papá." How could she still love him? Lo gripped the sides of her chair and pressed her tongue against the roof of her mouth to keep from saying anything.

The dinner continued as Lo's father and Juan Felipe discussed dull topics like business and Las Cuatro. "I'm happy that you're interested in my daughter, my boy," her father said. "Not just anyone would be suitable for her."

"Thank you, señor." Juan Felipe set his hand on Lo's thigh. She gripped her fork, for a moment pondering what would happen if she stabbed those wandering fingers of his. No, no, the blood would stain her new gown, which would be such a shame. "My father's worried that the arrival of Fortune's Kiss will turn Milagro upside down. We've already heard rumors of common families sending their eldest children so they too could become aristocrats. Isn't it absurd?"

"Indeed." Lo's father tipped his glass. "I'm none too concerned. None of that riffraff have the smarts needed to win the game."

Did they not believe the legends of how las grandes familias came to be? No, surely, they just did not want anyone else to benefit from Fortune Kiss's miraculous power. People as vile and greedy as her father and Juan Felipe would want to decide *who* could be among them. But didn't that make them just as bad as el orden antiguo?

Lo choked down the rest of her meal. Not soon enough, the meal ended and the servants cleared the table. Gracias a Dios, her father dismissed everyone before leaving.

"Shall we go for a stroll, Lorena?" The way Juan Felipe stared at Lo, eyes full of burning hunger, made her dinner threaten to come back up. He wanted to devour her like a second helping of flan de cajeta.

"I'm sorry. It's been a long day and I'm exhausted." Lo smiled sweetly. "Perhaps we can go a different day?"

Juan Felipe's mouth hung open. He wasn't used to being told no, especially not twice in one day. Still, they both knew he couldn't make a scene. Not here.

"Fine." His voice was cold. "I'll see you later, Lorena."

No, you won't. Lo waved as he left.

As Carmen took Sofía upstairs for her bath, Sera rushed out of the room, face red and mouth downturned, still feeling the sting of their father's dismissal.

As Papá walked into the kitchen, Lo could hear muffled yells and the sound of breaking glass seeping through the walls. Her father must have been letting the cooks and kitchen staff have it, likely blaming them for his coughing fit. Her cheek still tingled. She did not want to be in his line of fire, so she ran to her room.

The flickering candlelight cast a myriad of dancing shadows across Lo's bedroom wall. Even as she lay in bed, her heart refused to stop drumming, all her senses on high alert. The excitement of Fortune's Kiss pirouetted across her mind, alongside the horrible things that happened today.

After tomorrow, none of that would matter. No more lying or acting pleasant to make horrible people happy. As exciting as that was, a small voice in her head kept asking: *But what would you be without those things? Who are you if you aren't playing that role?*

She shook those thoughts away. That could be figured out later, once she was free, but for now, there was still much to be done. She strained her ears until distant sounds throughout the house had quieted. Then she rose from the bed, crept to her door, and peeked into the hallway. Not a light or noise. Holding her breath, she journeyed through the hall past Sera's and Sofía's rooms, then down the stairs. Everything inside her trembled. She half expected a servant to leap out of the shadows, but no, they were all asleep in their quarters. Soft moonlight seeped in through the windows, illuminating the way as she passed the kitchen and parlor to the other end of the hacienda.

Mamá's suite.

She reached for the doorknob, but hesitated. It had been years since she or anyone else had crossed the threshold. After Mamá left, it had become a forbidden area. The servants didn't even go in there to clean. Lo wiped her clammy palms on her nightgown and took a deep breath. There was no time for dawdling. As quietly as she could, she opened the door and stepped inside.

An overwhelming wave of nostalgia hit her. The familiarity, the memories, all of it was as thick as the dust coating the furniture. The suite was exactly how she remembered, though the room didn't feel as big as it once did. Moonlight wafted in from the balcony, spotlighting the mosaic tiled floor and luxurious rugs, along with the warm orange walls. The stone fireplace stood at the far end of the room, opposite her mother's bed, which was full of fluffy pillows and crisp white blankets. The only other sign of decay was the dried-out plants Mamá used to dote on.

Lo tried to soak it all in. If she shut her eyes, she swore she could catch a faint whiff of warm sunshine and rosemary. Mamá's signature scent.

As a child, this place had been her sanctuary. Back then, she thought it was normal for a husband and wife to sleep as far away from each other as possible.

She shuddered. The last time she visited this room had been on a muggy summer's night much like this one. A nightmare brought her here, one she couldn't remember, but it had been bad enough to send her scrambling inside. Mamá always let her snuggle up in bed with her whenever Lo got scared. And Mamá's tender fingers stroking her hair and the softly sung lullabies would vanquish any frightful thoughts or unsettling feelings.

Lo walked to the fireplace and crouched in front of it. Mamá had once told her of the hidden coins that were only to be used in an emergency by her and her sisters. Sure enough, behind the soot-stained cobwebs and rotted wood sat a pouch full of golden coins. A *lot* of them. Enough to attend an extravagant weeklong ball dressed as a new princess every night.

Beside the pouch, Mamá's silver comb sat with years of dust collected on its surface.

"Until I return, keep this hidden and safe for me."

Lo gently pulled it from its hiding spot. When she was little, the comb had nearly swallowed her small hand. Now it fit delicately in her palm. It was just as beautiful as she remembered, if not more. Even though she could never bring herself to wear it, it was her most prized possession.

She pulled the Fortune's Kiss poster from her nightgown pocket and smoothed it out on her lap. A teardrop hit the paper. Lo squeezed the poster and pressed her lips together to keep a sob at bay as more hot tears dripped down her cheeks. "I'm coming, Mamá. I promise."

No matter what, she would get her back. If she and Mayté won, she would use her wish to make it so. But Dios forbid, even if they didn't win, she would trade anything she could for Mamá. Sell her soul if she had to.

And maybe then, once she had Mamá back, Lo wouldn't be so broken.

As dusk's orange glow filled her bedroom the next evening, Lo got to work. Her father had been preoccupied the entire day and Lo hoped that he would stay that way. She grabbed her packed satchel and changed into a turquoise dress. The silk hem hovered inches above the floor. Lacy ruffles blossomed at the sleeves and around her neck. Subtle flowers and butterfly patterns winked when the light hit just right. Everything about the dress was elegant without being too constricting or heavy. She had to look her best, but also be prepared. No one could say for certain what awaited her inside Fortune's Kiss. She pulled her curls away from her face and pinned them back with her mother's comb. Only now did it feel right to wear it.

The door creaked open.

Lo's heart stopped.

Sera and Sofía stood in the doorway. Their bronze faces looked extra pale with red splotchy cheeks matching their bloodshot eyes.

"What happened?" Lo asked, unsure if she wanted to know the answer.

Sofía's lips quivered, and she burst into tears. "Don't leave us! Please!" She bolted into the room and hugged Lo's legs.

"Wh-wha—?" The walls wobbled and closed in.

Sera did a much better job at keeping her composure, though her eyes glittered with moisture. "Please don't go. If it's because of yesterday I'm so sorry, but you can't go to Fortune's Kiss. Papá says that everyone who goes never comes back."

Lo's blood ran cold.

He knew.

She couldn't even fathom what that man would do to her. She had to get out of here. *Now.*

Lo pushed past her sisters and ran as fast as she could.

"Lo, no!"

"Wait!"

But Lo couldn't stop. She flew down the stairs, fueled by pure adrenaline. The edges of her vision blurred, and her pulse drummed wildly. The parlor was the fastest way out. She rushed in but skidded to a stop.

Her father blocked the doorway. "Lorena."

How could her very own name bring about such a panic in her? Outside the window, the sun sank closer to the horizon, turning the room into a scarlet inferno.

The parlor may have been the biggest room in the hacienda, but at that moment, it felt tiny. Suffocating. She was trapped.

"You don't care about this family, do you?" Her father took a step closer, then another and another. "How could you *abandon* your sisters? Did you see how upset they were?" He backed Lo into a wall.

It wasn't abandonment if she was coming back for them. Because she would win Fortune's Kiss and use her riches to fix everything. Anything else wasn't an option. "I—"

"How could you leave *me*? After everything I've provided for you. Everything I've done to secure a future for you." He smashed his fist into the wall. Lo jumped. Tears sprang into her eyes.

Her father shook his head with a bitter chuckle. "I shouldn't be surprised. You really are just like your wretch of a mother." He pulled a crumpled sheet of paper from his breast pocket and held it up.

Lo's heart stopped.

It didn't matter that the paper was faded and tattered with age. She recognized the golden calavera. It hadn't changed in the last ten years. Fortune's Kiss.

"Juan Felipe told me about your fascination with Fortune's Kiss. How you asked about the entry fee, and when contestants would be chosen." Her father spat the words as if they were acid in his mouth.

No. Lo gripped the couch's plush backrest. Of course he'd told her father everything. How could she have been so foolish?

"Not that he needed to. I'm no imbecile. I knew that's where my greedy wife ran off to, and now that the Dios-forsaken abomination is back, it's only natural it would seduce you too. You have that same look in your eye as she did back then." Everything inside her screamed to run, but she couldn't move. "Eres una maldita egoísta!" He grabbed her by the shoulders and violently shook her. "You'll lose everything. Do you realize that? Leave here and you'll never return!" With every word, his booming voice beat into her skull like hot irons.

"I'D RATHER DIE THAN STAY HERE!" There. The unspoken truth hung between them. It was enough to get her father to stop shaking her, but she instantly regretted it. Now what would he do? She braced herself for his rage.

But it didn't come. Instead, her father burst out laughing. "Your mother said the same exact thing." He ripped the comb out of her hair. "This used to be hers. I remember her wearing something like this." How easily his large fingers could crack it in half.

Lo reached for it, but her father grabbed her wrist. Hard. Harder than he'd ever grabbed her before. She screamed.

"Why am I the villain?" he demanded, eyes wide. "You have things all mixed up in your little head. I did everything for your mother. She's the hateful one who left you and your sisters. One day you'll understand it was all her. She's the sinner. Not me." Snarling, he dragged her across the room.

"Stop! Let me go!" Lo screamed and struggled. "You're *hurting* me!" But it was useless. Her pain meant nothing to him.

"I should've broken her legs. Then she wouldn't have been able to run. And I could've taught her how to be a proper wife and mother."

Where he failed with Mamá, he would try to succeed with Lo.

"P-Papá," Lo whimpered. "I'm sorry. I wasn't thinking. I'm sorry." She managed a wobbly smile. "I'm just a stupid little girl."

But her father's eyes only darkened. "Oh, don't worry, Lorena. After I'm finished with you, Juan Felipe will keep you very good company. I've decided he's the one you'll marry. He's the only one who will be able to handle you."

The charade was over. The masks were off. There was no use in pretending. He was going to hurt her, badly, and then he was going to deliver her into the arms of someone who would do the same, or worse.

With a scream, she kicked his shin. Her father yowled in agony, loosening his grip. She shoved him as hard as she could.

He fell back into the shelf of vases, head smacking against the sharp corner. Glass rained down on him and shattered into pieces. He hit the floor. Blood pooled from his head.

Lo screamed and covered her mouth.

More and more blood flowed, oddly beautiful and rich like liquefied roses. For several seconds, she stood frozen, but everything inside her told her to move. She knelt, careful not to get any blood or glass on her dress. She plucked the comb from her father's still hand and slipped it into her pocket.

Her father gurgled, weak and pathetic. The life drained from his face along with his blood. Lo's heart rammed against her chest.

But what if he somehow survived? Then what would happen? What would he do to her sisters? *To her?*

Panic set in. She snatched a shard of glass, pointed and sharp as a knife. Her fingers wouldn't stop shaking. She couldn't breathe. Couldn't think.

She pressed the edge against his neck. Blood bubbled beneath the glass. This would kill him. There would be no turning back.

This was for her and her sisters.

And for Mamá.

Squeezing her eyes shut, she sank the edge of the glass into his skin, and slashed.

And then it was over.

She gasped. The bloodied shard slipped from her fingers and shattered. He was gone. He would never hurt her or her sisters ever again. The relief was so overwhelming, she blinked back tears.

Then she saw the blood again. Not as something beautiful and dreamlike, but *real.* Warm and sticky spatters stained her hands and gown. The metallic-scented scarlet sent her plummeting to reality. A wave of terror almost suffocated her. She *killed* her father. She was a *murderer.*

It wasn't supposed to happen like this. She would be locked away. Her sisters would hate her forever.

Lo stood on shaky feet, wiping her hands on her gown. Her pulse raced. Fortune's Kiss. Her last hope. It always had been. She needed to get there before it was too late. If she brought

Mamá back, her sisters would understand; she could tell them Lo did what she needed to do.

She ripped at the buttons of her bodice and pulled the dress off, not bothering to be careful. Threads snapped and the delicate ruffles tore. It didn't matter. Underneath, she wore a silky ivory slip. Gracias a Dios, it wasn't stained. She tossed the crumpled gown behind some vases and snatched a long cloak hanging near the door. Her heart pounded and her head swam, but pure adrenaline kept her moving.

"PAPÁ!" Sera screamed as she and Sofía ran into the room. Sofía burst into high-pitched wails and clung to Sera. All the while, Sera just stared at Lo, her dark eyes wide.

Lo jolted. She opened her mouth to say something. *Anything.*

He was going to hurt her, she wanted to explain. But more than that, she'd done this for them. To protect them. To keep them from experiencing the horrors her father put her through. But the words wouldn't come. Her throat closed up and her vision blurred with more tears. Time was running out. She bolted to the door. Ran through the garden as fast as she could. Sera didn't try to stop her, instead screaming for help. But that was all in vain. Their father was in El Infierno now.

Lo dashed onto the street, running farther and farther away from her cage. Like a bird escaping into the night. Free. She was free. Yet the joyous feeling didn't bloom inside her like she always imagined. Nothing would be the same ever again.

FIVE

Mayté

The sun sank under the horizon, and darkness dulled the sky. Mayté bounced on the balls of her feet. She would have paced back and forth, but there wasn't any room. Centro Street was even more packed than last time. Hopefuls and curious onlookers swarmed every which way. Children shouted in excitement and darted around, unsupervised, while a few opportunistic vendors tried to set up shop. Someone dragged around a mule; maybe that was their most prized possession. Voices clashed together in an unrecognizable jumble, but the excitement was almost palpable. If tasked with painting this chaotic scene, Mayté would have focused on portraying that feeling of expectation and energy, instead of getting all the ever-changing details correct.

She grasped one of her braids and tugged at the split ends. She was wearing her nicest ruffled blouse, and a long, bright red skirt. The outfit was supposed to be light and breezy, but she couldn't stop sweating.

Where was Lo?

The line started to crawl forward little by little, yet her best friend was nowhere in sight. Mayté stood on her tiptoes and scanned the crowd once again for a head full of long, bouncing curls. Was she running late? No. Lo would never be late for something so important. Could she have changed her mind? No way that could be either.

Had something happened to her?

Mayté's pulse thrummed louder. Should she go looking for her? She'd lose her spot in line, but if she ran the whole way, she might make it back in time. When were the doors supposed to close? What if she missed her chance? Then what?

But she couldn't leave Lo behind. It wouldn't be right. Her stomach churned.

Angry voices sliced the air.

"No cutting the line!"

"Who do you think you are?"

"Ay, I'm talking to you, girl!"

Lo pushed her way through the crowd. Warm relief flooded Mayté, starting at her fingertips and rushing to her toes. "Oh good!" She exhaled with relief, only for her stomach to drop. Lo was wearing a strange cloak. When the warm breeze wisped through, it revealed only a slip dress underneath. Men leered. Women whispered to each other in disapproval. All the while, Lo stared straight ahead—eyes glassy, expression dull. She didn't flinch when someone elbowed her. It was as if she were possessed by La Muerte.

"I was starting to worry something had happened," Mayté began cautiously.

Had something happened?

Lo flinched, face glistening and flushed. Then her lips quivered.

"Lo?"

With a sob Lo collapsed into her arms. Instinctively Mayté held her tight. Lo may have been the taller one, but at that moment she felt so frail. "What happened?" Mayté asked.

Lo looked up. Tears streaked her face, and her lips wouldn't stop trembling, but there was a fury and terror behind her red, puffy eyes. She looked away, shaking her head.

Mayté's own heart quivered. Lo wasn't one to cry. Not out here, in front of everyone. She always knew how to put on a sweet smile, saving her tears for the privacy of her pillow. Something was wrong. Very wrong, but she wouldn't force Lo to talk about it. Not now. All she could do was hug her best friend tighter. "Hey, it's okay now. Look, we're almost there, and once we get in, we're going to win."

Lo tearfully nodded. The two held each other as they waited in line. Soon, Lo's sobs quieted. As the evening breeze grew nippier, the crowd's swirling voices became louder.

"Look at all these fools in line, don't they know the house always wins?"

"They measure how much everyone's worth. That's how they're picking people. They only want the most valuable ones."

"Has anyone gotten chosen yet? Looks like everyone ahead went in, then got turned away."

Mayté winced, and she swore that Lo shivered. If she was turned away and had to return home—

No, she didn't even want to entertain that thought.

The line continued moving, and soon the gambling salon came into full view. Up close, it was much grander than Mayté could ever have imagined. In the dark, it glowed like a moonlit diadem. Unearthly vines and flowers slithered and sprouted around a golden calavera, the same as the one on the poster. The words *Fortune's Kiss* were etched in glimmering amber letters underneath the skull. No painting could ever do a wonder like this justice, but she sure would have loved the challenge of trying. Only darkness could be seen inside the rounded entry-way, and there wasn't a window in sight.

"Did you remember your most prized possession?" Mayté asked, digging through her satchel and pulling out a small painted piece of wood. "Good thing I never got rid of this." A painting of La Sirena from Lotería, Abuelita's favorite card. She always said she wished she lived in the sea, so beautiful and carefree.

Lo made a face. "You painted that?"

"I know, I know." Mayté snatched the painting back and studied it. "This was one of my first paintings, back before I knew what I was doing." And it showed. The proportions were way off with a giant head and a skinny tail that looked more like a snake. La Sirena's bare breasts were even worse, like deformed papayas. The outlines were much too wobbly, and the colors splotched unevenly without proper lighting or shading. Back then, she had thought of it as a masterpiece. Ha! "But Abuelita loved it and that's all that mattered. That's when I knew I wanted to paint for the rest of my life." If that didn't make it count as a prized possession, she didn't know what would.

"Here's mine." Lo pulled out the comb and put it in her hair. "It was my mother's. She used to wear it every day." Her eyes wouldn't meet Mayté's.

Was that why she was late? Had she had trouble getting the comb?

Mayté rubbed her arm and noticed something sticky and dark red on her palm and forearm. Paint? No. An icy chill stabbed her gut. *Blood.* But from where? She patted herself, and then it dawned on her. "Lo?"

"Next group, come forward!" A suited attendant called out as matching ushers herded their group inside. There had to be around fifty of them. Maybe more. Maybe less, Mayté couldn't focus on counting. Lo grabbed her hand. This was it.

Mayté expected to be greeted by sparkling chandeliers and statues made of pure gold, but inside was an endless abyss. So dark she could barely see her own hands in front of her, let alone the blood. She swore the sound of her own gulp echoed through the space. But the dark only lasted for a moment. Hundreds of tiny candles suddenly lit the large, circular lobby, casting an eerie glow over everyone as they gazed around in wonder. A smoky blue haze wafted around, and orange marigold petals flitted underfoot, guided by an invisible wind. Several doors stood ahead, ornate with glowing carvings of fierce alebrijes, supernatural guide animals adorned with colorful patterns. As if these were the gates to the underworld. A foxlike creature with a spiked mane captured Mayté's attention. Its narrow eyes made of sapphires glimmered in the dark, staring straight into her soul.

The group fell silent when the doors outside slammed shut. Several people jolted in panic, but all Mayté felt was electric excitement. Lo squeezed her hand tighter.

"Welcome, prospective players," a man's voice boomed. He stood at the center of the room, tall and spindly. He wore a black suit and matching top hat, along with a glowing white calavera mask. Surrounded by darkness, he looked like a floating skull. "You find yourselves in El Beso de la Fortuna. Fortune's Kiss." He bowed in a grand dramatic gesture. "But do any of you have what it takes to gamble?"

"Yes," Mayté whispered. She swore she felt Lo's speeding pulse through her clammy fingers. Or maybe it was her own heart, racing with anticipation.

"Let us find out, shall we?"

This was it. Mayté wet her lips and flexed her fingers.

"First . . ." The skulled announcer stepped back as the entire entryway changed before everyone's eyes. The candles' warm glow brightened, revealing a large banquet room with a long table in the center. The seats and silverware were all copper and amber. Golden fountains spurted wine. Shiny platters held delicacies like fresh seafood, carne asada, and tiny pastries that looked like they had been sprinkled with crushed moondust. "Allow me to introduce myself, my friends. I am your faithful host and guide. You may call me Misterioso. Not Señor Misterioso, just Misterioso, if you please. Now, then, make yourself at home." He beckoned for everyone to sit.

No one could deny such a request. Mayté and Lo took the nearest seats. Mayté grabbed a piece of shrimp. Despite her nerves, her mouth watered, but before she could take a bite, movement caught her eyes. Butterflies. Hundreds of orange butterflies flitted above, landing on the matching marigolds, which seemingly sprouted from the ceiling.

The crowd oohed and aahed. Even Lo seemed to perk up as she took it all in. Mayté looked around, trying to remember every last detail. How this would be a dream to paint! The warm glow in the dark clashing with the subtle cool haze wafting around. A fever dream with qualities of both her worst nightmare and most coveted fantasies. Her fingers twitched. What she would give for a canvas and paintbrush right now. Or even charcoal to draw on a napkin.

"This is but a mere taste of what the house offers its contestants," Misterioso said.

Dreams could come true here, Mayté thought.

"Now that you're comfortable, there's one more thing I must share. As I'm sure you all have heard, there are many rumors flying around about the price of entry. Like tiny little flies buzzing about, but now I'll tell you the truth." His words were light and airy. Half-singsong, half-taunting.

Mayté's heart skipped a beat.

Misterioso chuckled, feeding off the tension like a sweet nectar. "I would be lying if I said it wasn't a steep price to pay. The cost to enter Fortune's Kiss—is your greatest dream."

The entire room broke into confused murmurs.

"Our greatest dream?"

"What is that supposed to mean?"

"Are we giving up the chance for our biggest dreams to come true?"

Lo gasped. A wave of dizziness washed over Mayté. Her biggest dream was painting. It was *everything* to her. The only thing that truly made her forget her problems if even for a few moments at a time. She couldn't even imagine losing that part of her.

"Ah, but please keep in mind"—Misterioso's crisp voice cut through the whispers—"one cannot gamble without something to wager. This opens the realm of possibility and eliminates discrimination. Even those stricken with poverty have a dream that they can bet. A big risk isn't without a handsome reward. Beat the house and you can leave with your dreams intact along with a fortune and your wish granted. Any wish—without limitation. A fair trade-off, hmm?"

The dizzy tingle inside Mayté sparked into something stronger. The fortune itself would solve most of her problems. The wish would be the finishing touch to perfection.

But was it worth the risk? What if she lost? What would that look like? What would happen to her without her dream? She would be empty. Lifeless. Then a sickening revelation dawned on her.

"Are you okay?" Lo whispered.

Mayté shook her head. "Those who returned from Fortune's Kiss empty-handed . . . What if they were more than just
sad and humiliated? What if they were . . . empty? Because the
house stole their dreams away?"

Lo's eyes widened. She didn't argue. Those people who
returned from Fortune's Kiss had nothing left. Nothing to live
for. Abuelita used to point them out and click her tongue, warning Mayté and her brothers to never gamble. But Mayté had
always thought that was just Abuelita's overprotective paranoia.

"Ahem, it's not stealing if you willingly pay the price," Misterioso's voice cut through her thoughts. "In case any of you
came to that conclusion." His mirthful eyes flitted to Mayté,
before lingering on Lo.

There was no way he could have heard her from where he
stood. With a shiver, Mayté pulled her rebozo closer. This was a
fancy one she'd borrowed from her mother's closet. It was much
too stiff and scratchy and not as comforting as the one she had
left at Lo's.

"The house may be many things," he continued. "But we're
fair. If anyone here has second thoughts, you're free to go. We
won't judge you or hold it against you. Just know, if you agree to
stay, you won't be able to change your mind. And your dream
will be your collateral."

There was a pause. A moment where nothing happened and
no one moved, as if San Tiempo himself had frozen them. But
then all at once, chairs scraped against the floor. Most of the
room stood and made their way to the exit. Mayté chewed her
lip as she watched them.

"Ah, what a shame." Misterioso frowned. "Not everyone has
what it takes."

Mayté and Lo exchanged confused glances. The few left seated at the table looked just as baffled, but the rest of the crowd wore expressions of defeat. One of them covered their face and wept. Some consoled others, softly whispering that they would try again if Fortune's Kiss ever returned to Milagro.

Mayté once again caught Misterioso eyeing them. He chuckled. "The price of entry is a house secret, though they'll remember this part well enough."

"So, it's magic?" Lo murmured. "You make them forget?"

A magic like that was much more potent than anything in Milagro. Altering the memories of a large group of people was something only Los Santos should have been capable of doing. But what bothered Mayté even more was the deception of it all. All these years of *dreaming* of this. All that hope. Had it been misplaced? "I don't know about this anymore." She stood, but Lo grabbed her hand.

Fear and shadows danced across Lo's face, but there was something else. A desperation in her eyes that soon transformed as her jaw hardened with determination. "I won't let you lose your dream. We're going to win. And . . ." She took a shaky breath. "I need this."

So did Mayté. Memories of last night flooded her mind. If she left now, she would have to face her father's mess with those vile men. What would be worse? Being trapped with them, in a living nightmare? Or in a life where she couldn't even remember the one dream she had?

"We're *winning* this." Lo squeezed her hand.

"We're winning this," Mayté whispered back.

Yes, it was the only option.

Still, they had to be chosen first. For as large as the group had been, now only six remained—including her and Lo. There were hundreds of people still waiting to be let in. Among them, maybe a tenth would try to compete.

Misterioso cleared his throat. "Well, then. If everyone else is here to stay, let us begin." For a split second he looked disappointed. Maybe he had hoped more people would remain. With a flick of his wrist, a staff appeared in his gloved hand. Like his mask, the handle was bone-white. Bright orange marigolds gathered at the top where a lit candle rested. He held the staff to his lips and blew out the candle.

One by one, the doors at the far end of the room flew open. A gust of wind hit Mayté's face and extinguished all the candles at the table. Thick smoke surrounded her as she and Lo followed Misterioso and approached the door. The scent of woody musk filled her nostrils. Petals rained from the ceiling, making a path toward the door. She squinted and craned her neck to get a better look inside, but the haze was too thick. The only way to see was by going in.

Mayté turned to Lo. This could be the last time they saw each other. *No*, they were both going to get chosen. They had to. Lo flashed her a small smile. In the candlelight's glow, Mayté swore she saw tiny spatters of red on Lo's neck, but before she could get a closer look, the thickening smoke overtook them both.

All she could do was step into the pitch-black room. "Hello?"

Then all at once, the space lit up and burning candles surrounded her. A small wooden table stood in front of her. Atop it, a calavera. Plain and white, yet something told her it was the same one from the poster. Next to it sat a vial of amber liquid and a sign that read: MARÍA TERESA ROBLES, ARE YOU WILLING TO RISK EVERYTHING FOR A CHANCE TO BE KISSED BY FORTUNE?

"Yes," she whispered.

The sign changed. So quick, she swore it must have happened when she blinked. Now it read: DRINK AND LET YOUR SOUL BE MEASURED.

This was it. She took the vial in her hand, studying the liquid. It looked as if it were made of dwindling stars at the brink of dawn. A tingle of warmth seeped through the vial into her flesh and straight into her pounding heart. How many times had she gulped down potions from the street mercado? Just yesterday she had drunk the potion from Señor Vasquez. Sometimes they worked. Other times they gave her stomach cramps, but something about this felt so much more permanent.

Drinking this would reveal her fate.

She lifted the vial to her lips and took a shaky breath.

Then she gulped it all down. It tasted sweet and went down silky smooth, warming her insides. But soon, a strange aftertaste slithered up her throat. Bitter and fizzy, it burned her tongue and constricted her throat. Her legs buckled and the warmth became suffocating. Her rebozo slipped off. Chills and hot sweat overtook her body. Her head throbbed and her heartbeat sounded so distant as if her heart had been ripped from her chest.

All at once the candle flames went out, unleashing a thick blanket of smoke. Mayté choked back a cough and resisted the urge to cover her nose. The candles lit back up, this time a blazing haunting blue. Marigolds bloomed around the room's perimeter. One by one the petals plucked off and swirled through the air, surrounding her as if she were in the eye of an ethereal vortex.

The petals bit into her arm. She recoiled with a hiss. Scarlet blood bubbled up from her skin and glowed like a bright red energy spell. A strong smell of flowers and iron filled her nostrils. The calavera changed before her eyes.

Was any of this real? She gripped her head. Suddenly she was outside in the sunshine. Bright, burning sunshine. She squinted as the scent of paint comforted her. A girl with long black braids and a rebozo sat on a stool, painting a canvas.

Mayté rubbed her eyes. The girl was her.

Seagulls squawked and the ocean, glittering and lapis, splashed against the rocks. Where was this place? It certainly wasn't Milagro. Then everything changed and a crowd of nobles formed.

"Mayté! Mayté!" They cheered her name, voices full of adoration. "Show us your next masterpiece!"

The other Mayté stood ahead, looking happy. Happier than Mayté herself had felt in a long time. The other Mayté beamed, brown cheeks extra rosy, as she pulled away a cloth to reveal a finished painting. The crowd burst into applause and began bidding. Bidding honest-to-Dios coins on her painting.

Tears pricked Mayté's eyes. This was all she had ever wanted. But then she got a good look at the painting. A dark and drab little room with tattered curtains and light filtering through a tiny window. The cobwebs and dust in the painting looked so real. Too real.

The cheers and bidding transformed into screams and sobs. Then everything changed again. The azure sky transformed into a peeling ceiling. The salty ocean air shifted into something humid and musty.

"PLEASE DON'T! STOP!" Another scream chilled Mayté to her core. It was her own voice.

The door slammed open and Mayté saw herself fall to her hands and knees. The other Mayté's body shook as she sobbed. A purply bruise blossomed under her left eye.

Standing at the doorway were the men from last night. They stared with cruel amusement.

"She'll make us back what Robles took and then some."

This was the fate that awaited her if she wasn't chosen.

The door slammed, leaving Mayté alone with herself. The other Mayté curled into a ball. Seeing herself like this was strange and disturbing. More than anything, she wanted to tell herself that everything would be okay. But that would be lying. She took a step forward, toward her figure on the ground, but everything shifted once again.

Now the other Mayté wore a tattered dress and apron. Her cheeks were sunken in, and her eyes had the darkest of circles. She sat outside on the dusty road, alone and ignored in the street mercado as everyone else bustled about. She was away from those terrible men, but why did she look even more empty and broken?

A man walked by, lugging around a painted canvas depicting a scene. The other Mayté watched him.

Whenever Mayté saw others' artwork, it sparked something in her. Sometimes confidence, sometimes envy—but always inspiration. It got her fingers itching to create.

But the other Mayté's expression was as dull as ever. Unaffected. She put her head down.

The sickening realization hit Mayté so hard she almost vomited. This was her fate if she lost Fortune's Kiss. Her dreams and her talent, gone. Too empty to even be of use to those terrible men. Alone on the streets with nothing left.

But, but, *but* . . . What about everything she'd seen before that? When she was a famous painter. Surely that was her fate if she *won* Fortune's Kiss. Which left the vision of her with those men—her fate if she wasn't chosen to gamble. Everything melted away into nothing.

Several figures approached. One by one, they formed into boys she knew. Juan Felipe. Ernesto. Dominic. And many others. Each and every one of them walked past her, not even glancing her way. Instead, they surrounded Lo.

"Lorena! Lorena!"

"The most beautiful girl in Milagro."

"Your eyes sparkle like starlit diamonds."

"Your smile takes my breath away."

"I love you. I love you."

All their words, as sappy as could be, still sent pinpricks to Mayté's heart. *Always Lo. They notice her, but why not me? She doesn't care about them. She's so ungrateful. She has no clue how good she has it.*

Mayté jolted, stunned by her own nasty thoughts. Then she saw Carlos. Her mother pulled him into her arms and hugged him tight. The rest of her brothers surrounded them. None of them noticed her. They were too busy joyously laughing with each other.

"Carlito. My pride and joy. *My favorite.*" Her mother's whisper echoed inside Mayté's skull.

It's not fair. What has he done for this family that I couldn't? If they would just listen ... but they won't. Never have. Never will. They should all rot.

Good-for-nothing Carlos.

Selfish Lo.

They don't deserve what they—

"STOP!" Mayté screamed. But her head wouldn't shut up.

If the boys loved me, I would appreciate it. I wouldn't play games with them and talk badly behind their backs.

She dropped to her knees and gripped her head.

If my family trusted me, I could have used money from my paintings to help them. We wouldn't be so bad off. Father ruined everything. He's the one that should be punished. Not me.

Dios should strike them all down.

"NO!" Mayté pounded her fists against the floor. "No, no, no! I want them all to be happy." Her vision blurred with tears. "But I want to be happy too . . ."

Up ahead the skull sat on the table, but now the skull was painted with azure swirls and flowers. The same damn shade of blue she hadn't been able to afford at the shop.

Mayté jolted awake. Her muscles ached and her head throbbed. She lay sprawled on the cold hardwood floor.

Then it all came back. Fortune's Kiss. Measuring her soul. Everything she saw . . .

She sat up and gripped her forearm. Pinkish flesh puckered where the marigold petals had taken her blood. The room was no longer dark, revealing chipping, white walls. As if someone had trapped her inside an egg.

Had her fate been decided?

Only one way to find out. Trembling, she put her rebozo back on and stood. She pushed the door open. The lobby had changed. Before, everything had been shrouded in shadows and toed the line between fantasy and nightmare. Now the hall was pure light and grandeur. As if waking up from the most beautiful dream and realizing it was real. A circle of stark white walls surrounded her. Golden beads swooped from the ceiling like raindrops frozen in a spell. They glimmered and winked at Mayté. Ornate candelabras left behind an alluring glow that danced across the marble floor. Golden pillars glimmered. And she wasn't alone. A small group of people surrounded a table at the far end of the room.

She inched closer to get a better view. Framed portraits sat on the table, each of a different person. And there she was, lips curved into a tight smile. When was this picture taken? She had never liked showing her teeth in photographs. Her dark hair was pulled back into a low bun, and she wore a white blouse with a blue ribbon on the front. The girl behind the glass had a twinkle in her eye. As if she knew an exciting secret.

She had been chosen to gamble.

SIX

Lo

Lo stumbled out of the room. She couldn't get out of there fast enough. An icy sweat made her shiver. Her heart wouldn't stop pounding. Everything spun around her, too bright and shiny. When she closed her eyes, hellish images returned. The blood. So much blood. She swallowed back bile and the bitter aftertaste of that strange potion.

A group of people huddled together on the other side of the room. Their bodies blurred until she saw a familiar rebozo and long pair of braids. Mayté.

Just the sight of her best friend was enough to vanquish the hell in her head. Lo blinked back tears. Without a doubt they had both made it into Fortune's Kiss. "Mayté!" Lo almost tripped over her cloak as she rushed to her best friend.

Mayté whirled around and her face lit up. "Gracias a Dios!"

They held each other tight. The smell of cinnamon with the subtlest hint of paint hit her nose. Mayté's smell. The best and most comforting scent in all of Milagro.

"I'm so relieved," Lo cried out.

"Me too," Mayté said. "For a moment, I didn't think I'd made it."

"Yes, I was so worried, but as soon as I saw your rebozo, I knew everything was going to be all right." Lo tugged at the fabric.

"Ay, that's why I wear it. It's my signature look." Mayté twirled. Lo tried to scoff, but she couldn't stop smiling. "But wasn't it so strange?" Mayté asked. "Did you have to drink a potion too?"

Lo's heart stopped. She slowly nodded.

"Ah! Then maybe all of us had to. As soon as I drank it, I had these strange visions. I saw myself as a famous painter. It was amazing. All the nobles were bidding on my artwork. *Mine.*"

"Well, my father became a good man," Lo blurted before Mayté could ask what she had seen. "And my family was happy." She slipped on a smile, even though everything inside her churned like a sick storm. Lies. But reliving the truth even for a moment would make her vomit.

"Oh, really?"

Lo nodded. She couldn't meet her best friend's eyes. Her own gaze traveled to Mayté's skirt. Scarlet and flowing.

Just like her father's blood.

A chill gripped Lo and the tiniest of voices whispered in her ear. *What would your dear friend do if she knew you murdered your father?*

"Lo?" Mayté gave her a questioning look.

"You're both here too?" a new voice interrupted.

Lo gasped and Mayté's mouth dropped.

Dominic Castro waved. He wore a bright red cravat at his neck. In the candlelight, his white suit almost appeared to glow. "It's good to see some familiar faces. I was worried I wouldn't know anyone." His cheeks were flushed, and black hairs stuck to his forehead.

Lo fought a frown. She came to Fortune's Kiss to escape her suitors. Still, he was the least offensive of them. He had laughed at Juan Felipe when she snapped at him, so he had a sense of humor. She managed something of a smile. "Dominic, I never expected to see you here."

"Yeah, what *are* you doing here?" Mayté bluntly asked.

An heir from Las Cuatro didn't need Fortune's Kiss, especially the oldest son. Someone like Juan Felipe or even Ernesto would have likely used their wish to make their family the most powerful in all of Milagro. What was Dominic's end game? She would have to keep her eye on him.

"I could ask you the same." Dominic quirked an eyebrow.

"I think it's obvious why I'm here." Mayté rolled her eyes.

"You're right. I'm sorry." He offered a weak smile. A genuine-seeming gesture, but Lo knew all too well that everyone wore a mask.

Mayté huffed and tugged her rebozo.

"Well, I . . ." Lo tried her best to muster up naive innocence. "I thought Fortune's Kiss looked fun, you know?"

"You're gambling your dreams just for the fun of it?" Dominic stared at her as if he saw through to the truth of her sins.

No, no. That was the paranoia talking. It must have been a lingering side effect of that damn potion. "Maybe." Lo smiled, resisting the urge to pull her cloak tighter around her. She needed to get a grip.

Before Dominic could question her any further, Mayté suddenly gasped, loud and strangled as if someone punched her in the gut. *"Carlos?"*

"What?" Lo whirled around. Mayté's older brother came in from one of the doors, bewilderment written all over his brown face. It was really him.

"Wha—" He slowed to a stop, a wide-eyed gaze locked on Mayté. Until it flickered to Lo.

A warm tremor ran through her heart. Carlos's attire may not have been as extravagant as Dominic's; he didn't have a suit or cravat. Instead, he wore a white dress shirt. The top couple of buttons were missing. He also had on beige slacks with a patch on the knee that his mother must have sewn on. His thick, unkempt hair wisped into the tiniest of curls just under his ear. He looked handsome . . .

"Hello!" Dominic waved. "Another familiar—"

"What do you think you're doing here?" Mayté's words echoed, catching the attention of the other entrants, but she didn't seem to care. She balled up her fists.

"I could ask the same thing," Carlos said, voice steady. He was the calm to her fury. Always the water to her fire. "I'm here to save our family, *including you.*" Always the voice of reason, but this time his words didn't douse Mayté's flames. This time they were liquid fuel.

"Save . . . *me*?" Mayté growled. "*Now* you've decided to do something?" Her nostrils flared and her entire body shook. "All these *years* you could have stepped up to help, and only *now* you're trying?"

Oh. Lo had seen her best friend look like that one other time before. When they were only twelve and Carlos had just turned thirteen. The two had fought about something Lo couldn't remember, but the part that stayed forever in her mind was how Carlos spilled his horchata all over the table, soaking the pile of sketches Mayté had toiled over. He swore it was an accident, but didn't get far in his explanation, because Mayté gave him a black eye.

And now she was about to do it again.

"It's too late!" She stormed toward Carlos, but Lo snatched her arm just in time.

"Let me go," Mayté growled.

"No." Lo clung to her best friend tighter. Mayté would never hurt her, no matter how angry she got. "Listen." Lo leaned close and lowered her voice. "Don't do this. Not here. You might get kicked out for fighting, and we must win this. Don't forget what's on the line."

That seemed to be enough to calm her. "Fine," she huffed.

"I wish you would have told me you intended to come." Carlos pinched the bridge of his nose. "Now we're competing against each other for the same thing."

Mayté let out a soft, bitter chuckle. "That's where you're wrong. I'm here for *myself*. When I win, I'm taking my fortune and getting out of Milagro."

Carlos flinched, the pain of her words worse than a black eye. "What about our family?"

"What about them?" she scoffed. "Why should I help my family when they couldn't care less about me? Carlos, you know what would have happened if I'd stayed. No one was going to try to stop it."

Dominic quietly stared. Lo wanted to snap at him to mind his own business, but someone clapped.

"My, aren't you Las Cinco children so amusing." A petite woman strutted to the front of the group. She was wearing a gaudy gown with puffed sleeves, big ribbons, and long gloves. Underneath her ridiculously big hat—decked out with flowers, ribbons, and . . . a birdcage?—short brown tendrils curled into ribbons that framed her milky white face. No doubt this fashion atrocity was coveted in Hispana.

"Who is that?" Mayté whispered.

"Señora Montoya," Dominic answered.

"La Reina de Los Vampiros," Lo whispered back, ignoring Dominic.

Señora Montoya stopped in front of them. Her thick perfume was suffocating. Her children had been the ones in the gleaming white carriage who had nearly run them down yesterday, and Lo could see where they had gotten their haughty attitudes. Señora Montoya tapped her cheek as she eyed the four of them. "Oh, my. No, I meant *Las Cuatro*." Her cold smile cut through Mayté and Carlos. She wrinkled her tiny little nose. "I apologize."

Carlos looked down, and Mayté gripped her rebozo tighter. How dare she? Lo opened her mouth, but Mayté spoke first. "Once I win, Las Cuatro won't matter." She stared straight into Señora Montoya's eyes. The world spat on Mayté and tried its best to pull her down to the mud, but no matter what happened, she held her head up high. Lo admired that.

"Ohhhh," Señora Montoya squawked. "Is that so, dear? Well, I can assure you when *I* win, Las Cuatro will never be the same."

No doubt if this deranged woman won, she would use the fortune and power to make sure el orden antiguo ruled all of San Solera once again. If Mayté and Lo lost, they would eventually return to a nightmare. A world possibly even worse than the one they'd left.

"Then may the best person win," Lo said, voice as sharp and cold as a steel dagger.

"Ah, Lorena de León," Señora Montoya cooed. "You could've been a perfect match for my son, had it not been for that bullheaded father of yours."

"Sorry, I never heard he intended to court me," Lo muttered. This woman had no idea her father was dead. While it was nice to hear someone speak ill of that demon, Señora Montoya deserved a spot next to him in El Infierno.

Lo felt both Carlos and Dominic staring.

Señora Montoya clucked her tongue. "Shame. Shame. Shame. Just imagine how much better off you would have been. The union between our families would have been such a powerful and influential one. The first of its kind. It would have brought in a new era."

An era of el orden antiguo slowly but surely devouring las grandes familias.

"And you're quite pretty, with such lovely skin." Señora Montoya grabbed Lo's chin and inspected her face as if she were a doll. "And your children would have been even lovelier. My Lucas could have given you babies with sunshine hair and eyes as bright and blue as the sky. Wouldn't that have been nice?" Señora Montoya drawled, voice light and dreamy.

Lo's lip curled. She wanted to rip the woman's hands off her.

"Why is she certain that the babies would look like that?" Dominic whispered a bit too loudly. "Only Dios can control that." He looked so confused and concerned. Lo fought a smile at the blatant mockery. Señora Montoya, on the other hand, seemed anything but amused, but before she could spit out a retort, a puff of smoke erupted a few feet away from her.

"Ay, madre de Dios!" she shrieked. Several others in the group gasped and swore.

"Congratulations to all of you," a voice boomed. The smoke cleared, revealing Misterioso, only he looked much different. He had replaced his black suit with a white one, along with a golden cape and cravat. He wore a matching top hat, and now his skull mask covered only the top half of his face, stopping just below his upper lip. He flashed a wide grin and tipped his hat. His animated movements reminded Lo of a wind-up toy. "The house has deemed all eleven of your souls worthy."

"Eleven?" Señora Montoya murmured. "Was it not supposed to be just ten? Perhaps there was a mistake and *one* of us *isn't* worthy to be here." She sneered at Mayté and Carlos.

"Actually," Misterioso interrupted, somehow hearing her, "our Gamemakers couldn't decide on just ten, so eleven it is."

Señora Montoya spoke loudly this time. "But the rules—"

"*We* make the rules," Mysterioso corrected. "Which means *we* can decide to change them."

"I see." Señora Montoya looked away and her cheeks turned a delicious shade of pink. Served her right for being such a wretch.

"Though between us and the wall, I much prefer even numbers." Mysterioso made a show of acting as if this were a scandalous secret. "Now, then. Take a look at those around you. Until the game ends, they will be both your brethren and your competition."

Mayté and Carlos glowered at each other, while Dominic smiled at Lo. She bit back a scoff and studied the rest of her competition.

She had expected the crowd to be full of people like Mayté and Carlos—the lower class desperate to change their fates—but she instantly recognized a middle-aged man with light brown skin in a lavish suit. Don Martín Zelaya's ancestors were infamous for leading Ciudad Milagro back when it was first colonized. They could be considered the source of el orden, though by the way he eyed Señora Montoya, gaze thick with contempt, it was clear that he thought himself better than even her. With a grin full of straight teeth, and a head of abundant, graying hair, he was aging gracefully. Some might have even considered him quite handsome, but Lo knew better. He reminded her of her father. He had a coldness to him, all the way down to the icy undertones in his complexion.

Next to him stood Xiomara Fernandez, her burgundy lips turned up like a cursed crescent moon as she grinned and laughed at whatever Don Zelaya said. Her deep amber skin glowed against her plunging red gown and her crown of dark brown curls added to her allure. She sparkled like a jewel and by the confident way she carried herself, she knew it too. She often did business with Lo's father and the other noble families. Sometimes Lo wondered if she was one of her father's mistresses with the way she always came around the hacienda. Why would the likes of those two need Fortune's Kiss?

Lo caught a lighter-skinned woman staring at her. She had on a pink dress embroidered with a rainbow of flowers. Shiny raven hair hung freely just past her shoulders. "*Carmen?*" Lo whispered. She almost hadn't recognized her favorite maid out of her uniform, but she could never forget Carmen's kind and comforting face. As soon as they locked eyes, Carmen smiled and nodded at her. Lo's stomach churned. After everything Carmen had done to protect Lo and her sisters from her father, now Lo would repay her by competing against her and ruining her chances of making her dreams come true.

"On that note." Misterioso lifted a gloved finger, bone-white like the rest of his attire. It made the small bits of his visible brown skin stand out, but the real star of the show was his toothy grin, framed by the deepest dimples that Lo had ever seen. "Let us begin our first game."

"What?" Lo gasped and the rest of the competitors burst into confused murmurs.

"Already?"

"Don't we need to settle in?"

"But you just said—"

"Now, now," Misterioso cheerfully scolded. "The game will be explained in due time, and afterward we shall have our welcome dinner and then a tour of the salon. It will be very grand, so I sincerely hope you are all . . . able to make it." His gaze met every player. "Now come along," Misterioso said. "Everyone is awaiting your arrival."

Misterioso ushered them all onto the elevator. The circular box fit the final eleven with room to spare. He snapped his fingers, and the elevator began its steady ascent. Lo's stomach squeezed with anticipation. Dominic hovered around them as if he were one of his own loyal pooches, and Carlos kept trying to talk with Mayté only to be shushed and waved away each time.

"Young man." Misterioso turned to Carlos after his fourth failed attempt at speaking with Mayté. "The señorita didn't want to talk to you a moment ago, I don't think she will change her mind so quickly."

The other contestants chuckled, Dominic included.

Carlos's ears reddened, and he didn't say another word.

The elevator slowed to a stop. "This is where the magic happens," Misterioso declared as the doors opened. The group stepped into a large room and gaped at their surroundings. "Welcome, contestants, to the gaming den. This is where you will compete for Fortune's Kiss."

This room stretched out, full of different tables. Candle chandeliers dangled from above, illuminating a night sky mural above. Black velvet curtains covered each doorway, and golden skeletal sculptures stood guard. The walls and seats were the color of crushed rubies. Vines and orange marigolds slithered down marble pillars. Statues of alebrijes flanked the doors—scowling lions with feathered manes, butterfly wings, and the tail of a mermaid. The air carried a slight whiff of incense and forbidden magic. Everything about this space dripped with eerie luxury, suited for the nobles of the Underworld.

Applause filled the room. Lo flinched. She hadn't even noticed that there were other people. Croupiers dressed in black suits came forward, faces decorated to resemble calaveras.

"Wait!" Lo gasped and darted out from the group of players. What if Mamá was here among them, working off her debt? Her heart drummed as she gazed all around in search of bouncing, light brown curls and the kind smile she had missed for much too long.

"What on earth is she doing?" Señora Montoya scoffed. "A young lady should know how to compose herself."

Lo whirled around, ready to snap, but the grimace on Mayté's face silenced her. "I . . . I'm not doing anything," she muttered and, as she moved further into the center of the room, nearly ran into someone.

"Easy now, señorita." A young man steadied her by the shoulders. His dark suit was much more extravagant than the rest of the croupiers'. His jacket had purple accents and golden buckles, which matched his shoes and gloves. He also didn't have his face painted, but he didn't need it—his skin was ghostly pale. His black hair was slicked back into a low ponytail, and he had the most piercing blue eyes. Those blue eyes traveled down to her slip dress. Lo could have tried to cover up but didn't.

"Ah, yes." Misterioso took a step toward the man. "This is our Banker; he will oversee all the games." The two men were opposites. While Misterioso was bright and cheerful like a dancing skeleton, the Banker seemed dark and sinister like La Muerte. He couldn't have been much older than Carlos, yet here he was in a position of power. Interesting . . .

"A pleasure," the Banker said, his voice cool. "I look forward to watching the games unfold." He briefly gazed at the other players, but then returned his attention to Lo. The way he stared, surely he was enamored with her. "And it is especially a pleasure to meet a contestant as beautiful as yourself. What is your name?"

"Lorena de León."

"Welcome to Fortune's Kiss, Lorena." He took her hand and kissed it.

"Oh my, how the time has passed," Misterioso interjected, pulling a chained hourglass out of his pocket. Filled with black sand, the gold-trimmed glass barely fit in the palm of his hand. "Please have a seat and we'll get started."

As everyone sat at the circular table, the candelabras changed color from orange to pink, then to an eerie blue. The other croupiers' expectant gazes burned through Lo. A feeling she was all too familiar with. Her father had always paraded her around at parties, like a beautiful toy made for others to admire, but now, under so many eyes, it felt like she had been unveiled to the world. "Come on." She took Mayté by the arm and led her to the table. She sat directly across from the Banker.

"You've chosen the best seat in the house." The Banker leaned against the table, eyeing her with fascination.

Lo laughed. "We'll see if that's true."

Mayté fidgeted and grumbled something under her breath. She always got like that around Lo's suitors. Sometimes Lo wondered if her best friend envied her, but she never dared ask. She didn't want to know the answer. From the corner of her eyes, she caught Carlos staring, but Dominic took the other seat next to Lo before he could.

"Lorena." He leaned in closer. "May I ask, why are you wearing um . . . that." He nodded at her slip dress, eyes darting as if looking too long would turn him to stone.

"Oh. Well . . ." Lo tugged at her cloak. With everything happening she hadn't thought of a convincing excuse.

"Why does it matter to you? You shouldn't be staring." Carlos bumped into Dominic's chair as he walked by and sat next to him.

Lo bit back a smile. A thrill of warmth unfurled in her chest.

"Listen closely, dear contestants, because we will only explain the rules once," Misterioso bellowed.

The Banker snapped his fingers, and boards full of colorful squares appeared. Lotería boards. Lo gasped and grabbed Mayté's arm. "The game is Lotería."

"Our game!" Mayté sounded delighted. How many lazy afternoons had they spent as children playing with Mayté's abuela? It was as if the game had been made just for them.

Everyone at the table stared in awe as the boards orbited around the Banker.

"How did he do that?" Dominic whispered.

No one cast a spell or whispered an incantation; it just . . . happened. The other croupiers murmured to each other and pointed, not at the Banker, but at the contestants. As if they were the interesting part of this entire magic show.

The Banker shuffled the boards like a giant deck of cards. His gaze flicked to Lo, as if checking her reaction. Sure, she was entranced, but she made sure to play up the amazement and delight on her face. Satisfied, he looked away. "I'll deal this round."

"You all are familiar with Lotería, I'm sure." A board appeared in Misterioso's hand. Lo squinted. Some of the pictures looked familiar, like La Sirena, the mermaid with flowing black hair and a ruby red tail, and El Gallo, the lively rooster with fluffed-out feathers. But there were other images she didn't recognize, like the one of a a Xolo dog, and another with a shield made of steel. "As you know, you place beans on your board." He threw up his hands and thousands of tiny, hard beans rained down from the ceiling, pelting the players and bouncing endlessly off the table. No beans fell on the Banker, who looked quite amused.

"You will receive a bonus for filling a whole line." He ran his finger horizontally across the board, then vertically and diagonally. "Or if you fill up the big picture frame." He tapped the four outer corners. "Or the small picture frame," he said, pointing to the four center squares. "However, the true winner of Fortune's Kiss is the one who fills their entire board first."

"Easy," Mayté mumbled to herself, but Lo wasn't so sure.

Games with the objective of filling the entire board always held the most tension. By the end, several people would need only one more square to win. And now there were more than a handful of bronze coins and other tiny trinkets on the line.

Dominic's eyebrows scrunched. "But Lotería is purely luck. There's no skill in it at all."

"Are you certain of that?" Mayté scoffed, but for once Lo had to agree with her would-be suitor. Picking the correct board was purely at the mercy of San Fortuno.

"Ah, very good point, my boy." Misterioso materialized behind Dominic, giving his back a hearty pat. "Of course, our version of the game is much more exciting. I could explain, but I think it'll become clearer once we begin. Our first round will be unique.

In most instances, we choose the cards, or as some say, the cards will choose one of you, but this is your opportunity to be the one in control. Do I have any volunteers?"

"Me!" Mayté's hand shot up.

"Oh, no, no, no!" Señora Montoya stood. "If anyone should go first, it should be *me*." She waved around her cigarette, dumping ashes onto the player next to her. "That is the way Dios would have it."

Mayté's nostrils flared. "We aren't still living in the time of the crown, and anyhow, all of us were chosen. We're all on equal standing here. So I don't—"

Lo grabbed her arm. "Just let her go first," she whispered. "Then we'll see how this game is played."

A few croupiers at the nearest table snickered to each other. Lo glared at them.

Mayté's face reddened. "Fine." She slapped some beans away from the table.

"Very well," the Banker said. The cards floated in front of him, back sides facing Señora Montoya and the rest of the players. "Choose a card, choose your fate," he said, deep voice smooth and alluring.

"I will." Señora Montoya grabbed one of the cards and flipped it over. "Mmm." With a smirk, she appraised her board. "El Gorrito." She grabbed a bean between her thumb and index finger and placed it on her board. The bean glowed and melted away. With a flash, a giant El Gorrito card appeared in front of her, depicting a silky pink bonnet with white lace ruffles. Sofía and Sera had worn bonnets like that when they were babies. A tiny pang poked Lo's heart at the thought of her sisters.

"What is your wager?" the Banker asked.

"What is she supposed to bet?" Carlos said. "We don't have anything with us."

Lo patted her cloak and the realization hit her that Mamá's comb was gone along with her satchel. Mayté dug her hands through her skirt pockets, her painting must have been gone too. "Ah, never fear." Misterioso waggled his finger. "For this round, you may wager whatever your heart desires. The house always finds a way to claim what it's owed."

"Mm." Señora Montoya tapped her nails against the table in contemplation. "What shall I wager?"

"Maríana, you'd best make it something good," Don Zelaya said. "We want to start on a strong note."

Xiomara Fernandez leaned in and spoke softly to him. Her dark brown eyes looked almost fiery.

Señora Montoya's lips curled, and she turned away as if she had witnessed something vile and disgusting. "And you, Martín, best not shame our people with whom you associate." La Orden saw even the middle class as far beneath them. Still, Lo thought it was a smart strategy for Xiomara to find favor with Don Zelaya. "Enough banter, I wager a sizable amount of my family's fortune. I have so much of it, it's impossible to keep track of how big it is." Señora Montoya sneered. "Now, let's get this started."

"Ah, if you insist, señora." Misterioso shrugged, then snapped his fingers.

"Quickly, bebé," an eerie voice rumbled. "Like a good child, obey my words. Put on your bonnet and follow my lead." The same bonnet from the card appeared and flew to Señora Montoya.

Don Zelaya, Xiomara, and a couple of others at the table chuckled.

"What?" Señora Montoya swatted the bonnet away as if it were a fly. Her pale face flushed red. "What kind of nonsense is this?"

"Hurry, hurry," the card groaned as if in pain. "Put me on."

A pit formed in Lo's stomach. Mayté frowned, forehead creased. Dominic pressed a knuckle against his lips. Carlos folded his arms and squinted.

"Hurry . . . ," the card urged again.

"No," Señora Montoya snapped. "I'm not going to put on this silly thing. I thought this would be a real game. Is this entire thing just one big farce?"

The card flashed red.

Señora Montoya shrieked as she stumbled back. Bare feet poked out from under her gown. Her gaudy hat vanished, then her golden jewelry. Her gown transformed into tattered rags.

Don Zelaya and the others' amused whispers ceased.

"You lose," the Banker said, voice matter-of-fact. "You've lost your fortune and place as a noble. Your children are now destitute."

"What is the meaning of this?" Señora Montoya pounded her palms on the table, and beans went flying.

"Señora, you wagered a sizable amount, but you weren't specific. The price you paid *was* sizable, no?" Misterioso explained.

"But I didn't know!" Her voice shook. "Give it back!" Seeing Señora Montoya reduced to such a state should have felt vindicating, but instead it was disturbing. How easily could that happen to Lo or Mayté in another round? They needed to play carefully.

"Ah, I cannot do that, I'm afraid, but you have the chance to win it back," Misterioso said. "You must keep wagering until you pass El Gorrito's challenge. I have no fear that you won't be able to. You could say this challenge is so simple that even a baby could do it. Remember, in this round, you can bet anything your heart desires. *Anything.*"

"Fine." Señora Montoya snatched the bonnet and squished it onto her head. "Then I bet everything I have left. My home. My beauty. All of it." She smirked at the other contestants. "Just watch me win it back and more."

"That's the spirit." Misterioso grinned.

"Pick up a bean," the card groaned.

Señora Montoya plucked a bean between her fingers. She stumbled again as her high-heeled shoes reappeared on her feet along with a golden necklace at her throat. She smirked with triumph.

"What! This is nothing like Lotería," Mayté whispered.

"I'm confused," Dominic said as the rest of the table mumbled to themselves.

"Is this how all the challenges will be?"

"Everything we lose will just vanish into thin air? But you can get it back if you gamble more?"

"Is this going to put her at a large advantage?"

Lo frowned. Now that awful woman was going to win back everything with ease. It didn't feel fair. "Please . . . ," Lo whispered in prayer, squeezing her eyes shut. "Don't let her win. Don't let her win. Don't let her win." She prayed to Dios, and San Fortuno. She had stopped praying years ago when her pleadings went unanswered, but right now it was the only thing she could do.

"Pick up a handful of beans and count them," the card ordered.

Señora Montoya tittered with glee as she swiped a bunch of beans and used her finger to count them. "One, two, three, four, five, six, seven, eight, nine, ten, eleven, twelve. Twelve beans."

"That's too easy," someone at the table whispered.

Lo's heart sank.

But the card glowed red, and the room shook. The Banker looked up, startled. His icy blue eyes darted to Lo. His stare was so intense, she had to look away. Misterioso straightened, looking surprised as well. He grinned widely again, his eyes aglow with excitement. The dimples in his cheeks deepened, turning his expression into something almost dangerous. He nodded at the Banker, who quickly cleared his throat.

"Unfortunately, señora, you are wrong," he said, voice devoid of emotion.

Lo jolted.

"What?" Señora Montoya practically screamed as everyone else at the table glanced at each other in confusion.

"She . . . counted them right. I saw," Mayté whispered.

"There are twelve beans," Señora Montoya insisted. Her pale face reddened when the Banker shook his head. "Don't be foolish, the rest of you saw me count them." She held out her palm and counted the beans slowly and forcefully. "One. Two. Three. Four. Five," she spat. "Six. Seven. Eight. Nine. Ten . . ." She slowed, and her eyes widened. "Eleven . . . t-twelve . . ." But there was one more bean in her hand. *Thirteen.*

Everyone else at the table looked just as shocked.

"That can't be right," Mayté murmured.

"She had twelve, didn't she?" Xiomara asked Don Zelaya, who scratched his head in confusion.

But now she had thirteen. The only logical explanation was the impossible. Magic. "Mayté." Lo tugged her best friend's rebozo. "Do you think . . ."

Without warning, the card flew at Señora Montoya's head.

Something warm squirted onto Lo and everyone else. Señora Montoya's body fell with a loud *thud*. A river of crimson blood flowed, staining her gown and furs. *Blood.* Blood on Lo, on her face and hair. All over her dress. Spatters of red on Mayté's white shirt. Bloody freckles on her nose and cheeks. Smears on Dominic. Droplets staining Carlos's dress shirt. The sickening scent of iron filled the air.

"¡Dios mío! Her head! Her head's gone!"

The contestants flew from their seats. A shrill scream erupted. It took a second for Lo to realize it was her own. The Banker casually blotted his face with a handkerchief. His cold gaze flicked to Lo, before he turned away.

Mayté stared at Señora Montoya's body. No, her corpse. Mayté's body trembled and her eyes filled with tears.

If Lo hadn't stopped her, it would've been Mayté on the floor, head cleanly severed. Her heart raced faster than it ever had before. Her stomach fluttered and she wanted to vomit. She stumbled back into Carlos, who steadied her. Lo's heart pounded so hard. Carlos spoke fast and frantically, but she couldn't make out his words.

"And there we have it," Misterioso said, holding both hands out like a performer. "Maríana Montoya wagered *everything*, which of course includes her life."

This is not a game. This is el infierno, Lo thought. It was the only explanation. She was being punished for killing her father.

Fortune's Kiss was supposed to fix everything, but now it would be their damnation.

SEVEN

Mayté

Mayté didn't remember when or how she got on the floor. Maybe her legs gave out on her, or maybe she chose to sit. It didn't matter. Not when everything else erupted into pure chaos. People around her screamed, sobbed, and shouted, but the silence from the croupiers was even louder. They draped a blanket over Señora Montoya's body. *Her headless corpse.* Where had her head even gone? Mayté stopped herself from looking. She didn't want to know. The croupiers carried Señora Montoya's body off as if she were a freshly killed mule deer. The rest of them ambled about, quietly sweeping up the beans from the floor and table, while others started washing away the blood.

Fortune's Kiss wasn't a castle of dreams gilded in gold, it was an altar dripping with blood, and the eleven—*now ten*—contestants were sacrificial offerings.

It wasn't supposed to be like this.

"Please, señor!" Xiomara yelled at Misterioso, burgundy lips quivering. Almost as stark as the spatters of blood on her cheek. "I don't want to play anymore!"

Misterioso clicked his tongue and lifted a hand. Not even the smallest drop of blood stained his suit. "It's Misterioso, and unfortunately, you've made a commitment to see this through . . . until the end."

The end. Those two simple words filled Mayté's veins with ice.

"We didn't know what kind of game this would be!" a man snapped.

"Y-you can't just force us to stay," another man joined in.

Mayté had recognized them the moment she sat down at the table. The first man was the awful owner of the paint shop, while the other was Señor Vásquez, the owner of the elote stand. She felt almost numb to this discovery. The day she crossed paths with both of them was also the day Fortune's Kiss had returned.

That day, they were all damned.

"I'm afraid you've already paid the entry fee. There is nothing we can do."

"No! You can't hold us all hostage!" The shopkeeper bolted past Misterioso straight for the elevators. He pounded the button, but the doors wouldn't open. He whirled around, dark eyes wild. His wiry mustache and beard had taken the brunt of the blood.

"Hostage? You came here willingly." Misterioso chuckled, unfazed. How many times had he gone through this with past contestants? "Trust me when I say if you fold now, you will leave in a much worse state than Maríana Montoya."

"THIS IS MADNESS!" the shopkeeper screamed.

Mayté would have welcomed the opportunity to see that stingy weasel in distress, if her own stomach hadn't been churning.

The shopkeeper pleaded with the other croupiers. "Can't you see how terrible this is?" When they ignored him, he turned to the Banker, who looked quite upset—at the blood staining his suit. "Please! If you have any heart at all, tell him to let us go!"

The Banker tossed aside a bloodied handkerchief. "Nothing I can do about it, señor. This is the game. You'd do well to play your hardest, and pray you win."

The shopkeeper backed away, trembling. Mayté's own fingers wouldn't stop shaking and her chest was tighter than the corsets she used to wear. What had she done? Why had she come here? Her heart twisted in her chest. Why had she brought that poster to Lo?

Lo.

As if a curse had broken, Mayté searched for her best friend. She stood up on shaky legs, only to find herself face-to-face with Carlos.

He touched her arm. "Are you ok—"

"Don't!" She wrenched away. It didn't matter that everyone was staring, because among them stood Lo. She was the bloodiest of all. Splatters of bright red covered her slip like rose petals on fresh snow. She stared, unblinking, at the spot where the death had happened.

Without a word, Mayté rushed over and hugged her tight. It didn't matter that they were both drenched in sweat, or that they trembled like newborn pups. Mayté wasn't sure if she felt Lo's racing heart, or if it was her own heart throbbing erratically. "Thank you," she choked. "Thank you for not letting me play that horrific game."

For several moments, Lo stood stiffly, but soon hugged her back tightly.

The biggest lump formed in Mayté's throat. Her vision swam. She pressed her quivering lips together and swallowed the swirling terror and sorrow. She couldn't cry. She had to be strong, no matter what.

"On that note," Misterioso declared, casual as could be, as if he weren't responsible for this bloodbath. "I promised all of you a grand dinner and tour. If we want to do that before the night's end, we should be off."

It was not a suggestion. Several croupiers ushered them to the elevator. Mayté glanced back. The Banker headed in the opposite direction. The rest of the croupiers continued cleaning. She caught one staring at her. His painted face looked almost sympathetic.

Or maybe it was something her mind conjured up, desperate for someone, anyone, to see how horrific this entire thing was. Before she could figure out if it was real or not, he turned away. Mayté and Lo clutched each other tight until they reached the dining room.

The pungent yet rich aroma of spices and fried meat filled the air as everyone stepped off the elevator. Such savory scents should have made Mayté's mouth water, but instead she almost gagged. She gripped her stomach as everyone ambled to a large table that was covered with a silky white tablecloth and marigold centerpieces. How could she eat when the smell of blood lingered in her nostrils?

From the corner of her eye, she spotted Carlos inching his way closer. Her fury toward him faded into terror. What if he met the same fate as Señora Montoya? Just looking at him made her mind conjure up scenarios of his death. She swallowed the urge to retch. She couldn't do this. Not now.

Next to her stood Dominic. This entire time, he had been eerily quiet. He stared straight ahead, face pale and cheeks feverish. "Come sit with us, Dominic." She tapped his arm, causing him to flinch.

"Oh." He blinked. "Yes. Of course." With a weak smile, he followed Mayté and Lo to the table and sat on Mayté's right, while Lo took her left. Carlos snagged the seat next to Lo.

"I don't want to talk to him," she told Lo out of the corner of her mouth. *"Please."* Her voice cracked.

"Don't worry," Lo whispered before turning to Carlos. "Hi."

"Lo, are you—are you two okay?" He leaned forward, trying to catch Mayté's eyes.

Mayté quickly turned away as a line of servers came over, holding platters covered by golden cloches. They each wore identical skull masks and moved in swift coordination as if they had rehearsed this over and over again.

Were these people here working off their debts?

That would mean that not everyone who played died a horrific death.

Maybe things weren't as bad as she thought. But Señora Montoya . . . No matter what, she couldn't get that image out of her head.

One by one the servers set the platters in front of everyone at the table. All ten of them. There was an empty spot across the table where Señora Montoya would have sat. The golden cloche, without a single fingerprint or blemish, reflected the exhaustion and horror on Mayté's face. *And the blood.* Spatters all over her face and blouse. She would have tried to wipe it off, but all at once, the servers lifted the cloches from everyone's plates. Warm steam and a familiar spicy smell hit her nose.

"For the first course of our welcome feast, we have soup made for joyous festivities such as this: menudo rojo!" Misterioso announced as the servers poured everyone water and wine. The contestants squirmed as they stared at their steaming bowl of tripe soup. White hominy floated in the cream-colored broth. Misterioso was mistaken. This was menudo blanco. Mayté squinted. The tiniest bit of red floated in the center of her bowl. Then it spread, just like a bloody cloud—until the entire soup turned red. She gasped.

Lo gave her a questioning look. Mayté shook her head. Had it been her imagination?

"Enjoy your meal," Misterioso said.

But no one touched their menudo, or even made a move to sip their drinks. Mayté couldn't eat.

"Oh, come now." Misterioso paced around the outer edge of the circular table. When he crossed behind Mayté, the hairs on her arms stood. "Being here and competing for the chance to be kissed by fortune, is this not what you wanted? Out of thousands of people, *you* were chosen. You made it through the first game as well. This is a time to celebrate!"

Someone let out a small sob. Mayté couldn't bring herself to look and see who it was. She wouldn't be able to handle it. She glanced at Lo, who kept reaching for her spoon, only to draw back at the last second. Before she could stop herself, her gaze traveled to Carlos. He frowned at his bowl. He wasn't one for outbursts or crying. Instead, whenever he got upset, he became quiet, as if retreating somewhere deep in his mind. The time their father gambled away all the coins he had been saving, he didn't yell at him or complain. None of that. He just went to his room and didn't talk to anyone for the rest of the night.

What must he be feeling in this moment?

She almost hated that she let herself wonder.

"But please also keep this in mind." Misterioso continued his pacing. "Maríana Montoya specifically wagered *everything*. Of course, something so broad includes her very life and soul."

Soul? A sharp cold jolted down Mayté's spine.

"There are rules within the chaos of the house," Misterioso went on. "For some rounds, you will choose your wagers yourselves. For others, the house chooses what you'll wager."

What? That sounded even worse! Distressed gasps and frantic mumbles filled the room.

"Ah, but don't be alarmed," Misterioso cooed as if comforting a child mid-tantrum. "I can assure you that the house will not ask for your lives so quickly. Imagine how boring it would be if everyone dropped like flies so suddenly."

Boring? Who would be bored? she wondered. Was this all for Misterioso's sick entertainment?

"Perhaps *you* will get the chance to choose what you wager in another round or two," Misterioso said. "Not everyone has to wager so much, especially not all at once. You may play much more conservatively if you wish."

"Ah, but those who play it safe never emerge victorious," Don Zelaya said, wearing the slimiest of smirks. "We should bet big! But unlike Montoya, Dios rest her soul, I'll play it *smart*."

"I like the way you think!" Misterioso grabbed a goblet of wine from one of the servers and raised it. "¡Salud!" But before he or Don Zelaya could drink, Xiomara retched and turned away from the table. She vomited all over the floor. Mayté didn't see it, but she didn't have to. She wasn't sure what sickened her more: the sloshing splash or Xiomara's whimpering groans.

"Oh dear." Misterioso handed off his goblet to a server. "We'll get that cleaned up right away."

A few of the servers rushed to clean up the mess, while another led Xiomara into a hallway.

"If anyone else needs to excuse themselves, you may follow them to the lavatory," Misterioso said. "But do keep in mind, there are no exits, so if your intent is to escape, don't bother."

Dominic snatched his napkin and pressed it against his mouth, suppressing a gag. He jumped from his seat, almost knocking over his chair, and rushed into the hallway.

"Now, please, you must be hungry," Misterioso urged.

"How can you expect us to eat after that bloodbath!" The shopkeeper threw his bowl off the table, sending glass and menudo flying. Much in the same way Mayté had thrown the pot of paint. That felt like a lifetime ago. "Stop telling us to eat, because WE CAN'T!" He pounded his fist, shaking the entire table. Next to him, a woman burst into anguished sobs. It took a moment, but Mayté recognized her. She was one of Lo's maids. The only one who still treated Mayté like a princess even after her family lost everything rather than gossiping like everyone else. It was terrible to see someone as kind as her stuck in this horrific place.

But then it dawned on Mayté. She knew most of these contestants. Was everyone here connected in some way?

A spoon clinked against a bowl. Lo took a delicate sip of menudo, then another spoonful and another.

"How can you keep it down?" Mayté whispered.

"A good bowl of menudo always c-c-comforts me," she whispered back. Her answer may have sounded confident, but her fingers shook, dribbling soup onto the tablecloth. For Lo's sake, Mayté didn't call her bluff.

"This is the best food I've had in ages," a man gruffed before slurping a spoonful. Mayté looked up at him and froze. The vaquero from last night. The exact one who had grabbed her. Outfitted in a dress shirt and without his hat or bandanna, she almost hadn't recognized him, but his voice gave it all away. Her scalp tingled and the lump in her throat grew as she stared. Broth dribbled down his scruffy chin. He wiped his mouth with his sleeve and continued shoveling in the soup. Then he glanced in her direction.

She had to get away. "E-e-excuse me." She shot up from her seat, only to crash into someone. "S-s-sorry."

"No, I should have watched where I was walking." It was the croupier who had been staring at her earlier. Up close, the paint on his face was full of haunting detail. An intricately patterned spiderweb emerged from his dark brown hair, which was styled away from his face. Painted black swirls at his chin emphasized his sharp jaw. A stitched smile had been painted at his lips; his frown fought with the cartoony illusion. Hazel eyes popped against the black paint, and thick eyebrows furrowed with concern. "I know you must not be very hungry," he said, lowering his voice. "But you should at least stay hydrated." He pointed to the glass of water at her place. "Tonight's dessert is pan dulce. I've found sweets go down much easier, and you'll feel better if you eat a little. Trust me." His lips curved into a slight smile. "If you have time, maybe stop by the library. It's a good place to sit and think."

"I—okay. Y-y-yes," Mayté stammered as her face flushed. "Thank you." Unsure what else to do, she sat back down.

The croupier continued on his way until Misterioso pulled him aside, giving him orders of some kind. As the two spoke, the croupier kept glancing at Mayté with those hazel eyes. Or was it all in her head? For all she knew he could have been eyeing Lo, next to her, just like every other boy.

Mayté took the smallest sip of water. Then another, and another. The cool liquid soothed her dry throat. When she looked back up, the croupier was gone.

As promised, pan dulce was the final course of the hellish meal. The servers set down a platter spilling over with colorful pastries and cookies, but unlike those at the street mercado, which might or might not have been stale, these were clearly just pulled from the oven. The sweet warm scent brought Mayté's curdled stomach back to life. Flecks of sugar winked under the light of the chandelier, and vibrant shades of pink and rich chocolaty brown begged to be devoured.

She grabbed a polvoron rosa and took a bite. It crumbled onto the table and melted in her mouth. The subtle sweetness tasted so much like home, it almost brought tears to her eyes. She barely touched the rest of her meal, but before Misterioso gathered everyone for a tour of Fortune's Kiss, she had eaten a concha and two empanadas. She felt better, but only a little.

As Misterioso led them back into the elevator, no one said a word. It seemed everyone had accepted their fate.

Or so Mayté thought.

As soon as the doors opened, the shopkeeper bolted out, sprinting down the hall without looking back.

No one chased him. Misterioso didn't even bat an eye. Instead, the masked man stepped out of the elevator with an amused chuckle. "Let us continue."

Mayté was no expert on architecture, but Fortune's Kiss seemed much bigger on the inside than the outside. From the street she would have guessed it was around five floors, yet they had already seen five and the elevator continued to ascend.

"The library," Misterioso said as the doors opened. Mayté could see the enormous room—a whole floor, it seemed—filled with wall-to-wall shelves of books.

The croupier. This was the place he meant . . .

The doors opened on another floor and there was a theater with twinkling lights and plush seats. Misterioso told them that live entertainment played there every evening. On another floor there was an indoor garden full of marigolds in different shades of pink, yellow, and of course, orange. The walls emulated the night sky, showing deep violet clouds and stars glittering like diamonds. Fireflies danced, aglow among the crosses sticking up from the ground. Was this actually a graveyard? If it was, Misterioso didn't say a word about it. Everything about this place was beautiful, yet no one marveled aloud. Someone sniffled. Dominic coughed. No matter how breathtaking this place was, it didn't change the terrible truth.

As they continued, things grew uncanny. The skulls on the walls seemed to be watching them. There were altars to Santos Sagrados she didn't recognize. The candles cast strange shadows across everyone's faces. As he led the group, Misterioso moved in grand, sweeping, exaggerated motion. Like a living, breathing skeleton, taking them through el infierno.

The tour ended in a large, circular lobby much like the entrance to Fortune's Kiss. Ten doors, black as the night stood out against the walls, white as bone. A chandelier hung overhead, lighting up several seats around a center table. A common area of sorts.

"Wait a moment." Misterioso held out a hand, then nodded at a door on the other side of the hall. As if on cue, it slammed open and out stumbled the shopkeeper. His face was drenched in sweat and his wild eyes grew at the sight of the group.

"But I—I . . . ?"

"Thought you could escape?" Misterioso casually drummed his fingers against a statue of an alebrije octopus. It wasn't until he ran his hand over one of the tentacles that Mayté realized they were snakes—each with gaping mouths revealing ivory fangs and forked tongues embedded with rubies. "The only way you're leaving the house is by losing or folding, I'm afraid."

The shopkeeper's shoulders sagged. It looked like at any moment, he would weep.

"You've missed the tour as well." Misterioso's voice darkened. "You will have to hope that someone else will be willing to show you around later. For now, I have something for each of you." He dug through his pocket and revealed a handful of keys. He then handed them over one by one. A single person per room. Mayté rubbed her shivering arms. She didn't want to be alone. Not yet.

"Mayté!" Carlos caught her off-guard and grabbed her arm before she could escape.

"I told you to leave me alone!" Mayté snapped. She couldn't even look him in the eye.

"I'm not leaving my *sister* alone," Carlos countered. "That game was . . ." He shuddered and shook his head. "Are you okay?"

"Do I look okay?" She gestured at the crusted-over blood on her blouse.

"This is why you need to get out of here while you can. The both of you." He briefly glanced at Lo, who seemed too stunned to respond.

"Bet low if you have the opportunity and fold quickly. I'll stay and handle everything."

"What?" Mayté broke free. "Do you know what you're saying? We gave our dreams to be here and I'm sure we're not getting that back if we fold. Why should *I* be the one to give that up? Have you considered giving up *your* dream? Do you even have one?"

"I—" Carlos blinked. His gaze briefly flicked to Lo again. "Of course I do! But survival is the most important part. You can't dream if *you're dead!*"

"Then go back! Live on and take care of Ma and everyone else!" She shut her mouth at the sight of the Banker strolling over.

"Lorena." He ignored Mayté and Carlos. "I have a special key for you." He twirled a golden key that made the black ones Misterioso had handed out look plain and useless. "For the finest suite here," he said, smooth as silk.

Mayté raised an eyebrow, and Carlos stiffened.

"Ah, but I have already handed out the keys." Misterioso walked over.

"Mm, perhaps, but this is *my* favor to Lorena." The Banker took Lo's hand and placed the key in her palm. "This key will transform your suite into a bigger one with two beds. You may invite anyone you wish to stay with you," he purred.

"Really?" Lo beamed and looked to Mayté. Now they would be able to stay in the suite. It was an unbelievable relief. A miracle.

Lo held the key to the light. The tip was a calavera accented with golden swirls and glimmering diamonds for eyes. "It's beautiful."

"But not as beautiful as you, señorita." The Banker smugly glanced at Misterioso, whose smile turned stiff. He looked between the Banker and Lo.

The tension in the air was so strong, Mayté could almost visualize it. Dark scribbles on parchment on the verge of ripping. Surely the two men were fighting for Lo's attention. Even in the world of Fortune's Kiss, her beauty did not go unnoticed. The tiniest flame of envy lit in Mayté's belly, but she quickly extinguished it. She hadn't wanted to be alone for the night, so this was a good thing.

"Well, thank you. It means the world to me," Lo said, then tugged Mayté's arm. "Come on. I need to sit for a while."

Now that the adrenaline had faded, Mayté's temples throbbed, and her shoulders burned. Her legs could barely carry her forward.

Lo led her to the door and fiddled with the lock until it opened. Mayté followed her inside and pulled the door shut behind her, but not before peeking out to see the two men glaring at each other.

And Carlos frowning at her.

She quickly closed the door.

Damn him.

But also, damn her. She didn't mean what she said. She didn't want Carlos to give up his dream. Whatever it might have been. Didn't want him to die, either. They needed to figure out a way to both survive. But how? The thought was way too overwhelming.

"Damn everything," she whispered.

A sob cut through the air.

Lo sank to the floor and covered her face. Her wail echoed against the walls of the cavernous room.

EIGHT

Lo

Lo couldn't stop sobbing. Her shoulders shook and she couldn't breathe. It had taken everything in her to keep it together during dinner. The moment it was just her and Mayté, she completely crumbled. She was a murderer and now trapped here, doomed to a fate even grislier than the one that had met her father.

"Lo." Mayté stepped in front of her, but Lo barely saw her. Instead, her gaze locked onto a painted calavera atop the vanity. Golden and covered in wilted roses, it faced her as if staring straight into her soul.

The same exact calavera she had seen after drinking that Dios-forsaken potion.

Suddenly, she was back in that dark room surrounded by only candles and bloody carnage. *No. No, no, no.* She bit her lip until she tasted metal. "M-M-Mayté—" Her mouth dried up and the rest of her words shriveled into her throat.

Lo's best friend was still there, but now the old blood staining her own face and blouse was the brightest and freshest of red. So fresh, it glimmered under the candlelight. Then there was her skirt. Lo didn't know where the scarlet fabric ended and the blood began, but, like a waterfall, it flowed down her legs. No, *waterfall* wasn't the right word. Waterfalls flowed fast, but the blood oozed. The crimson puddle pooling under Mayté's feet crept toward Lo. She stumbled back with a yelp.

"Lo?"

It was Mayté's voice, but when Lo looked up, a figure stared at her with cold, dead eyes. Blood spurted from his neck where she had slit his throat. She tried to run but got tangled in her cloak.

Her father. He was here for her.

"Lo."

She wanted to scream but couldn't.

"Lo?"

No matter how hard she tried.

"Lorena!" Mayté's voice cut through the dark and suddenly everything was back to normal. No more fresh blood on the floor, or on Mayté. The painted calavera was nowhere to be seen.

Mayté hugged her tight. "I'm here. It's okay."

Nothing was okay. Lo whimpered, "I'm sorry. I'm so sorry!"

"For what?" Mayté held her.

"You were going to leave, but I made you stay." Her vision swam with endless tears. "A-a-and now—"

"No," Mayté whispered. She brushed away the curls that stuck to Lo's wet cheeks. "We made a promise to each other. And I think—maybe it's good that we're here." She averted her gaze and chewed her lip.

"Why?" Lo whispered.

Mayté took a shaky breath. "Last night when Carlos needed help finding my father . . ." She shuddered. "There was a group of men waiting at our home. Thugs."

Lo's stomach lurched.

"They came for the money my father owed them, but he couldn't pay, s-s-so they . . . they were going to take me instead."

"No!" Lo gasped. She gripped her cloak tighter around her shoulders. If she had been there, she didn't know what she would have done.

Mayté nodded. She managed the slightest bit of a smile. "Here . . . at least here I have a chance. But, Lo." Her expression turned worried. "You have to tell me the truth. Something happened with you before we entered Fortune's Kiss, didn't it?"

Lo couldn't hide the fear on her face.

"That's why you were almost late, and why you're dressed this way." Mayté tugged at the cloak. "What happened?"

If Mayté knew, what would she—

"Lo." Mayté squeezed her hand. "You know you can tell me anything."

That was true. Mayté was the only one who knew the extent of the terrible things her father had done. Lo was the only one who knew what Mayté's family had to endure.

But this was different.

Wasn't it?

"Lo, please," Mayté pressed.

"B-b-before I left, my father tried to stop me." The words dribbled out, shaky and uncertain. "He found out my plan and wasn't g-g-going to let me leave. He threatened me. Wanted to hurt me. He grabbed me and I pushed him." The tears came back as the memories flooded in. "He fell into a shelf of v-v-vases a-a-and—"

Mayté hugged her tight and Lo lost the last thread of composure she had so desperately clung to. She could have continued. Should have. But then Sera's face filled her mind. Sofía's terrified, heartbroken wails rang in her ears. Would Mayté react the same way?

Lo had already lost her sisters. She couldn't lose her best friend.

"H-h-he's dead." She sobbed even harder.

"Oh, Lo . . ." Mayté rubbed her back.

"It's . . . my fault," she whispered.

"No," Mayté soothed, "it was an accident."

It wasn't.

"Anyone who knows the truth wouldn't hold it against you."

But it was all a lie.

Lo was a murderer.

But if being a liar meant keeping Mayté, then so be it.

"We'll clear your name when we get back to Milagro, but first we have to win this."

"Y-y-yes. You're right. Thank you." Lo hiccupped and wiped her face. Maybe it was wrong, but it felt like a weight had been lifted off her chest. With her father gone, the chains had been broken. She was free. And when she was victorious, she would find a way to make her life exactly what she wanted it to be. "I'm glad we get to share a suite. It's so beautiful." She smiled at Mayté to let her know she was okay now. The two finally had the chance to look around.

The room was marvelous. It made her own bedroom look plain in comparison. Two huge fluffy canopy beds with flowing orange curtains took up opposite ends of the bedroom. With the balcony doors open, bringing in the evening breeze, the curtains billowed like magical flames. Milky moonbeams cast their enchanting glow. The rest of the room was dark. The walls were a deep slate, with charcoal-black furniture. Soft candlelight illuminated the bouquets of marigolds on the table along with a tray of chocolates. The room was eerie, yet oddly calming in comparison to everything else in the house.

The walk-in closet could have been a room of its own. It was full of extravagant gowns, all in different jewel tones. Bold sapphires, mystical emeralds, romantic amethysts . . . with all the silk, lace, and tulle, it must have cost thousands of gold coins to make them. Then there were the vanity drawers spilling with jewelry. Necklaces, chokers, earrings, and bracelets. All gold and silver with jewels that sparkled brighter than the stars outside. While Mayté marveled at a pair of golden hoop earrings encrusted with diamonds, Lo stepped into the bathroom.

It was just like stepping inside a rosebud, with red walls on all sides. She never would have considered that such a color could feel so otherworldly. Black and white tiles led to a circular marble tub. Rose vines slithered down the wall like a curtain next to the tub, giving off their subtle sweet scent. "Let's wash up," Lo called into the dressing room. "Then we can figure out a plan for the rest of the games."

After her bath, Lo scrunched the excess water from her curls and changed into a flowing white nightgown with a high collar and puff sleeves. The soft satin soothed her skin, which she had scrubbed raw to ensure that every last flake of dried blood came off. Now she was spotless. A clean slate. This was her fresh start.

In the bedroom, Mayté sat on the bed nearest the balcony. Her long black hair hung freely down to her waist. So soft and glossy, those tresses would have been the envy of every noble girl who struggled to tame her hair with hot irons and beauty spells. A shame she rarely wore it down, but she always complained that it got in the way. Even when she restrained it with braids and buns, she somehow managed to get paint in it.

Staring off into space, Mayté ran a brush through her hair over and over again. Her eyes were still the slightest bit red and puffy. Maybe she cried while Lo was in the bath? Right now, Mayté was the stronger one, but they were both teetering on the edge. Every so often, Mayté paused to tug at her lacy nightgown, which kept slipping off her shoulder. It wasn't until Lo sat next to her that Mayté seemed to notice her. "Oh. How was your bath?"

"Warm. Refreshing." Lo scooted closer. "Are you ready?"

Mayté set aside the brush and took a deep breath. Then she re-braided her hair into one thick plait, reusing her red ribbon instead of one of the many jeweled hair accessories the room had to offer. The treasures in here had surely been bought with blood. "Okay."

As disappointing as it was to see her gorgeous hair pulled back, Lo knew that in that moment, Mayté meant business when she quickly said, "Señora Montoya died because she wagered everything, including her life. She didn't seem to fully understand what she was doing, but . . . I don't quite understand the rules either. This isn't like the Lotería we're used to."

Lo nodded. "It seems like the only thing they have in common is that you win by filling your board."

"If we don't figure out how to play properly, we might be the next to die." Mayté chewed her lower lip.

"That won't happen," Lo insisted. She held out her palm, still slightly scarred from their blood pact all those years ago.

With a small smile, Mayté held up her own scarred palm and pressed it against Lo's. Then she lowered her hand. "With Carlos here too, I'm wondering if there's a way we can all win."

Lo truly hoped so, but in all the legends of Fortune's Kiss winners, the victors were either one or a pair. Never a trio. "First, let's focus on learning the game and surviving. We need to find out something about the next round that could help us get ahead, and I'm certain the people who work here may have an inkling about that. For example"—she leaned against the pillow and smiled coyly—"that handsome croupier from dinner."

"Wh-wha—?" Mayté sputtered. Her spine stiffened straight as a board.

"I saw you," Lo teased in a singsong voice. "I heard what he said. *I've found sweets go down much easier.*" She tried to impersonate the deep timbre of his voice.

"You heard that?" Mayté shrieked.

Lo chuckled. From a young age, she had learned to use her ears. Listen for footsteps from her father. The heavier the sound, the more likely he was to be furious or drunk. Mamá had taught her that. She used her ears to her advantage in every situation after that. People talked louder than they realized. "He seemed quite concerned," she said. "Smitten, even."

"He was just being nice." Mayté grabbed a pillow and squeezed it against her chest.

"Maybe so, but men are only kind when they want something in return."

Mayté looked like she wanted to say something, but then seemed to change her mind. She looked away instead.

"Use that to your advantage. He'll become soft like clay. *Or* think of him as a blank canvas, free for you to paint your masterpiece on."

"Blank canvases aren't soft," Mayté muttered, but Lo ignored her.

"Get as much information as you can from him about the house and the games. We need every advantage if we're going to survive and win."

"Ugh! I'll try," she growled, but her red cheeks revealed that she was more flustered than anything. "No promises it'll work. I'm not good at this stuff like you."

"Nonsense!" Lo retorted. "You've already caught his attention. All you have to do is be yourself."

Mayté responded, not with words, but by hiding her face behind the pillow.

"And while you do that, I think I'll see what I can find out from Misterioso. He seemed quite sore after the Banker gave me this room. I can use that to butter him up."

Mayté's head shot up from the pillow, face no longer flushed. "Lo, be careful. After everything that happened tonight, he seemed . . . jolly? It felt sadistic. He's dangerous."

Lo couldn't help but scoff. She wasn't scared. No man could frighten her more than her father. "Maybe you're right, but we both have to do everything we can." She glanced out at the balcony. The full moon shone bright like a glowing opal, but she swore the dark spots made it look like a round calavera. "We should probably try to sleep. Who knows how early in the morning the next game will be."

Mayté shuddered. "I don't think I'll be able to sleep after . . . all that."

"I know." Lo took Mayté's hand and ran her thumb over the fading scar. Mayté's skin was rougher than Lo's, with some dry spots and a callus or two on her fingers. It was as if her scar hadn't healed as much either; it was pinker and the flesh still felt a bit jagged. "Remember what you told me? We just need to do our best and keep going."

Mayté nodded with a small smile. "As long as we stick together, we'll have an advantage over everyone else."

Lo knew it was true. As long as they were together, everything would be okay.

NINE

Mayté

Mayté spun around the dance floor. The cool night breeze invigorated her, and the colorful string of lights dangling above glowed extra bright against the black sky. With every twirl, her azure skirt fanned out around her like endless ocean waves. The cheerful pops of accordions and guitars, paired with rhythmic clapping from the crowd, pumped through her veins. She clapped her hands and stamped her feet in time with everyone else. These were the dances she had been taught by instructors before her father's disgrace. Despite everything, her arms and legs never forgot the swift movements. They were ingrained in both her heart and body.

All the boys wanted a turn to dance with her. Juan Felipe, Ernesto, and even Dominic. Their sombreros and embroidered suits glittered under the winking lights.

Lo was nowhere to be found.

Soon another boy pushed his way to the front and asked for a dance. She didn't recognize him, but he had the most beautiful hazel eyes she had ever seen. He took her by the hand and wrapped an arm around her waist. This dance would be different.

"Stop this at once!" a woman's voice boomed. As she commanded, everything ceased. The music, the cheering, even the boy released Mayté and stepped back.

The crowd parted and Señora Montoya marched to Mayté. Her long-sleeved gown made of bright red satin looked out of place, but somehow less absurd than the bonnet she wore. She looked even paler than usual, and that was saying a lot for La Reina de Los Vampiros. "Imposter!" The woman pointed a bony finger at Mayté. The blue veins in her wrist almost glowed. "You don't belong here!"

Mayté's face burned, and she blinked back tears.

Señora Montoya burst into cruel laughter. "You know what you are, so why are you here?"

Mayté squeezed her trembling fingers into fists. "Because it's not fair! I didn't tell my father to ruin everything! I want to be with the people I grew up with! I want suitors! I WANT THE LIFE I WAS PROMISED!" Her voice shattered and tears dripped down her cheeks. She was angry. So angry. And when she got that angry, she cried.

Señora Montoya stuck out her lower lip, then sneered. "Scream and cry all you want, but that won't change a thing."

She knew that already. She'd spent endless hours crying and crying until there were no more tears left in her. She hoped and prayed that Dios would see her pain and somehow, miraculously, fix things. But it never happened.

Her gorgeous dress began to melt away. The elusive azure dripped down like the paint she couldn't afford. It wasn't fair. Why did this have to happen to *her*? What sin did *she* commit to deserve this? Why?

"Now look at you!" Señora Montoya cackled.

"CÁLLATE!" Mayté screamed. "Why are you even here, you're supposed to be—" She slapped a hand over her mouth, stopping herself from finishing that thought. Her stomach twisted itself into anxious knots.

"What?" Señora Montoya made a strange face and tilted her head to the side. "Dead?" Her bonnet glowed, the ribbons constricting tighter and tighter around her neck. Her eyes bulged.

"NO! STOP!" Mayté turned away just as blood spattered on the poles next to her. "No . . . no, no, no." She gripped her head. "I'm sorry! I—I didn't mean to say it—" She fell to her knees. The lights above swirled around and became too bright. Nauseatingly so. She couldn't hold it in any longer. She vomited.

Mayté's eyes snapped open. Everything was dark and she lay in a fluffy bed with silky sheets. She was no longer on the dance floor covered in blood. Gracias a Dios. But what was that? That dream—*nightmare*—was the most chilling thing her mind had ever conjured. And reality wasn't much better.

Her eyes adjusted to the dark. The suite was the same as when she had fallen asleep. The balcony to her right, the bathroom straight ahead. The suite's door creaked shut, causing her to flinch. Lo wasn't in her bed. She'd left.

Mayté kicked away the blankets, but then shivered. The room was ice cold. She scurried to the closet where she found the most luxurious robe made of white silk with azure patterns. Of course. The color seemed destined to haunt her until the end of time. Still, she slipped it on and as much as she would've denied it, the robe was a warm, comforting hug. The way the sleeves puffed out at her shoulders and the long train trailing behind her as she tiptoed toward the door made her feel like a queen.

But this wasn't her castle.

She found an unlit candelabra on the table. But where were the matches? She reached for a drawer and nearly yelped when the candelabra lit on its own, casting an eerie glow throughout the room that clashed with the calming moonlight. Like a battle between El Cielo and El Infierno. She snatched the candelabra and left the room.

"Lo?" she called. But it seemed she was too late. Not a soul stood in the common area. She walked along the circular lobby, running her hand along the wall and doors. Was everyone else asleep? How could they be after the carnage they had witnessed?

Carlos was in one of these rooms. How was he doing? She didn't want to think about him, but she couldn't help it. What she needed to do was find out the rules of this damn place as quickly as possible. Then she could figure out a way for the three of them to win.

Was that why Lo left? Was she off to get information from Misterioso?

Mayté's stomach lurched. A haze of smoke and silence surrounded her. So quiet, she swore she heard a heartbeat—not her own heart thudding, but a rhythmic vibration inside the walls. The floor rumbled under her bare feet. It was as if the house was alive and breathing, but surely it was just paranoia—something left over from her nightmare. Still, her senses were on high alert. It felt like, at any moment, a hand would reach out from the dark and behead her.

Should she look for the croupier? she wondered. Was he even awake at this hour?

There was no way she would be able to get back to sleep, so she stepped into the elevator, but couldn't remember where anything was. That blasted tour was all a blur of beauty and blood. She pressed the button for the fifth floor and hoped for the best. At the very least, she could figure things out depending on where she ended up.

The doors opened and she journeyed through a dark hallway. As she passed by, lanterns on the walls lit up, but their flames were so dull, she could barely see much more than a few feet ahead. It soon sank in that this wasn't a place Misterioso showed them during the tour. It couldn't have been. This was just a long stretch of hallways lined with doors. So many doors. Every corner was just another long hallway full of them.

"Hello?" Mayté whispered.

No answer.

She tried one of the doorknobs. Locked. She tried another and another, but those were locked too. Maybe she wasn't supposed to be there. She turned and went back the way she came, or at least the way she thought she came, but the elevator was nowhere in sight.

No, this couldn't be right. Panic squeezed at her chest, and she walked faster and faster until she broke into a full sprint through the endless labyrinth of hallways and doors that led nowhere. What if she couldn't find her way out?

What if no one found her?

What if she died here?

What if—?

She found a flight of stairs and nearly stumbled as she rushed down them, through the next door and into—the library.

In the dark, the room looked sinister, but the burning fireplace on the far end of the room cast a warm glow.

How did she get here?

If you have time, maybe stop by the library. It's a good place to sit and think. The croupier's words filled her head.

Holding her breath, she took a few cautious steps. How many books did this room hold? There had to be hundreds at the very least. Almost every inch of the walls had shelves filled with them, their bindings all different colors and widths. It reminded her of a mosaic. Her fingers twitched. Recreating this in a painting would be a challenge, but sometimes she found comfort in drawing the same shapes over and over. The tiny little differences were what kept the task from becoming maddening.

She continued along, gazing above at the books near the ceiling. She would need a ladder to reach those. Were there special books hidden away up there, to keep their secrets? A rule book, perhaps? Or maybe that was where the worst books went. The ones with little value. Maybe the true treasures were but an arm's reach away.

"It's you."

Mayté jumped back as a teenage boy stepped out of the shadows, hazel eyes twinkling. The most beautiful eyes she had ever seen. "I just came to read," he said, flashing a knowing grin. "It's been a tough shift."

It was him. The croupier. She almost hadn't recognized him without the face paint. Earlier he had looked haunting, like a living skeleton, but now he looked quite . . .

Handsome.

She squinted, studying him hard. His face was the color of the buildings in Milagro during sunset: a soft golden bronze, yet his complexion looked almost dull compared to his hazel eyes. As if some of the color had been drained. He wore a black dress shirt and slacks. His tousled brown hair hung near his sharp jawline. He watched her in amusement.

Her heart skipped several beats, and she swore the fireplace blazed brighter, filling the library with heat.

This was a golden opportunity. Almost too perfect to be real. Had the house really kissed her with such fortune? It baffled her, but she would be a fool to question it. "You—you're the one from dinner."

"You recognize me." His eyes crinkled and he looked pleased.

"Of course. I'm an artist so I have to be observant about people's faces." She ignored her pounding heart and stood taller.

"It's an honor to have an artiste in my presence." He bowed, clearly playing along, but it felt more fun than condescending.

Mayté couldn't stop grinning.

"I've been wanting to meet the world-famous Mayté. *Just Mayté*," he said.

Her smile fell. "How did you—?"

"Did you like the pan dulce?" he asked as he turned to the fireplace, which cast dark shadows over his face.

She hesitated. The question hung in the air, but she had come here for *different* answers. "Yes, it was good, and you were right—it made me feel a little better. Thank you. My stomach's still a bit unsettled," she admitted.

He seemed almost relieved. Or was she just being paranoid? "Ah!" His face lit up. "Wait a moment." He held up a finger before dashing off.

Now alone, Mayté's head caught up with her racing heart. She needed to focus on her mission. Get answers. Hints. Rules. Anything she could find out from him. She crept closer to the fireplace and warmed her hands before they could tremble.

"I'm back."

Mayté whirled around. Her heart fluttered like a butterfly trapped in a glass jar.

The croupier held out a saucer and teacup.

The butterfly in her heart slowed. She took the saucer and cup. "Isn't it a bit late for coffee?" She raised an eyebrow.

He chuckled and shook his head. "No, no, it's cinnamon tea." Taking a closer look, a couple of cinnamon sticks poked out from the liquid. She hesitated. Abuelita always warned her never to accept a drink from a stranger. Wicked men slipped dangerous potions into drinks.

"You don't like cinnamon?" He frowned, heavy eyebrows furrowed.

"No, no." Without thinking, she took a small sip, careful not to burn her tongue. How could she let a simple frown pressure her so easily? But if she acted too suspicious, he might not want to tell her anything.

The tea tasted good. Surprisingly sweet, the velvety hot liquid went down smooth. The soft spice warmed her down to her toes. "Mmm . . ." She took another sip, then another and another, each one bigger than the last. Surely if this were laced with a potion, she would have noticed by now. "It's really good." Her shoulders relaxed and she sat on the plush sofa nearest the fireplace.

The croupier sat next to her. "That's the best cure you're going to find for an upset stomach. Even better than a potion."

"Ohh. Mmm. It tastes much better than a potion. That's for sure." Mayté took another sip. "The cooks here are really good."

"I made it," he corrected her. "It's a recipe I've always known. I think." He looked away and rubbed the back of his neck. "I take it you can't sleep."

"After seeing a woman beheaded? No, actually, I can't."

Even though her tone was harsh, the croupier flashed the smallest of understanding smiles. "You grow numb to it after a while."

"Seeing enough of *that* to get used to it? That would be even worse."

The croupier frowned. "You're right. It is."

There was a pause where all she could hear was the crackling flames consuming the firewood. It was warm. A sleepy, calming warmth. This was the most relaxed she had felt since arriving. "Is this room magic?"

"Hmm?"

"It's just . . . being in here is making me feel really good."

"Oh, it's not the room. It's the house. It feeds off the emotions of you and the other players and gives them back to you. Right now, it's reflecting your pleasant feelings. I feel it too. You're a very calming person to be around." There was that smile again. So charming. The room grew even warmer, and the candlelight dimmed, becoming almost dreamlike.

"What really brought you here at such an hour?" Mayté asked.

"I already told you." He chuckled. "I came to read. This is a library, after all. The books change each time the house moves, so I have plenty to read." He beckoned at the thousands of shelves all around them. "No matter what's going on, I can grab a book and be transported to another place. The house has every book one can dream of reading. I know I'll never run out." His words were cheerful, but the way he spoke them sounded more wistful than anything.

Mayté racked her brain for a clever response. Flirting was Lo's thing. She was a performer. But Mayté had zero talent in that medium.

As a child, when she first began drawing, she used to place her paper on top of her favorite Lotería cards and trace over them. The lines were rigid and awkward, but it helped her learn. Now she would have to do the same. What would Lo do in this situation? She imagined her best friend, sweet and smiling. The warm firelight casting a glow on her pretty face and bouncy curls.

With her own twitchy smile, Mayté scooted a tad closer to the croupier. "Be honest. Did you really come here *just* to read, or did you come hoping to see me?" *Dios.* As soon as she said it, she wanted to curl up into a ball and die. She was nothing like Lo. Didn't have the beauty or charisma to pull this off.

He chuckled again. "I think perhaps it was *you* who wanted to see *me.*"

"Wh-wh-what?" Mayté stiffened.

"Everyone here knows the house has a way of leading people to what they desire."

Mayté didn't know where to look. His hazel eyes made her insides twist and the way he smiled made the rest of her feel warm and melty. The chandelier above glittered and the smell of cinnamon filled the air.

"Maybe that's why the house wouldn't let me sleep. It knew you wanted to see me." He rested his head on his palm. "So, tell me, *why* did you want to see me?"

"I—I— Well . . ." What was she supposed to say? That she wanted to use him for information? What would Lo do at a time like this? No, Lo was too crafty to even find herself in such a bind. Mayté reached for her teacup to take another drink but fumbled. The steamy liquid sloshed around, burning heat bit through her finger. "Ow!"

"Are you okay?" The croupier took the saucer and teacup and set it on the side table.

"I'm fine." Mayté rubbed her finger. The skin was red and tender, and already she felt a burn blister forming.

"You've burned yourself," he said as if reading her mind.

"Don't worry. It's fine." How many times had she singed herself frying tortillas for herself and her brother?

But the croupier shook his head and gently took her hand. "It'll just be a distraction and you need all the concentration you can get during the games." He lifted her hand toward his mouth. "May I?"

Her heart skipped. "Uh. Sure. Yeah." But what was he going to do? He pressed her finger against his parted lips. His tongue brushed against it. Warm. It sent a flood of heat down her arm. But soon a familiar cool sensation chased away the warmth. The pleasant, relieving sort of cool. The kind that vanquished her stinging skin.

"Alivio Frío?" she whispered. Abuelita always insisted on cooking for fiestas. Always complained that the servants' cooking didn't have the same magic to it. And she was adamant that Mayté learn her recipes so she could pass them on to her children, and so on. She learned how to make delicious chicken and rice, fresh tortillas, and many other dishes, but a memory of the time they made tamales filled her head. Abuelita warned Mayté to wash her hands after touching the serrano peppers, but Mayté didn't listen and accidentally rubbed her eyes. All these years later, she could still remember the fiery pain. Her eyes instantly began to burn, and she screamed her head off. Abuelita quickly came to the rescue with an icy blue Alivio Frío potion. Just a drop in each eye and she felt instant relief.

The croupier quickly looked away as he lowered her hand. Was he blushing?

Mayté swore she could feel the heat of embarrassment radiating off him. She studied her finger. The blister had already shrunk, and the redness had dulled into a faint pink. "How did you . . . ?" Why would he consume such a potion?

His eyebrows furrowed.

"What is it?" she whispered.

Clunk!

The two whirled around, but no one was there. A book with an azure casing lay on the floor not even a foot away. It must have fallen off the shelf.

"I really can't stay much longer." He stood.

"Wait. Can I at least know your name?"

He bowed. "Alejandro."

"And you already know mine."

He nodded, eyes dancing.

"*How* did you know?" Maybe it was risky to ask, but she couldn't help it.

Alejandro picked up the book. "You could say I've read up a bit on the contestants. We croupiers don't have that much to entertain ourselves with."

It was a simple enough answer, but her stomach clenched as if telling her that there was more to it than just that. The way he looked at her, it was as if he knew something she didn't. Wanted something from her too, but the most frightening part of it was that she found it all oddly . . . thrilling. "Wait!" She reached back and grabbed his arm. She couldn't let him slip away without getting any information. "I—I'm a bit nervous about tomorrow." She chewed her lower lip and chose her next words carefully. "Is there anything I should bring with me? Which of Los Santos should I pray to tonight?"

Alejandro looked over his shoulder, then leaned in close. It was so sudden. Every part of Mayté froze except her heart. Was he going to kiss her? What would she do? What *should* she do? But he wasn't going for her lips. Instead, he whispered in her ear: "Just bring your wits, and remember: the house has a way of leading people to what they desire. Focus on what you want most, but be careful. The magic comes at a price, and those with wicked intentions pay a steeper one."

"W-w-wha—?"

He pulled away before she could ask more. "I'll come see you again, but I really have to go." With that, he left the library.

Now alone, Mayté rubbed her finger, which had stayed cool to the point of numbness. A smoky haze filled the air as the fireplace's glow dulled. The room had changed from pleasant to ghostly once again. She got out of there as quickly as she could, but once she returned to the hallway, her unease morphed into excitement. If Alejandro was right, if she could keep calm and focus on what she wanted, maybe she could win the next game.

As if to prove that theory true, she found her way back to the suite with no problem. She threw the door open and grinned at the sight of Lo back in bed. "You'll never guess what I found out."

But Lo didn't respond, or even stir. She was sound asleep.

Mayté couldn't help but wonder if Lo had actually left the room earlier.

Or if had been just an illusion.

TEN

Lo

For as long as Lo could remember, there was always someone there to wake her up in the mornings. Whether it was one of the maids gently calling her name, or Sera roughly shaking her and babbling on about being late for breakfast. Sometimes it was Sofía pouncing on her like a kitten. In the distant dreamy past, it was Mamá climbing into the bed and endlessly kissing her cheeks and forehead until she gave in and woke up.

But this time, she wasn't in her familiar bed in her bedroom. Instead, she woke in the grand suite of Fortune's Kiss. Sunlight streamed in through the balcony, illuminating Mayté, who sat on her own bed. She would have looked like an angel if it weren't for the shadows rimmed under her puffy eyes.

"You look—"

"I know." With a groan, Mayté rubbed the goo from her eyes. "I did not sleep well at all. I had a horrible nightmare about . . . the game." She looked toward the balcony. Outside, the sky was a blanket of gray with threads of blue and sunlight poking out here and there. Not quite foreboding, but not happy and cheerful either. Lo squinted. Fortune's Kiss should have been nestled around the buildings of Milagro. A brightly colored centerpiece among the dull and drab stucco. Yet there were no other buildings in sight. It was as if they were no longer in Milagro, but some other world. A horrible deadly one hidden behind gold and jewels. She gripped the blankets as memories of yesterday and the reality of the situation sank in once again.

"So, you . . . you didn't wake up at all last night?" Mayté asked.

Lo's heart skipped a beat. She had woken up last night and had snuck out of the room to search for Mamá. Not that she got far. The strange noises the house made and the uncanny feeling of being watched sent her scurrying back to the room. Mayté didn't need to know about that. "I actually slept pretty good." That part was true at least. She couldn't recall her dreams, but the black nothingness wrapped in the silky warmth of her blankets had been so wonderful. "Are you sure you don't want to try and get a little more sleep?" She could have easily fallen back into slumber if she let herself. That sounded better than facing the game. At least for a bit longer.

"I—" Mayté furrowed her eyebrows. "I saw you leave. I—I thought I did, but when I returned you were sound asleep."

Lo could have easily told the truth, but no, she didn't want to see the look on her best friend's face or have to hear the words that everyone had told her for years.

Your mother is never returning.

"You left?" Lo asked instead.

"Yeah." Her eyes darted. "I ran into Alejandro. The croupier."

"Oh?" Lo pushed the blankets away, both intrigued and relieved that the focus was off her.

"But what did I see then if you didn't leave?"

Or not.

"Maybe it was your mind playing tricks on you in the dark," Lo quickly said. Inwardly, she told herself she would tell Mayté everything after she found Mamá. That would negate the lies, right? "Especially given how frightening everything has been."

She was ready to change the subject once and for all. "So, the croupier's name is Alejandro? What did he say? Were you able to get any information out of him?"

"Kind of. He said that the house has a way of leading people to what they desire. And it already has. I think it led me to him last night." She twirled the long wisps of hair as if deep in thought.

"Really?" Lo almost choked. Then why hadn't the house led her to Mamá . . . ? Was it because she hadn't tried hard enough? That had to be it. "Did he say anything else about . . . how that works?"

"Oh, he also said the house feeds off the players' emotions and reflects them back. When we were in the library, I guess I was feeling calm and relaxed, so the room began to feel extra warm and pleasant."

"I see." That was a lot to take in. It wasn't exactly the clear-cut hint that she had hoped for, but maybe there was a way they could use this information. "Do you think that it can be controlled? What if we go into the next game feeling calm, positive, confident, and aware of our desires to survive and win? Would the house . . . help?"

"I don't know." Mayté frowned. "It almost sounds too good to be true."

"It definitely does. But it's the only thing we have to work with for now. Let's try it and see."

"Yeah." Mayté still sounded uncertain.

"What's wrong?"

"It's just . . ." She rubbed her arms as if trying to warm up. "Alejandro. It almost seemed like he wanted something from me."

Oh. Was that all? "He probably wants *you*. That's how men are, but you get to use that to your advantage. Dangle his desire before him until he gives you what *you* want."

"Mm." Mayté looked down.

Lo hopped off the bed and moved to the walk-in closet. "We should get dressed. If we're going to project confidence, we need to look the part."

Long ago, Lo had learned that a gown could make all the difference in how others perceived her. Luxurious garments impressed the nobles. The latest fashions caught the eye of the other young women, but it was a balance. Dressing too beautifully could easily cause envy. Something a bit more fitted and revealing made her suitors even easier to manipulate.

Staying calm, confident, and positive. Desiring to do well in the next round. That was today's objective. The best way to do that was to wear something that made her feel gorgeous, all while being just comfortable enough. And maybe this would help her understand the house better. Maybe she could use that magic to find Mamá.

She decided on a soft pink silk gown with a waterfall of lace ruffles down the front and at the sleeves. She tied her curls back with a matching pink ribbon.

Unsurprisingly, Mayté went for something much simpler, claiming it was easier to move around in—a baby blue cotton gown. A chiffon flower bloomed just under her breasts where the gown hugged her the tightest, before blossoming out around her hips. The quarter-length sleeves and bodice were made of cream-colored lace. It may have been less extravagant than Lo's gown, but it was still much nicer than what Mayté usually wore, shabby rebozos and all. Now if only Lo could get her to wear her long, silky hair in anything other than her signature braid.

The two left their suite. If Lo allowed herself, she could imagine that things were the way they used to be. Back when Mayté was still a part of las grandes familias. The two of them arm in arm, giggling about the boys who would one day become their suitors.

But the door to the room directly across from them flew open, crashed into the wall, and out stepped Dominic. "Oops. Oh! Good morning!" He waved before rushing over. He was wearing tan woolen trousers with a matching silk waistcoat with a rose pattern detail. His white oversized sleeves flared out, and, as always, he wore a cravat. Everything about him looked bright and cheerful—both his clothes and his big, toothy grin. Aside from his puffy eyes and flushed cheeks, he looked good. "I'm so glad to see you both. I was worried I'd be the last one up. It always takes me a while to get going in the mornings."

And we're expected to care? Why? Lo was close to saying it, but it must have shone on her face, because Mayté lightly pinched her arm. Lo raised an eyebrow and narrowed her eyes.

Mayté pursed her lips and lowered her chin.

Fine.

Lo mustered up her friendliest voice. "So how did you sleep, Dom?"

"Eh. As good as I could, given everything." He shivered. "I'm just glad we all made it through the night."

"Me too," Mayté said, and it sounded like she meant it.

The elevator doors soon opened, and they stepped inside. "Do either of you remember which floor the dining room is on?" Dominic scratched the back of his head.

"Twelfth." Mayté pressed the button. "Just under the gambling den."

Directly under the bloodbath.

Someone slipped through the doors just as they began to close. The man was rather muscular and imposing. He wouldn't have made it through if the opening had been any smaller.

"Good morning," Dominic said.

The man gruffed something unintelligible.

Mayté stiffened before looking down, as if her blue satin shoes were the most important thing on this elevator. As if her life depended on them. From her peripheral vision, Lo studied the stranger. His eyes squinted into narrowed slits as if any bit of light pained him. The deep bags under his eyes were from many restless nights. Unkempt hair curled around his ears, and his chin scruff was in the awkward phase between shadow and beard. What looked like a knife scar marred the side of his beige face. His navy dress shirt and black waistcoat should have made him look like a noble, but the way his shirt was half tucked in and not even properly buttoned gave him away. Who was he?

"I wonder what's for breakfast," Dominic babbled, oblivious, as the elevator made its ascent. "I wasn't feeling well during dinner, so I didn't get to eat that much. Even though I'm nervous, I'm actually starving, so I hope it's something good. It seems like they have competent cooks here. Maybe even better than the ones back home. I think—"

"Enough!" The man slammed the side of his fist against the wall.

Mayté jumped and let out the tiniest of yelps.

Who is this man? Lo clenched her fists.

Dominic stared up at the man, who was twice his size both in height and broadness. "I'm sorry?" he asked rather boldly instead of cowering away.

"Ay," the man growled. "I don't wanna hear you running your mouth again, you hear?"

"Well, yes, my ears work."

Whoa. Lo glanced at Dominic from the corner of her eye. Bold. Impressive. As much as she didn't want to admit it.

This further agitated the man. "Next time I'll shut you up myself." He stormed off as soon as the doors opened.

Mayté let out a soft sigh. Her shoulders lowered from their perch just below her ears, but her eyebrows still furrowed with apprehension.

More than anything, Lo wanted to ask what was going on. Mayté clearly knew the man, but not well enough for him to instantly recognize her. If Dominic hadn't been around, she would have asked, but that would have to wait. For now, all she could do was follow them into the dining room.

The sweet smell of pancakes and pastries danced through the air, along with the spicy tang of fresh salsas and pico de gallo. Servers bustled about offering different options. Fresh fruits like mangoes, plantains, huayas, and zapotes, along with a variety of egg dishes. Chorizo con huevos, huevos veracruzanos, and entomatadas rellenas de huevo. Lo's stomach buzzed with hunger.

No one was sobbing or vomiting at this meal, thankfully, though the place didn't have the atmosphere of a joyous feast either. All that could be heard were forks and knives scraping against plates as the players ate. Some were more ravenous than others, clearly starved after not eating much at dinner. Everyone kept their heads down.

Except Carlos.

He rose from his seat, eyes locked on Mayté. Lo's heart skipped a beat. He wore a brown suit and a matching cravat. It once again made her nostalgic for the old days. In another life, she would have chosen to wed him.

"Mierda," Mayté whispered as Carlos strode toward them.

"Maybe it'll be good to talk to him," Lo said, voice soft. "It could help you feel better. You want to *feel* your best for the next round, remember?"

Mayté shook her head. "I can't deal with him. Not yet."

"Come on." Dominic took both girls by the arm and led them to the other side of the table. "There's three seats over here." Three seats with no extra spot for Carlos. The group quickly sat down. Carlos slowed to a stop and frowned before walking away.

"Thank you," Mayté whispered.

Dominic gave her a kind smile.

"Lorena?"

Lo turned and gasped with delight. Carmen was seated next to her.

"Are you all right?" The maid took her hand and gave it a squeeze. She looked stunning. No longer was her black hair in a tight bun. Soft waves framed her face, making her look younger, less severe. Her off-the-shoulder scarlet gown was embroidered with intricate silver and gold patterns that shimmered in the candlelight. Despite that, the brightest part of her was her smile. She beamed from ear to ear. Up close, Lo could make out every pale freckle and the occasional brown mole sprinkled across her nose and dusting her chin, likely from the endless hours tending the gardens and hanging freshly washed linens. The sun may not have burned her olive skin so easily, but it still left its mark. Sera often warned Sofía she would look like Carmen one day if she stayed outside with the horses too long and Lo saw now just how beautiful and sun-kissed Carmen truly was.

"I'm as okay as I can be," Lo said. "Are you?"

"Yes. Now that I'm here, all I can do is try my best." Carmen plucked a little cake dusted in sugar with the tiniest strawberry on top off her plate. She took a bite and winced. It was the joyful kind of face someone made after biting into something unexpectedly sweet. It made Lo's teeth tingle. Carmen licked the sugar off her lips before continuing. "I'm sure it's the same for you." Her warm eyes sparked with sympathy. The unspoken hung between them like a silky thin strand of a spiderweb. *Lo's father.* They were both flies caught in the web, desperate to escape the carnivorous spider.

"If I may ask . . . when did you leave for Fortune's Kiss?" Lo toyed with her silverware. Did Carmen know what Lo had done to her father?

"Very early in the day. I volunteered to run some errands but didn't come back. I don't know if I would've had the courage to go if anyone had tried to stop me."

She had left before the incident. There was no way she could have known.

Lo felt a prickle on the back of her neck and turned to see Dominic staring. She hadn't realized she was gripping her knife tight until his gaze flicked to her hand. With a jolt, she quickly dropped the knife to the table and smiled. "What? Do I have something on my face?" But before he could answer, she turned back to Carmen. "I'm sure you've heard rumors about my mother." Walls may not truly have ears, but the house staff did, and she was certain those who worked in the de León household knew of every scandalous thing that transpired within its walls. Maybe Carmen knew something about Mamá.

If the staff at Fortune's Kiss were anything like the workers at home, they could know something about Mamá too. "Some say she came here, in fact." Lo spoke louder and glanced back to see if that had caught the attention of any of the servers. If any of them knew anything, it would seem that they had their poker faces mastered. They stared straight ahead, almost as if they had no emotion.

"Oh, yes." Carmen nodded and popped the rest of her cake in her mouth. The time it took for her to chew and swallow it felt excruciatingly long. "I know some people believe she simply ran off, but I truly believe that she came here. That's what inspired me to come. I remember when I first started working at your home, everyone talked about it, but no one dared say anything in front of your father."

Lo bit back the urge to ask what Carmen and the other staff thought had happened to Mamá.

"I was only a teenager. Not much older than you." Her smile turned bitter. "With a newborn. Shunned by most of my family and the Church. My abuelo took me in and watched over my son while I worked. Now Abuelo's health is poor, and every year he grows more and more forgetful. I knew we were in a bubble that would soon pop. But from the moment I heard what your mother had done, I knew I had to come here too once the opportunity arose. Even just the slightest chance of winning a better life for what's left of my little family . . . It's the only thing that has kept me going."

"I . . . I had no idea," Lo whispered. Even though Carmen was her favorite, she had never thought to ask about her personal life.

Carmen was always so warm and gentle when brushing Sofía's tangly curls, and endlessly patient whenever Sera went off on her pompous tangents. Most of all, she was dogged in the way she looked out for Lo.

It was because Carmen was a mother, Lo realized. She came here for the sake of her child.

Just like Mamá.

She felt sick. No matter how much she favored Carmen, how much she respected her, Carmen could not win Fortune's Kiss, for her winning would lead to Lo and Mayté losing, and Lo could never allow that to happen.

A server set a plate of berry panqueques in front of Lo. She stabbed her fork into it, causing crushed strawberries and raspberries to ooze out like fresh blood. Her heart skipped a beat, but she reminded herself to keep calm. Calm and confident, like a winner.

Carmen smiled at her once again, before digging into her own plate of pancakes. Lo wanted to press more about Mamá, but movement from the corner of her eye caught her attention. Carlos. He came over with a steaming mug. Up close, Lo could see the shadow of unshaven hair forming above his lips.

"Mayté," he said.

Mayté bit into her chorizo con huevos. Her eyes watered as if the spiced sausage had an extra kick to it. But Lo knew that wasn't the cause.

"I brought you some café. It'll help wake you up," Carlos said. He held the mug out to her, but she continued scarfing down the orangey eggs as if they were manna sent from San Proveedor.

"I don't think she wants any." Dominic stood. "But I'll take some." He took the mug and Carlos's mouth hung open. Dominic lifted the mug to his mouth, about to take a swig, but then seemed to change his mind. "Or would you rather have it, Lorena?"

"Oh, thank you so much, Dominic." Lo took the mug, careful not to burn her fingers. She took a sip, not bothering to blow on the steaming liquid. The pain made her forget her unease. "Mmm." She closed her eyes. It went down smooth and rich, with the slightest hint of spicy cinnamon. It heightened her senses and chased away the heaviness around her eyes. When she looked back up, her heart skipped a beat: Carlos's entire face had turned red and he stood rigid with his arms close to his sides, hands balled up into fists—just like Mayté whenever something enraged her. The thing was, Carlos was usually the cool-headed one. The one who shrugged off problems. Now he was a vat of boiling potions, unstable and ready to explode.

"You should finish your breakfast, Carlos, before it gets cold," Dominic said. He acted nonchalant, but there was a knowing glimmer in his brown eyes. He was about to sit down when Carlos snatched his arm. His chair toppled with a loud clang. Everyone else stopped what they were doing and stared. Even Mayté froze mid-chew, but didn't look up.

"Just because you're one of her suitors doesn't mean you can act so damn entitled." Carlos grabbed Dominic's collar, yanking him closer.

Dominic simply gripped Carlos's arms. "This has nothing to do with Lorena." His voice was surprisingly steady. "Your sister has made it clear that she doesn't want to talk to you right now."

Carlos growled. "It really pisses me off how you're acting so friendly and familiar with her. Why now? You wanted nothing to do with either of us before."

Mayté's shoulders shook and her face was just as red as Carlos's. She looked as if she might burst into tears.

"I know it won't mean much to you," Dominic said. "But I've been occupied with some other matters—"

Carlos drew back his fist, ready to punch.

"Stop!" Lo jumped up from her seat. Not for Dominic, but for Mayté. Carlos froze instantly, as if her words were infused with magic. She had that effect, even on him, without trying. "Enough, Carlos." She grasped his arm. He didn't look particularly muscular, but his arms were strong. Likely from the strenuous odd jobs he had to do to keep his family afloat. "It won't help anyone if you make a scene." She looked up at Carlos.

"Yes, please don't do that." A new voice chimed in.

Lo and the boys whirled around with a jolt. Misterioso stood inches behind them. When had he even arrived? With a jovial grin, he tipped his white top hat.

Lo's heart skipped several beats. "Thank you," she said.

He gave Carlos and Dominic a hardy smack on the back, before turning to the table now filled with the rest of the players. Just like last night, one seat remained empty. "Top of the morning to you, dear contestants. I hope everyone rested well."

No one said they had. Someone coughed. Another person mumbled something under their breath.

Misterioso ignored the lukewarm response. "Our next game will be in . . ." He checked his giant hourglass. "An hour's time. Don't be tardy. Our croupiers and most certainly our Banker do not enjoy waiting. Now, then. I'm sure you're curious about what's to come. Each day, there will be two rounds." He held up two fingers. Even when wearing gloves, it was obvious that his fingers were long and bony. "One in the afternoon, and one in the evening. This will go on day by day until the winner or winners are declared."

Lo's stomach lurched.

"In the past, the eliminations have taken as long as a week. I wish you all the best of luck and a satisfying breakfast," he said with a bow.

Carlos turned back to Mayté, but she still refused to look his way. His face twisted with pain and anger. "Tch." He stomped to the elevator.

Mayté lowered her head and roughly wiped at her eyes.

"Listen," Lo whispered. "Try not to let him get to you. Remember our plan."

"I know," Mayté's voice cracked, but then with a stubborn grunt she took a big bite of food. Good.

Lo needed to focus on her plan too. From the corner of her eye, she watched Misterioso as he moved around the table. Her heart beat faster as she plotted and planned. Maybe he was the one she should have pursued all along instead of searching for Mamá last night. She shoveled down the rest of her breakfast before turning to Mayté. "I'll see you in the next round." There wasn't any time to explain herself. She practically jumped out of her seat and rushed after Misterioso as he stepped into the elevator. "Mind if I join you?" She slipped through the doors just before they closed.

"Oh! Lorena." Misterioso looked surprised and eyed her up and down. Displeasure sparked in his dark eyes, visible even behind his mask. "Shouldn't you finish your meal? There will be no time for eating once the next round begins."

That wasn't the reaction she had been expecting. Most men would be more than pleased to have a private moment with her like this, but Misterioso pulled out a cigar and began puffing away. He seemed less than interested.

Lo carried on, undeterred. "I'm a light eater," she replied. The elevator slowed to a stop. She needed to hurry. "And I wanted to make sure all was well after last night. I hope it's okay that I accepted that key from the Banker." She twirled one of her curls. *Come on. Take the bait.*

Misterioso exhaled a puff of smoke and pulled the cigar away from his lips. A few glowing cinders flitted to the floor, transforming into marigold petals. His narrowed gaze turned almost wary. "All will be well as long as you remember you are simply a contestant. Nothing more."

Lo's eyes widened. "I—"

"Do not get it confused." With a ding, the door opened and Misterioso stepped out, leaving behind a puff of smoke. For a moment, it looked like a skull.

"Wait." She tried to follow, but someone grabbed her arm.

"I wouldn't do that if I were you." The Banker stood among the smoky haze. Had he been in the elevator this entire time? He smirked, as if amused by her shock.

Lo recovered quickly. "Oh, so I have a guardian angel now?"

The Banker let out a breath, a mixture between a sigh and laugh. "You could say I'm looking out for you. Trust me when I say Misterioso holds his cards close to his chest."

Very well, Lo thought. Change of plans. The energy coming off the Banker was decidedly different from Misterioso's. "What about you?" Lo curled her lips into a smile. She didn't make a move to pull her arm out of his grasp.

"What *about* me?" The Banker raised an eyebrow, blue eyes gleaming.

"Maybe we can help each other out, hmm?"

"Oh. And how can we do that?" he replied.

Lo laughed. There was something about the Banker that made him easy to talk to. Something almost familiar, but she couldn't quite put her finger on it. She playfully looked out toward the hall, needing those precious few seconds to choose her words carefully. The long hallway was barren, save for a large mirror at the end. She turned back to him. "Well, you see, I—"

Wait.

She glanced back at the hallway. No longer was there a mirror, if there had even been one in the first place: a woman stood with her back to her. With her voluptuous curls, the color of dulce de leche, she could have been Lo's reflection, her double. But she wasn't, and that was the most terrifying part. Because at that moment, Lo knew she wasn't looking at some mysterious doppelgänger, but someone very familiar. "M-Mamá?" she choked. She rushed out of the elevator, forgetting about the Banker and everything else. She stumbled over her gown. When she looked back up, the figure was gone.

"Wha—"

A door slammed.

Cursing the lacy frills of her dress, Lo scooped them up and followed the sound. She turned the corner and found a single door. She yanked it open and barreled inside. But what she found was an empty room. Completely empty. White walls. A wood floor. No windows.

No Mamá.

The door slammed shut behind her. She whirled around and jiggled the doorknob, but the door wouldn't budge. No. This couldn't be happening. She tried the knob again, before pounding and kicking at the door. She was trapped.

When she turned back around, her heart stopped. The room had completely changed. No longer empty, it was Mamá's suite in their hacienda.

Sometimes when Lo closed her eyes and concentrated hard enough, she could remember times when Mamá was still around. Softly singing alabados as Lo fell asleep in her arms. Sitting at Lo's bedside and soaking rags in water mixed with Alivio Frío and putting them on Lo's forehead whenever she was sick with a fever. Laughing until she snorted at the silliest of jokes.

But this time, Lo didn't have to close her eyes for the memories to unfold.

Mamá's gown fluttered around as she rushed around the suite, packing a small satchel.

"*Mamá,*" Lo whispered, the memory overtaking her. "*What are you doing?*"

Mamá whirled around; in the glow of the night, she looked like Santa Belleza. "*Oh, Lorena.*" *The tightness in her bronze face unraveled.*

Back then, Lo couldn't comprehend her facial expression, but thinking back, it was probably a blessing.

"*What are you doing awake?*" *Mamá caught her in a hug. Much tighter and longer than the usual embrace.*

Lo hugged herself, desperate to recapture the feelings of comfort and safety.

"*I had a bad dream. Why are you awake, Mamá?*" *Lo asked, clinging to Mother's dress.* "*Are you going somewhere?*"

"*Yes.*" *Mamá knelt and took Lo's hands.* "*But you must not tell anyone.*"

"*Why?*"

"*Because it's a surprise.*"

"*Oh!*" *Lo beamed, bouncing on her toes. Surprises were the best. Better than a brand-new dress or the sweetest flan.* "*I won't tell anyone. I promise.*"

"*Good girl.*" *Mamá kissed her forehead with a loud smooching pop.* "*My clever, clever girl.*" *She stroked Lo's cheek.* "*I'm going to Fortune's Kiss.*"

"*Wow! Really?*" *Lo's heart did somersaults inside her chest. Earlier that day she and Mayté had been talking about Fortune's Kiss. They didn't know much about it, but it sounded magical and exciting.* "*Can I come too?*"

"*Oh, no, no, no.*" *Mamá shook her head and grasped Lo's shoulders.* "*I won't be gone for long, and I'll bring back a surprise for you and your sisters; so, remember, you mustn't tell anyone.*"

Back then Lo envisioned gifts. Toys and new dresses. But now she knew the surprise would have been much more meaningful than those. Mamá intended to have enough money for all of them to escape from Father and start a new life together.

"When will you come back?"

Mamá looked away and bit her lip. "I don't know for sure, but I'll see you soon." She looked back at Lo, her smile sincere. "I promise. Okay?"

"Okay," Lo said, satisfied.

"Oh, Lorena, my precious mamita." Mamá hugged her once again, even tighter than before. "I love you so, so much."

"I love you too, Mamá."

Lo should have never let her leave. It was the biggest mistake of her life. She wasn't sure when she ended up on the floor, but she stared up at the ceiling, full of cobwebs and dust from years of neglect.

Maybe she shouldn't have come to Fortune's Kiss either. Maybe she was doomed to the same fate as Mamá, trapped here.

Forever and ever.

With no one to know where she had gone.

ELEVEN

Mayté

Mayté was certain that she would never get used to riding elevators. Her stomach flipped endlessly, sloshing the contents of her breakfast around. Her head pounded and her ears popped, the closer she soared to the thirteenth floor. The gaming den.

The game would begin again. The next hour could be her last.

Memories of her nightmare still seared her mind, but when she tried to push them away, she could only think of Alejandro and the library. If it wasn't for her finger, which still felt the slightest bit numb, she would have chalked it all up as a dream. A strange and wonderful one.

Everyone here knows the house has a way of leading people to what they desire.

She couldn't let herself forget that. She needed to stay positive, confident, and most of all remember what she desired most. *Winning.*

Her thoughts drifted to Carlos. If she could win, he could lose. She dug her nails into her palms. Why did he have to come here too? *Why?*

"Do you always look so angry when you're nervous?" Dominic's question pulled her out of her thoughts. Honestly, she had nearly forgotten he was in the elevator with her.

"What?"

"You look angry," he explained. "But I figure you'd be nervous. At least that's how I feel right now."

It should have been annoying, but she found it more amusing than anything. "I guess I'm just a mess right now," she admitted. A jumble of baffling emotions. The most confusing part of it all was how, right at this moment, she was alone with the boy she once had fancied, yet he was the last thing on her mind.

"Don't worry. I'm sure that's how everyone here feels, even if they don't act like it."

The elevator abruptly stopped and the door slowly opened. A lively buzz of chattering voices filled her ears, and the musky scent of fresh marigolds hit her nose. Bright neon spotlights in shades of orange, green, and pink stung her eyes. But as soon as her vision adjusted, fear seized her heart.

The vaquero leaned against the nearest gold-encrusted pillar, smoking the fattest cigar she had ever seen. He glanced in their direction. Sweat pooled under her arms and she gasped for air.

"Mayté." Dominic moved in front of her. "Listen." He cleared his throat. "Before everything gets frightening again, I just wanted to say that I'm here if you ever need to talk."

She must have looked confused, because he quickly added, "If you need the perspective of someone outside your situation. I'm a good listener, you know, and even better at keeping secrets."

"Dominic . . . thank you. I appreciate it, but . . ." She shook her head. If she let herself get too close to him, then she would worry about him too. "I don't have anything to talk about." She forced a smile.

"All right." Dominic didn't seem bothered. "If you ever change your mind, the offer stands." He held out his arm.

Mayté wasn't sure what came over her, but she took his arm and let him lead her into the heart of the salon. They walked past the vaquero, with Dominic blocking her from his view. If Mayté hadn't known better, it would have seemed like Dominic was doing this on purpose to protect her.

The big round table came into view. Every last bloodstain and spatter had been scrubbed off the carpet and walls. It was as if Señora Montoya hadn't even existed, much less lost her life here. Surely, if Mayté tried hard enough, she could pretend that none of it had ever happened.

A few contestants already sat. Carlos was among them, but not for long: he jumped up from his seat and stormed toward them. Clearly, he had purposefully chosen the seat across from the elevators so he could ambush Mayté as soon as possible.

"Go save a seat for me and Lorena," she told Dominic. He didn't need to get swept up in this again. Carlos was *her* problem.

"If you say so." Dominic looked reluctant, but thankfully she didn't have to tell him twice. He strode toward the table. Just in time, too, because, not even a second later, Carlos stepped into view.

"You know he's just being kind so he can get to Lo."

Mayté crossed her arms. "You aren't Dominic Castro, so how would you know that?" This wasn't the first time they'd fought. Over the years, they'd argued about anything and everything. She got on him when he ate the last of the tortillas. He scolded her for staining the table with her paint. He got riled up when she used to tease him in front of Lo. She hated when he used to tell his friends that her hair smelled like musty paintbrushes. No matter how big their fights were, they would always be fine in a matter of hours. He was her brother. She could never be truly angry with him. She loved him.

And that was what made this so hard.

From the corner of her eye, she saw the vaquero. He was staring at them, clearly curious. If he hadn't recognized her before, he would surely recognize her and Carlos together. She needed to end this *now*. "Please, let's just focus on the game. Bet low, and, no matter what, *don't* fold." She turned away, but he grabbed her arm.

"How am I supposed to 'just' focus on the game when you're here? You're my little sister."

Now the vaquero was really staring.

"Carlos—"

"I'm supposed to protect our family. After everything that happened with Father, it was all put on me. I know you don't think I'm trying, but I really am. That's why I'm here. Do you think I wanted to risk my dreams just for myself? I—"

"Enough!" Panic tore through her vocal cords. "Please."

Carlos's eyes widened, taking her in. No doubt he knew *something* was wrong, he just couldn't put his finger on what. "Mayté," he whispered.

"Contestants," Misterioso called out with enthusiasm and bravado. "Please make your way to your seats. Our second game will begin soon."

Mayté broke free from Carlos and rushed to the table, not daring to look back. Her heart pounded. She had never really stopped to consider Carlos's position. Ma doted on him, but that came with extra pressure. He must have felt obligated to come here. Not just for himself or his own gain . . .

No, she couldn't think about that right now. She needed to keep it together. Dominic was now at the table alone; Lo was nowhere in sight. Where was she? A new kind of anxiety clawed at her throat. "Have you seen Lorena?" she asked him.

"She's not with you?"

Mayté shook her head and dug her teeth into her bottom lip. What would happen if Lo didn't make it to the game?

Once everyone took their seats, the tiniest of leafy green buds sprouted on the table top. Thousands of them. All at once, their sprouts opened and a bean popped out. *Plip plip plip.* They landed on the table with tiny thunks.

"Whoa," Dominic whispered in amazement. Everyone else around the table looked just as awed—and yes, it was truly magical, but Mayté couldn't appreciate it. *Stop. Calm down.*

Carlos sat down across from her. He looked around the room, likely searching for Lo as well. Mayté caught a familiar face staring at her. Señor Vásquez, the elote stand owner. It felt like a lifetime ago that she'd painted him a sign for his stand. His dark eyes flicked with recognition, then he flashed a sad smile. A lump formed in her throat. Both of them were full of dreams, and now they were trapped here fighting for their lives.

"It is time for our second game of Fortune's Kiss!" Misterioso shouted. "But first"—he wagged his finger; his voice carried through the entire gaming den as if his lungs were lined with magic—"several introductions are in order. You already know me, your humble Master of Ceremonies." He dramatically bowed, unbothered by the silence and anxious tension in the room. "Dealing for this afternoon's round is our newest croupier, Alejandro."

Mayté's heart stuttered.

Alejandro strode to the front of the den, as nonchalant as could be before taking his place at the inner center of the round table. His face was once again painted to look like a calavera.

"Where's the Banker?" Xiomara asked.

Alejandro simply put a finger to his mouth.

"Ah, a secret he'll never tell," Misterioso joined in.

A secret. At that exact moment, Alejandro glanced Mayté's way. His hazel eyes held her captive; his finger still hovered over his painted lips. Heat bloomed in her cheeks. The gesture was supposed to be all a show, but something told her that there was a hidden double meaning just for her. Yet, at the same time, there was something expectant in his gaze. As if she were the one who held the answer to the darkest secret.

Why did that make her heart race?

"Did you sleep well, señorita?"

It took her a second to realize that Alejandro was asking *her.* "I—er—yes." Her face warmed and she began to sweat. The feeling grew even more intense when Alejandro flashed a charming grin.

"Good. I'm glad. A beauty like you needs all the rest she can get. I hope you're in good spirits today."

Mayté's mouth hung open. Had she heard him right? No boy had ever spoken so boldly to her. "I—I—th-thank—"

But before she could stammer out something that wasn't nonsensical, Misterioso spoke over her. "Now, then, if you will spare me a few more moments, I will formally introduce you to our contestants." He waved his hand, and the air next to him shimmered and changed.

Mayté leaned closer to get a better look. Back when they had been kids, she and Lo used to pretend they saw mirages in the fountain garden, visions conjured up from nothing. This was exactly that, except that this wasn't make-believe: it was completely real.

An image of an altar covered in orange marigolds and candles appeared. The centerpiece was a large black and white photograph of Señora Montoya. Mayté's stomach churned.

The woman's light eyes stared straight on. Aside from her hair, her smirking lips were the darkest part of the photo. Thin, with razor-sharp points forming a Cupid's bow. She was the embodiment of hubris.

"It isn't every day that a contestant goes for broke so early in the game." Misterioso chuckled. "Maríana Montoya wanted to go first, and she certainly got her wish. Dios rest her soul."

Mayté gulped down bile and stared hard at the altar. Perfume bottles sat next to Señora Montoya's photo, along with a hand fan and her cigarette holder. Jewelry encrusted in alabaster pearls and iridescent opals dangled off the edges of the altar. A pure white calavera wearing an extravagant scarlet hat covered in colorful flowers and feathers sat next to the photo as well—though, on closer inspection, the calavera truly wasn't white: brownish cracks and decay were just below the surface. A beetle-like insect darted from one eyehole to the next. The calavera was painted with red around the lips and blue and black around the eyes, mimicking makeup, but it looked uncanny. Like an animated corpse masquerading as the living.

"But no need to worry, we have respectfully cremated Maríanna." Misterioso sounded cheerful as always. Did he show any other emotions, aside from playful joy? Mayté couldn't imagine the man angry, let alone sorrowful.

A chill settled over her. An urn sat next to the skull, ivory and trimmed in gold.

"Please take a moment to remember Maríanna." Misterioso snapped his fingers—and, in a puff of smoke, Señora Montoya appeared in the empty seat between the shopkeeper and Carmen.

Dominic gasped. Everyone at the table stared. Señora Montoya stared back, a demure smile on her lips.

Alejandro sharply cleared his throat. Mayté turned to him. He stared straight at her very deeply and intensely.

A sickening slice filled the air. Someone screamed. From her peripheral vision, she saw Dominic flinch.

Mayté forced herself to stare into Alejandro's hazel eyes. *They are so beautiful. The most beautiful eyes I've ever seen.* She told herself that over and over again. Anything to keep her distracted.

It felt like an agonizing eternity, but soon Misterioso began introducing the surviving contestants one by one. Mayté could hardly focus. Where was Lo? She kept glancing toward the elevators.

Dominic elbowed her. With a smile, he nodded toward Misterioso.

"—Teresa Robles, who happens to be the sister of Carlos Robles. But don't be mistaken. They aren't twins."

Wait. He was introducing her like *that*? She didn't want to be known as Carlos's sister. This was the place where her family lineage wasn't supposed to matter.

"However, unlike her brother, her ambitions are not to restore her family's fortune and reputation, but for herself. She dreams of becoming a world-famous artiste."

¡Dios mío! When Misterioso put it like that, it made her sound like a selfish ass—and her brother a righteous martyr!

Misterioso continued. "Last, but most certainly not least, is Lorena de León." He gestured toward the table, but his smile faltered. "Lorena? Where is Lorena?"

Mayté began to sweat.

"Has she *forfeited*?" Misterioso dramatically asked. He knew the answer, but by the way he grinned, Mayté couldn't tell if the answer was good or bad.

Letting her go off was a terrible mistake. Mayté couldn't breathe. If she had to go through Fortune's Kiss alone . . .

Please, please, please. Bring Lo in here. Now. Please. She clasped her hands together until her knuckles throbbed.

A ding sounded. Every single person in the room turned toward the elevator as the doors opened and out stepped Lo. She stumbled, eyes wide and darting.

Something was wrong. Dread rushed through Mayté. She gripped the seat cushion.

"There she is!" Misterioso gasped. "Lorena de León. Heir of the Cuatro Grandes. The most beautiful bachelorette in Milagro. Perhaps even in San Solera, hmm?"

One of the croupiers whistled, and some others cheered.

"She has her pick of any suitor she desires, yet she has decided to come here and gamble."

More cheers and fanfare.

With her most beguiling smile, Lo spun around and curtsied. The croupiers went wild. They clapped, and their joyous yells became almost deafening.

Prickles of jealousy jabbed Mayté's heart like tiny fingers. But why did she feel like this? It didn't matter what the croupiers thought of her. She just needed to win the game. She choked down her envy and glanced back. Suddenly the cheers stopped. The croupiers stood at their tables silently watching, some even looking bored. Her mouth dried. Had all the cheering been in her head? Had the house somehow done this?

She let out a shaky breath as Lo sat next to her. "Where were you? Are you okay?"

"I'll explain later," Lo whispered, breathless. Her cheeks were flushed, and her bronze complexion glistened under the lights. "Don't forget our plan for this round. Oh." She looked at Alejandro, then glanced around the room. "The Banker's not dealing this round?"

"Afraid not," Alejandro said, leaning against the table. He raised an eyebrow at Lo. "Disappointed?"

Lo rested her chin in her palms. "I'm not sure. Haven't decided yet."

Mayté's stomach twisted. No. She chided herself. This was all a part of the plan. If anyone could get information out of Alejandro, it would be Lo. She was irresistible. More potent than any Quiéreme potion, Lo glowed like pure magic; next to her, Mayté was dull. Forgettable. No one ever gave her a second glance once Lo came into the picture.

But maybe she wanted to be the one to get the information from him.

"Well, I'm not disappointed," she blurted before she could stop herself. "I like you more than the Banker."

Alejandro blinked in surprise, but then smirked and nodded.

"Good." Lo's whisper startled her. "Keep it up. He's already at your mercy."

Mayté nervously laughed and resisted the urge to fan her face. They *were* on the same team, she reminded herself. This was all part of winning—surviving. Despite all the things she imagined, things seemingly aimed at making her resentful and angry, she had to cling to that thought for dear life. Alejandro wanted something from her, and she would use that to get exactly what she *needed*.

"Now that everyone is here and introduced, let us get started!" Misterioso said.

Alejandro closed his eyes, and his eyebrows furrowed in concentration. Bursts of lights flashed around him as Lotería boards appeared. "Choose a board, but choose wisely." He spoke dryly. Almost as if this were the last thing he wanted to be doing.

One by one, each player chose one of the boards floating around him. Just like a normal game of Lotería, no one could see the front of their board until they chose it. Most would say it was all down to pure luck, but Abuelita would have begged to differ. It was about each player's energy. And maybe the house would feel the same way, Mayté thought. She had silently begged for Lo to enter the gaming den, and a second later, she had. If she could will that to happen, then surely she could will herself into picking a lucky board.

When her turn finally came, she closed her eyes and held out her hand, slowly, ever so slowly, hovering it back and forth. *Feel for the heart in your fingertip. Follow, and let it decide.* Abuelita's words replayed in her mind. It was her philosophy when playing, and she almost always won. She'd had bags and bags of bronze coins to prove it.

She focused as hard as she could until she swore she felt a pulse in the tip of her finger. It was brief. Maybe even imagined. But there was no time to doubt herself. She reached out and grabbed a board. When she opened her eyes, Alejandro flashed an amused grin at her. Her face warmed. Lo lightly poked her under the table before closing her eyes and choosing her own board.

Soon, Alejandro snapped his fingers and a card deck appeared in his hands. He shuffled it, tossing cards around and letting them spin around him. His fingers moved so fast, they were almost a blur; he didn't let a single card fall to the floor. One seemingly slipped away, but he kicked up his leg, balancing the card on the tip of his shiny black shoe. He kicked it back up and caught it up with the rest of the cards. Lo squealed, and Dominic clapped his hands. Truly, it was spellbinding.

So spellbinding, in fact, that Mayté almost forgot to look at her board. She flipped it over and studied the different images. As usual, there were 16 spaces total: four down and four across. Some of the pictures were familiar, but many were not. The Lotería she knew by heart had fifty-four cards in all. One afternoon, many years ago, she had asked Carlos to help her figure out what the odds of winning were. She never cared for her studies, always succumbing to the urge to sketch in her workbooks instead, while Carlos seemed to be the exact opposite. He couldn't draw much more than wobbly stick figures, yet he excelled at academics. Unfortunately, Lo had kept distracting him by sashaying around and trying to get him to focus on her. Eventually, she resorted to tickling him. They never did figure out what the odds were.

"For this round, the house will choose what you wager," Misterioso said. "Your possessions are on the line this time. The round will last until a player gets a lotería."

Mayté didn't have many earthly possessions. Just some old paintings and art supplies, along with borrowed jewelry from Lo, and Abuelita's favorite rebozo. Her gaze darted to Carlos. He didn't have much of anything either. At least in this round, neither of them had much to lose.

Alejandro held up a card. "La Garza," he called out, voice loud and clear. The card showed a white heron standing in the water, plucking out a fish.

The card glowed, and Mayté didn't dare breathe. What would happen? Would someone die?

Something flew out of the card and landed on the table with a thunk. Lo shrieked. A fish. Don Zelaya and Xiomara burst out laughing. A huge white blur of a heron darted out of the card and scooped up the fish. It flew around the gaming room higher and higher until it disappeared.

"Don't forget to place your beans on your board if you have La Garza," Misterioso said.

Mayté looked down: sure enough, her board had La Garza on the bottom row, third column. She plucked up a bean and dropped it onto her board as a few others did the same. As soon as the bean landed, it melted into the La Garza space, causing it to glow.

"El Nopal." Alejandro held up another card.

Bright green cacti sprouted around the gambling den. Most from the carpet and some from the walls. Some were tiny, while others kept growing more and more, some with heads with pink flowers.

Mayté's heart skipped. El Nopal was on her board next to La Garza. She snatched a bean and placed it down. The plan was working. She had fixed her mind and followed her heart, and the house had given her a lucky board. She needed just two more matches to get a horizontal lotería, and then the round would end. Next to her, Lo placed a bean, while Dominic frowned at his board, unlucky and beanless.

This was more like the Lotería she knew and loved, save for the spectacle whenever a new card was called out. But memories of last night wouldn't allow her to fully relax. This game was deadly.

"El Borracho." Alejandro held up a card with a man holding a bottle of liquor. The card glowed, and out stumbled the drunkard, still holding his bottle. Several people at the table gasped. El Borracho swayed as he eyed the contestants.

Mayté's heart stopped. With his messy dark brown hair and the sloppy stubble dotting his chin and upper lip, he looked almost exactly like her father, albeit much younger. Without graying hair and deep wrinkles, but still it was uncanny. She couldn't help but glance at Carlos. He sat stiffly, mouth hanging open.

El Borracho lifted his bottle, sloshing around the alcohol inside, before pointing it at Carlos.

"Ah, I must inform you that this is a special card," Misteri-oso said. "Cards like this one will challenge a player for a wager. Carlos, my boy, you will wager the jar you've hidden under your bed."

What? Mayté sat up straighter.

The jar? How on earth did he know about that?

Misterioso snapped his fingers, and Carlos's jar appeared on the table with a clang as coins smacked against the glass. It was a quarter full of bronze coins. Barely enough to buy much of anything.

"Once upon a time, this jar had been much fuller, if it weren't for certain thieving hands," Mysterioso declared.

It was true. Carlos had been saving coins ever since he was ten. The jar had been almost overflowing at one point. Before their father found it. Carlos kept hiding it in different spots over the years, but their father had kept finding it. As if he hadn't already stolen enough. Mayté's teeth chattered.

"Perhaps you can win back those stolen coins. Or perhaps not. Are you ready?" Misterioso asked.

"Er . . ." Carlos stared at the drunk man as if he had seen a ghost.

"We must begin. Are you ready?" Misterioso repeated.

"Uh." Carlos's face reddened. "Yes."

"¡Toma!" El Borracho slurred and tossed his bottle at Carlos demanding he drink. Dios. He even sounded like their father. Or was Mayté just imagining it? Her heart pounded violently; she couldn't think straight.

Carlos managed to catch the bottle. His eyes were wide with terror as he held the rim to his lips and began to chug.

"¡Toma! ¡Toma!" El Borracho demanded. The vaquero joined in along with Don Zelaya and Xiomara.

"¡Toma!"

"¡Toma!"

"¡Toma!"

Carlos's eyes watered and his face twisted, but he kept drinking.

Mayté winced. From here, she could smell the alcohol. It stung her nose as it infiltrated her sinuses. It must have been strong, but Carlos was drinking for his life. If he stopped, who knew what would happen.

Please. Don't stop drinking.

Carlos's body twitched, and his chest heaved.

"Come on, Carlos. You can do it!" Lo cheered.

He squeezed his eyes shut and kept drinking until there was no liquid left. With a loud gasp, he dropped the bottle. It shattered into thousands of pieces. Several people at the table cheered.

"No vomites," El Borracho growled before vanishing.

Golden coins dropped into the jar until it overflowed.

"Congratulations." Misterioso applauded. "If you can make it through the entire round without vomiting, you'll keep your reward. Now, put your bean over the El Borracho space, if you please."

Carlos nodded blankly and fell back in his seat, nearly toppling over. He grabbed a handful of beans and fumbled around, barely able to put one in the right spot. How could he have gotten so intoxicated in such a short amount of time? The booze must have been infused with magic: it was the only explanation.

With shaky fingers, Mayté put a bean down. Only one more until she got lotería. She chewed her lip and glanced at Carlos. What would happen if he vomited? Would he die too?

Alejandro called out the next card. "El Cantarito." The card showed an ornate clay pitcher painted orange with white patterns. "Damn it," Mayté whispered. That space wasn't on her board. She tried not to watch the others put down their beans. A flurry of waitresses rushed to the table. Each wore off-the-shoulder gowns that hugged their torsos and hips like gloves. The gowns and their matching floppy feathered hats were all in different jewel tones. Ruby red, sapphire blue, amethyst purple . . . Stark white calavera masks obscured their faces. All at once, they set clay cups in front of every contestant.

The liquid began to bubble inside the cups. Next ice cubes appeared, followed by a slice of grapefruit. The rims glittered as salt formed.

No one made a move to take a drink.

"Oh, come, now." Misterioso chuckled. "It's quite delicious, if I do say so myself."

Carlos gagged and slapped a hand over his mouth. His chest heaved.

No, no, no. Mayté grabbed Lo's hand.

Lo squeezed back. "Hum, Carlos!" she called out and hummed an aimless tune.

Carlos furrowed his eyebrows, but he hummed too. At first it sounded strained and off-key, but he soon matched Lo's tune. The panic in his eyes softened. Could something so simple chase away nausea? He flashed a grateful look at Lo. Mayté quickly looked away, blinking back tears. She took a shaky sip of El Cantarito. It was shockingly sweet, but it burned on the way down. Everyone else drank too, some sipping, while others chugged it down. That seemed to satisfy Misterioso, who nodded at Alejandro.

"El Soldado." The card showed a man clad in San Sol-era's orange-and-yellow military uniform. He stood stiff as a board, rifle at his side. But suddenly he marched out of the card and pointed his rifle straight at Carmen, who flinched and whimpered.

Lo gasped.

"El Soldado has chosen you, Carmen. He commands that you wager the land your abuelo plans to leave you after his passing." A slip of paper appeared and slowly descended to the middle of the table.

"It's . . ." Dominic craned his neck to get a good look. "It's a deed."

Carmen wrung her trembling hands.

"Answer three of my questions correctly," El Soldado barked. "One: How many floors are in the salon?"

"Th-thirteen."

"Correct," El Soldado said. "Second question: What is the name of the croupier dealing to you?"

Carmen's eyes widened, and the others looked to each other, unsure. Mayté normally wasn't the best with names. She found it easier to remember people by their faces. Unusual eyes or an intriguing birthmark caught her attention better than just a name. And yet, she remembered Alejandro's name. It was ingrained in her mind.

Lo knew his name too. She stiffened and stared at Car-men, frantic.

"Uh . . ." Carmen looked around. Beads of sweat formed at her brow. "G-Gerardo?"

Mayté winced. Alejandro raised an eyebrow, as if offended by the name.

"Wrong," El Soldado said.

"I'm afraid you've lost this wager," Misterioso nodded at the table. The deed combusted into flames, quickly crumbling into ash.

"No." Carmen covered her mouth.

"You'll have to keep wagering until you pass the card's challenge. Next will be your abuela's wedding ring."

Carmen held out her hand. A golden band sat snug on her ring finger. Her lips quivered. The land was likely worth more coins than the ring, but it was clear that the ring meant more to her. Mayté completely understood. She would never forgive her father for selling off her grandmother's ring and squandering away the money.

"The croupier's name. What is it?" El Soldado demanded.

Carmen let out a shaky sigh.

She wasn't going to be able to guess it, and then what?

"Antonio?"

"Still incorrect," Misterioso said.

The ring vanished. Carmen jolted. Her light brown cheeks were flushed and her eyes filled with tears.

"Keep in mind, we cannot move on until you pass this challenge," Misterioso said as he tapped his foot and checked his hourglass.

"I don't have anything left to wager." Carmen's voice shook.

"Oh, nonsense!" Misterioso turned cheerful once again. "You have your son, of course. You brought him into this world. He's your possession. Ten years old. The innocent little thing has no clue that you're here right now."

Mayté's blood ran cold.

"No." Lo grabbed Mayté's arms. She was completely helpless. They both were.

Murmurs echoed through the room.

"Will she do it?"

"There's no other choice."

"Well, this is a fascinating turn of events," Don Zelaya said unashamedly.

"No!" Carmen snapped, her voice panicked. "No, no, no. I'd give my own life before that."

"Very well. It's not against the rules to offer a counter-wager as long as it's worth at least the value of what was originally proposed." Misterioso grinned. "Now, if you could answer El Soldado's question. The name of the croupier, please?"

This was Carmen's last chance. If she failed, she was gone. Carmen just stood there. With a small sob, she covered her face. She didn't know his name.

"Carmen," Lo whispered.

What was she doing?

"Don't tell me you're going to help her," Don Zelaya loudly interrupted. "Why, that sounds like cheating." He smugly sipped his drink.

"Actually, most anything goes during these games," Misterioso said. "The contestants may interact with each other during the challenges. But beware, the path to el infierno was paved with intentions both wicked and noble."

Mayté and Lo exchanged glances. They would have to keep that in mind. "It's Alejandro," Lo softly said. It was up to Carmen if she would trust her or not.

"Alejandro," Carmen blurted.

"Correct."

Carmen wiped her eyes and mouthed something to Lo. Probably a thank-you, but her lips trembled so much that Mayté couldn't be sure.

"One final question," El Soldado said. "What astronomical event occurs around the time that Fortune's Kiss chooses a new location?"

Carmen's face lit up, and Lo whimpered with relief. An easy question. One that anyone remotely interested in Fortune's Kiss would know.

"The equinox."

Wait—

An explosive shot rang through the gambling den. Carmen froze. Blood pooled at her chest. Right at her heart. Her wide eyes glazed over and she fell backward. Lo screamed. Carlos began to hum, head down. Mayté's ears rung.

"Close, but not quite. It's the solstice, not the equinox, unfortunately." Misterioso didn't sound the least bit sorry.

In contrast to last night, everyone at the table was quiet. Subdued. No one jumped up from their seats, screaming and desperate to escape. Maybe because the futility of it all had sunk in. Dominic rubbed his mouth and fiddled with his cravat. The vaquero downed his entire drink and snatched the one from the person seated next to him.

Lo trembled. Mayté grabbed her hand. Lo's eyes watered, and she looked absolutely horrified, but then she took a breath and her face hardened into something determined. Mayté caught Alejandro staring, observing them almost wistfully.

You grow numb to it after a while.

Mayté covered her mouth. She still wanted to cry. Just like last night, but this time it wasn't as much of a surprise. It was shocking, yes, but it didn't completely blindside her this time. In the game, lives would be lost.

And there was nothing she could do about it.

The other croupiers took Carmen's body away. It was much less messy, though someone had to wipe away the blood spatters from the wall. Mayté shuddered.

She *had* to win.

And figure out how to do so with both Lo and Carlos.

The game continued. "La Botella." Alejandro held up a card that had what appeared to be a liquor bottle on it. However, Mayté had never seen a bright turquoise liquor before. Probably spiked with some kind of potion. The card glowed, and the bottle floated out. It flew to the table, hovering in front of Señor Vásquez. He reached for the bottle, but then hesitated.

"The matter, old man? Can't hold your liquor?" the vaquero taunted.

"La Botella has chosen you, Daniel Vásquez. You must take it," Misterioso said.

Señor Vásquez's eyes widened and his wide shoulders shook as he took the bottle. The fear on his face was almost palpable.

"You must either drink or pass it on for someone else to drink," Misterioso explained. "Whether the contents inside are helpful or poisonous is a mystery." He put a gloved finger to his lips. "You will wager—"

"No!" Señor Vásquez blurted. "I can't do this. I want to fold."

Mayté's eyes widened, and everyone else at the table stared at Señor Vásquez.

"Remember, señor, what you gave up to compete here." Misterioso's voice sharpened into something deadly. "If you fold now, you'll leave with your life but lose your dream."

"I—I don't want to do this anymore." Señor Vásquez's mustache. He ran a trembling hand through his thick, curly hair. "I don't want someone else to die because I'm here."

Misterioso clicked his tongue. "Very well. If you are certain, then you only have to repeat the words 'I fold.' But understand, you have been warned."

Alejandro shifted on his feet and drummed his fingers against the table. His lips thinned into a straight line, and even with all the makeup, Mayté could read his dread clear as day.

Losing one's dream was a fate worse than death.

"Señor Vásquez, don't!" she blurted just as he said, "I fold."

As soon as the words left his lips, he suddenly stiffened. The life left his dark brown eyes, and his shoulders drooped.

Next to him, Xiomara nudged his arm. "Señor?"

He grunted in response and stared straight ahead. It was as if everything that made him *him* was sucked dry. Gone was his jovial aura. Now he seemed dull. Not quite empty. More like miserable. A croupier took him by the arm and led him to the elevator.

Alejandro looked away, focusing on his deck of cards. Mayté's heart sank.

Misterioso spoke. "Folding may be the safer option, as one can leave with their life; however, it comes at a cost. Daniel Vásquez had much higher ambitions than his elote stand. He dreamed of becoming a world-famous chef, making people happy with his delectable dishes." Misterioso patted his stomach. "Trust me. I've tasted his elote. Unfortunately, we all will suffer, as we will never be able to partake in his delicious dishes ever again." Despite his words, his grin remained, unchanging.

Mayté stopped breathing.

"Because he folded, he has lost his knack and desire for cooking. His sense of smell and taste are also gone, which means he can never enjoy food again."

"Dios mío," Mayté choked out. She couldn't even begin to imagine. If she folded, would she lose her ability to paint? Lose her eyesight and the feeling in her fingers so she could never even pick up a paintbrush again? The thought shook her to her very core. Folding was absolutely not an option. She frowned at her board. La Botella, the card that Alejandro had most recently dealt, and the one that led to Señor Vásquez's demise, was the last space she needed to fill a horizontal row. She placed the bean down and called out, voice weak, "Loteria!"

"Wonderful!" Misterioso said. "Our second round has ended!"

Mayté let out a breath. Not a moment too soon. The rest of them were safe.

For now.

TWELVE

Lo

Lo collapsed onto her bed as soon as she and Mayté returned to their suite. *Carmen. Poor Carmen.* Yet, the more Lo thought of it, the more numb she became. Carmen hadn't deserved to die. She was kind. She was only trying to protect her son. Like Mamá had been trying to protect Lo and her sisters. But no, there was no use in dwelling on that. She and Mayté had survived the round. Mayté even had gotten lotería. That was the thing that mattered. Life would go on. As long as they survived.

After the game had ended, Misterioso had dismissed them. They were free to do as they pleased until the next round that evening. Lunch wouldn't be formally served, but instead everyone could order what they wanted. Apparently, the cooks could make any dish the contestants dreamed of. All they had to do was ring the bell on the table next to the door, and, like magic, a servant would deliver the meal they desired most.

Lo sat up, leaning against the fluffy, silken pillows, which must have been spun with magic, because just resting against them eased the tension in her tight shoulders.

"Dios mio." Mayté leaned against the door and covered her face. "Those poor people." Her voice shook. "They didn't deserve any of that." She kept her hands pressed against her face and gulped down shaky breaths.

"I know," Lo whispered. She couldn't stand the sight of her best friend being so upset. "But you did wonderfully. You got lotería."

Mayté slowly lowered her hands. Her eyes glistened. Lo patted the bed next to her. When Mayté sat, Lo put her arm around her. "Let's wish for desserts from far-off countries and then taste them all." Anything to get their minds off what had just happened. "I want to try those pastel cookie cakes with cream in the middle—oh, and the balls of dough with ice cream inside. We can make that our theme. Only the finest desserts with a special surprise hidden within."

"That sounds great, but . . . I'm not hungry." Mayté looked down. In her gown, she resembled a princess from a storybook. Troubled and beautiful. But there was no Prince Charming to rescue her.

Not that either of them needed that.

"Lo, what happened before the game? Where were you?"

Lo tried to explain everything. It was hard to put it into words when she still couldn't quite wrap her mind around it herself. She told Mayté about trying to talk to Misterioso and her encounter with the Banker and, as briefly as possible, about how she had wandered into a room just like Mamá's and gotten trapped. She hated the strange look of discomfort and sympathy that crossed her best friend's face at the mention of Mamá. It almost made her wish she hadn't said anything. "There was no way out, but then I heard your voice."

Mayté's eyes grew.

"You called my name, and then suddenly I was back in that empty room and I was able to leave. I ran as fast as I could to the elevator."

"Lo!" Mayté grabbed her hands. "The whole time, I was so worried. I started thinking and trying to will you to the gaming den—it worked!" She sounded breathless. "I willed myself to choose a lucky board. And I did! Alejandro was right. Maybe we can actually win this!" She jumped to her feet. "I need to find him. Maybe he'll be able to tell me how we can save Carlos, too. Do you want to come?"

Lo almost agreed, but the house seemed to be giving in to *Mayté's* desires. Lo herself was getting nowhere. If she were, she would have found Mamá by now. "No, I think it'll be best if you go alone. Alejandro trusts you. He may not be so open to divulging information if I tag along."

"Are you sure?"

"Positive." Lo needed to figure out how to make herself useful. "Let me know what you find out—and please make sure you eat something."

"Save me some of those sweets, okay?" With a smile and a wave, Mayté left.

Lo lifted her hand in a wave, but as soon as the door shut, she lowered it and squeezed the plush blankets until her knuckles turned white. A lump formed in her throat. She couldn't let herself be the reason Mayté lost the game. But she couldn't stop thinking about Mamá either. Lo knew in her heart; she was here somewhere . . .

She walked to the table by the door and picked up the bell. Tiny and silver, it tinkled when she shook it. She didn't know what she desired anymore. The thought of sweets now made her stomach churn.

Nothing happened. Maybe the house knew she had lost her appetite.

Defeated, she returned to her bed. More than anything, she wanted a nap, but when she closed her eyes, all she could see were scattered memories from earlier. Mamá in the hallway. Finding herself trapped in that room. Carmen crumpling to the ground. Lo replayed all of it.

As she began to doze off, dreamlike fantasies mingled with her memories. This time, she caught up to Mamá. Grabbed her arm before she could vanish into thin air. Mamá slowly turned back, thick curls obscuring the side of her face.

BANG!

Gunshots rang through the air once again. Blood spurted from Mamá's chest.

Lo yelped, but the ringing in her ears was even louder. Mamá's arm slipped from Lo's grip as she toppled to the floor, into a pile of orange marigolds. A gust of wind blew the petals away, revealing not Mamá, but Carmen. She lay in a puddle of blood, bright and red like the roses she had formerly—and tirelessly—tended to.

A young child screamed and wailed. "Mamá! Mamá!"

Lo realized that she was the one screaming. She slapped a hand over her mouth and sat up.

Her chest heaved, and a cold sweat chilled her. It wasn't real. That wasn't how it happened.

But what if Mamá *had* died like Carmen? The two were connected by the same motivation, like a ribbon intertwining their hearts. What if the same ribbon of fate had strangled them both?

No. Lo abruptly sat up, ignoring the ache in the back of her skull. It wasn't true.

Her mind wandered to her sisters. How were they doing? Maybe now, with their father gone, Sera would be able to do more than just studying and needlework. Maybe Sofía would be able to spend her days in the stable without interruption.

Lo missed them.

She desperately wanted to see them. Her heart raced. "Please . . . ," she whispered. "Let me see them." If it worked for Mayté, then it could work for her. "Show me my sisters."

Just when she was about to give up, the mirror across the room flickered. Her reflection morphed into the image of her sisters. They both sat on a bed. Sera brushed through Sofia's curly hair.

Lo scrambled to get a closer look. Were they okay? Were they sad? Were they taken care of? Were they—

The image changed into her father lying in a pool of blood.

With a scream, Lo recoiled. Why was this happening? Her hand shot to the vanity, knocking over jewelry as she searched for something to destroy the mirror, but when she looked back up the glass was back to normal.

Did her sisters hate her for killing their father?

Murder was a sin. She had heard that preached countless times. But what about when the person in question was a monster? Her father would have done terrible things to her—and eventually her sisters—if she hadn't acted.

He'd *deserved* to die.

A knock at the door tore her from her thoughts. That must be lunch after all. She hopped off the bed and hurried to answer the door. What she didn't expect to see was the Banker holding a tray with a silver-domed platter. "Hello," he greeted her, voice smooth as silk.

"It's you." Lo stepped back, letting him into the room. A familiar scent hit her nose, but she couldn't quite place it. "You actually came." She felt like a fish about to be beheaded, wide eyes, gaping mouth and all. She quickly pulled herself together, glancing at the tray in his hands. "You aren't a servant."

"I'm not. I could say something fanciful like perhaps it was your desires that pulled me here, but in reality I was intrigued by our conversation earlier." He set the platter on the table and leaned against the wall with a smile. His gaze never left her.

Maybe now things would finally go her way.

"Couldn't it be both?" She sweetly smiled.

"You think so?"

"I *know* so. What's your name?" Lo approached him. "Surely it's not Señor Banker."

"You're right." He pushed off the wall and closed the space between them. "However, I don't give away that information for free." He leaned in close. Much closer than a proper gentleman should be to a lady he wasn't promised to. Their lips were mere inches away from each other.

"Oh, really?" she purred, matching his boldness. This was fun. When all else failed, mimicking one's opponent's energy always worked. Let them think they had control over the interaction. "I must thank you for this wonderful suite."

"And how will you do that?" he asked. For just a moment—in the blink of an eye, really—his wolfish grin slipped and his eyes dulled as if his mind had gone elsewhere. In that moment, Lo realized exactly why this was so fun. Men were always a game to her, a self-imposed competition to see how quickly she could get what she wanted, but, for the first time, she had a companion playing with her. *Playing her* as much as she played him. Flirting with him felt so familiar, because he treated her exactly how she treated other men: saying and doing all the right things until he won his prize.

But what was that prize for him? What did he want from her?

This had never happened before. She didn't know what to say. "I—I'll have to think about it."

"Mm." The Banker slickly moved away. "Do that, and perhaps you can tell me another time." He turned for the door.

"Wait!"

He ignored her.

There was no time for careful words. "Can't you see that I'm going to win this entire game?" Both Fortune's Kiss and whatever was going on between the both of them. "You would be wise to ally with me."

She had never played the game like this. It felt raw. There was no hiding behind masks or the armor of flirtation. This was a risk that could very well backfire, but, after all, she had come here to gamble.

The Banker paused, halfway out of the room. Then, with a chuckle, he stepped back in and closed the door. "Oh? Is that so?"

"You see it, do you not? My potential. My wits. My *charm*. Or was it wrong of me to assume that you are not a fool?"

He smirked, icy eyes aglow with a hunger. A strange kind of hunger. Not one of lust, but of something else. What was his game?

"If you are so sure of yourself, why do you want me as an ally? What is it you think you need from me?"

"Lots of things." Lo folded her arms. "Tell me: What is the secret to the game?"

He chuckled. "Did you not just say you were going to win?"

"Yes. And I would like to do it as quickly and easily as possible."

He raised an eyebrow, but that must have been a good-enough answer. "I could never tell you how to win—it would make the game far too short." He paused. "María Teresa's strategy seems to be working well for her."

Lo bit back a gasp. He knew. But how? She could have asked, but no. "It's not working for me," she admitted instead.

"Are you sure about that?" He tugged at his cufflinks. "You willed the house to kill Montoya."

"What?" Lo's knees buckled. The beans Señora Montoya had counted had magically changed. She'd had nothing to do with it.

"Do you not recall whispering a prayer for her to lose?" The Banker smirked. "It was remarkable, really. I haven't seen anyone do that so early in the game in quite a while. Of course, with powerful magic comes a price, and something like that costs quite a lot."

Lo rubbed her temple and sat in the chair nearest the table. Is this why nothing after that moment had seemed to go her way? "Does this mean I'll have hallucinations of my mother for the rest of the game?"

The Banker sat across from her. "You cling to the hope that your mother is here. Trapped and scared like a prisoner," he mocked. "Yet everyone else around you is certain that she is dead or long gone. Do you truly think so many people could be wrong?"

Hearing her worst fears spoken aloud was more than Lo could take. "Don't try to fool me." She smacked her palms against the table, shaking the platter with her hidden lunch on it. "I know she's here." She hated the way her voice wavered.

The Banker leaned back in his chair, unfazed. "If finding her is what you desire most, *if* you survive, the house will surely show you the truth. Just be careful not to wish *too* hard. You might find yourself in the afterlife."

She might . . . Wait. Was he implying that Mamá truly was dead? It had to be a trick, right? "Wh-what do you—"

"Lorena, you talk about your mother, but didn't you make a pact to leave with your little friend and the boy you fancy so? Neither of them knows just how focused you are on her, do they?" He watched her expectantly. "The house is not fond of indecisive people."

Lo stiffened. She had come here for Mamá, but she had also come for Mayté. They had vowed to win together. And the idea of harm coming to Carlos made her sick with fear. Why did she have to choose? "I just don't want to worry them, and surely there's a way to get her back *and* win."

The Banker stood.

"*Is* there a way?" she growled.

But he still ignored her. "I've grown bored. If you can think of another way to entertain me, come find me." He opened the door, but then turned back. "You should eat that before it gets cold." He slammed the door behind himself.

Lo frowned at the platter and lifted the lid.

Paella. Most of the dish was normal enough. Saffron rice, bright green limes, and salmon-pink prawns. Any other person wouldn't have given it a second thought, but Lo did. The dish was missing something: mussels, their shells black as obsidian.

Mamá loved paella. She used to ask the cooks to make it at least once a week, but always requested that the mussels be left out, because she hated them. She found them odd and inconvenient to eat. Yet she never minded the prawns staring up at her with their beady black eyes.

Lo's hands quaked. This was a sick joke. The Banker must have been in on it, delivering her mother's favorite dish.

Another knock sounded at the door. She scrambled to answer it. Maybe it was the Banker wanting to see her reaction to the food. This time she would pull him into the room and not allow him to leave, until he gave her some answers. But when she opened the door, she found Carlos.

He leaned against the door frame, his dark eyes scanning the room. Displeasure pinched his flushed face. He reeked and was still clearly drunk from the liquor El Borracho had forced him to drink. Carlos wasn't one for alcohol. He never took more than a few sips, always scrunching up his face and shaking his head before pushing the drink away. It was honestly impressive that he had managed to best El Borracho. "Where's Mayté?"

"I'm not sure." It was somewhat true. Lo didn't know exactly where Mayté had ventured off to.

"Mierda." Carlos rubbed his face. "This isn't how it's supposed to be!" he shouted.

The alcohol had only made him angrier. But Lo wasn't scared of him. Deep in her heart, she knew he wouldn't hurt anyone. Even in this state, he was as harmless as a rabbit.

"I was supposed to fix everything. For both of you. You two weren't supposed to come here." He clumsily pressed his fist against the door frame as if he wanted to punch it, but couldn't quite bring himself to.

Lo's heart jumped. He was going to fix things—for *both* of them?

What was the wish *he* wanted?

"But now, I could never ask Mayté to give up her dream. And I would never forgive myself if anything happened to either of you. How . . . how did this happen, Lo?" His voice cracked. "We were supposed to be happy. How did everything go so wrong?" He tried to take a step, but ended up stumbling.

"Careful." She steadied him, but it was awkward since he was much taller than she was.

He pressed his palms into the wall on either side of Lo and stared down at her. "Most of all," his voice softened, "I regret not being more open with you. I wish things could have been different."

The boy you fancy so . . .

The Banker's teasing voice filled her head. Lo's heart pounded. "Me too." And she truly meant it. "Carlos." She hugged him. Whether she was doing it to comfort him or herself, she couldn't decide.

The moment the Robleses had fallen from grace, Carlos had stopped being an option. Her father would never have allowed him to pursue her. They both knew that. Yet the flame inside her heart that glowed for him had never dulled. It wasn't something as simple as blowing it out. Over the years, she had simply become good at hiding it.

But now there was no one else here to see it.

Carlos may have been a mess in this moment, but the way his eyes took her in made her feel as if *she* were the one who was intoxicated. Seeing him in this state should have repelled her, but instead she found him handsome. Maybe the most handsome he had ever been. His gaze landed on her lips. Lo swallowed.

She wasn't sure who had leaned in first, but suddenly their lips found each other. The kiss was short, sloppy, and warm. It ended much too fast.

Because even if there was no one to stop them, there was too much at stake to let themselves get swept away.

"We need to"—Lo gulped down air—"find a way for all three of us to win. That's what Mayté wants more than anything."

Carlos stumbled past her and sat on the bed. He looked up at her. Not with hunger like her suitors, or with mysterious arrogance like the Banker. Instead, his dark brown eyes gleamed with sorrow. "I don't know if that's possible," he whispered. "But we know at least two can conquer the game. So, no matter what, you and Mayté have to win."

"But, Carlos—"

He shook his head and stood. "Please, do what you can to protect my sister and yourself." He strode past her, seemingly sobered up by determination. "I'll see you later, Lo." With eyes still full of sadness, he left the room.

THIRTEEN

Mayté

Mayté strode the hallways with determination. Along the way, she passed Don Zelaya and Xiomara exploring the house, their eyes wide with wonder. Was the house leading them to what *they* desired most? Were they aware of the possibility? She certainly hoped not. She and Lo needed every advantage they could get.

She rounded the corner, glad that she remembered the way to the library. Her heart pounded with anticipation. She hoped more than anything that Alejandro would be in there, but even if he wasn't, maybe she could uncover some clues hidden away in the books. Maybe, just maybe, she could find a way for three people to win.

With a deep breath, she pushed open the door and stepped inside.

But this wasn't the library.

Instead of endless bookshelves crowding the walls and a cozy fire giving off a soft glow, this room was much simpler and brighter. The blue sky shone through the floor-to-ceiling windows, revealing an azure ocean in the distance. This had to be an illusion, right? Fortune's Kiss had been nestled inland, in the heart of Milagro.

Against the wall was a shelf full of gleaming arrows that looked as if they had been dipped in crystallized light. Next to them were archery bows gilded in gold. Further ahead were targets. Once upon a time, she had learned archery. Abuelita had insisted that Mayté hone many skills so she could stay well rounded. Back then, it had been a fun way to blow off steam. Her aim had been quite sharp, too. But that was then. After her family had lost everything, they could no longer afford to pay for lessons, and even if they somehow could have, they needed her home to look after her brothers.

Surely she had become quite rusty. Still—

She grabbed a bow and arrow and took aim. That part, she still remembered. Her fingers trembled—and she lowered the bow with a sigh.

A mixture of sorrow and frustration clawed at her throat.

Archery—a reminder of what her life once had been and never could be again.

Where had the library gone? That was where she needed to be. Not here. If the house kept shifting the rooms around, it could take hours to find it. She didn't have that kind of time. Or patience.

But maybe she could use this moment to test the house's magic. What she wanted most was to talk with Alejandro and discover the key to winning the game. She closed her eyes and focused on that desire. But her mind drifted to her art. Painting always calmed her and helped her gather her thoughts.

The bow slipped from her fingers and landed with a clang. The noise was much softer than it should have been. As if the bow wasn't nearly so big and heavy as it had seemed. Mayté's eyes snapped open, and she gasped. It wasn't a bow on the floor, but instead a painter's pallet. In her hand, the arrow was now a paintbrush.

The shelf was full of tubes of paint and other supplies. The targets had transformed into blank canvases. The room had morphed into something just for her—a studio. She picked up the palette and squirted paint on it. Then she snatched several brushes and approached the canvases. She chose the one in the center. It didn't take long for her to begin painting. First the sky with smooth puffs of white clouds and the glowing orb that was the sun. It was easy, since azure paint was in endless supply here. *Ironic.* She didn't try to make it polished or perfect; instead, she focused on the effect of each stroke. It felt like flying.

Before she knew it, she began painting a portrait of Alejandro against the beautiful blue backdrop. His face had ingrained itself in her mind. His charming smile. His bright hazel eyes and his stark black hair.

This, her art, was the reason she was here risking it all. She couldn't let herself forget. Her mother had told her to marry a good suitor who would let her paint. But that soon changed to: *"Painting is only for the privileged."* Then to: *"You don't have time to paint."* And in a way, her mother was right. The only time she truly had to herself was in the dark of night and the wee hours of the morning when everyone else was slumbering.

Her hand trembled. What if this was her last painting? She couldn't shake what had happened to Señor Vásquez. How many people had she encountered in Milagro who had suffered the same fate? The beggars who barely lifted their heads and didn't notice when people dropped a coin into their cup. The vendors who suddenly stopped selling their wares at the street mercado. The nobles everyone whispered about who no longer left their homes.

No matter what, she had to find a way to make it out of here with Lo, Carlos, and all their dreams intact.

And she would. This painting was proof that the house favored her; with its magic, they would win.

"Agh!" Something sharp dug into her palm, and she dropped the paintbrush. But it was an arrow once again. The palette in her hand shifted back into a bow before her eyes. Mayté set it aside and studied her palm. The razor-thin cut was just deep enough to draw a thread of blood. And the painting? She braced herself to see what had happened to her work.

The canvas had changed back into a target, but the painting of Alejandro's face remained, run through with several arrows.

A pit formed in her stomach.

The door creaked open. "Er, am I interrupting something?" Dominic raised an eyebrow at the image on the target.

Mayté's face warmed. To someone just stepping in, it probably looked like she was using Alejandro's face for target practice. "N-no! I was just painting, a-and the house suddenly changed." She yanked at one of the arrows, but it wouldn't budge. "I know what this looks like, but really—"

"Relax." Dominic stepped next to her, a smile playing on his lips. "I know what you mean. The house keeps changing things around. I thought it was just subtle differences like the décor, or finding a door that hadn't been there a few hours earlier, but it can completely transform—right in front of us."

She had thought the house was mainly changing for her. Was she mistaken? She didn't dare mention anything specific about it out loud. "It's very strange, isn't it?"

"Yes." Dominic pressed his hands against the window and stared out at the ocean in awe, but there was a sadness in his eyes. "If not for the stakes, it would actually be a wonderful place to stay."

Mayté twisted her hands together. It didn't matter how the place dazzled. The stakes were everything.

"I've been meaning to ask." He turned to her, eyes bright and cheerful once again. "My mother commissioned you, right? For a painting of the dogs?"

"Er, yes." Mayté slowly nodded. Dios, that whole ordeal felt like a lifetime ago. It gave her mixed feelings. A part of her wanted to be back home in a world where she and those she cared for were safe, but then she remembered how dire things had been when she left. It was a lose-lose scenario. "I'm surprised you know about it."

"Of course I do." Dominic laughed. "I was the one who wanted the painting."

"What?" Mayté bit back a gasp.

Dominic scratched the back of his head. "Come on. It's not *that* surprising. I've always loved art, but anything I try to make looks like a chicken dipped its claws and beak in paint and went to town with a canvas."

Mayté burst out laughing. "Everyone has to start somewhere, you know?"

"Maybe, but I remember how you drew when we were kids. It always looked so good. I was a little jealous."

"Really?" She had never thought anyone noticed or cared about her drawings back then. Except for Abuelita and Lo, of course.

"And now look at you." He gestured at the ruined canvas. "Even after that boy is gone, the painting will remain. That's amazing. An artist can take any view, any idea, any person, and make them . . . immortal."

That was surprisingly insightful and deeper than she would have expected from someone like him. "And you wanted to immortalize—your dogs?"

"Something like that. If anything was to happen, I wanted to always be able to have them in eyesight."

Mayté felt her heart soften. Even though she thought they looked more like oversized rats, it was endearing how much Dominic cared for them.

But dogs usually lived several years. It seemed a bit premature to want to immortalize them.

"I never got to finish it. I was almost done, but I couldn't afford to get the supplies I needed. Sorry."

"Oh, if I had known, I would have bought your supplies and lent you a room in my hacienda to work in peace."

"Really?" She felt warm, but then a swell of sorrow chased the feeling away. They were both in Fortune's Kiss. She couldn't let herself grow attached to another person. Her life, along with Lo's and Carlos's lives, depended on it.

"Mayté?" Dominic's voice softened.

"Yes?"

"I just want you to know, I really am sorry."

"It's fine," she said. "I don't think the commission was meant to get finished."

"No, not about that. About the way everyone in las grandes familias treated you. I should've defended you. Or, at least, ignored everyone and still talked to you. I think we could've been good friends."

She didn't know what to say. The young girl inside her who was still so incredibly hurt felt overjoyed, but the rest of her was strangely numb. "I used to have the biggest crush on you, you know."

Now it was Dominic's turn to look shocked. "Really? I—I had no idea." He didn't add any confession of his own feelings. Mayté knew he had never felt the same way about her, but it was okay. Now that it was out there, the lovestruck girl inside her could get over it.

"It's fine. I know you're hoping to win Lo's affections. Good luck."

Dominic stammered. It looked like he wanted to say something more, but then closed his mouth. He cleared his throat and shuffled his feet before filling the awkward silence. "Once we get out of here . . . can you paint a portrait of me instead? I've been thinking about that lately, and I would prefer that."

Mayté frowned. He spoke as if they just had to survive a few more rounds, and then they'd all be free, but no. It wasn't that simple. Nothing about this place was. "Dominic—"

"I know," he interrupted. "But then again, anything is possible here. Look at where we're standing." He gestured out the window at the sparkling blue sea. "We've seen all the terrible stuff that can happen, but surely there are good things that can happen too."

It was . . . optimistic. Foolishly so. But in that moment, after all the horror, Mayté truly hoped he was right. "If that happens, I'll paint you the best portrait you've ever seen."

But until that happened, she had to focus on her own plan. She rubbed the cut on her hand.

"Thanks, Mayté." Dominic grinned, then patted his stomach. "I'm getting hungry. Want to get some lunch?"

"I'm going to stay a little longer."

"All right, but make sure you eat something before the next round."

"Sure."

After Dominic left, she turned back around and gasped. The painting supplies had returned, and the targets shifted back into canvases. The painting of Alejandro was once again pristine and perfect.

"Is that a painting of me?"

Mayté jolted. She had been so shocked by the morphing painting that she hadn't heard anyone else approach.

It was Alejandro.

He still wore his uniform, face paint and all. The sight of him brought back a flood of memories from today's game. Carmen jolting as the bullet pierced her heart. Bright red blood spurting from her chest. The life leaving her eyes in a heartbeat. Then Señor Vásquez, giving up his hopes and dreams so he would not have anyone's blood on his hands. Did he regret it by now? A lump formed in her throat.

"It is me, right?" Alejandro pointed at the canvas. He looked delighted.

"I—I—" There was no way to hide it or even explain herself.

"You're very talented. It's an honor." His grin sent warmth to her stomach. "Though the hair's a bit . . ." He leaned closer, studying the painting. "Is my hair really so flat?"

"Of course not!" Mayté bit back a laugh. "I'm not the best at drawing figures without a reference," she admitted.

"Well, here I am now." He sat on a stool and raked his fingers through his dark hair until it looked absolutely fluffed out.

"You want me to paint another one?"

"Just a sketch will do." His stare intensified. He raised an eyebrow, narrowed his eyes, and posed with his lips curled into a roguish half grin.

She bit back a laugh and grabbed a piece of charcoal, all while ignoring the heat swirling behind her cheeks. It was hard to tear her gaze away from his face and draw, and even when she did, she felt his eyes on her. It made her feel self-conscious and squirmy.

"What's the matter?" he asked.

"What you said during the game. Your comment about desires. It really helped, you know," she said, changing the subject.

"I'm glad." His posing relaxed, but he still looked at her.

She *wanted* him to keep looking at her.

She *needed* him to look away.

"Do you have ... any other morsels of truth for me?" she asked as she looked over her shoulder. Something about this place felt less private than last night. Maybe because they didn't have the cover of dark to hide behind, or the whispers of shadows to drown out their words.

"You mean like how sweets go down easier." He flashed a grin; even his teeth were charming—the way they dug into his lower lip slightly. "I can't say much more than what I've already told you." He gestured at the blank canvas next to hers. "May I?"

"Sure." She handed him the charcoal and watched in curiosity as he sketched something in bold, assured strokes. It was messy. His hand moved so fast. Mayté always worked slowly, contemplating every line, but Alejandro was quick and confident. When anything looked like a mistake, somehow it worked inside his composition. Every few seconds, he paused to look at her. Wait. Was he drawing *her*? Every time his eyes locked onto hers, her heart thrummed against her chest. All she could do was stand there awkwardly, unsure what to do.

Soon the messy scratches formed into a girl with a braid. It was stylized, with eyes much too big for her head and lips that looked more like a heart. It was incredibly charming—even more so since he did it in only a few minutes.

"Since you painted me ..." He flashed a lopsided grin. "What do you think?"

"It's ... it's lovely! And you did it so fast. Much faster than I ever could. Are you an artist?"

Alejandro set down the charcoal with a frown. "I . . ." His eyes lit up as if the most mesmerizing spell washed over him. "I think I am."

"What do you mean, 'you think'? If you make art, you're an artist. Simple as that." That was something she was firm about.

He chuckled. "Then I suppose I am . . ."

"How did you come to be a croupier here?" she asked.

"I was once a player in the game, just like you." He hesitated as if carefully choosing his words. "I bet everything but my life itself and lost. I was given a choice—return home without my dreams, or stay here and work."

"How long have you been here?"

He shook his head. "Weeks? Years? I can't remember."

Mayté's mouth hung open. At least some of the rumors about this place had been true.

"Everyone here has competed in the game at one time or another. I've been a dish scrubber, a butler, and now here I am."

"Could you work your way up to become like the Banker or Misterioso?"

"The Banker, maybe. Rumors say he lost but showed much promise. Whatever that may mean." His eyebrows creased. "But Misterioso . . . I'm not sure. *No one* is certain how he came to be."

Mayté's tried to wrap her head around this new information. "So, losing isn't always a death sentence. And if you don't have to give up your dreams, maybe it's not so bad."

Alejandro jumped as if she had slapped him.

"What's wrong?"

He looked over his shoulder once, and then a second time. He rubbed his mouth. Then, without warning, he pulled her into his arms. Her cheek pressed against his chest. Her heart pounded wildly. She would have pushed him away if she hadn't been so shocked.

Holding her tight, he whispered in her ear: "There are ears everywhere." Keeping an arm around her, he grabbed the charcoal and wrote on the canvas in shaky letters.

THE HOUSE HAS MY SOUL.

"What?" Mayté gasped. "That's—"

Alejandro pressed his hand against her mouth. He shook his head and put a finger to his lips.

Mayté's head raced faster. The soul was the place where hope was born, where love manifested, where . . . memories lived.

Alejandro slowly lowered his hand from her mouth. His eyes glowed like gems dipped in sorrow.

A lump formed in her throat. It all made sense now. The reason why he seemed uncertain about so many things. She couldn't imagine it—all of his memories *gone*. No sense of where he had come from, or who he was. What he did . . . or who he loved. Her eyes stung, but now wasn't the time to cry. She grabbed her paintbrush, squeezing it tight to keep her fingers from trembling. She painted under Alejandro's words.

CAN WE WIN?

She had to know. Was everything she was fighting for futile?

Alejandro started to write an answer, but he hesitated. Clearly the answer was much more complicated than a yes or a no. And by the way his jaw clenched, it was an answer Mayté wouldn't like.

"It's not fair," she whispered, her voice barely audible.

Something tickled her finger. She looked down and screamed. The biggest centipede she had ever seen curled around her finger where she once had held the paintbrush. She flailed and fell backward. All the paint supplies on the shelf had transformed into centipedes, spiders, scorpions. They all crawled toward her with shocking speed. She tried to get away, but they climbed onto her legs, biting and stinging her.

"NO!" she shrieked.

Something grabbed her from behind. She sobbed.

"Mayté, Mayté," Alejandro whispered. "The house is messing with you. Just breathe."

He held her tight. She took deep breaths as warm hands gently took her wrists. When she opened her eyes, the creatures were gone. Paintbrushes and tubes of paint lay scattered around her. Her legs didn't itch or burn.

Alejandro scooted in front of her. His hazel eyes were wide with concern.

She opened her mouth, but only a whimper came out.

"Shh, it's okay." His voice was soft and soothing. "I—I may have said too much. The house . . . reacts. It can take scheming as a threat." He took her hands and helped her up. Behind his warmth and strength, Mayté felt a tremor. "You should return to your room." There was a warning behind his suggestion. "And please, be careful during the next round."

Everything comes at a price.

What was the price for knowing the gambling house's magic—or for using it during the game?

As Alejandro led her to the door, her stomach twisted into tighter knots.

The house had helped her up until now. Was she suddenly losing its favor?

FOURTEEN

Lo

Lo couldn't begin to express how relieved she was when Mayté walked into the suite. That feeling vanished at the sight of her best friend's pinched face. "What happened?" Lo stood from the bed.

"I saw Alejandro." Mayté whispered.

Lo closed the gap between them. "Did he do something to you?"

"We talked. I—I found out that he played the game in the past. When he lost, he was given the choice to work here or return to Milagro like Señor Vásquez, b-b-but—" She shuddered.

Lo pulled her close. "Please tell me."

She breathed the words: "The house has his soul."

"Wha . . . what does that mean?" Lo whispered.

"His feelings. Memories. Everything that makes him who he is!" Mayté covered her face with her hands and cried aloud, "There's no good way out. The only way is to win."

Lo stared as the words sank in. "Is . . . is it like that for *every-one* here?"

"Most likely."

Lo rubbed her mouth. Dare she mention Mamá? Mayté wouldn't like it, but Lo couldn't hold it in any longer. She would just have to convince her that Mamá was here. "There's something I need to show you." She scurried to the table and lifted the platter lid, revealing the untouched paella. "This is what came. My mother's favorite meal. Made her special way, without the mussels. Supposedly what I desired to eat most, but I hadn't even been thinking of it."

Mayté opened her mouth, but Lo wasn't done.

"The Banker brought it. And he tried to make me think she's dead, but it must be a trick. The house must not want me to find her."

Mayté's face fell. "Lo." Her voice was soft and regretful.

Lo's heart plummeted. "You don't believe me?"

"It's not that. But are you sure the house isn't just trying to fool you? It showed you your mother and almost made you miss the last round. Don't you think it's trying to distract you from winning?"

Mamá wasn't *just* a distraction. Lo's throat burned, and the angry heat spread all the way to the palms of her hands. "We're using the house, so how can it be tricking us?"

"That's exactly the problem, I think." Mayté went on to explain her time with Alejandro and how the art supplies had suddenly transformed. "Alejandro said everything comes at a price, and it's even steeper for those with bad intentions."

"*Our* intentions are bad?" Lo asked with a frown.

"Well, we're trying to gain an advantage, bend the rules, which means other people will die, or be damned. I think the house is turning on us, if it hasn't been toying with us from the very beginning. It's showing us illusions to distract us—" Mayté interrupted herself with a gasp. "And now I think about it, it might be trying to mess with how we feel about each other."

Lo shook her head. What did Mayté mean? She explained that, during the last game, the house made her think the croupiers were all cheering for Lo. "It was like it was trying to make me jealous."

Lo bit back the urge to sarcastically ask if Mayté had always been jealous of her. But no, maybe Mayté was right. Maybe at this very moment the house was trying to make her resent her best friend.

Mayté was just trying to protect Lo's feelings and keep her from getting her hopes up. Right? Lo tried to subdue her anger. "Okay. We have to survive to win, and if that costs us something, we'll just have to endure it. In the end, it'll be worth it. For the next round, we have to block out everything else and be ready for whatever the house tries to throw at us. Right?"

Mayté was supposed to agree. She was bold and determined, always recovering from setbacks, but this time her wide eyes filled with tears. She collapsed onto the bed. "But even if we survive this next round, I don't think three people have ever won. I—I don't think they can," she whimpered.

"Mayté." Lo sat next to her and put an arm around her. A lump formed in her own throat. Was it true? It couldn't be. She wouldn't let it be. "I spoke with the Banker." She used the frill on her sleeve to dab at the tears on Mayté's cheek. "He came to the room and told me a bit about the game. He said any number of people can win, so long as they make it to the final round." The lie slipped off her tongue, cool and smooth as sugared cream, yet something lurched in the depths of her stomach. She had lied many times. To her father, her suitors, and many others.

Never to Mayté.

Not until Fortune's Kiss.

But this was different than those other lies. This was a *good* lie. One purely for Mayté's sake. One that would keep her safe. If

Mayté thought there was hope, she would keep fighting. Because the only sure way to lose was giving up.

"That's what we have to focus on," Lo urged. "Making it to the end."

"Okay." Mayté rubbed the tears from her face. "One step at a time. I can do that."

Good. Lo took her best friend's hands and led her to the table. "We should eat before the next round."

As they ate, they discussed strategies. Different ways they could will the house to tilt the game in their favor without being obvious. In the end, they decided it was best to see if they could bend the game so that the players were able to choose their own wagers. That way, they could all keep their wagering low.

Even better would be making it so none of them was chosen for a challenge. That way, there was no risk of losing at all. It was bolder, perhaps riskier, but it was worth a try.

With that resolved, the two left the room arm and arm. Throughout the entire walk and elevator ride, Lo repeated the same mantra in her head.

Allow everyone to make their own wagers. Don't challenge me, Mayté, or Carlos.

Soon they reached the gaming den. Everyone else was already seated. Mayté made a beeline for the two seats next to Dominic. He must have saved the seats for them. As Lo sat, she noticed a middle-aged man with a mustache staring at them. She didn't know who he was, nor did she particularly care. He wasn't a noble, and he didn't seem like a threat. He would probably die in the next round.

"Ah, a pleasure you can join us, señorita." The man folded his arms. "Not that I should be surprised that you're the one holding all this up."

Excuse me? Lo bit back her words. The man hadn't addressed her, but instead Mayté, who bristled and tensed her jaw. Did they know each other?

"Who is he?" Lo whispered.

"The asshole that wouldn't sell me supplies for my commission," Mayté said loudly.

Everyone else looked between the man and Mayté. The man's left eye twitched and his golden-brown face turned a bright scarlet, bordering on purple.

"I'm not surprised you had to come here after being so stingy," Mayté continued. "Treating customers like that, people probably took their business elsewhere."

"So, he's the reason I didn't get my commission?" Dominic blurted.

"Enough," Mayté said. "I can handle this myself." Even though she had scolded him, Dominic's lips tugged into a grin. Mayté returned a secret smile.

Envy simmered inside Lo, tiny bubbles pricking against her heart. Since when was she an outsider between these two? She squeezed her hands together and tried to focus on her desires for this round, her mantra. Her gaze drifted to Carlos, who sat next to the shopkeeper. He flashed a small smile. Her face warmed.

She had almost forgotten about the quick kiss they had shared when he was drunk. Did Carlos remember it? He looked much better now. His cheeks were no longer red, and his eyes no longer seemed unfocused.

If he *did* remember—she bit her lip—had he enjoyed it as much as she had?

The elevator dinged, and the doors opened. But it wasn't Misterioso. Instead, it was the burly grump from the elevator ride that morning.

The shopkeeper groaned in disdain and checked his pocket watch.

Mayté quickly glanced away. She looked like she was going to be sick. Every fiber in Lo went on high alert. Even the hairs on her arms stood on end. Why was Mayté so frightened of him? Lo kept her eye on him as he rounded the table like a caged jaguar.

"Could you sit down, señor?" the shopkeeper grouched.

The man ignored him and pointed. First at Mayté, then at Carlos. "Robles's kids. I knew you looked familiar."

Mayté froze. Her eyes were wide. She looked absolutely panic-stricken.

He headed straight for her. "Your old man's so pathetic, you both had to come here, hmm? Since you owe me a debt, maybe this is the place to collect what I'm owed." His eyes were fixed on Mayté.

"Whoa, whoa, whoa." Dominic started to get up, but Lo beat him.

"Who are you?" She stared at the man straight on. She wasn't scared. He was nothing to her. "What do you want with my friend?"

"First off, linda." He eyed her up and down. "The name is Rodrigo Domingo."

Lo continued to stare, not even pretending to be impressed.

"Their pendejo father, José Robles, owes me a lot of money. Too much." His face twisted. "Why else would I be here? But you see, Robles and I came to an agreement." Rodrigo gestured at Mayté. "If he couldn't come up with the coins, we'd take his daughter instead."

Lo's vision flashed red. This was one of the vaqueros Mayté had told her about. She would never have thought such a lowlife would be permitted to gamble in Fortune's Kiss.

"I could get my money's worth from her. Put her to work, and then—"

The rest of his words blurred together. Lo clenched her trembling fists and bit the inside of her cheek until she tasted blood. No. No. No. NO. Mayté wasn't a piece of property to be sold off. She was worth more than every gold coin in existence combined. She could barely think straight, but she managed to growl out the only words that came to mind. "If you so much as lay a finger on her—"

Rodrigo burst out laughing. "Then what will you do, cariño?" He leaned closer.

Kill you.

Rip your face off.

Break those fingers of yours one by one.

She opened her mouth to speak.

"Ah, you've already gathered. Wonderful." Misterioso appeared between Lo and Rodrigo, breaking them up. Lo hadn't even heard the elevator ding. "Ready or not, it's time for the next round."

Rodrigo rudely winked at Lo. She stared back at him. Slowly, she smiled—an expression that sent her message to him loud and clear. *If you try anything, I will kill you.*

The look seemed to catch him off guard. He startled. Satisfied, Lo took her seat.

The Banker took his spot at the center of the table. It seemed to be his turn to deal. His icy blue eyes honed in on Lo. "Did you enjoy your meal?"

He was messing with her.

"I did, actually." She rested her chin in her hands. "Thank you."

What other secrets did he carry with him? Lo would have to find out, but for now, she needed to focus on getting through this round.

"Let us begin!" Misterioso exclaimed. "This round will last only for five turns. You will be able to choose what you wager."

Underneath the table, Lo snatched Mayté's hand. It had worked. They had bent the house to their will. She did her best to keep a straight face. Everyone else around the table seemed equal parts pleased and relieved. Lo glanced at the Banker. He raised an eyebrow and locked eyes with her. He looked perplexed. Lo simply smiled at him, silently scolding him for underestimating her.

"We ended off the last round with María Teresa getting the first lotería of the game," Misterioso explained. "Every time a player fills their board enough for a lotería, they may draw a special card. These cards do not pose a challenge or need a wager from you, but instead can be to your benefit. They can be used at any time. Anyone who has that card on their board may place a bean down as soon as the card is revealed. Please choose a card, María Teresa."

The cards floated in front of the Banker face down. Mayté reached out, but then hesitated and studied the cards.

Lo prayed. *Please let her pick a good card.*

After what felt like an eternity, Mayté pressed her finger against one of the cards. It flipped over, revealing a silver shield. El Escudo. The card floated to Mayté's hand. She grinned.

"Once activated, this card will defend the user from harm, or protect them from performing a challenge, one time," Misterioso said.

Perfect! Lo thought. Having this in her back pocket was wonderful.

The Banker drew the first card. "El Cazo." The card was simply a cooking pot. Soft clangs filled the air, followed by the scent of savory meats sizzling over chiles and other bold spices. It brought back memories of when she had been a child—sometimes she would sneak into the kitchen and watch the servants bustle around as they prepared dinner.

She and several others put down a bean. The next couple of cards were similarly surreal, yet ultimately uneventful. El Gallo brought about the crow of a rooster while El Conquistador summoned war cries, the clanging of swords, and screams of the innocent. Lo stole a glance at Don Zelaya, who looked around without even an ounce of remorse or guilt about his ancestors.

Lo's board began to fill up nicely. So far, so good. Only two more turns left.

She snuck a peek at Mayté's board. Only two more beans and she would get another lotería. La Sirena, the mermaid, was one of the cards Mayté needed.

Draw La Sirena next. Lo dug her fingers into the frills on her gown.

"La Sirena."

Lo's eyes snapped open. Amazing! It had worked again!

The Banker stared straight at her as he held up a familiar card with a mermaid. But this time the card glowed.

"Oh no," someone whispered.

The vaquero, *Rodrigo*, whistled. "This should be good."

Lo braced herself for what was to come.

A mermaid crawled out of the card. Her sopping black hair flopped over her bare chest. Her long red tail writhed behind her. Lo wasn't sure if it was breathtaking or grotesque. La Sirena had a beautiful face. Sparkling blue eyes and full red lips accented by the peachy undertones of her skin. But Lo couldn't tell if those lips of hers were upturned in playful mischief or pure malice.

"Unlike other special cards which present a challenge, La Sirena will simply predict the future of a chosen player. Whether that player heeds the prediction as fact or treats it as fiction is up to them. Now let's see who she will choose." There was a sinister note in Misterioso's delighted tone.

"You." La Sirena pointed a long red nail at Mayté.

It was fitting. Mayté had brought the painting of La Sirena as her prized possession. Lo held her breath.

Mayté lifted her chin and sat up straighter. To anyone else, she looked confident, but Lo saw the way she fiddled with a bean as her thick eyebrows twitched.

"María Teresa Robles," La Sirena drawled, half speaking, half singing. The sound was both enthralling and haunting. Everyone at the table fell silent. Even Rodrigo kept his nasty mouth shut. Lo's heart pounded harder. What would she say? Could she possibly predict if Mayté would win?

Or die?

"Before your time here ends," La Sirena's voice rose, "your heart shall be torn in two."

Mayté jolted. "Wh—! By who?"

With a smirk, La Sirena simply put a finger to her lips and vanished.

"Unfortunately, La Sirena finds it pleasing to be vague," Misterioso said. "But a broken heart, hmm? Isn't that rather intriguing?"

"Ah, young love," Don Zelaya scoffed and Xiomara snickered. All the while, Mayté stared straight ahead, face clearly distressed.

Who would dare break her heart? The thought made Lo furious.

Could it be Alejandro? Maybe she shouldn't have pushed Mayté to flirt with him . . .

"And be sure to put down a bean if La Sirena is on your board," Misterioso reminded them with a chuckle.

"Oh." Mayté set a bean down.

"Lotería!" Rodrigo leaned back in his chair, arms folded and smug.

What? No! Under the table, Lo grabbed bunches of her gown and squeezed as tightly as she could. It was the only thing she could do to hold back the anger bubbling inside her. The Banker caught her eye again. This time, he raised an eyebrow as if to say *I told you so.*

Everything comes at a price.

The Banker turned away and checked Rodrigo's board. He snapped his finger, summoning a bigger projection of the board for everyone to see. The four corners of his card had beans.

With a sneer, Rodrigo snatched a card from the Banker and held it up. "El Valiente!" he cheered. The card depicted a man holding a serape and a bloodied dagger.

"If you could leave the announcing to me and the Banker, señor." Misterioso huffed and dramatically cleared his throat. "El Valiente!" he shouted and theatrically raised an arm. "This card will give the player access to El Valiente's items. It's up to you how you would like to use them."

Rodrigo stroked his chin while staring at Mayté.

Lo clenched her fists. How she wanted that card. Then she would have plunged El Valiente's dagger straight into Rodrigo's chest.

"Don't forget I have El Escudo." Mayté held up her card, the shield. Her voice trembled the slightest bit, but her burning scowl spoke much louder. "You don't scare me."

Rodrigo chuckled. "Whatever you say, muchacha."

No one else got lotería, though Lo was very close to getting one in a couple of spots.

"El Perrito." The Banker held up the next card. A gray Xolo leaped from the card and ran straight for Dominic.

"Aw. Hello!" he cooed and scratched the dog behind its ears. The dog's thin tail wagged around endlessly and it jumped up at Dominic with its bony legs, revealing its white stomach. "You look just like my perritos."

"Ah, El Perrito has chosen you, Dominic. What do you wager?"

What kind of challenge would a dog offer? Beating it in a race? Getting it to do tricks?

"I wager one gold coin, please," Dominic said.

"Very well," Misterioso said. "Now, for your challenge, you must kill this dog with your bare hands."

Mayté covered her mouth. Xiomara gasped. Next to her, Don Zelaya simply folded his hands and stared on with curiosity. Carlos looked down, and the shopkeeper looked away.

"Fun," Rodrigo whispered with a cruel snicker.

As for Dominic, he stood slowly.

With a whine, the dog sat and stared at him expectantly. It panted, pink tongue flopped out. The way its mouth curved made it look like it was smiling.

It had no idea what was about to happen.

"No," Dominic blurted. "I can't do that. I *won't*. Take my coin."

"I can do that, but the challenge will not end. You'll have to keep wagering higher and higher until you vanquish it," Misterioso said.

"NO!" Dominic yelled.

"We won't be able to move on until you do. Either the dog dies, or you," Misterioso said, voice dull. "Unless . . . you would rather fold?"

Mayté let out a sharp breath.

"N-no . . ." Dominic's wide eyes watered. His lips moved, but no sound came out.

No doubt he would be the next to die. Lo felt . . . nothing. No, actually, she felt the teeniest, tiniest bit of relief. One fewer person to worry about.

"What will you do, Dominic Castro?" Misterioso asked.

Still panting, the dog approached Dominic. He backed into his chair and fell.

Rodrigo burst out laughing.

Dominic coughed into his sleeve. Loud rasping coughs. The kind that sounded painful.

"I hope he's not ill," Xiomara murmured. "I don't want to catch anything."

Still hacking, Dominic hunched over.

Mayté turned to Lo, eyes wide with terror.

Was this because he was about to die?

"Dominic, please make your choice," Misterioso said, voice growing stern. "Failure to take action can be seen as breaking the rules, and rule breakers automatically forfeit at the end of the round."

"Ay, just take your chair and clobber it," Rodrigo said.

Dominic began to weep. El Perrito came over and licked his face.

This was the end.

"Enough!" Mayté held out her card to Dominic. "Use it."

"Wha—?" He looked up, red cheeks streaked with tears. "No! I can't! I could never. I—"

"It isn't your choice," Mayté said.

"No!" Dominic shouted.

"Wait!" Lo exclaimed.

Mayté took the card and held it up. It flashed, and a silver shield appeared between Dominic and El Perro.

El Perrito yapped and joyfully play-bowed before vanishing.

Dominic's cherry lips quivered, and he nodded. "Thank you, Mayté."

"Well, then, that was certainly a turn of events." For once, Misterioso didn't sound so enthused.

Lo fumed. She turned to Mayté, but stopped herself from saying anything. She was the one who had told Mayté that whoever made it to the final round would survive. Of course she would help Dominic.

But there were more important people to worry about.

"You're welcome," Mayté whispered. The gentleness in her eyes was like a burning acid to Lo. What if Dominic was the one who would break Mayté's heart? She'd always had her little crush on him, no matter how much she tried to deny it.

"That's five turns, I suppose," Misterioso said with a shrug. His nonchalance was a bit surprising. Lo imagined he would have been agitated at the lack of death.

Everyone at the table let out a breath of relief.

"I'm starving." Rodrigo shot up from his chair and headed for the elevator.

"Wait a moment, if you please," Misterioso said, sounding quite gratified with himself. "This round may be over, but we're going straight to the next one."

The other contestants gasped. Lo shot a worried glance at Mayté. There would be no time to rest or strategize.

"This is hardly fair!" the shopkeeper yelled. "You can't keep stringing us along like this."

"Fair?" Misterioso tilted his head to the side, and his eyes narrowed. His toothy smile vanished. He stalked across the room, taking big strides. "As a Gamemaker, *I* can make the rules as I see fit, señor." He turned to the group. "You have unlocked sudden death. In this round, each player's wager will be the same. Everyone will wager their lives. The round will continue indefinitely until two players have been eliminated." He stopped behind Lo and Mayté, placing his hands on the backs of their chairs. "This time, using anything except your *own* wits and skills"—he locked eyes with Lo, then flicked his sharp gaze to Mayté—"won't help."

FIFTEEN

Mayté

Everything comes at a price.

Alejandro's words pounded through Mayté's aching head. This is what he had meant. The bigger the magic, the steeper the cost. How could she have been so foolish?

And now, when they needed a magical advantage the most, she and Lo couldn't use it. How were they going to survive?

"Sudden death?" The Banker raised an eyebrow at Misterioso. His eyes narrowed into slits; the only thing sharper was his razor-like grin. He carelessly shuffled his deck. "What brought this about?"

Misterioso's jaw ticked, yet his smile remained. "I have caught wind that there has been meddling. Someone has been feeding a player information."

Mayté's heart stopped. He knew about her and Alejandro. Could the house have somehow told him? What would that mean—

But Misterioso's gaze landed on Lo and the Banker.

"Oh, my." The Banker's smirk became shameless. "I wonder who could have possibly done that."

"I have my suspicions," Misterioso said.

"Do you?" The Banker leaned against the table. "Regardless, I wonder what our other Gamemaker will think of this new change. Guess we will have to find out."

Misterioso ground his teeth, but, as if catching himself, he turned away. "I am simply trying to keep balance within the house!"

"I see," the Banker sighed, unconvinced.

Lo watched the men in fascination.

Such an odd exchange—

"There will be six left," Carlos murmured, tearing Mayté from her thoughts. "We each have a twenty-five percent chance of getting eliminated."

Right. There were more frightening things to focus on.

Twenty-five percent Mayté would die.

Twenty-five percent Lo would die.

Twenty-five percent Carlos would die.

Carlos. He had no idea this was all her fault.

"I'm sure you're all wondering how we shall proceed," Misterioso spat. "You all will split into two groups of four." He lifted four long fingers to demonstrate. "In this *thrilling* round, each group will play indefinitely until one person in each group is eliminated. Are you ready?" His words carried a timbre of excitement, as if he couldn't wait for them to die.

None of the players responded. Dominic dabbed at his mouth with a handkerchief. Xiomara looked away. The shopkeeper glared at Misterioso, and Rodrigo flashed a crude gesture.

"Mayté," Lo whispered in her ear. "We should split up."

"Yes." If they played at the same table, it would only worsen their odds of both surviving. Mayté let out a shaky breath.

Dios, if you're listening—Abuelita, if you're watching, please give me your strength.

"Also." Lo nudged Mayté. "You're worth more than anyone else here. Think of yourself first. You need to survive this round, no matter what."

Mayté nodded. The two released each other and went in opposite directions. She headed for the table Alejandro stood at. He might not be able to help her, but still she found the game wasn't as horrific when Alejandro was the dealer. She thought back to their time in the archery range . . . art studio? The silly faces he made while posing made her smile. His gentle hands and sweet words calmed her, warmed her insides.

La Sirena's face appeared in her mind. *Your heart shall be torn in two.*

Dread ran down her spine, and her strides slowed. Alejandro. He was the first person who came to her mind. The way La Sirena put her finger to her lips. It was just like when Alejandro did so. What if he broke her heart? But . . . wouldn't she have to give him her heart for him to break it?

Even from afar, his hazel eyes homed in on her. Face grim, he wouldn't look away.

Had he already stolen her heart right out from under her nose?

Carlos stepped next to her. She gasped. If he played with her, that would worsen his chances. "Y-you can't do this!" She grabbed his sleeve.

"I can't let you compete alone."

Her eyes filled with tears. She had tried to hide her true feelings behind anger, tried to avoid them, but now she had to face them head-on. "Carlos, you can't. I—I don't want you to die!"

His lips curled into a half smile, but he couldn't hide the fear in his eyes. "I don't want you to die either. That's why I'm going to do whatever I can to protect you. Okay?"

"But—"

"Ever since Father . . . I became the person who was supposed to take care of our family. I thought I was doing the most I could do, but I've let you down so much, haven't I?"

She bit down on her lip to keep it from quivering. All this time, she had yearned for her family to acknowledge her sacrifices. To validate her hardships.

"Think of it as recompense," he finished.

Knowing that her brother saw her, that he cared for her, was a comfort. But she also felt a twinge of guilt. He had come here for his own reasons.

"Yeah, well." She yanked his arm. "I'm going to do anything I can to protect you too, menso!" she snapped.

Carlos chuckled, and the tension melted from his face. "Good luck, Mayté."

"Good luck." She pulled herself together. Only one person would die in this round. It didn't have to be her or Carlos.

The two siblings sat next to each other.

"Milagro," Alejandro softly whispered.

"What?" She looked up at him.

His hazel eyes were wide and brimming with something she couldn't quite recognize. If emotions were paint, her best guess would have been to mix together awe and terror, but quickly the fear took over. He opened his mouth to say something, but then looked down and drummed his fingers on the table. Instead, he pulled out a napkin from his pocket and scrawled something on it. He slid it to Mayté face down, but shook his head before she could grab it. "After the round," he said, voice thick with trepidation.

She nodded and slipped the napkin into her pocket. Normally, curiosity would have gnawed at her, but right now she just needed to survive. *Carlos* needed to survive too.

Carlos looked between Mayté and Alejandro in confusion. Mayté shook her head. She would explain things to him later. When they were safe. Carlos nodded in understanding.

"L-let's get this over with, I suppose." The shopkeeper pulled out the seat next to her, but Rodrigo shoved him out of the way. Mayté's heart dropped to the icy depths of her stomach.

"Sorry, amigo, but this seat's taken." Rodrigo plopped down and turned to Mayté and Carlos with a nasty grin. "I was hopin' to get a game in with Robles's kids. This'll be fun." He cracked his knuckles.

"Ay yai yai. Not for the rest of us." With a grumble, the shopkeeper took the last available seat.

This was the worst possible combination for Mayté. Stuck in a game with her brother who needed to survive, the stingy shopkeeper who hated her, and this thug who was out to get her. Also, he had the El Valiente card, which would give him access to a dagger. That made him the most dangerous player at the table.

At the other table sat Lo, Dominic, Don Zelaya, and Xiomara. At least Lo would have an easier time surviving. The only one of that bunch who was a threat was Don Zelaya.

The same masked dancers came over and passed out goblets of drinks to all eight contestants. Their bright gowns sashayed around them as they moved from person to person. Mayté pushed her drink away. It wouldn't help her.

Alejandro shuffled the cards. They flew from hand to hand and swirled around his body, unleashing a chilly breeze. Alejandro closed his eyes in concentration. He looked serene and graceful. One with the wind. Like San Viento.

"Stop," Rodrigo barked.

Alejandro jolted, but easily caught every last card before any could fall.

"I'll make this nice and quick for everyone." Rodrigo's lips slithered into a snakelike grin.

Blood pounded in Mayté's ear.

Rodrigo took a big slurp of his drink and wiped his mouth with the back of his hand. "Each of you needs to give me something." His slimy gaze skimmed over the shopkeeper and then Carlos, before lingering on Mayté. "Whoever has the least to offer me dies." He held up his El Valiente card. "Easy as that."

"Wha—?" the shopkeeper sputtered.

"Can he really do that?" Carlos demanded.

Mayté shot Alejandro a frantic look.

"We need to play the game properly," Alejandro said, voice clipped. "It's not your turn."

"Nonsense!" Misterioso drawled. "It's a legal move. El Valiente can be thrown whenever the player chooses. Unless—are *you* trying to meddle with my players as well?"

Alejandro's eyes flickered with fear. "Of course not." He looked down. "Proceed."

Mayté couldn't breathe.

Rodrigo leaned back in his seat, resting his boots on the table. "Start making offers. Wow me."

"Very well." The shopkeeper sighed and stroked his mustache. His eyes gleamed and his fretting frown turned smug. "Spare my life and you can take my shop. Do with it as you please." Instead of looking to see Rodrigo's reaction, he turned to Mayté and Carlos. His face oozed with triumph. They all knew that neither of them could trump his offer.

"Ah, your shop, hmm?" Rodrigo twirled his stubby sausage of a finger. "Yes, yes, I could sell it for quite a lot. I'm sure. Now you." He nodded at Carlos.

What could he possibly offer? Neither he nor Mayté had much of anything.

She gripped the table to keep from slipping out of her seat. What was there for her to give? A few paintings?

"I'll give my winnings from the last round," Carlos said. "And anything else I win in the coming rounds as well, but only if you leave me and my sister alone."

"Carlos," Mayté gasped. "You don't have to—"

"No." He turned to her, gaze hardened with determination. "This is what I should have done from the very beginning. I should have protected you from those monsters the minute they showed up at our place."

"Well, isn't that sweet?" Rodrigo sighed. "I dunno, though. I got burned once, taking on a loan from your family. How do I know you won't stiff me like your old man did?" He turned to Mayté, scooting closer. "Bet you wish now you hadn't given up El Escudo like a fool. That little boy can't help you now." He grabbed her braid and twirled it around his finger.

"Don't touch me!" She yanked away.

Rodrigo snickered. "Why not? Actually"—his voice lowered and he grabbed her chin—"you have something much more valuable than either of these two."

Disgust and horror swirled through her, but soon anger joined in. *Never ever ever.* "I SAID DON'T TOUCH ME!" She snatched her drink and threw it on him, goblet and all.

It smashed into his head, soaking his face and shirt. With a roar, he released her and furiously swiped at his face. "THAT'S IT!" He smashed his fist into the table, shaking it and causing the other drinks to slosh over.

"Hey!" The shopkeeper snatched up his Lotería board before it could get wet.

"¡Ten cuidado!" Alejandro spat a warning, voice barely above a whisper. The whites of his widened eyes were stark against the black paint.

Mayté looked back.

Rodrigo tossed back his colorful serape. Time slowed. The cloth was a bright yellow like the sun, with vibrant stripes of green, rich as the leaves in summer and red like fresh blood. Something gleamed in his hand. A dagger. El Valiente.

"¡Estás muerta, maldita!" He lunged for her.

"NO!" Mayté shrieked and tumbled backward out of her seat. Pain shot up her tailbone. She couldn't get up fast enough. Spilled liquid seeped through her gown, which was way too tight and constricting. She couldn't move. She felt like a crab trapped in a fisherman's net.

"DON'T HURT HER!" Lo shot up from her seat and rushed for them, but suddenly recoiled. She threw her drink. It bounced off the air, spraying liquid back at her. An invisible wall had formed around the table. No one could get through it.

And no one inside could escape.

Alejandro stood in his spot. He looked absolutely frantic, but didn't make a move. Croupiers couldn't interfere with the game . . .

Rodrigo lumbered over, wearing a sick grin.

Mayté tried to get up and run away, but he snatched her by the arm. Was she about to die? She blindly flailed and kicked, but it did no good.

Carlos rushed behind Rodrigo and threw the serape over his head before tackling him. Suddenly free, Mayté stumbled back.

"You can die too!" Rodrigo slashed Carlos's arm. Carlos clutched his arm as scarlet seeped through his sleeve.

Mayté screamed.

Images of the past filled her head. Carlos with his thick head of black hair and chubby cheeks letting her snuggle close whenever she had a nightmare. Carlos crying when he lost his tooth and dropped it before he could show Ma. Carlos helping her with her studies.

Carlos at her side when the world they had grown up with crumbled around them.

And now, Carlos with her in the most terrifying trial of their lives.

She couldn't let him die.

Rodrigo yanked Carlos by the collar, but before he could do anything, Mayté crashed into him. The dagger dropped to the floor with a clatter. She scrambled to grab it. Anything to keep it away from him. Just when her fingers tightened around the handle, he grabbed her neck. Hard. A strangled choke burst from her lips.

"Ay, you are just as annoying as your old man." Rodrigo squeezed her neck. She couldn't breathe. Couldn't think. Black dots filled her vision.

"But hey," he spat and wiped his mouth. "Killing you both will end sudden death for everyone. So, congrats."

Squish. The sickening sound of a blade piercing through flesh.

Mayté dropped to the floor.

Blood stained her hands and dress.

She stared at the dagger sticking out of Rodrigo's chest. She had plunged it into him. Rodrigo coughed up blood and collapsed. His wide eyes locked onto Mayté. Blazing with fury, but only for a moment as the life drained from him. Seconds passed, or maybe it was minutes, she couldn't be sure, but soon Rodrigo stopped moving and breathing. Dead.

"Mayté." Carlos pulled her to her feet. She hadn't even noticed him come over.

She'd killed someone.

"Mayté!" Carlos grabbed her shoulders. Firm without being too rough. He stared into her eyes.

"I—I—"

"You *saved* me," he urged. "And yourself."

But she never would have been able to do so if Carlos hadn't defended her first.

Her vision blurred. All along, she had only wanted someone to protect her. All these years, she had been desperate for it. That night when Rodrigo and the other thugs threatened her, she had yearned for someone to stand up for her. Carlos had done just that. With a bitter sob, she crumbled into her big brother's arms.

"I'm so sorry, Mayté." Carlos hugged her tight. "That I didn't do anything sooner and it had to come to this."

"I'm sorry for pushing you away. We . . . we have to work together!"

"I know. And we will."

No matter what, they would figure out a way for the three of them to win. She stuffed a hand in her pocket. Her fingers skimmed the napkin Alejandro had given her.

"Congratulations to the surviving players!" Misterioso boomed. "Everyone, please return to your seats and we will begin round two."

Mayté pulled away from Carlos. All of the relief and warmth from her tears turned to ice. It wasn't over. She turned to see her best friend standing nearby, terror written all over her face.

It was Lo's turn to survive sudden death.

SIXTEEN

Lo

Lo's heart wouldn't stop pounding. A group of workers took Rodrigo's corpse away. They didn't bother to remove the dagger from his chest, but they didn't have to. El Valiente's dagger and blanket soon vanished on their own.

Seven players left.

Six after this next round.

Gracias a Dios, Mayté was okay. Carlos too. When that man went after Mayté, Lo wanted nothing more than to kill him. But she had been powerless to do anything.

She returned to her seat next to Dominic and glanced toward the other side of the room. The shopkeeper already sat, hands folded and lips moving as if silently thanking Dios. Arm in arm, Mayté and Carlos headed for their own seats. Carlos grunted in pain as a worker bandaged him up. Mayté locked eyes with Lo and nodded. Lo nodded back. She would survive this. *She had to.*

When she turned back, she caught the Banker staring.

"Interesting round, no?" He carelessly juggled cards one by one. Each card returned to his opposite hand like a boomerang.

Lo gave him a withering look.

"Don't look at me like that." He leaned closer. "I tried to warn you."

Everything comes at a price.

"Yes, well, you weren't specific enough about the consequences."

"Ah, but revealing too much would be cheating." He put a finger to his lips. "*Supposedly*, the house doesn't tolerate cheaters."

Lo pursed her lips. She tilted her head toward his ear and lowered her voice. "What was that between you and Misterioso?"

"It would seem he is somehow under the impression that I'm feeding you clues. Absurd, no?"

And yet, he hadn't denied it. Lo felt like a pawn in the Banker's game, yet she still couldn't figure out his goal. Usually, she was the one in control, moving around the hearts of men for her own gain. Being on the other side of it was unexpectedly thrilling.

Because she couldn't wait to take over the game and make it her own.

"I see, but it almost seems like you *want* Misterioso to believe we're in cahoots."

The Banker smirked.

"Why?" Lo pressed.

"I think you'll find it more pertinent to focus on the matter at hand. This may very well be your final round." It wasn't so much a threat as it was a vague warning. The playful excitement drained from his face. It was almost as if he were certain she would die.

And that made her hell-bent on proving him wrong.

"Round two of sudden death." Misterioso strutted along the table and waved his arm for the crowd. "Let us begin."

"Don't forget that anything goes, this round." The Banker shuffled the cards around.

"Oh, really?" Lo smirked. "Does that mean you'll be able to play with us too, Señor Banker?"

But before the Banker could respond, one of the dancers sauntered over and whispered something in his ear. His face became deadly serious, and he nodded before stepping away from the table.

The dancer stepped into his place. "I am Pearla, and I will deal this round," she said, voice cold.

Lo raised an eyebrow. She caught the Banker's eye, and he simply half shrugged, before tossing the deck to Pearla, who caught it with ease. Her frilly dress was black as obsidian, and she wore a matching veil, obscuring her hair. Lustrous black pearls, shining in different deep shades of blues, greens, and purples adorned her bodice. That, combined with the skull mask, fully covering her face, made her look more sinister than the Banker ever had.

"This is an unexpected change," Misterioso drawled. There was a tense undertone in his voice.

"I wanted to see this sudden death for myself," Pearla simply said.

Misterioso stiffened. Lo would have loved to see what his face looked behind his mask. It surely hid a lot.

Pearla called out cards, voice loud and booming. She dealt fluidly, as if she had done so many times before. Lo couldn't swallow back a feeling of unease. There may have been a strange tension between Misterioso and the Banker, but it had strengthened tenfold with Pearla here.

"Oh, what a shame," Don Zelaya said with a triumphant smirk. "You don't have your little joven to help you. Don't think we haven't noticed that you both are the reason we're in this situation." With a chuckle, he raised his glass to Xiomara, who happily clinked her glass against his.

He couldn't have been more wrong, but Lo ignored him. She wouldn't let him frazzle her.

The first few cards were uneventful. El Melon. Pearla flicked her wrist and plates of fresh melon landed on the table. Then La Mariposa, where hundreds of orange monarch butterflies fluttered and flitted about. Xiomara oohed and ahhed, while Dominic caught one on his finger. Don Zelaya swatted at the ones that flew too close. Lo didn't care so much about the butterflies. What she found much more delightful was the fact that her board was filling up.

"Lotería!" Xiomara proudly called out and waved her arms.

Lo's smile fell.

Pearla checked Xiomara's board before snapping her fingers. The board then appeared for everyone to see. She had a vertical line filled with beans. Damn it. Lo had only needed one more card in several spots to get lotería.

"Congratulations, Xiomara," Misterioso said. "Now choose a card."

Pearla held out several cards. Xiomara scrunched up her deep amber face in concentration before plucking one and holding it up. "La Corona." A card with a golden crown covered in red rubies.

"Ah, a powerful card," Misterioso said. "You will become a monarch within the game. You can order anyone to do your bidding and they will have to obey. How fortunate indeed."

"Yikes," Dominic whispered.

Lo gulped. At any moment, Xiomara could command one of them to kill themselves. She could end the round—if she was smart enough to do so. Don Zelaya leaned over and whispered something in her ear. With a nod, Xiomara handed the card to him.

"What are you doing?" Lo asked.

"What does it look like?" Xiomara scoffed. "We're working together. No one said that was against the rules."

It wasn't a surprise that Lo and Mayté weren't the only alliance here, but that made Don Zelaya and Xiomara even more dangerous.

A plan formed in Lo's mind. She covered her mouth, feigning distress.

"What's the matter?" Xiomara taunted. "Are you upset that I made an alliance with the best contestant here?" She ran her nail down Don Zelaya's arm.

"No, I'm worried about you," Lo said, her eyes wide. "It seems more like he's using you. If you are a team, why would he take such a powerful card from you?"

Xiomara stiffened, and Don Zelaya's bushy eyebrows shot up.

"Wouldn't it make more sense if you *shared* your cards?" Lo shook her head sadly at Xiomara, a pitying smile on her lips. "I would *never* allow a man to control me like that."

Xiomara faltered, no longer looking smug.

"Ah, but you're misunderstanding," Don Zelaya said as he patted Xiomara's hand. "Your father is the one who keeps track of your family's fortune. Correct, Lorena? I, too, had that task for my family." He spoke calmly. Even sweetly, but it was all a facade to hide poisonous condescension. It was the same way most of her suitors talked to her. "Because of that, I've become adept at managing resources. It only makes sense, no?"

"But isn't Xiomara a businesswoman?" Dominic asked, his gaze finding Lo. "I know she did a lot of business with my family, so—"

"Enough talk." Pearla cut him off, voice sharp and cold. "We continue." She drew the next card. "La Botella." The card flashed, and the same bottle floated out, turquoise liquid sloshing like the stormy seas.

"La Botella has returned," Misterioso said, voice full of excitement and wonder. He was even louder than before, as if he wanted his words to overpower Pearla. "This was the card that made Daniel Vásquez forfeit. The user must either drink the contents of La Botella or persuade someone else to do so. Whether the effect of this drink is positive or negative is a mystery."

La Botella floated to Xiomara. Her eyes widened.

"You are the chosen one, Xiomara. Remember, your life is your wager. What will your next move be?" Misterioso asked. "Will you drink La Botella, or attempt to pass it on to someone else?"

Drinking from the bottle was way too risky, Lo thought. If it had a bad effect, who knew what it could be? At best, it could make her weak, leaving her vulnerable to her opponents.

Xiomara turned to Don Zelaya. "What should I do?"

He stroked his chin, gaze flicking to Dominic and Lo. He had the same strategy in mind. He was going to try to make one of them drink it.

Lo's heart pounded. She needed to think fast.

"Dom." She scooted closer to him. "Listen." She lowered her voice, but made sure it was still loud enough for Don Zelaya and Xiomara to hear. "If they make one of us drink it, we'll be okay. Say I drink it. If the effect is bad, I completely trust that you'll watch over me, and I'll watch you if it's the other way around."

Dominic's dark eyes flicked with confusion.

Lo stared at him hard. *Play along.*

He suddenly took her hands. "Yes, Lorena. Of course. I trust you with my life, but look at the positive side too. The potion might be a lucky one and have an effect that will help us win this round."

Lo smiled at Dominic before nodding seriously. "Ah, you could be right." He had caught on quickly. Maybe she had underestimated Dominic . . .

Beads of sweat formed on Don Zelaya's brow, and Xiomara fidgeted. They had fallen for it. "What should I do?" she whispered almost frantically.

"Drink it," he finally said.

Lo bit back a victorious grin.

Xiomara's sharp eyebrows furrowed. "B-but I—"

She didn't fully trust him.

"Drink it," he repeated, more forcefully. In that moment, Don Zelaya revealed his hand. He saw Xiomara as nothing but a pawn. Why else wouldn't *he* offer to take the drink?

Xiomara was a smart woman. She knew the truth now. Her frown deepened, but then she flinched when the bottle began to fizz and spurt out smoke.

"Time is running out." Misterioso strode by. "If you idle too long, you will *lose*."

Xiomara's eyes widened.

Don Zelaya growled. If Xiomara forfeited, he would lose his possible gains if the potion turned out to be lucky.

Xiomara squeezed her eyes shut and clenched her hands atop the table. "O-okay." She sniffed the bottle, then took the smallest and most cautious of sips. Her face scrunched, and she quickly lowered the bottle. "It's so bitter."

"Well, you already started, so just keep drinking," Don Zelaya coaxed. When Xiomara hesitated, he took the bottle and gingerly grabbed her chin, so he could pour the drink into her mouth. It was such a gentle movement. Xiomara could have easily pushed him away, but she didn't. "If you don't finish it, you'll die." Her wide brown eyes watered, and liquid dribbled down her chin, staining her gown. As soon as the bottle emptied, she pulled away and coughed. Her head bobbed, and her eyelids drooped.

"Ah, it appears La Botella was filled with sueño dulce," Misterioso announced in excitement.

Xiomara whimpered, blinking hard and trying to keep her eyes open.

"Shhh, it's okay." Don Zelaya stroked her cheek, grin bordering on malicious. "I'll take care of you."

Xiomara slurred and lowered her head until it rested on the table.

Lo's stomach churned with both excitement and disgust. Her plan had worked, but now she wished she had figured out a way to get that slimy Don Zelaya to consume the sleeping potion instead.

Pearla drew the next card. "El Gorrito."

"Ah, yet another repeat," Misterioso said. "Remember, Maríana Montoya did not defeat the challenge. This card will remain in the deck until someone can best it."

The card flashed and transformed into a bonnet. Lo squinted. This El Gorrito was different from the one that had slain Señora Montoya. She couldn't remember what the previous one had looked like, but she swore it wasn't silken white trimmed in gold and pearls. It had looked much plainer, hadn't it? *Drip drip drip.* Drops of scarlet blood dripped slowly from the inside of the bonnet like a spout left on just enough for the smallest bit of water to seep through. *Drip drip drip.*

"El Gorrito, whom do you choose?" Misterioso asked.

"The heir of Las Cuatro," El Gorrito groaned, voice thick and pained.

Lo's blood ran cold. This voice was different than before. It was familiar, but from where—

Then she remembered.

Señora Montoya's voice.

Did the cards all take something from those they defeated?

"The Castro boy," Señora Montoya rasped. Her voice sent tingles across Lo's skin. The sound of her sisters sobbing. The sound of her father stomping around upstairs. A noise that brought nothing but dread.

"Me?" Dominic pointed to himself, as if there were several other Castros in this game.

"Listen carefully," Lo whispered. "You have to do whatever the card tells you *exactly* how it tells you." For now, she would much rather keep Dominic around and get rid of Don Zelaya. "You can do it." With an encouraging smile, she patted his arm.

"Dominic Castro, your life is on the line," Misterioso said. "You must pass three of El Gorrito's challenges in order to survive."

One mistake and it would all be over.

"Can you accomplish what I could not?" The card—no, Señora Montoya—asked. "Put me on your head."

Dominic practically tumbled out of his seat and snatched the bonnet from the air. He slammed it onto his head, but then winced. Thick blood oozed down the sides. He raised his arms, about to rip off the bonnet, but then froze, catching himself.

The blood was just another distraction, designed to make him fail. "Stay focused, Dom!" Lo cheered him on

"Now kiss the cheek to the one to your left."

Lo sat to his left, but he foolishly turned to Xiomara. No. No. No. "Dom," Lo whispered.

Catching himself once again, he turned to her and leaned in, giving her a quick peck on the right cheek.

"One more task," Señora Montoya growled. Lo could picture her milky face pinched and annoyed, lips curled with hatred. She wanted to drag Dominic to El Infierno with her.

By now, Dominic's entire body trembled. Blood dripped down his chin, staining his shirt, coating his eyelashes, and covering his lips. He didn't dare wipe it away. Lo didn't blame him. Who knew if that would count against him?

"Shake hands with my greatest rival at this table."

Dominic hesitated as he stared at the three of them.

The answer was clearly Don Zelaya. He was the biggest threat in this game.

But instead, Dominic turned and held his hand out to Lo. A small trail of blood made its way to his shoulder, snaking down his sleeve.

"What? Are you sure?" Lo stammered.

He nodded, looking scared but certain. She slowly raised her hand and he grabbed it, shaking it.

"You have youth . . . and beauty." Dominic spat away blood. "You're the most sought-after young woman in Milagro and rejected the chance to become her daughter-in-law. She can't stand the thought of someone from your bloodline getting so much adoration. From the moment your paths crossed in here, she has looked only at you."

"Correct," Señora Montoya said, sounding like she wanted to scream. "You . . . win."

Dominic ripped off the bonnet, and it vanished. Some of the croupiers clapped for him. With a triumphant grin, he wiped his bloody face and shook out his hair like a dog.

"Congratulations," Misterioso said, with a voice equal parts eager and amused. "My, this round is a long one." He clasped his hands together and grinned, clearly still riding the sickening high from Rodrigo's death.

"Then please let it end," Mayté mumbled from her seat. Next to her, Carlos nodded.

"Every game has a loser," Misterioso said as if he hadn't heard her. "And I'm curious who it will be."

Pearla drew the next card. "La Dama." The card flashed, flipped out of her hand, and grew in size. A woman stepped out. She wore a ruffled gown the color of a deep blush. Purple ruffles and stripes of white silk accented her figure and gathered at her decolletage. For a moment, all Lo could focus on was the gown. It was as if her mind refused to comprehend anything else, but once it did, her blood ran cold.

Mamá!

Thick, bouncy brown curls hung at her waist. Her droopy brown eyes sparkled, and her full lips curled into a knowing smile. Golden bronze skin glowed under the candlelight. It really was her. She looked exactly the way she had when she had left Lo. Without even a sign of wrinkles or aging. She didn't have streaks of gray in her hair or puffy eyebags like Mayté's mother, or fine lines on her forehead and around her mouth like Señora Montoya. She looked the way Lo remembered her. Nothing about her had changed. Not even the length of her hair or the way she parted it to the side.

Mamá locked eyes with her. Her smile grew as she crooked her finger, beckoning for her.

Just like she always used to do. Mamá would never call out to her. Instead, she would wiggle her finger, and Lo always knew to come. They were connected like that. It wasn't until she was much older that she realized that Mamá probably did that so as to not draw her father's attention. Better to stay hidden, and in such a large hacienda, it usually worked. How many times had Lo pretended not to hear when her father called for her?

"La Dama has chosen you, Lorena. Your life is on the line."

She stared at Mamá, searching for any sort of reaction, but Mamá simply smiled.

Lo's stomach flip-flopped. Why wasn't she saying anything? "Ma—"

"Vamos a bailar." Mamá cut her off and pulled her into a dance. She swung her hips and twirled her skirt, all while staring expectantly at Lo.

Lo wanted to argue. Scream at Mamá to just stop and talk to her. She had so many questions. But she had to remind herself that this was a challenge. The questions could wait. Lo stood, and music filled the air. The shake of maracas. The lively strum of guitars. But there wasn't a musician in sight. Mamá had always loved to dance. At every fiesta, she spent most of the night on the dance floor twirling around and clapping her hands. Smiling and accepting dances from any man who would ask.

And then afterward she and Lo's father would scream at each other until the wee hours of the morning. He always hated that she danced. Accused her of being unfaithful with every man she danced with. But most of all, Lo was sure he just hated seeing her happy.

The music swelled louder as Lo approached Mamá. She grabbed the ruffled hem of her gown and twirled around. Mamá spun with her. The memories of all her dance lessons came back. The countless hours learning how to move her legs and twirl around in her dress.

Good girl.

Look at my bonita mamita.

Soon you'll be dancing like your Mamá.

Lo glanced back at the table. Don Zelaya stared, deep wrinkles cutting into his forehead. Dominic covered his mouth and looked away. The Banker lingered near the other croupiers. He watched with interest.

Her heart flipped in her chest.

Still moving, she turned to the other table where Mayté and Carlos sat. Carlos looked perplexed, but Mayté had tears streaming down her face.

Why would she be so sad?

This was supposed to be a happy moment. She finally found Mamá.

Mayté tugged Carlos's shirt and whispered something into his ear. His face transformed from confusion into pure sorrow and pity as he gazed at Lo.

But why?

Something was wrong.

"Mamá," Lo murmured as the two circled each other. But Mamá didn't react.

The music grew louder and off-key. It rang through her skull, and Lo almost tripped over herself.

This wasn't Mamá.

It was a card.

And if the card took on Mamá's form . . .

She was dead. Just like Señora Montoya.

This card had killed her.

Mamá was gone.

She died—here.

All this time, everyone else had been right. Lo had been the delusional one.

The world blurred with tears. She wanted to fall to the floor in grief. But her body kept dancing. If she stopped now, she wouldn't survive.

She caught sight of Mayté, who suddenly looked smug. Fury bubbled in Lo's veins. No, that couldn't be right. This was another trick from the house. Lo spun with La Dama. When she glanced at Mayté a moment later, tears once again soaked her friend's cheeks. That was the truth, but somehow it made Lo feel even angrier.

And soon, but not soon enough, the music stopped. La Dama curtsied before vanishing.

"Congratulations, Lorena," Misterioso said. "Now return to your seat and place a bean over La Dama."

Returning to her seat felt like a blur. She could barely remember putting a bean down. She gripped the edge of the chair, tempted to yank it up and hurl it across the room. But she resisted the urge. *Barely.*

"Lorena?" Dominic whispered.

She looked away, only to see Don Zelaya staring curiously at her, as if watching a performance. But this was real life.

Keep it together. She still needed to survive this round.

"We continue." Pearla drew the next card and called out, but Lo barely heard her. Her heart wouldn't stop pounding and her face flushed with unpleasant heat. The fiery rage burned inside her cheeks and stomach.

This house had stolen Mamá from her. *It* was the reason her life was as miserable as el infierno.

A bony arm stuck out of the card, flesh grayish and dead. A decaying finger pointed at Don Zelaya.

"Are you okay?" Dominic asked.

"Yes, yes," she gritted out, on the verge of snapping. "What is this card?"

He warily eyed the card. "El Enterrado."

The buried. Lo swallowed down her fear. This wasn't the first card that wasn't normally in Lotería, but something about it was extra strange. Her heart raced with dread.

"Very well." Don Zelaya rubbed his hands together. "This should be interesting."

Pearla chuckled. "He's a bold one."

"Bold indeed," Misterioso murmured just as the floor rumbled.

"Whoa." Dominic stood.

Lo and Don Zelaya did the same. Xiomara remained asleep, even as the table jerked around.

Dominic backed up until he couldn't move any longer. Just like the previous round, they were trapped inside invisible walls with whatever was about to happen.

"Beware," Misterioso boomed. "El Enterrado won't give up until it takes someone with it."

That same hand from the card shot up from the floor next to Don Zelaya. If he hadn't stumbled away, it would have snatched his ankle. It didn't stop there; more and more hands broke through the floor in pursuit of him, each looking more decrepit than the last. Rotting flesh hung from stained bones.

Lo felt grim satisfaction. If he was smart, he would use his La Corona card to call off the hands. Otherwise, there was no way he would survive this. He wasn't quick and spry like

Dominic or Carlos. He turned to Xiomara, who hadn't stirred from all the chaos.

Xiomara—oh no.

"Don't!" Dominic yelled.

But it was too late. Don Zelaya snatched Xiomara by the arm. She jolted awake with a sputter, but couldn't move in time. He pushed her to the floor, and the hands snatched her arms and legs, pulling them through the broken floor. She screamed and writhed but couldn't break free. The hands pulled her deeper and deeper until only her head down to her neck stuck up from the floor.

"Why?" She sobbed, but it quickly transformed into an enraged scream, so loud and piercing that it made Lo's skull ache. But more than that, she felt the betrayal. She could almost taste the bitter pain and revolting rage in her voice: "AFTER EVERYTHING I'VE GIVEN YOU!"

"And I thank you for that. Truly." Don Zelaya took a cautious step closer. No more hands tried to attack him. El Enterrado was appeased. Now that it was safe, he crouched in front of her. "I was hoping to keep you around longer." He grabbed her chin. "But alas . . ."

"¡Hijo de puta!" Xiomara bared her teeth, but soon her eyes widened with horror. Another hand shot up and yanked her by the dark brown hair. Two more hands grabbed her face, pulling down through the floor. She screamed and cried until her head was completely under. The marble suddenly repaired itself, cutting off her screams and entombing her.

She was gone.

Dead.

Just like Mamá.

Don Zelaya dusted himself off and stood.

"And that concludes sudden death!" Misterioso cheer-fully announced. "There are now six contestants left. Six out of eleven. A little over half. Be prepared; the latter part of our games always goes much quicker than the first."

Lo clenched her fists, the truth pounding through her. The house had killed Mamá. It had stolen her from Lo and her sisters. She caught Pearla staring at her, brown eyes visible from under her mask.

"Congratulations on surviving another round," Pearla said, voice almost taunting.

What was the point of surviving if Mamá was gone?

The Banker came over and took back the deck from Pearla. The woman spoke to him, voice hushed. He glanced at Lo, a strange look on his face. Was that concern? After all this time, *now* he had the gall to act as if he cared? His gaze lingered on her for another moment before he followed Pearla.

What was the point of any of that?

Lo stormed off. Past Mayté and Carlos.

"Lo?" Mayté called after her.

Lo whirled around. "You were right about my mother. You were right, and I was a fool. Are you happy?" She ran out of the room. Tears slid down her cheeks, but burning rage evaporated them. Lo was going to destroy Fortune's Kiss and avenge Mamá. She had never been so sure of anything in her life.

As she rode the elevator alone, the pieces of her plan fell into place. She would burn the place down. It was only fitting, since Fortune's Kiss had made all their lives into a living el infierno.

And she would use the house's own magic against it. "Lead me to your demise," she hissed under her breath as the doors opened. "I don't care what it costs me." She swiped at her drip-ping nose, not even recoiling as thick blood stained her fingers.

Whether illusion or real, she didn't care. *Show me how to destroy this place. Show me now.*

A cluster of monarch butterflies fluttered by. Were they remnants of La Mariposa? She chased after them through a winding hallway until one by one they dropped dead, transforming into orange marigold petals. A gust of wind blew the petals down a hallway full of doors. Maybe she was onto something.

She tried a door. Locked. Then another and another. Still locked. Was every door here barred to her? She pressed her ear to one but couldn't make out any sounds. What could be behind them? It had to be something important. She pounded her fist against the wood.

"The answer is behind this door. Show me," she whispered. Still locked. The fiery anger inside her blazed hotter. She tried the next one and the next one, yanking harder and harder. This hall of doors seemed endless, but it didn't matter. She would stay here until the end of eternity if she had to. "Give me something I can use. Anything!" she spat and yanked the next one.

It flew open.

Lo peeked inside. It was empty and pitch-black, an endless abyss. If she stepped inside, she feared she might suffocate in a glob of inky blackness. Her eyes soon adjusted to the dark, or maybe the room itself changed, revealing a study.

She rushed inside. The crackling fireplace cast an eerie glow throughout the room. There was a desk along with shelves full of books and other knickknacks. A dog slept on the rug by the fireplace. No, not a dog. It had horns and spikes growing along its tail. Spots on its dark fur glowed bright orange. An alebrije. Lo froze. Until she realized it was just a statue.

She let out a sharp breath. There wasn't time for paranoia. This place had to have some kind of clue. She hurried to the desk, searching through the stack of papers and yanking the drawers until something gleaming and silver caught her eye. A letter opener. The handle had ornate carvings of skulls and flowers, but the part that interested her most was the sharp blade. She lightly touched it with her finger. With the right amount of force, it could do quite a bit of damage. She stuffed it down her bodice. The cool metal chilled her skin.

One of the drawers slammed shut. She jumped away, heart racing. Everything inside her screamed at her to run, but that was exactly why she needed to stay.

Sprawled across the desk was a map of San Solera and the surrounding countries. Circles in blood red ink covered the parchment. This included Ciudad Milagro. Was this a map of the places Fortune's Kiss had visited? Could this be the study of one of the Gamemakers?

Lo snooped further. There was a cabinet full of potion bottles, all colorful and glowing bright. She frowned. It would have been helpful to have her best friend with her. Mayté always kept tabs on the potions being sold at the street mercado. They should have been working together, but now Lo was in too deep. If she left, the house might not let her return to this place.

On the next shelf was a thick ledger full of names. Workers, maybe, or perhaps contestants. She couldn't tell with just the light from the fireplace, it was too dark to make sense of the names.

The candles flickered, suddenly going out. A burnt smell filled her nostrils, and tendrils of smoke curled like fingers warning her to keep quiet.

Her breathing became shaky. She slammed the booklet shut.

The next shelf was full of framed photographs of people. An altar of sorts. One caught her eye—an image of what appeared to be a man in a suit, but most of the face had been scribbled out. Next to it was a stack of documents; the name and other identifying information on them had been blotted out as well. She studied the photograph again, squinting. The bottom part of the face hadn't been fully scribbled out. She caught bits of wide grin, angular jaw, and deep-set dimples. "Misterioso?"

Was this information about the Gamemakers? Why would the house send her here? Unless—she remembered the strange tension with the Banker and Misterioso, how the sensation only thickened when Pearla came onto the scene. Lo studied the papers more closely and found that someone had jotted down words in neat script.

Is there another copy?

She set down the page and found a framed photograph of the Banker. He looked exactly the same. Long hair slicked back into a low ponytail and all. On his lapel, he wore a Hispana crest. Lo swallowed hard. Many members of el orden antiguo wore them like a badge of honor. To think she had been trying to conspire with a member of La Orden. There was a twinge of bitter disgust, but apathy washed it away. With Mamá gone, nothing mattered anymore.

Next to his frame was a locket and a piece of paper. Lo grabbed the locket and studied it. The gold had begun to tarnish. She flipped it open and found a cameo of a girl. She was beautiful with rich brown skin, bright red lips, and the most striking golden eyes Lo had ever seen. Her black hair was pulled up into a loose bun, and wavy tendrils of hair framed her face. An old lover, maybe?

Lo set down the locket and found a folded-up piece of parchment.

Mi vida,

By the time you read this, I'll already be gone. I know I promised—but I couldn't stand by and let you be disowned for my sake. Not without doing something about it. I'm going to win. That's a promise I will stand by. I'll bring back enough of a fortune so we can run away and never worry about your family. Then they'll regret everything they've said about me and my bloodline. Please wait for me.

With all my love,
Ana Lùcia

Lo read it again. Wait. This Ana Lùcia came to Fortune's Kiss in order to be with the Banker? But then how did he end up here as well? He must have followed her. Then . . . she must not have won the game.

Was there a way Lo could use this information to her advantage?

Then she heard the sounds. Distant wails of agony. Rasping breath and pounding on the walls. There was something nearby. She backed up against the wall next to the fireplace, and what she saw on the mantle took her breath away: Mamá's comb. The one Lo had brought as her most prized possession. Mayté's painting had been taken away too, along with everyone else's prized possession, Lo imagined, but only Mamá's comb was here. The house was taunting her. And it was really beginning to piss her off.

She snatched the comb, barely feeling the blast of hot air and smoke from the fireplace. The comb was just as she had left it. Without a scratch or chip. Her gaze traveled upward, and the comb slipped from her fingers. The painting above the fireplace showed Mamá. She stared at Lo, a knowing smile playing on her lips.

A scream bubbled in Lo's throat, but then in the blink of an eye, Mamá winked.

"What do you think you're doing in here?"

She whirled around and found herself face to mask with Misterioso. His lips, the only visible part of his face, curled down into a snarl.

"I—I—" She cleared her throat, regaining her composure. "Oh, I'm sorry." She channeled innocence. "The door was unlocked. I didn't know we weren't allowed in here." When she glanced back at the painting, it had changed once again now portraying a calavera sitting among decaying marigolds.

"I never showed this room on tour, as it is private." Misterioso moved closer, backing her into a corner. "I know you're up to something."

Lo frowned. He seemed . . . threatened by her. But why? He was the man in control of this murderous place, and she was just a girl. He had every reason to consider her harmless, yet he didn't.

"I simply wandered in here. I'm sorry."

"No one wanders in here by chance," he countered. "I don't take kindly to contestants lying to me." His voice lowered. "The house will not stand for cheaters. The Banker let you in here, didn't he?"

Lo's eyes widened.

"Actually, I did not." The Banker stepped into the room. Misterioso growled under his breath.

"I also have to wonder why *you* are in here, Misterioso." The Banker tilted his head to the side. "This is not your study."

Then whose was it? The Banker had made reference to another Gamemaker. Was it theirs?

Misterioso said nothing. A vein stood out from his neck.

The Banker's smirk grew. "But if you allow Lorena to leave, I will not mention this."

Lo took the opportunity to rush to his side.

Misterioso gritted his teeth. "Very well. Just bear in mind, if a player sniffs around where they do not belong, the outcome may not be good for *any* of us."

It was a threat, yet the Banker didn't seem the least bit bothered. "I'm well aware." He offered his arm. Lo let him lead her out of the study. Once they were out of earshot, he turned to her.

"Lorena," he began, voice soft and serious.

There was his disgusting pity again. It didn't suit him the least bit. "Whose study is that?" she interrupted.

He frowned.

She thought *Fine. Be that way.* "Do you regret gambling here for a woman?"

The Banker stared straight ahead, but Lo felt his forearm tense up. "The outside world no longer matters to me."

The answer felt stale. Over-rehearsed.

"You followed her here the first chance you got. But here you remain. Which means she must have failed in the games. She's dead, isn't she?"

He turned to her, eyes flashing, but then looked away as if putting himself back together.

"A tragedy," she continued. "One that must have caused you great pain, and yet, now you damn everyone else foolish enough to wager away their souls. How can you live with yourself?"

"Lorena," he croaked. "I think I know what you want."

He knew that she wanted to destroy the house? Not likely.

"I can help you."

"How?" Now she was intrigued.

He glanced over his shoulder. "Not here. Not like this. It's a delicate line, and if we are careless, it could have disastrous consequences."

What was he getting at? What did he think she wanted?

He slipped a golden key into her hand. "On the tenth floor past the fountain, there is a locked elevator. Get onto it and go to the top floor. My chambers are the first door on the left. Meet me there." Without another word, he walked off.

Lo watched him go. Her fingers wrapped around the key. It could be a trap, but if anyone had the power to destroy the house, it was him. And she would do anything to gain that power, no matter the price.

SEVENTEEN

Mayté

You were right about my mother. Are you happy?

Lo's harsh words had carved a hole in Mayté's heart, leaving behind sadness and guilt. She hated that she was right. Normally, being right was something she prided herself in. She may not have been the most beautiful girl, but she liked to think her instincts made up for it. This time, she wished her gut had failed her. She shouldn't have been so dismissive when Lo brought up the paella. Or maybe she should have been honest with her best friend sooner. She wasn't sure which one was better. All she knew was that Lo was in more pain than she could even begin to imagine.

Next to Mayté sat Carlos. They were the only ones in the common area between the players' suites. Misterioso had boasted that tonight's feast would be extra grand, with a whole roasted pig and dishes from around the world. The thought soured her stomach.

Mayté and Carlos had looked everywhere for Lo, but hadn't found her.

"From now on, you, me, and Lo are working together," she whispered because if she spoke any louder, her voice might shatter into a million pieces. "We'll get to the final round. We'll be unstoppable."

Carlos managed a smile, then winced. His bandaged arm was still painful.

All the fiery anger she had felt, the fear that plagued her all this time, subsided into soft warmth. For the first time in a very long time, she and Carlos felt like true siblings. Do or die until the very end.

If they could all make it through the final round, they would be safe. Lo had told her that. So why did her stomach lurch? As if there were some other catch. Maybe the Banker had lied. Everything came at a price, and surely there was more to it.

She didn't want anyone else to suffer or die.

But she didn't want to give up on her own life and dreams either.

And for that to become reality, people would have to lose and pay the ultimate price. The cost of her beautiful dream was bloody horror.

She chewed her lower lip and twirled the wispy strands of hair at her temple.

"Mayté." It wasn't until Carlos touched her arm that she realized how hard she was pulling at her hair.

He gripped his arm, letting out several curses under his breath. It was getting worse.

"Should we go tell—?" she began.

"They won't do anything," he replied. "It happened during the round, so it's fair game." When he lifted his hand, blood seeped through the bandage. "I'll be okay. Let's keep looking for Lo."

"But—you'll be at a disadvantage next round! We have to do something," Mayté said, panicked. There were only six people left, and Misterioso was certainly going to make sure more of them got eliminated quickly.

"I think I might be able to help."

Mayté looked up just in time to catch a glass bottle that Dominic had tossed in her direction. It was half full of what looked like liquid opals. In the light, the silvery liquid gleamed different shades of pinks and purples. "What is this?"

"Dedo de Dios." Dominic was standing in the connecting doorway of his room. He had washed up and changed into a fresh suit. His eyes looked extra puffy, and his cheeks were flushed bright red.

"What?" Mayté and Carlos gasped. Dedo de Dios was incredibly expensive and as rare as the flowers needed for it, which bloomed only during full moons. The potion was known to heal wounds and even some diseases.

"Where did you get this?" Mayté asked.

"Brought it with me. Just in case." Dominic grinned, but his eyes didn't have their usual shine. "I don't have much use for it. Keep whatever you don't use, okay?"

Smuggling in a potion in case something terrible happened. Clever.

"Hey." Carlos turned around in his seat to face him, expression somber and the slightest bit regretful. "Thank you." Any ill will between them had been buried away.

"You're welcome." Dominic backed into his room and closed the door. Even someone as cheerful as him couldn't stay that way in this hellish place.

Mayté opened the potion as Carlos undid his bandages. The liquid's scent filled the air. When she closed her eyes, it reminded her of an early spring morning when the cool air smelled fresh and carried the subtle scent of newly bloomed flowers.

As she sprinkled the potion onto Carlos's wound, his skin repaired itself.

Carlos sucked in a breath. The tension in his jaw and shoulders loosened.

Gracias a Dios. Mayté let her fingers relax. Would the house make Dominic pay for smuggling in a potion? Would that be something that needed payment? She would have to ask Alejandro.

Wait! Alejandro.

She pulled the napkin out of her pocket. With everything that had happened, she had nearly forgotten. Her heart raced as she studied it. There was a smudged note scrawled in charcoal: *LIBRARY AT MIDNIGHT—A*

There were still several hours before then. "Come on." Mayté stuffed the napkin back in her pocket and stood. "Let's keep looking for Lo."

They had searched for what felt like hours, but Lo was nowhere to be found. Mayté's insides twisted with more and more worry with every passing moment.

It was nearly midnight. She had to meet Alejandro.

The elevator doors opened, and Mayté rushed down the hall toward the library. Soft light from the wall lanterns washed over her. Her heart wouldn't stop pounding.

When she pushed open the creaky door, everything in the room had once again changed. If it could even be considered a room. The sky was a deep purple, and the full moon shone high above. There were no walls, just an endless expanse of cobblestone, and buildings tall enough to touch the stars. Bright lights from lampposts and windows cut through the dark and illuminated the deep blue river ahead.

This wasn't Milagro.

She had never seen a place like this before. Was this even in San Solera?

Despite the unfamiliarity, it was beautiful. *So beautiful.* Slowly, almost shakily, she approached the metal fence overlooking the river. Nearby rose bushes exhaled their dreamy scent. A cool breeze pulled at her braids as she stared out at the lake and city.

Her fingers twitched, wanting to paint a replica of this exact scene. Golden lights popping in the dark night, the silver moon reflecting in the waters, soft roses and harsh architecture.

To find herself in a place like this and create art. This was what she wanted. More than anything. She blinked back tears.

Would she ever get there? Or would she die inside Fortune's Kiss?

She wiped her eyes and looked away. As beautiful as this place was, there was something uncanny lurking between the lights and buildings. There wasn't a soul in sight. This shouldn't have been a surprise. It was all just a mirage, yet it bothered her that there wasn't a single figure in any of the windows. No carriages on the streets, either. It was just Mayté. Or was it? She spotted something approaching her. In the dark, it looked like a shadow come to life. Her heart jumped into her throat.

The stranger stepped under the light of a lamppost. Alejandro.

Mayté huffed. "You scared me!"

He took a step closer.

"The room changed, but you still came. Is this even still considered the library?"

Alejandro came closer, but kept quiet. He stared at her, hazel eyes tired and intense. He had washed the paint off his face, but clearly had been much too hasty as traces of black surrounded his eyes. The first few buttons on his wrinkled dress shirt were unbuttoned. He stopped in front of her, still wordless. As if he had consumed the potion El Silencio.

"Alejan—"

He suddenly hugged her, taking her breath away. Gentle, yet strong, he held her close. The subtle odor of paint and incense mixed with fresh lemongrass filled her nostrils.

"I was so worried. I'm glad—so glad you're okay." He buried his face in her neck.

The sky lightened into a dreamy purple. The stars glittered brighter, reflecting off the dew on the roses. Feeling his skin against hers sent shock waves of warmth all the way down to her toes. Her face must have been brighter than the moon. She was certain it would have reflected a vivid pink against the river's glimmering water.

"I'm so sorry. The sudden death was all my fault." He held her tighter. "I never should have told you about the house's magic."

"No. It's okay. You tried to warn me about keeping my intentions pure, but I didn't listen. I just wanted"—her voice cracked—"my best friend, my brother, and myself to survive."

"That sounds pure to me." He held her tighter. "This damn place has a warped sense of morality."

Pressed up against his chest like this, her pulse pounded even harder. Or maybe it was Alejandro's heart she felt. She wasn't sure.

But she liked it.

She had never been hugged by a boy before. Save her brothers—and her father, long ago—but that was different. No one outside of her family and Lo had cared for her so strongly. How many nights had she lain in bed, fantasizing about situations just like this? Yearning for this type of warmth, but also not fully understanding what it would feel like. Slowly, and almost shakily, she lifted her hands to return his embrace.

"I've been so selfish," he whispered.

Your heart shall be torn in two.

La Sirena's prophecy hit her like a bolt of lightning. She wanted to ignore it. Pretend it was all just a lie.

But she couldn't.

"What do you mean?" Her hold on him loosened. A thick purple fog rolled through. It obscured the moon and the tops of the buildings. Hazy. Uncertain. Treacherous.

"I . . ." Alejandro looked down. "I've been using you."

"What?" Mayté wrenched away from him. Distant rumbles filled the air and streaks of lightning cut through the sky. She turned away , pinpricks of pain racing across her chest, followed by heat. Angry, furious heat. She whirled around to face him with a growl. "I've been using you too!"

His eyes grew as wide as an owl's.

She jabbed her finger against his chest. "I was using you to learn more about the game, but you're easy to talk to, and I . . . I enjoy being around you, so."

"That's not using me." He stepped closer.

She didn't back away.

"That's survival."

"Then how were you using me?" She forced out the question before she could take it back.

"The thing is, I don't feel much of anything anymore." Alejandro slowly released her. "Even the most potent potions—the ones that should cause pain—do nothing to me."

She thought of the numbing sensation she'd felt from his lips last night. Was that why he resorted to Frío Alivio?

"But *you* make me feel something, Mayté."

Her heart swelled. "I mentioned how I enjoyed reading; well, the most fascinating part of Fortune Kiss's library are the soul books." Alejandro reached into his rucksack. She hadn't even noticed that he had one with him. He pulled out a book with an azure cover. "These books are made to fit the player's desires. I read them once new players are chosen. I've always held on to a hope that seeing other's dreams on the pages would help me remember mine." He held up the book, showing her the cover.

Mayté gasped. In golden swirly letters, it read: *María Teresa Robles.* She tore her gaze away, only to find that they were both back in the library. The fireplace roared to life.

Her fingers trembled as she took the book from Alejandro. Ever so carefully, she sat in the nearest seat and studied the cover. What could possibly be inside a book about herself? Abuelita used to read her illustrated stories she'd bought from the street mercado. Fairy tales about princesses getting rescued, peasants meeting Los Santos, and brujas unleashing magnificent curses on the cruelest of people.

Mayté imagined her own tragic fairy tale about a princess losing her crown and castle after her fool of a father gambled the throne away. She wet her lips and lifted the cover.

What she saw took her breath away.

Page upon page full of gorgeous paintings. The kind she could only dream of creating. Scattered between were photos of beautiful scenery. The same city she was in. The calming beach. A sunset view on a mountain. A field full of flowering cacti. An endless ocean on a cloudless day. "What is this?"

"Your wishes and dreams." Alejandro peered over her shoulder. His face was so close, she could see just how long his dark eyelashes were and count the string of moles on his cheek. They looked like half of a crescent moon. "The books appear as soon as contestants are chosen. Most are full of palaces overflowing with gold. Some are . . . not so beautiful to look at." He frowned. "But your book is full of the most beautiful dreams I've ever seen. The pages show you have a pure heart." His warm breath sent pleasant chills down her neck. "I knew I had to meet you. And you're just as beautiful on the outside as the dreams inside of you."

No boy had ever appreciated her so intensely. She swallowed the biggest lump in her throat. It was something she could only have dreamed of, but now that it was happening, she didn't know what to do or say.

He continued, "I'm not sure if it's the magic of the book, or *you*, but my memory has been coming back in bits and pieces."

Mayté followed his gaze to the fireplace. The flames transformed, revealing a boy sitting on the street, sketching on parchment as a crowd gathered around. Some threw coins into his cup and in return he handed them his drawing, but when he looked inside the cup, the flames weakened, fizzling into smoke.

"I came from Milagro, and I had nothing. Except my drawings." His voice became distant. Not quite dreamy, more like recollecting a recurring nightmare. "I drew charcoal portraits. Quick. Fast. People enjoyed them, yet no one wants to pay an artist what they're worth."

Mayté nodded for she knew exactly what he meant. It was the very reason she fought tooth and nail for patrons like Dominic's mother, because most everyone else expected masterpieces for very little pay. "You came here to fund your dream."

"I believe so, but that part is still foggy."

"I don't understand how you're using me, though." She looked back at the shelf. Each book was a vastly different color, but every name was printed in that same swirly gold. What did the other contestants have inside their books?

The fire crackled; several embers flew out like angry little spirits. Alejandro flinched and gripped the back of the seat. "I know. And we don't have much time until people start looking for us. There's one more thing I need to show you."

Alejandro led Mayté through the twisting hallways of the house. But this time they ended up somewhere completely unfamiliar to her. A different elevator. This one was a claustrophobic box that could fit only four people at the most.

Alejandro leaned against the wall, hands in his pockets, staring at the floor numbers as they grew higher. His face was completely unreadable.

"I shouldn't be in here." Mayté nervously ran her fingers over her braid. "You'll get in trouble if someone finds out."

"It's okay." He flashed a small smile. "I made my choice that night we met in the library."

"What do you mean?" she asked, just as the elevator dinged and the door opened. The panel no longer showed a floor number, but instead a calavera.

He took her hand once again. "I need to show you what Fortune's Kiss really is." He led her down another hallway. Marigolds dusted the floor and a sweet-smelling smoke wafted through the dim air. They passed by several doors, each large and gilded in gold. Mayté couldn't imagine what secrets were locked behind them, but Alejandro instead led her to a red door at the end of the hall. Hazy wisps slipped through the keyhole like ghostly fingers. He fished a large black key from his pocket. "Where did you—?" Mayté started.

"Misterioso," Alejandro finished. "Plucked it right from his pocket." With a small smirk, he stuck the key into the hole. "Perhaps I was a pickpocket as well." He unlocked the door and yanked it open with a grunt.

A blast of wind and smoke hit Mayté's face. Marigold petals fluttered around her robe. It reminded her of when she had first come here. The ritual that measured her soul. Back then, she had been filled with a jittery concoction of excitement and nerves. Hubris. Foolish, foolish hubris. But this time, as she stepped into the dim room, her stomach churned with nothing but pure dread.

The biggest altar loomed before her, stretching out to cover the walls. Similar to altars to the dead and Los Santos, it was full of framed photos, painted calaveras, candles, and other trinkets. Hundreds of them. Something about this was off. It wasn't somber or reverent, but felt more like an elegant abomination. "What is this?" she whispered.

"El Beso de la Fortuna," Alejandro answered. "Behind the golden possibilities, beautiful illusions, and mystical decadence, this is the truth of Fortune's Kiss." He knelt at the center of the room.

Mayté had been so focused on the altar that she hadn't noticed the floor. There was a circular pool filled with what looked like molten gold. It glowed bright, not burningly so like the sun, but it was brighter than the moon, washing Alejandro's face in glittering light. The ocean flowed in waves, but this pulsated. Almost like a beating heart. She knelt next to him.

A pleasant feeling washed over her. Suddenly she was wide-awake, and not the least bit fatigued. The confusion and anxiety racing through her mind calmed into lovely bliss.

"You feel it, don't you?" Alejandro studied her.

"I think so." She had never gotten drunk, much less had more than a few sips of alcohol, but this was how she imagined intoxication would feel: the way people swayed and smiled without the slightest care as they acted like complete fools. She rested her head on Alejandro's shoulder.

"At one time this was a potion, but after absorbing so many hopes, dreams, emotions, lives, and souls, it has become the heart of the house."

"What?" Mayté jolted. That was enough to sober her up.

"*This* is what makes the house aware and sentient. It takes in what you give it and amplifies it." He stared at the pool, eyes narrowed. "The Gamemakers swim in it, but like everything else here, it comes at a price. There are whispers that it amplifies something dark inside you and corrupts your soul. Like Misterioso and the Banker. They're different from the rest of the staff. They have their memories, yet they've lost their empathy. Misterioso has been here the longest, and he's the most callous of all. Rumor has it that Gamemakers from the past eventually lose their minds. Everyone wonders if Misterioso will be the next one."

"How . . ." Her voice came out hoarse. "How do you know this?"

"Because . . ." Alejandro hesitated. Mouth shut tight, he ran his tongue over his teeth. "I was on my way to becoming a Gamemaker. All of them were players once—" He ran a hand through his thick hair. "They promise you things—a bit of freedom, some of your memories. Thing is, I only have two choices.

Either I become a Gamemaker, feeding off pain and the misery of others, or I let the house consume every last bit of me until there's nothing left. I can't grow older here. Can't die by my own hand. I've—I've tried." He frowned, then clenched his fists so hard that his knuckles turned white. "I'm stuck." His voice was hoarse with grief.

"That's horrible." Mayté's voice cracked. Anything short of winning, even surviving, was still damnation. "It all feels so . . . hopeless."

"I know." He stared at her, hazel eyes shimmering in a golden haze. "But there's more to the story." He pointed to a painting on the far wall. The canvas stretched out to an amazing length, but even more shocking was the way the image shifted and changed.

First it showed a young woman, the most beautiful woman Mayté had ever seen. The woman lit a candle. The dancing flame almost looked alive. For a second, Mayté lost herself trying to figure out how she could replicate the effect in her own paintings, but Alejandro's voice pulled her out of her head.

"There was once a mortal woman who prayed to San Fortuno every night, for her family was very cruel and wanted to marry her off to the highest bidder."

The woman in the painting pressed her palms together in prayer and squeezed her tearful eyes closed. The entire room lit up as a figure bathed in light appeared before her.

"San Fortuno heard her prayers and became quite fond of her. To the point that he eventually appeared to her whenever she prayed. The two inevitably fell in love."

The woman stepped into the light and embraced San Fortuno. It was a sight that was both beautiful and frightening.

"To protect his love, San Fortuno created a potion, El Beso de la Fortuna."

The painting changed once again, revealing a vial filled with a glittering golden potion. As soon as a drop hit the ground, everything transformed into a flurry of painted colors.

"The purpose of the potion was to create a place for the woman and San Fortuno to hide together, the woman away from her family and San Fortuno away from the judgment of Dios and the other Santos. The potion reflected their feelings of love, joy, and safety with each other, and made the house a paradise on earth."

As the typhoon of colors slowed, Mayté gasped. Now the painting was an exact replica of Fortune's Kiss, but on a smaller scale. Colorful alebrijes danced across the canvas, more vibrant and surreal than any of the wooden sculptures sold at the mercado.

"The house attracted the guiding animals from the dream world. The alebrijes quickly took to the maiden and became guardians of the house." Alejandro's expression turned grim. Dark splotches appeared on the painting, forming into a group of figures closing in on the house. Red spatters stained the canvas as the dark forms slayed the alebrijes. "Eventually, the woman's suitors found the hideaway. They broke into the house. The enchantment continued to work, but now the house fed off the woman's fear and murderous rage toward the men. The house attacked them until they became a part of it too."

The painting moved into a chaotic mess of colors and smears. To some it might have looked completely abstract, but Mayté saw the frenzy of anger and terror in the deep reds and erratic lines. Saw the men fleeing as shadows grabbed them and forced them into the walls. She expected everything to become peaceful after that, but the entire painting shook both inside and out. The canvas spat out streaks of paint onto the floor. A deep red. Almost black. Like blood.

"San Fortuno lost control of the house, and the woman became trapped inside. When Dios found out, he banished San Fortuno forever."

Tears prick the corners of Mayté's eyes. It wasn't fair. The young woman just wanted to be free and happy. Other people stole that from her. Other people twisted her dream.

"Without her love, the woman was beside herself. She became the first Gamemaker," Alejandro said. "Luring people in so the house could feed on their souls." He motioned to the house's heart. "The pool of golden potion. This is the result. The sole thing keeping the house and its magic alive. They say that without it, the house would collapse on itself."

Mayté slowly backed away from the pool. Suddenly the pleasant warmth felt sinful. "So, the woman is here? She's the one in charge?"

Alejandro shook his head. "Not long after, she went mad and let the house consume her. By then, there were other Gamemakers to take her place, and the cycle continues endlessly, because—"

"Everything comes at a price," Mayté whispered. Her eyes stung. Was she destined to become another story with a sad ending? The sight of that cursed pool made her sick to her stomach. She turned away and noticed that the painting had changed once again.

It now showed the woman and San Fortuno embracing once again, as glittering light consumed them. The image shifted into

a game card. Mayté inched closer and squinted, trying to make
out the words on the card. "El Beso de la Fortuna?"

"Yes," Alejandro's voice trembled. "This card always appears
during the final round. If someone with a pure heart claims
the card, something miraculous will happen. But if anyone else
does, it will simply further corrupt them. I . . ." He stuffed his
hands in his pockets. "I've never seen the miracle, but, as I've
read everyone's soul book, I've searched for the right person to
make it happen. Mayté, your heart is pure. I know you can make
the miracle happen, and I . . ." He clamped his mouth shut and
shook his head.

"Alejandro, is this what you meant by 'using' me?"

He wouldn't look at her. That all but confirmed it. He needed
her to make the miracle happen. Despite everything, he had
hope after all.

She took his hands. "That's not using me. That's survival."
She repeated his words and truly meant it.

"I thought that maybe your miracle could save us both." He
tilted his head up just enough to lock eyes with her. "But meeting you and finding bits and pieces of my memories and feelings. That's enough of a miracle for me."

The words took her breath away. The silence between them
stretched, yet it felt like his eyes said so many things. Things she
didn't quite understand. She wanted to stay like this and deci-
pher all of it, but a small voice in her head told her this wasn't
the time. They needed to survive first. "Does the person who
gets the card win?"

"By then it's usually down to multiple players needing one
more card to completely fill their board. El Beso de la Fortuna
is that card."

"But that card's not on my board. I don't think it's on Lo's board either. D-doesn't that mean we're destined to lose?"

"No, no. That's the magic of the card. It will always change the board to become the final card needed. I've never seen it show up the same way twice, but there is always a challenge or struggle in order to claim it."

"Okay." Mayté turned away, heart pounding. This was the final piece to the puzzle. The way she would win. But as quickly as her heart had soared, it plummeted when she remembered Carlos and even Dominic. Would there be a way for them all to win? "How powerful is the card?" she asked. "Is it possible for—"

The sight of something familiar cut off her words.

A framed photo of Señora Montoya along with her fan, cigarette holder, and jewelry. A rotting calavera wearing a scarlet hat sat on the table next to it. The same one that Misterioso had shown everyone during the second game. "These are the altars of the dead players?"

"And anyone else who has lost the game," Alejandro said. "I'm sure mine is somewhere among them, but these"—he beckoned at the nearest shelf in front of them—"are the most recent. There's also the card that bested them." He pointed at the El Gorrito card next to Señora Montoya's calavera.

Mayté studied the other photos. Was it wrong to look at them? It felt like she was intruding on something sacred, but she couldn't tear her gaze away. Xiomara's calavera was the color of the cheap jewelry from the street mercado. Streams of dark blue were under the eyeholes like tears. There were ledgers and contracts and coins surrounding her photo and calavera. La Botella was the card lying next to them. Mayté swallowed hard. Thinking about what had happened to Xiomara made her feel sick.

Then there was Rodrigo's part of the altar. El Valiente was the card lying next to his photo. His calavera was cracked in places and brown and rotting. The teeth were even worse, completely black in spots and pure gold in others. He had his sombrero, along with other weapons and empty booze bottles, among his belongings.

Lo's maid, Carmen, and Señor Vásquez, the elote man, were even harder to look at. Carmen's skull was beautiful. A lively pink covered in hearts and roses. Her only belonging was a photo of a young boy. Her son? She had refused to wager him, sacrificing her own life instead. Señor Vásquez's calavera was bright yellow and orange with green cilantro leaves sprouting out of it. She swore she could smell the spicy savory twang of elote just standing by it. He had little jars of different spices and papers with scrawled-up blueprints for restaurants, along with napkins with little recipes jotted down. He wasn't dead, but the house had stolen away any chance for him to make his dreams come true.

Mayté's eyes burned. She didn't want to look anymore, but couldn't stop herself. Then she saw it. A photograph of a man. One that she instantly recognized. Her legs almost gave out on her.

Alejandro put an arm around her, steadying her. "What is it?"

"M—my . . ." She could barely gag out the words. "My father."

She reached past the other photos and skulls, snatching the framed photograph. His hair was thick and black. He didn't have deep wrinkles around his mouth and puffy eye bags. His eyes didn't look dead.

He was actually smiling.

When was the last time she had seen her father truly smile?

"B-but how . . ." She picked up the card, El Borracho, and let it slip between her fingers. Then she grabbed the calavera. It looked normal enough. A crisp white painted with colorful flowers and patterns. The most striking part was the bright purple mustache. But the longer she stared at it, the more the colors drained and dulled. A brownish liquid leaked from the mouth and dribbled onto her arm. It reeked of rancid spirits. "H—he's alive . . ."

"Then he must have forfeited," Alejandro said, voice soft and hesitant. "Did—did he suddenly stop being the person you knew?"

Mayté slowly nodded, too stunned to wipe her arm. "He lost our family's fortune, but wouldn't say what truly had happened. He would hardly say anything at all. He became a deadbeat, frequenting the cantinas and binging on drinks spiked with strange potions. Always accumulating new debts he couldn't pay off."

"Fortune's Kiss stole away his drive and ambition."

All the misfortune, the humiliation, burdens, fear of an unstable future: it was because of Fortune's Kiss.

This place was supposed to be her salvation, but it was the very thing that damned her family. Her throat tightened as she held the frame and calavera to her heaving chest. All these years, she had gobbled up the lies of this place like sweet little corncakes. Now she was trapped—with poison eating away at her. The true price of entry was the house's best-kept secret. She still remembered the way the people who decided not to compete seemed to be magically deluded into thinking they had been turned away. It was the only way to keep naïve fools like her coming in. She and Carlos came here to break the cycle in the only way they could imagine, but instead they were pawns destined to continue it.

Unless she did something. And she would. Somehow. She had lost enough to this cursed place.

Lo's mother was surely among the pictures of those defeated. Mayté wasn't sure if she wanted to look for her. Would telling Lo the truth behind her mother's death give her closure, or just add to the torment?

Before she could decide, the doorknob jangled. Alejandro snatched her arms and pulled the both of them under the table just as the door opened. Alejandro practically folded himself over her, so he could snatch her long robe and pull it closer. The two of them were a tangle of arms and legs. Mayté's heart pounded hard. Too scared to even breathe, she pressed her cheek against his chest.

A pair of long legs clad in white pants stepped into the room. Misterioso. He took a few steps, clearly looking around. But why wasn't he leaving? This room wasn't particularly big.

Alejandro let out the softest of curses and turned to the wall, pressing his hand into different spots. Soon the wall melted away, revealing an opening. A secret passage? He pushed Mayté toward the opening.

"Alejandro," Misterioso growled.

Mayté's heart dropped. Alejandro squeezed his eyes shut and gritted his teeth.

"I know you're in here." Misterioso stopped in front of the table where they were hiding. If Mayté had reached out, she could have grabbed his leg. Dios, at any moment he could peer under there and see them. "I know you've taken my keys as well. Do you truly think it's wise to poke your nose where it doesn't belong?"

Alejandro shoved Mayté toward the tunnel. *Go,* he mouthed.

And you? Mayté mouthed back.

He shook his head harshly and glared, dark-rimmed eyes wide with urgency. Then, before she could stop him, he stepped out from under the table.

"I'm right here. I'm sorry. I just couldn't wait to see what—"

Crash!

Mayté bit back a scream as glass shattered. She should have gone into the tunnel, but she peeked out from under the table just in time to see Misterioso yank Alejandro by the collar, pulling him from a pile of broken photograph frames and other shattered trinkets. Already Alejandro's cheek glowed bright red.

"What were you doing in here?" Misterioso's voice boomed. He violently shook Alejandro, slamming him into the table. More and more trinkets shattered. "You brought *her* in here, didn't you? You're in on this too! ANSWER ME!"

He's going mad.

Sickening chills ran down her spine.

"I—" Alejandro let out a strangled gasp when Misterioso grabbed his neck. Alejandro's face reddened before slowly turning blue.

"If you've done anything to jeopardize the game, I'll—"

"NO!" Mayté dropped the calavera and portrait and darted out from under the table and slammed into Misterioso's back. "Let him go!" Frantic, she pounded her fists against his back, but he still wouldn't release Alejandro. "Stop! Stop!" She reached up for his face, aiming for the eyes, and ripped at his mask, nearly pulling it off.

Misterioso howled, and Alejandro collapsed, coughing.

Mayté stumbled back as Misterioso dropped to his knees and frantically covered his face.

Alejandro leaped up and snatched Mayté's hand, dragging her back under the table to the tunnel. "We need to go *now.*"

We. That was the part that mattered most.

"Stop!" Misterioso roared.

She snatched up the calavera and her father's portrait just before Alejandro pushed her into the tunnel.

"You can't run—"

Alejandro closed the secret door, muffling the rest of Misterioso's words. Clutching her father's portrait and calavera to her chest with one hand, Mayté crawled as fast as she could. They were safe. But for how long?

EIGHTEEN

Lo

Lo lingered in front of the door to the Banker's chambers. She could have knocked. Should have. He had the power to destroy the house.

But she didn't trust him.

What if this was a trap? A play in his game. She refused to let herself fall as his pawn. And who was to say that she even needed him? "Give me the power that the Banker has. Show me how to get it," she softly demanded and mentally willed it until her temples throbbed.

For a moment nothing happened, but then the red door at the end of the hall glowed bright. Like rubies dipped in starlight. That was where her answer led. She moved toward it.

With every step she took, the house rebelled against her. The lights flickered and the floor shook underneath her feet, causing her to stumble. The corridor shifted before her eyes, sometimes looking decrepit and destroyed, and other times filled with thick smoke making it hard to breathe. But the one part that never changed was that door. She had to get there.

Finally she reached the door and pulled. To her surprise, it opened!

This was it. Her answer to destroying this damn place. She rushed through the threshold.

Only to find herself back in the same hallway. The same door behind her.

"No." She tried to go through the door again, but it was the same result. The house creaked and groaned, but she swore someone was whispering in her ear.

Turn back.

Give up.

"Never!" she yelled. "I don't care about the price, just let. Me. THROUGH!" With a growl, she pushed her way through the door once again—and stepped into a new room.

It was dim. Candles flickered along the walls. There was a scent that was disturbingly familiar. It grew progressively darker the deeper into the room she got. The candles' glow grew weaker and weaker.

She could sense someone in the shadows.

He stepped forward.

Her heart froze.

Her father, Salvador de León, stood before her. Blood gushed from his head and throat, but he was alive, breathing, and sneering in that nasty way she knew all too well. "Surprised?"

Lo stumbled back. A bloody puddle formed under him, growing larger and larger by the second.

"Did you really think you could kill me so easily?" Her father came closer, shoes squelching through the blood. "Did you really expect Fortune's Kiss to solve *all* your problems?"

Lo was stuck in place. This wasn't real. It couldn't be.

"I'm just surprised you've lasted this long. A girl like you doesn't have the wits for these games. Someone should have killed you by now." He lunged for her.

Lo screamed and stumbled back. She turned and ran in the other direction. Pounding footsteps chased after her.

The room stretched before her, on and on. It felt endless. She passed the same candles on the wall. The same doors.

No! No matter how fast she ran, chest heaving and lungs burning, she wasn't getting anywhere. Yet every time she looked back, her father was closer, arms outstretched and deranged grin growing.

If he caught her, he would kill her.

Lo stumbled to the nearest closet door. She bolted through it and slammed herself against the door, pressing it shut. Her father pounded against the door, trying to force it open.

She couldn't stay like this forever. Eventually he would overpower her. She searched for another escape, but when she glanced back, the candles flamed to life. She wasn't in a closet at all, but a room in the hacienda. She was back home. "HELP! SOMEONE HELP!" she cried out as the door jiggled. Her father was forcing his way through.

But her sisters didn't come running down the stairs. No servants dashed in from the kitchen. No one was coming to save her.

The door flew open, narrowly missing her face. She stumbled, but managed to stay upright and ran as fast as she could. She knew this place by heart, but of course so did her father. His fingers grazed the back of her gown, nearly taking hold of her.

"LEAVE ME ALONE!" She rushed through the kitchen, then into the dining room.

Her father sprinted ahead around the table, blocking her way. Lo backed away, and he did the same. Each time she tried to move around the table, he mimicked her movement. "Run as much as you want, but you aren't getting away," he shouted. "And once I catch you, you'll never leave my sight ever again." He smashed his fists against the table, knocking over empty glasses and plates. Their shatters on the floor were as loud as gunshots. "You'll marry Juan Felipe and it'll be a grand wedding." Church bells echoed through the room. "I told him to do whatever is necessary to make you submit. Oh, but don't worry, I'm sure you'll calm down once you start birthing children. Even Loretta did. For a little while."

Lo gripped the table as a wave of nausea washed over her. The wail of a newborn baby grated inside her ears. Had the births of her and her sisters broken Mamá's spirit? Or had her father tried to use them as leverage for Mamá to stay? The room spun.

If she married Juan Felipe and had his children, the cycle would continue.

And she would rather die than have that happen.

"Now get over here!" Her father flipped the table. Lo scrambled away from the shattering glass and thudding chairs.

He snatched her arm and slammed her against a shelf. A huge pot fell inches away from her and shattered. This was the spot where she had killed him. *He was supposed to be dead.*

"STAY AWAY FROM ME!" She pulled the letter opener out of its place in her bodice. She plunged it deep into his chest.

He stumbled back, releasing her. Lo yanked the dagger out. Blood sprayed everywhere, but she stabbed him again and again.

This was for the years of torment he had put her through. *Stab.*

This was for brainwashing her sisters with his conditional love. *Stab.*

For making Mamá his prisoner. *Stab.*

It was his fault she had left. His fault Lo was like this. His fault she was broken.

Stab.

Stab.

STAB!

At some point they both ended up on the floor, in a puddle of his blood.

Suddenly the room changed. She was no longer in the hacienda. The soft orange glow from hundreds of candles revealed that she was back in Fortune's Kiss, red door once again looming before her like a prize earned with blood. The body didn't belong to her father. Another man lay dead at her feet.

Lo gasped and clutched the bloodied letter opener tighter.

She couldn't stay here. With trembling fingers, she pulled open the door and rushed through it.

Warm humid air curled around her as she stepped onto pearlescent tiles. Waterfalls flowed from the walls into a large pool. Milky beams of moonlight drifted down through the glass ceiling, reflecting off the water like a mirror.

Her shoulders drooped. There was nothing in here that could help her destroy the house. And yet—she couldn't take her eyes off the pool. Her breath hitched and her heart raced. Something about it drew her closer.

She took off her shoes and descended the steps leading into the water. She dipped her toes in and felt her anxieties and rage swirl into something else: a delicious warmth that enveloped her skin. With a sigh, she closed her eyes.

A flicker of light caught her eye. On a nearby table, golden hair pins glimmered in the moonlight. There was no time to question it. She quickly pinned up her curls, then stripped off her dress and tossed the bloodied mess aside before descending into the warm waters.

This felt good. She could have stayed until the dark sky brightened with dawn's pinky-golden glow. She was at ease. She wore no mask. Felt no need to pretend she was anyone or anything other than what she was right at this moment.

Gently she wiped the blood from her skin. Tendrils of pink swirled around her, and the waters carried it away.

As soon as she was certain that every last bit of blood had washed off, she looked up and gasped. The room had completely changed. Warm candlelight bathed the space, and altars surrounded her. The waters had turned gold. Glittering. *Perfect.*

She couldn't quite understand it, but in that moment something inside her had changed. She knew things she didn't understand yet.

Everything felt right.

NINETEEN

Mayté

Mayté and Alejandro didn't stop running until they reached the library. Once inside, they worked together to push the plush chairs in front of the door.

Alejandro paced in front of the makeshift barricade like a caged animal. Every little crackle from the fireplace made him jump until he suddenly whirled around and grabbed her shoulders. "You need to return to your room."

"No!" Mayté squirmed away. "He was going to *kill* you, Alejandro. And I . . . I can't live another second in here!" She blinked back angry tears. "I can't let this place take any more people I care about. This is all wrong!"

"Mayté." Alejandro's voice hardened into a warning, yet his eyes spilled over with pain.

"I know," she choked out. He didn't have to tell her.

There wasn't enough time to search the entire library. If they were going to find a way, they needed it *now*. She gripped the edges of the bookshelf. "Please," she whispered. "Please. I'm desperate. I'll do anything." A hot tear slipped down her cheek. "Show me the information I need to get out of this." She grabbed a book and flipped it open.

A list of names. A record. Slowly she sank into the nearest chair.

"What is it?" Alejandro whispered.

Mayté couldn't stop to answer. Her eyes scanned the page, trying to make sense of the names. "Winners," she whispered to herself. Listed was every winner followed by the final card they had used.

El Beso de la Fortuna.

El Beso de la Fortuna.

El Beso de la Fortuna.

She already knew that. How was this supposed to help her? Still, something in her gut told her not to push this aside just yet. She flipped through a couple more pages and found another set of entries. Endless wealth. A lifetime of treasure. Wait. These were the wishes of those who had won. Mayté read faster.

Ruler of her family.

King of his nation.

Owner of all the properties in the city.

Every winner received a single wish. It was another fact she already knew. *Free everyone.* That didn't feel like enough. Lo, Carlos, Dominic, and Mayté herself had reasons for coming here. Desperate dreams that only magic could solve. They would just be returning to Milagro, problems and all.

There had to be more to it. There was a reason the house had led her to choose this book. Then she saw it. A different kind of wish printed in glimmering gold letters.

Mayté gasped.

"What? What?" Alejandro asked.

"I know how we're going to get everyone out!" She jumped from her seat and paced. "Even you!"

Alejandro looked baffled, but there was the slightest glimmer of hope in his hazel eyes.

Mayté could already imagine a future where everyone was free from this place. Lo, Carlos, Dominic . . . and Alejandro.

"I still don't understand," Alejandro said. "What did you read—"

The door burst open, toppling over the chairs blocking it.

Mayté yelped, and Alejandro moved in front of her.

Time was up.

But it wasn't a furious Misterioso that had come into the room. No. Dominic had stumbled inside. Maybe the house had led him to her. It was actually the only explanation.

Mayté felt herself relax, but only for a moment.

Dominic's face was pale and his hair drenched in sweat. "Mayté." He wheezed air. "I had to get to you. Something's wrong with Lorena."

"Where is she?" She rushed for the door, but Dominic grabbed her arms. "What happened?" Mayté demanded.

Dominic stared at her, eyes wide and full of terror.

If Lo got hurt, she would never forgive herself. She shouldn't have stopped looking for her. Damn it. Damn it all.

"TELL ME!"

Dominic took a rasping breath. "I got lost and wandered onto an elevator. When the door opened, I saw Lorena and she . . . was on top of someone." He choked, as if unsure if he wanted to cry or wretch.

Mayté's stomach twisted.

"She was hurting them. M-maybe even *killing* them."

No. She shook out of his grip and backed away.

Dominic talked faster and faster. "There was blood. So much blood. That's all I saw. I pressed the button as fast as I could. I had to get out of there."

It had to be a mistake. Maybe another illusion. Maybe it was still punishing Dominic for giving the potion to Carlos. That was the only explanation. Because Lo would never—

"Attention, contestants." Misterioso's voice chimed through the room, an agitated growl evident in his words.

Mayté and Alejandro exchanged fearful glances.

"We are moving up the penultimate round. Please be in the gaming den within the next half hour. The wager for this round will be your souls."

TWENTY

Lo

Lo finished washing up and climbed out of the pool. She had felt nothing but euphoria while in the warm, golden liquid, but as soon as she spotted her bloodied gown, the feeling faded. Brownish red spatters stained the delicate pink fabric. There was no way to hide it. People would see when she returned to the game.

Mayté would see. Lo couldn't bear the thought of her best friend screaming in horror like Sofia had, or staring accusingly like Sera.

Unsure of what to do, Lo turned away and gasped. Hanging from a rack was a towel and a black gown.

That definitely hadn't been there when she got in here.

The house knew. And yet . . . instead of judging her, it was helping her hide her sins. Like an old friend in on the secret. With a smile, Lo dried off before slipping on the gown.

It was beautiful. The most beautiful thing she had ever worn. The long sleeves flared out like chiffon flowers at her forearms. The collar was made out of raven feathers, and the plunging bodice was gilded in gold. She admired her reflection in the pool. She looked like the queen of Fortune's Kiss.

She turned to leave, but paused and dipped the letter opener in the pool, washing the blood off. She slipped it back down her bodice.

She was ready for the next round.

The house no longer felt like an impossible maze or an ever-changing labyrinth. Somehow, Lo knew exactly where to go. She strode the hallways with confidence, but paused when she heard voices.

Whispers leaked from a cracked door. Mayté's whispers. Lo could recognize her best friend's voice from anywhere. She grinned and moved closer to the door, just about to push it open.

"Are you sure about this?"

The sound of a deep voice made her stop. Who was Mayté talking to? Lo leaned closer to the opening in the door and peeked just in time to see Mayté rush over to someone. Her long robes spilled out behind her like moonbeams as she hugged the person. Holding her breath, Lo squinted, nose inches away from the cracks. Alejandro.

"Yes, yes, I'm positive!" Mayté's voice rang out with absolute joy. The kind that was infectious. Lo found herself smiling. Mayté was surely using Alejandro for hints at surviving this next round. Smart. "Once I use El Beso de la Fortuna to win, I'll get you out of here. I promise!"

Lo's heart stopped.

She was planning on escaping with *him*? What about everything they had been through? Their promises? *Their pact.*

No. This couldn't be real. This was an illusion from the house. It was trying to make her hate her best friend.

But no matter how hard she squeezed her eyes shut and bit the insides of her cheeks, it wouldn't end. She fought against the thought that wormed its way through her skull.

This is real.

A stab of betrayal and shot straight to Lo's heart. She swore that she felt the blood draining from her body, leaving behind an empty cold.

Was Mayté just going to leave her here to die? It was impossible to wrap her mind around it. This couldn't be, yet the truth shone before her. The girl she'd thought was her best friend was plotting with some worthless boy behind Lo's back.

Behind my back.

"Don't look at me like that!" Mayté grabbed Alejandro's shoulders. "We're doing this. It's going to work! It has to."

"Mayté! Oh, Mayté!" Alejandro suddenly lifted her up in the air. Mayté shrieked and the two burst into laughter. Then they kissed.

Lo backed away, shaking. She was too numb to feel the achy lump in her throat.

"As soon as we get back to Milagro, I'll teach you how to paint."

"I think I'd much rather see *you* paint. But I can show you my drawings."

"Perfect. We'll make art together."

Lo stormed off, unable to take any more of it. With every step, the walls swayed.

How could Mayté do this to her? How could she let herself fall for him? Was it because he was the first boy to show her the least bit of attention? Was Mayté that pathetic? That desperate? Didn't she realize men couldn't be trusted, especially the ones here?

La Sirena was right, Alejandro was going to shatter Mayté's heart the first chance he had.

But maybe she deserved it.

Lo reached the elevator and smashed her palm against the button.

"Lo?"

Lo bit down on her lip and clenched her fists, before turning to see Mayté rush over.

"I . . . I'm so sorry." Mayté's eyes filled with tears.

Sorry?

"I shouldn't have been so dismissive about your mother. I never wanted to be right about her." With a small whimper, Mayté hugged her.

The hug should have been warm and comforting. Just hours earlier, it would have been something she desperately needed, but now Lo stiffened and didn't return the embrace. A silence lingered between the two. But it wasn't the normal kind of silence. The kind on cool summer mornings where Mayté toiled away trying to paint the distant mountains as Lo lay in the grass. This silence, in the midst of lies, deception, and betrayal . . . this silence was deadly.

"It's fine. I'll get over it." And she would, once she destroyed everything.

Mayté pulled away and looked Lo up and down. "Your dress," she said with a frown.

"That other gown was becoming too stuffy," Lo answered simply.

Mayté's eyebrows knit and her eyes slowly grew as if she were looking at Lo for the first time.

Lo's stomach sank. Mayté was making her nervous. Why was she acting like that? It was almost as if she were frightened.

Did she know what Lo had done? She couldn't have, and yet . . .

Ding.

The elevator doors opened. Lo waited for Mayté to step inside, but she didn't. "What's the matter?" Lo asked.

Mayté slowly backed away. Each tiny step chipped further and further into Lo's already wounded heart. "I should probably change out of my nightgown. You go on without me." She wouldn't meet her eyes.

A part of Lo wanted to tell her no, but another part of her, the part that was numb, wanted to just leave without her. That was the part she listened to. Without a word, she turned away and stepped into the elevator to head to the second to last round of Fortune's Kiss.

She should have been scared. Terrified, even, yet her pounding heart calmed. It didn't matter. Mayté talked about El Beso de la Fortuna. She said getting that would help her win. It was a card. Lo felt it in her gut. She would get it, and bringing the house down would be her winning wish.

And she wasn't going to let any worthless people get in her way.

TWENTY-ONE

Mayté

Mayté was supposed to return to the suite and change out of her nightgown and robe. But now she found herself stuck. So many thoughts bounced through her head and competed for her full attention. The discovery of the El Beso de la Fortuna card. Knowing exactly what she had to do to free everyone from the house. The brief taste of Alejandro's lips against hers. But, most of all, her thoughts kept returning to Lo.

Lo had seemed so strange. As if she were a completely different person. Not the dearest friend Mayté had grown up with. There was something odd about her demeanor. She looked beautiful in her black gown. But all the gowns in their suite had been bright and colorful. Not the color of shadows in the night.

When she had looked at Lo, she'd felt something off, but she couldn't figure out *why* or *what* it could be.

"Mayté? What are you doing in your nightgown?"

Carlos approached her in front of the elevator, clad in a suit. His dark eyes squinted with exhaustion.

Mayté clutched her satchel tighter. Inside was her father's framed photo and calavera. This was the moment she most dreaded. She pushed the button to call the elevator if only to buy her an extra second to pull herself together. "I need to tell you something."

"What is it?"

The elevator doors opened, they got in, and Mayté looked to the ceiling, blinking back tears. She had never noticed that it was painted to match the night sky: stars winked and glistened like gems floating in a sea of ink.

"Mayté, what happened?"

She took a shaky breath. "F-fa—" She snapped her mouth shut before her voice could completely shatter. If she dared speak, she would completely break down, and that wouldn't help anything. She needed to collect herself, so, instead, she pulled out the photograph and calavera and forced them into her brother's hands.

"Wha—?" Carlos flinched as he studied the photograph. "Where did you get this?"

"Father gambled here," she blurted out. It was painful and her vision blurred, but there was also a relief. Just like ripping out a splinter. "This . . ." She took a shaky breath as a hot tear crawled down her cheek. "This is what happened to our family's fortune."

Carlos didn't say a word. Instead, he just stood there, mouth agape. But soon his eyes twitched and his lips curled. He hurled the calavera at the wall. It shattered into thousands of pieces, leaving a spatter of brown. He shouted a string of curses. Mayté felt every vile word because the exact same thing had gone through her head. "Why?" His shouting and anger morphed into tears. "He had *everything.* So why?" The frame slipped from his fingers and landed with a thud. "Why would he come here?"

"I have no idea." Mayté knelt to pick up the photograph. A long crack stretched along the glass. She changed her mind and instead hugged her brother. The two stood like that for several moments as the elevator ascended. Just silence, and the tears dripping down their faces. She finally broke that silence. "We're here because of him, and if we lose . . ."

"We'll either die a gruesome death or live to become just like him," Carlos croaked.

Their father had destroyed their future. Becoming like him was a fate worse than death. "The only way to avoid that is to win," Mayté said. "And I know exactly how to do it; I know a way that we can *all* escape from here."

Carlos's eyebrows rose.

"So, please." She wiped her tears. "You have to trust me and make sure you keep surviving. Okay?" Now she was more determined than ever to save everyone.

"I should have trusted you from the very beginning," Carlos said as the doors opened.

She gave his arm one final squeeze before the two stepped out into the gaming den, leaving behind the remnants of their father's greatest mistake.

Lo was already seated between Dominic and the shopkeeper. She wouldn't even look in Mayté's direction.

Carlos glanced between the two girls, but said nothing as he and Mayté took the only two seats left.

What was going on with Lo? Even the Banker, who stood at the table shuffling cards, kept glancing at her, a mixture of bewilderment and concern in his blue eyes. He was usually as slick as a serpent. Smug and nonchalant, but right now he looked disturbed.

Misterioso strode into the room. "Everyone's here. Let's begin!" he growled.

Mayté didn't dare look as he rested his hand on the back of her chair; she felt his imposing presence directly behind her.

"This round should be short and straightforward," he spat. "Souls are on the line. We play until one person is eliminated."

Mayté broke into a sweat. One person. After that would be the final round. El Beso de la Fortuna would surely appear then. But they still needed to get through this round. She glanced around the table. Carlos, Dominic, Lo, even the shopkeeper: she couldn't stand the thought of any of them dying.

But one of them would have to.

"Understood?" Misterioso drummed his fingers against the back of her seat. She felt each of those forceful taps in her heart. She finally dared a look up at him, and froze. He had swapped out his white calavera mask for a black one. It was made from harsh angles and looked almost decayed. The large round eye-holes emphasized the murderous way he stared down at her.

"Wait a minute," the shopkeeper said, stealing away Misterioso's attention.

No longer under his terrifying scrutiny, Mayté let herself breathe.

"We're not all here. What about Don Zelaya?" the shopkeeper asked.

Her heart thudded.

"That's right. Where is he?" Carlos murmured as he looked around the room.

"I'm afraid Don Martín Zelaya is no longer with us," Misterioso said plainly.

"He dropped out of the game?" the shopkeeper spat in disbelief. "What a foolish move."

Dominic looked down, conflict written all over his face.

And Lo? She stared calmly, straight ahead.

Had Lo killed Don Zelaya? He was a nasty, horrible monster. He must have threatened Lo somehow. Had he done something to her? Was that why she was acting so strangely?

"Banker, begin the game," Mysterioso said.

Everything felt wrong. Yet the game began as usual with the Banker calling out cards and everyone placing beans on their boards. Cards like El Tifón, which unleashed strong winds through the gambling den; El Venado, which summoned a herd of deer that walked around and munched on the vases of marigolds; and La Sandia, which prompted the servers to set out plates of sliced watermelon. Lo took a big bite of hers and wiped away the dribbling juices from her chin.

She still wouldn't look at Mayté. Instead, she studied her board. "Oh! Lotería!" she shouted and flicked her hand.

The Banker leaned over to check her card. Even he looked like he didn't believe it.

"Congratulations." Misterioso waved his cane, and an image of Lo's board appeared. It showed beans covering the first row and column. "Double lotería. How fortunate for you." But he hardly sounded pleased. "You may draw two cards."

Lo plucked two cards from the Banker and held them high for everyone to see.

There was El Cotorro, which showed a green parakeet on a branch; the other one was La Corona. The same card that Xiomara had given Don Zelaya.

"We . . ." Misterioso's eyes widened as if he were taken aback. Seeing the man who had presided over so much carnage made Mayté feel ill. Something was seriously wrong. "We'll start with El Cotorro," he said, voice strained and flat. "This card can be used on another player, who then must truthfully answer your questions or else lose their wager."

"Then I'll use it now," Lo said.

"On whom?" Misterioso asked, looking oddly relieved.

Lo pointed at Mayté.

"Me?" Mayté asked in disbelief. "Why me?"

Misterioso eyed Lo suspiciously. "In order to keep your soul, you must answer Lorena's questions truthfully."

The room spun. Why would Lo do this?

No one had actually lost their soul in sudden death, but Mayté was almost certain what losing meant: sharing the same fate as Senor Vasquez, if not something much worse.

The card flashed and a parakeet flew out of it. Its colorful tail feathers trailed behind it like elegant ribbons as it landed on Lo's shoulder.

"Ask as many questions as you wish until El Cotorro stops you."

Lo gently stroked her finger under the bird's chin. "Mayté, are you jealous of me?"

Mayté's heart stopped.

Lo simply stared inquisitively with a knowing smile.

Mayté's face burned. She became hyperaware of all the eyes on her. The gazes from the other croupiers, the other contestants. But most of all, she felt Lo's eyes.

"I—I—yes." Mayté couldn't lie. "I have been jealous of you." She looked down.

"Truth," El Cotorro squawked.

"Why?" Lo asked.

Mayté's head shot back up. Lo still smiled, brown eyes cold. Mayté clenched her fist, nails digging into her palms. "B—because all the boys adore you. They've always paid more attention to you and not me." Her voice cracked. Vocalizing her darkest feelings—everything she despised about herself—hurt.

"You're the prettier one. And you've never had to worry about money." She sucked in her cheeks, willing herself not to cry.

"Truth," El Cotorro squawked again.

That wasn't the full story. The truth was that it wasn't Lo's fault, and Mayté never held it against her. "But, Lo, I—"

"What about the croupier, Alejandro?"

Mayté's heart stopped.

"What do you think of him?"

"H—he's handsome. And kind. And . . . he makes me feel safe," she rasped.

"Truth."

"Please, no more," Mayté whispered.

But Lo ignored her. "Do you want to save him?"

The uncomfortable, slimy humiliation hardened into piercing thorns. How did Lo know about that? "Y—yes."

The room spun. If Lo kept prodding, would she make Mayté reveal the plan about El Beso de la Fortuna? Misterioso circled the table like a hungry shark, glaring eyes trained on her.

"Truth." El Cotorro flew from Lo's shoulder and headed for Mayté. "Reversal, reversal," it squawked and landed on her shoulders. It dug its talons in, but she barely felt it. Her entire body was a mixture of terror and fury.

No one said anything. Not even Misterioso. Not until the Banker cleared his throat.

"A reversal," Misterioso said quietly. He didn't smile. "María Teresa, you may ask Lorena a question, which she must truthfully answer."

"What? Why?" Lo demanded.

"Everything comes at a price," El Cotorro squawked.

Her lips pursed.

Mayté's heart skipped. So many questions came to mind. Why was Lo doing this? What had happened? Were they still friends? Had Lo really killed Don Zelaya?

But she had to choose her question carefully.

Lo had been strange and cruel. Mayté needed to know that the Lo she loved was still there. That her heart was still beating.

"Lo, if there was a way to save everyone here, would you?"

Carlos sat up straighter. Dominic looked down. Lo stared blankly.

Yes, Mayté thought, you would save everyone. You would. Because you're a good person. You're my best friend. You're—

"No," Lo finally answered.

Mayté gripped the table. If she hadn't, she might have fallen from her seat.

"Truth." El Cotorro stayed on her shoulder. She had time for another question.

"Have you killed anyone?"

Lo jolted. Her wide eyes begged Mayté to take the question back. But she couldn't. Even if she wanted to.

Carlos made a small noise, while Dominic kept his head down.

"Yes."

"Who?" She blurted before El Cotorro flew off.

Lo's face pinched. She looked down. "Don Zelaya and . . . my father." The way she said that last part. It wasn't an accident, was it?

Mayté couldn't believe it. *Didn't want to.*

But Lo didn't want to save everyone . . .

And Lo had lied to her about her father. What else had she lied about?

Her best friend was a murderer.

El Cotorro flew around the room.

"Let's get the game moving," Lo muttered, voice cold. She held up the La Corona. She wouldn't look at Mayté. "What does this one do?"

The Banker's eyes darted all around and Misterioso gritted his teeth. Was that fear?

"I'm sure you recall, that's the card that Don Zelaya received," he replied. "*How fitting.*"

Lo scoffed. "Tell me what the card does. Now." The card flashed and vanished into a million tiny lights that gathered atop Lo's head and transformed into a crown.

Misterioso grunted as if pained. "The card allows you to order anyone to do your bidding and they will have to obey."

When Xiomara first drew the card, Mayté thought it only would work on the other players. That they would have to obey the order or lose the wager, but she had been dead wrong. The card's magic forced the commanded to obey. If the orders worked on Misterioso, would it work on *everyone* in the house?

"Lo!" Mayté gasped. "Command Misterioso to free us all!"

Dominic coughed and Carlos stared between Mayté and Lo. Even the shopkeeper, who had looked groggy and grumpy, perked up.

"Why?" Lo asked, her voice stone-cold.

Her words were like a punch in the gut. Mayté couldn't breathe.

"Lo!" Carlos snapped.

"What are you doing, you stupid girl?" the shopkeeper screamed. "You're going to get us all killed."

"Enough," Lo snapped. "I've grown quite bored of this round. Let's end it." She pointed at the shopkeeper. "You're going to listen to *me*."

"What?" He jumped up from his seat, but this time there was more than just snobbish irritation on his face. There was fear. Pure terror. "Wh-what are you saying? Y-you're not going to kill me, are you? You can't do that."

"Don't!" Mayté blurted. Now Lo turned to her, but Mayté wished she hadn't. The nasty scowl on Lo's face made her stomach ache. "Please. Think, Lo. You can free us all, right now."

"He humiliated you," Lo growled. "He prevented you from finishing your commission: he doesn't deserve to be free."

"Wha—?" The shopkeeper stood. "It was nothing personal. Truly! I have a family to feed. My wife had just had twins. W-we weren't prepared. W-we—"

"Oh, how ironic," Lo mocked. "The reason you came here is the reason you'll die."

"LORENA." Mayté pounded the table. "Don't. You. Dare." No one else deserved to die. No matter how terrible they were.

Lo's eyes widened. Mayté rarely called her by her full name. A wounded look crossed her face, and she looked away. "I'll be merciful this time." She folded her hands together, resting her chin atop her fingers. "Señor Shopkeeper, I order you to fold."

"What?" the shopkeeper squawked.

"No," Mayté gasped. "If he forfeits, he'll—"

Lo simply lifted a hand, cutting her off. "Misterioso, he will work here instead."

Misterioso looked bewildered. "Very well," he said.

Lo looked satisfied. "See? He won't die or lose his soul. Are you happy, Mayté?"

"I—I—" Mayté stammered. Her hands wouldn't stop shaking. No. This was all wrong. Now he would be just like Alejandro, trapped, unhappy, losing his humanity bit by bit, for eternity. She whispered. "Why are you doing this?"

"I'm just playing the game," Lo replied simply. "I'm keeping *our* promise and doing my best to make sure *we* win." She turned back to the shopkeeper. "Go ahead!"

"I—I forfeit." The shopkeeper broke down into bitter weeping.

Mayté looked away and swallowed hard.

"Well, then," Misterioso said, sounding exhausted. "Antonio Rivera has been eliminated. I suppose this concludes this round. Our final round will begin in two hours."

"Good." Lo stood and dusted off her black gown. "Misterioso, Banker, follow me." She waltzed toward the elevator.

The Banker gasped and Misterioso cursed, but the two followed her, steps wobbling and strained as if they couldn't control their bodies.

Was the card still in effect? The crown hadn't vanished from Lo's head.

"Wait!" Mayté chased after her.

Lo whirled around. "Don't follow me!"

Mayté's legs abruptly froze, nearly causing her to fall over. She couldn't move them, no matter how hard she tried.

"All the rest of you, too."

All Mayté could do was watch helplessly as Lo, Misterioso, and the Banker stepped into the elevator. She couldn't do anything to stop the doors from closing. The last thing she saw was Lo's face. Cold, with a dark glint in her brown eyes.

TWENTY-TWO

Lo

Now it was just the three of them. Lo couldn't let herself think. Not fully. She couldn't give herself time to regret punishing Mayté. Nothing mattered. Not until she destroyed the house. "Show me, how did the Banker and Misterioso come to be in their positions?" This time her command wasn't directed at a living person, but the house itself.

A mirrored wall changed, the reflection shifting to the Banker standing in front of a pool. The same one she'd washed in. He looked different. His long black hair hung freely, and his dark suit was much less flashy than what he wore to the games, but the most striking part was his face. Dark circles hung under his eyes and his expression held a sense of devastation.

He stepped into the water, clothes and all. When he emerged, he looked sure and refreshed. The familiar smirk played on his lips.

The reflection shifted again, revealing a man running through the house as it rumbled. Dozens of alebrijes, creatures of all shapes and sizes, pursued him. He ducked away as claws and tusks jutted out, trying to gut him. The floor beneath him opened, and he jumped. He landed in the pool room and for a moment was submerged in the waters. He emerged from them and frantically knocked over a table full of trinkets. A mask lay among them. He snatched it and put it on, before turning back to face the alebrijes. One by one, they vanished. The man grinned, revealing deep-set dimples. Misterioso.

It all clicked together like beans being placed on a Lotería board.

She'd wanted to destroy the house—commanded it to show her how.

The house led her to the same pool. Which she had bathed in, and now she was powerful. Just as powerful, she sensed, as the two men before her.

She reached up and adjusted the crown on her head. No wonder they both seemed so skittish.

"Which one of you two is in charge?" she asked.

"Neither," the Banker said.

Interesting.

"Very well." She pointed to the Banker. "You will take me to the one in charge." The elevator doors opened, but before Lo and the Banker could step out, Misterioso blocked the way.

"No! Enough!" He flinched as if the words themselves pained him. He was resisting her orders. Just barely, but it was still enough for him to corner her against the wall.

"Don't touch me!" she snapped just as he reached for her.

His arms shook and he grunted, fighting against himself.

"Oh, Misterioso." She stroked the side of his mask before sneering. "Don't make me rip off your mask. We both know what happens if I do." For some reason, the house had wanted him dead, yet now it couldn't recognize him from behind the mask.

That was enough to get him to stumble back, hands up in surrender.

Lo hooked arms with the Banker. "Now, shall we?"

Silently, as if defeated, Banker led her into another elevator. They soon reached the familiar hallway with the red door at the end. It wasn't a surprise that the main Gamemaker would reside on this mysterious floor. The Banker stared straight ahead, face full of concern. It was quite amusing to see him finally squirm.

"Lorena, what have you done?"

"I made myself like you."

The way he recoiled amused her. "What's the matter? Don't want to share the power of the house?"

"It wasn't supposed to happen like this. Why didn't you come to my chambers like I asked?" He spoke almost frantically.

"Don't worry." She patted his arm, feeling him shiver. "I won't hurt you as long as you do as I say. Tell me your name."

His eyes widened.

She simply grinned at him.

When he had the upper hand, he'd held on to his name as if it were some kind of prize. Lo wanted it. "Tell me."

He sighed. "Miguel."

"Miguel," she repeated in amusement. "Miguel Ángel?" The archangel's name was incredibly popular in Milagro.

"Yes, but I'm no angel. I go only by Miguel now."

"I suppose we have more in common than you thought." She stroked his cheek. He flinched. "I thought this was a game to you. Is it no longer fun? Now will you take me more seriously, Miguel?"

"Is this what you really want?" he whispered.

"Yes." She lifted her chin. "Why are you even questioning me, Señor Gamemaker? You have what *you* want, don't you?"

"No," he croaked.

"What exactly happened with your precious little Ana Lùcia? Tell me."

His face pinched. "She . . . became a Gamemaker . . ." He spat out the words as if they burned his mouth. They stopped in front of a door. "Please, you don't want to do this!"

"Wait a moment." Lo giggled. "Your beloved became a Gamemaker? Oh! I understand. She must be the one in charge here. You don't want me to destroy her."

"Lorena—"

"Well, that's just too bad." She pushed past him and flung the door open, revealing a suite fit for a king. Hundreds—no, thousands of candles illuminated the room. Golden flames clashed with the silver moonlight leaking through the floor-to-ceiling windows. Everything looked as if it had been dipped in gold and sprinkled with crushed diamonds. The glittery glass floor, the plush furniture, the fur rugs, and the velvet curtains. The back wall was pure gold with different gems poking out. Bloodred rubies, fiery amber, tearstained aquamarine, along with glittering opals and diamonds. Sitting in the center of the shining extravagance was a woman sipping wine.

It wasn't Ana Lùcia.

Bouncy brown curls framed her beautiful bronze face. Inquisitive eyes stared at Lo. Familiar ones.

"Lorena," she sighed.

The room's glittering opulence became dizzying. Lo's legs almost gave out on her. This was another trick of the house, or her broken mind had finally turned against her.

It was Mamá.

She wore a tailored suit, a marigold at her lapel.

"Hija." Mamá set aside the wine and slowly stood.

Dios, this was real. It really *was* Mamá.

"You're . . . alive!" Lo choked. The joy coursing through her was almost too much to handle. She *knew* it. Everyone else had been wrong. She rushed to Mamá to hug her, but her mind caught up with her heart.

Mamá was safe. She wasn't tied up or hurt. Her eyes weren't bloodshot after endlessly crying. There was no villain holding her captive. In fact, it looked like she had been living like a queen.

Lo stopped in front of her. Strange—they were the same height. Lo no longer had to look up to meet her eyes.

Just like the illusion created by La Dama, Mamá hadn't aged a day since she left, but there was something different about her.

Her eyes lacked their warm sparkle. No matter how terrible her father was, no matter how loudly he screamed at her or how vile his threats, Mamá could always pull herself together with a playful wink and sweet smile for her daughters. But now she stared blankly, calm and cool.

"I thought you were dead . . . La Dama—"

"I know," Mamá said. "Everyone else was convinced of my demise. You have a much stronger will. While it's admirable, some things are better kept secret." She sat back down. "Now, please, sit. Your feet must be hurting."

She remembered. As a child, Lo had complained of her achy feet whenever she had to walk for a long time. Her father would snarl at her to stop complaining, but Mamá would pick her up and carry her the rest of the way.

Lo shook her head. "No, thank you. I'll stand."

Mamá's eyebrows twisted, but she looked more amused than hurt.

"What happened to you?"

"I could ask you the same, Lorena. I see you've found your way to the heart of Fortune's Kiss."

Lo stared. How did she—

"It was a little premature. Though it *is* fortunate that you discovered it on your own," Mamá continued. "If someone had led you there, that would have been cheating. Cheaters can't win. Their souls are consumed by the house once the game ends."

Lo shook her head. "What?"

"You'll see soon enough. Mayté is cheating with one of my croupiers. It's a shame, too. I was beginning to grow fond of Alejandro. I had such high hopes for him."

Lo's heart pounded wildly. She backed away. There was too much to process.

"Though Misterioso may get to them first. He's the only one who loathes cheating more than the house itself."

"What? No!" Lo snapped. She had to think. She still had her crown. "I order you not to let that happen!"

"Oh, my!" Mamá chuckled and stood. With an icy smile, she smacked the crown off Lo's head. It landed with a thud and vanished into smoke. "That won't work with me. But don't fret," she cooed as if consoling a small child. "Perhaps Alejandro will die first. Since Mayté never asked him to cheat with her, the house may consider his death fair payment and spare her."

The room spun. Lo couldn't breathe. She was the one who had told Mayté to talk to Alejandro in the first place.

Mamá studied her with uncaring amusement.

For years, all Lo had ever wanted was a reunion with Mamá. Now . . . who was this person?

"You *won* the game, didn't you?" It hadn't quite sunk in until now. She had asked Miguel to lead her to the one in charge. *Mamá* was the one in charge.

Lo knew it was true, yet terror filled her veins when Mamá simply nodded.

"Why didn't you come home?" Lo asked. It was the most she could muster without breaking.

Mamá simply smiled. "There was more for me here."

Lo's heart stopped. In the end, her mother had simply abandoned her. Her father was right. And Lo had refused to believe that it was even a possibility.

"I had my reasons, Lorena. Your father's wealth kept you and your sisters safe and comfortable. If he had gotten anywhere near me, he would've likely killed—"

"He's dead," Lo blurted. "I did it myself."

"I know. When we measured your soul, we saw everything."

Lo bit her lip. She didn't know what to say. None of it made sense. "Do you know how terrible things have been for us? He brainwashed Sera and Sofía. They think that his cruelty is love. And me? He wanted to marry me off to a man *just like him?*"

"Who?" Mamá asked as if it was all harmless gossip.

"Juan Felipe Garcia," Lo spat.

"Ah." She crossed her legs. "He was a vile child. Spoiled, always getting what he wanted. His mother told me he would erupt into tantrums and bite her until she bled. It's no surprise he grew up to be a pig."

"Mamá," Lo snapped in disbelief. "Father hurt me. Before I killed him, he became wild. He threatened me. I didn't know what he would do." An angry sob tore past her throat. "That's what you left me with."

"But you're here now. And you're doing quite well at the games. You may even win."

Lo backed away. *May?* She couldn't believe her ears. Mamá was the person in charge of this el infierno.

Lo backed into a shelf, causing the contents to topple over. A skull mask and a black veil caught her eye. The same one that Pearla wore during sudden death. "Y-you're . . ."

"Yes." Mamá sighed. "I had to make sure you knew I was gone, because I'm no longer the woman you knew."

"You're right," Lo rasped. "That woman would have done anything to protect her daughters."

"Ah, but I have done so much for you from the moment you arrived, Lorena. I asked Miguel to look out for you. I added an extra contestant to the game so Mayté could compete with you. I even made sure you and Mayté got to sleep in the finest suite."

Lo felt numb. It all made sense. But: "You . . . you still promised to return, and you *didn't*."

"I had every intention of returning. But once I was given the choice, I didn't want to leave Fortune's Kiss. It became . . . everything to me."

Each of her words was like a venomous barb latching on to her heart.

Lo had come here for her Mamá. This woman wasn't her. Not anymore.

There was nothing left here to fight for.

Nothing worth saving.

And then a small voice inside her whispered, "Except Mayté." *Mayté.*

The red haze that had surrounded her every thought began to dissipate, and for a moment everything became clear as a cloudless morning.

Without another word, Lo ran from the room. *Take me to Mayté. Take me straight to her.* But the house wasn't leading her in any particular direction. Was her power gone? Had her mother removed it?

She lifted her skirts and sprinted to the elevator. She kept smacking the button until the doors opened. She had to find Mayté before it was too late.

The elevator descended, but not fast enough. Soon Lo heard muffled shouts.

"Stop! Don't hurt her! It's me you want! STOP!"

The doors opened and Lo stumbled into the gaming den. A crowd of croupiers surrounded a table.

"Stop!" Alejandro yelled, as other croupiers held him back. His makeup was smeared and his left eye bruised and swollen. Blood dribbled down his busted lip. His wide eyes were trained on something across the room.

Lo's heart almost stopped.

Misterioso had Mayté by the neck, pinned against the main table. "You've made enough of a mockery of my game!" he snarled. "And now that you've cheated, the house won't care what I do to you!"

Lo's vision flashed red. "STOP!"

"L-Lo," Mayté whimpered.

"Cheaters cannot win," Misterioso hissed. "Either I deal with them or the house will."

He was right. Lo's mother had said as much.

But there was a way out.

Alejandro met Lo's eyes. He knew it, too: the one way they could give Mayté a chance to survive.

"Please," he said quietly. "I'm begging you." He lowered his head.

Lo knew exactly what Alejandro was asking. She knew what she had to do.

She strode toward him.

"Lo?" Mayté whimpered.

"Lo? What are you—?" Carlos. He was being restrained at another table. Dominic was with him. "Stop!"

Lo couldn't feel her own heart pounding anymore. Maybe it was gone. Destroyed.

She pulled the letter opener out of her bodice.

It had to be done. Lo believed her mother. It was her house, after all.

This was the *only* way.

Lo plunged the letter opener deep into Alejandro's heart.

TWENTY-THREE

Mayté

This wasn't real.

The other croupiers released Alejandro. He dropped onto the floor, a bloodied dagger in his chest.

This was a terrible nightmare.

Mayté knew she would wake up and thank Dios that none of it was real. She would wake up. *She had to.* But the longer she stood there, looking between Lo and the boy she cared for, the more it sank in.

Lo had stabbed Alejandro. She had killed him.

Mayté screamed.

Misterioso backed away, hissing curses under his breath.

"Wh-wh-why?" Mayté's lips wobbled.

"It was the only way to save you," Lo responded.

Mayté dropped to her knees and crawled over to Alejandro. A pool of blood had already formed around him. His face twisted in pain and his chest heaved. She didn't know what to do. An icy shock flowed through her. Even her tears felt cold as they dripped down her cheek.

Alejandro! No one was trying to help him. Why weren't they?

The elevator doors opened and the Banker stepped out, face extra pale. He didn't spare a glance at the bloody sight before him. "She's amused. She wants to push up the final round." With a sigh, he shook his head. "Someone clean this mess up." He headed back for the elevator.

"Go with him. All of you," Lo ordered Misterioso and the other croupiers with a growl. Even without the magic of La Carona, they obeyed. After they left, Lo herself sauntered to the elevator without looking back.

Carlos and Dominic remained, yet Mayté barely noticed them. The rest of the gambling den blurred around her until all she could see was Alejandro. With a sob, she folded herself over him. It didn't matter that blood stained her robe and nightgown. "A-Alejandro . . . ?" If she could race back to Carlos's suite, perhaps there was a little bit of Dominic's potion. "I have a bit of Dedo de Dios."

"No," Alejandro said, voice soft. He grabbed her hand, squeezing it: his fingers felt weak. "Stay . . . with me . . ." Tears coated his dark lashes. His lips twitched into a smile. Even as the life gradually dulled from his hazel eyes, they were still as beautiful as ever.

"Win . . . the game . . . be . . . happy."

"NO!" Mayté sobbed and pressed his hand against her cheek. His knuckles felt cold.

They were supposed to leave *together*.

All of the could-have-beens swirled through her mind. Beautiful, but faded as the harsh grays of reality overtook them. They would never get to step into Milagro together. She would never get to show him the beautiful sunrise and the way the soft amber and pink hues painted over the distant mountains. He would never taste elote fresh off the grill or pick out a colorful serape to drape over the grass as the two of them lounged in the fountain garden. They would never make art together or know what could have happened between them outside of this hellish place. All of their beautiful hopes and wishes were now tainted with blood.

Alejandro tried to stroke her cheek, but his arm fell. He stiffened. He was gone. *Dead.*

Mayté took Alejandro's hand and pressed it against her cheek. "NO," she whispered.

There was nothing she could do to get him back.

She sat there with him, not knowing how much time had passed. It could have been a few minutes or several hours, but soon she heard footsteps. It wasn't Carlos and Dominic come to comfort her. No.

"Señorita, we need to—"

"NO!" She laid herself on top of Alejandro, holding him tight. They weren't going to take him away. She wouldn't allow it.

But she was powerless. They easily pulled her up and dragged her into the elevator.

"Don't touch her!" Carlos snapped, but the workers restrained him and Dominic, forcing them into the elevator as well.

A scream tore through Mayté's raw throat. "ALEJANDRO!" The doors closed.

Mayté stayed in the elevator, curled up on the floor. Carlos and Dominic tried to console her, but she barely heard them. Soon the workers returned and dragged her back into the gaming den, now cleaned and sterilized. But Mayté remembered what had happened here. She would never forget. As soon as they released her, she crumpled to the floor, where she remained and bitterly wept.

Dominic knelt next to her and hugged her tight. Her throat was too hoarse to sob anymore. All she could do was squeeze her eyes shut.

"Damn them," Carlos spat.

"To El Infierno," Dominic agreed before glancing over his shoulder at the figure who had just entered the room.

Mayté bristled when she caught sight of a black gown lingering near the gaming table. *She* was here. *Lo.* Mayté couldn't bear to look at her.

Dominic held Mayté tight.

"Why? Why would Dios allow this to happen?" Mayté rasped.

"I don't know," Dominic whispered. He suddenly burst into hacking coughs. A painful kind full of wheezing.

Bright red blood stained his hand and dribbled down the corner of his mouth.

"Dominic . . ." Mayté looked at him. A ring of purple accentuated his puffy, bloodshot eyes. His cheeks looked sunken and feverish, and his brown skin had lost its golden glow.

"I'm sorry," he whispered. "It always happens at the worst time . . ."

"What? What's going on?"

"I didn't come here for riches or to make Lorena my bride." He hacked into his hands, and let out a gasping breath. He held up both hands, soaked with bright red blood. "I'm dying."

Mayté froze and Carlos's eyes widened.

Lo stood still.

"D-dying?" Mayté whispered.

Dominic nodded and wiped his hand with his handkerchief. "It's been almost a year. No one knows what's wrong. We've tried the best doctors in San Solera, the most well-known curanderas who reside in the district. Not even the most powerful potions work for long. I brought along Dedo de Dios in hopes that it would hold off my fits until my wish was granted, but even that has stopped working. And now, it's worse than it's ever been." He spit out more blood.

Mayté's eyes filled with fresh tears.

A butler approached. She wouldn't have paid him a second thought, but Dominic and Carlos stared hard at him, a look of horror growing on their faces. When Mayté looked again, she understood why.

It was Antonio, the shopkeeper. There were many reasons she didn't recognize him. For one, he had his hair slicked back, and his mustache was trimmed, but most of all it was the vacant look in his eye. He didn't stare at Mayté with contempt. Now he looked like a lifeless doll. Did he remember who he had been mere hours ago?

Misterioso and the Banker walked into the gaming den, trailed by a woman. Mayté choked. She had the same bouncy brown curls and lithe frame as Lo's mother.

Lo hissed and looked away.

"Welcome to our final round," Misterioso announced, a tense undertone in his words. "Gracing us with her presence is our supreme Gamemaker, Loretta de León." His grin twisted into a sneer.

Mayté felt even more numb and empty than before.

Loretta de León.

They had all thought she was dead. Lo had been right all along.

The shopkeeper pulled out a chair for Loretta. With a satisfied smirk, she sat down, crossed her legs, and rested her chin in her hand. Like a queen sitting atop her throne. The true reina del Beso de la Fortuna.

"May San Fortuno show you favor," she drawled.

The woman Mayté had grown up around had seemed so kind and loving. But she had been here in this place for so long. She was cold, flat, bored. The house must have corrupted her.

Just like it had somehow corrupted Lo.

"For our final round, our remaining contestants will play until someone fills their entire board. But beware, the cards have become even more dangerous." Misterioso spoke playfully, as if they were children and he was warning them about El Cucuy. "Let us see how you four fare, shall we? Once again, your wagers are your souls. Good luck."

This was it. The final round. Deep down, Mayté had always known she would make it this far, and yet, *and yet,* this wasn't how she had imagined it at all. She couldn't even bring herself to look at Lo. Instead, she walked over to Dominic and helped him to his seat. She gave Carlos's arm a light squeeze. She made a silent vow. She would do anything she could to keep anyone else from dying.

And it was clear that she would have to do that without Lo's help.

Mayté took a shaky breath and wiped the tears from her eyes. The only available seat was one next to Lo. She took it, and focused on the Banker as he stepped to the center of the table and shuffled the cards. His downcast eyes were the same color as the ocean during a storm.

Lo ignored Mayté and stared directly at him. "You knew about Loretta this entire time. You were working for her. Played me for a fool." Her tone wasn't accusing. No, her voice was devoid of any emotion.

The Banker frowned as if he wanted to say something, but changed his mind. Instead, he began drawing cards. It felt like a surreal blur. All Mayté could truly focus on was filling her board. There was La Campana, which caused a loud bell to ring. The sound echoed against her already throbbing skull. Then there was El Coraje. The strange card depicted a flaming heart with two disembodied hands underneath. A blast of heat erupted from the card washing over everyone at the table. Mayté's heart slammed against her ribcage as dizzying adrenaline made her want to fly out of her seat. Surely this card represented anger. Thoughts of Alejandro, Lo, and all the injustices of the house consumed her, but she couldn't become reckless.

Dominic frowned and Carlos squeezed a handful of beans—everyone at the table had something to be angry about—yet Lo sat calmly.

"This is getting a bit boring, hmm?" A twisted grin formed on Loretta's gorgeous face. "Misterioso, I hope the other rounds you hosted haven't been so dull."

This earned a glare from Misterioso. There was something between the two of them. A power struggle of sorts. Misterioso was the face of Fortune's Kiss. The one who guided everyone to their damnation, while Loretta ruled from the shadows. They were both equally wicked, but in different ways, and it seemed Misterioso didn't want Loretta's darkness to dull his spotlight.

Loretta's smile grew as she clearly relished his anger. "Let's liven it up, shall we? I suggest you hold on to your hats."

"El Abysmo," the Banker called and held up a card.

Mayté didn't have the chance to fully study the purple card before a strong wind rushed around the room.

In the center, a void opened, pulling objects toward it and sucking them inside.

A black hole.

Mayté gripped the table and held on tight.

TWENTY-FOUR

Lo

El Abysmo grew by the second, greedily consuming everything it could. Vases, statues, chairs, and anything else unfortunate enough to find itself in its path. Mayté shrieked. Dominic toppled from his chair. Carlos clung to the table for dear life—was it anchored to the floor?

Nearby, the Banker simply shuffled his deck, casually catching a stray card before El Abysmo could steal it away.

There was something *almost* beautiful about the chaos. Bits of gold and jewels mixed with the flying debris. The winds violently tugged Lo's curls and skirts. El Abysmo would grow, she knew, until it had its sacrifice. One of them would die. She laughed. Perhaps it would be her!

Loretta stayed in her throne with that pathetic shopkeeper at her side, fanning her.

El Abysmo's inhale intensified. Lo fumbled around for something to cling to as her curls whipped her face. She lost her footing. She closed her eyes.

Death could be a relief.

Something yanked her arm, stopping her tumble toward El Abysmo. She watched in shock as several chairs disappeared into the gaping black.

Carlos had been the one to grab her. With a grunt, he pulled her against him. His other arm was wrapped tight around the sturdy-looking leg of a table.

Lo's eyes widened as she and Carlos looked at each other, the wind howling around them. "Why?" It was all she could get out. Why would he save her, after everything she'd done?

Carlos yelled over the noise, yet the rest of the world seemed to soften until all she could focus on was him. "If I won, I would have helped my family, restored Las Cinco . . . and convinced your father to allow me to marry you. You would never have had to depend on him again."

Their noses nearly touched. She could make out each of his eyelashes and the tiniest few freckles on his brown face.

He could have used his wish on anything. He could have asked for enough power and wealth to attract *any* woman. One who wasn't broken, like she was.

And yet—

His eyebrows furrowed. "Now I just want us to make it out of here. Alive."

Lo's fluttering heart slowed. What did *she* want? When this began, she could have confidently answered: she wanted Mamá. A way for her family to start anew.

Hours ago, she also could have answered: destroy Fortune's Kiss.

But now . . . now everything felt empty and dull. As if her soul were already claimed by this wretched place.

Carlos was kind, but as much as she cared about him, they could never be together. Maybe in another world. Another life. One where her mother never left and Señor Robles didn't destroy his family. But in this life, no. She hugged him tighter and buried her face in his chest. Her pounding heart was almost as loud as the howling winds.

Maybe they could have stayed like this forever, but El Abysmo had a different idea. The force grew even more powerful, pulling Carlos and Lo's feet off the floor. Carlos gritted his teeth as he struggled to hold on.

But what about Mayté?

There was something that Lo wanted: for her best friend to be safe. She frantically looked around. Wreckage flew through the air. The debris circled the black hole in the room's center.

Mayté and Dominic held on to a different table. Dominic coughed and coughed. His chest convulsed.

As Lo stared, he lost hold of the table—

And plummeted toward the spinning vortex.

TWENTY-FIVE

Mayté

Time slowed. One moment, Dominic was next to her, clinging to the table for dear life. The next, he was gone, sliding toward El Abysmo—its mouth ravenous and greedy, ready to swallow him whole.

"DOMINIC!" Mayté caught him by the arm. Her feet flew from under her, and the two plummeted toward the black hole. She barely managed to grab part of a curtain. It was enough to stop their momentum. She cried out. It felt like her arm would rip off at any moment, but she refused to let go. She couldn't. *Wouldn't.* A loud rip filled the air. The curtain's threads began to pop and unravel.

"Mayté." Dominic looked back at her. His bloodstained lips curved into a half smile.

Her blood ran cold.

"Remember me, Mayté." He shook free from her weak grip.

Mayté screamed, "No!" The force of El Abysmo dragged him into the black hole. As soon as it swallowed him, it vanished. She fell to the floor just as the curtain tore.

He was gone.

Mayté slammed her fist into the floor with a screaming sob.

Dominic.

Would the house never be satisfied? How much more horror did they have to endure?

Misterioso spoke, but she couldn't make out his words over the roar in her ears. She didn't want to.

She glanced at Carlos, who helped Lo back to the table.

Was it even possible to save them? Mayté didn't know anymore.

"Señorita." Antonio the shopkeeper knelt before her. "You must return to the table so the game can continue."

Mayté wanted to lash out at him, but she bit her tongue. It wasn't his fault. He was just another victim of this Dios forsaken place.

She stood on shaky legs. The gambling den was in shambles. Tables and chairs were strewn around the room, vases and statues cracked. But despite it all, the golden embellishments shone brighter than ever.

Carlos and Lo found seats at the table. Her brother looked miserable, cradling his head in hands, and Lo . . .

Lo looked calm. Bored, even.

"Do you remember all the times we would play Lotería with your abuela? We'd beg and beg Carlos to play with us. He never would." Lo sighed, her eyes never leaving Mayté. "I'm glad we finally got the chance."

She spoke so calmly. It made Mayté sick.

She slid into a seat between Lo and Carlos. What horror would await them next? She studied her board. Only a few more beans left. El Beso de la Fortuna would appear soon. Could they survive that long?

The Banker drew the next card. "El Espejo," he called out.

Loretta and Misterioso grinned, but the Banker's voice was devoid of any emotion. Like Lo's.

Mayté thought of Alejandro. He had told her this place hardened a person. Made it so they couldn't feel anything at all.

The card glowed and morphed into a full-length mirror. The reflection inside showed Lo, who smirked, pressing her palms against the inside of the glass.

"Lorena, El Espejo has chosen to challenge you," Misterioso said. "Let us see if you can best it."

Matching the smirk of her reflection, Lo stood and approached the mirror.

"You must face yourself, Lorena de León," the reflection purred. "Do you have what it takes?"

"Of course I do." Lorena stopped in front of the mirror.

"Very well," the reflection replied. "Everything here comes at a price. And yet you kept pushing your will onto the house."

"I know," Lo said, voice dull. "The price was more than worth it."

"Are you so certain?" Smirk growing, the reflection pressed both hands against the glass and leaned close. "You found your mother and gained the secrets of the house, yet you lost your dearest friend. Now nothing will ever be the same. She'll never love you again."

Mayté's chest tightened.

Lo turned to her, eyes wide, and for just a moment she looked like her old self. Mayté quickly looked away, her own heart pounding. Lo did destroy their friendship. It had begun crumbling when she used El Cotorro on her, but the final blow was when she plunged that dagger into Alejandro's heart. Everything the both of them shared: hardships, hopes, dreams, wishes, memories. All of that was dead.

"I'm not sorry," Lo whispered. "And I never will be. It was the only way to save her."

What?

"Lo!" Carlos jumped from his seat. "Watch out—"

Lo shrieked.

Mayté turned back just as the reflection reached through the glass. It pulled Lo inside the mirror and disappeared. The real Lo pounded against the glass. "Let me out!" But a moment later, she stopped. Placed her hands at her sides. Her face impassive. Mayté's breath caught in her throat. She had accepted her fate.

Mayté expected the mirror to vanish. Or glass shards to brutally cut into Lo, but she remained in place. Trapped. Would she stay that way for the rest of eternity?

She deserved it. Lo was a murderer. She claimed to have done this to save her, but how could Mayté believe that? She was a liar. She'd ripped out Mayté's heart and stabbed it just like she'd stabbed Alejandro.

Mayté scoffed. The mirror. In her head, she knew it was a fitting punishment.

But her heart . . . Her heart couldn't bear it.

Carlos pounded his fist against the table.

"What a shame," Misterioso sneered.

"Truly," Loretta agreed. "She had so much potential." Her eyes narrowed, becoming almost as sharp as her smile. "You must be relieved, Misterioso."

Misterioso sputtered. "That conniving girl wanted to bring down the house. I find solace that she is no longer a threat."

"A threat," Loretta mused. "What an interesting choice of words."

Lo sank to her knees inside the mirror, head down, her long curls obscuring her face like a curtain.

"And we continue," Loretta ordered, not the least bit bothered by her daughter's fate. "Only two players left."

Mayté blinked back tears as she stared at the mirror. The glass of Lo's prison was half-transparent, half-reflective. Through that reflection, she saw the Banker frowning, a conflicted look on his face, but he didn't falter for much longer. "El Ángelito." The card depicted an angel clad in white robes and surrounded by golden lights.

The brightness stung Mayté's eyes. She gasped at her reflection. The light formed a golden halo behind her head. Just like the paintings of Los Santos and the angels in the cathedrals.

"El Ángelito has chosen you, María Teresa," Misterioso announced. His mask didn't obscure the agitated twitch in his eyes. "You must choose to restore the life of one player the game has taken."

"R-restore?" Mayté choked. "What does that mean?"

Loretta looked bored. "The house keeps the souls of those who have perished playing the game . . . and those who will soon perish." She glanced toward her daughter. "You can undo that."

The house keeps . . . Mayté covered her mouth. Then that meant Alejandro, Dominic, and all the other innocents who died here didn't have the relief of joining Dios in the afterlife. They were trapped in this el infierno for the rest of eternity.

It wasn't fair.

It wasn't right.

"Wait. I could save . . . Alejandro!" She gasped. "Alejandro! I want to save him!" She slapped her shaking palms against the table.

"Oh." Loretta smiled.

Misterioso chuckled.

A sob lodged itself in Mayté's throat. "W-what . . . ?"

"I'm afraid I should have been clearer," Misterioso drawled. "Lorena killed Alejandro. Not the house. Not the game. He is ineligible for salvation."

"That's not fair!" Mayté replied.

"Ah, but as Gamemakers we can do anything we want. Fair or not." Loretta leaned back in her seat. "Such delicious entertainment!"

A tear rolled down Mayté's cheek. This had always been a sadistic game to them. She knew it, but it still shocked her how utterly evil these people were. She put her head on the table and wept.

A warm hand found her shoulder. "Mayté," Carlos whispered.

Yes. She had to act. There were others she could choose. Dominic, or Carmen, or . . .

"Mayté." Carlos turned his head toward the mirror, his gesture full of meaning.

Lo placed a palm against the glass. Her head bowed.

No. Lo was not one of those innocent people . . .

"Mayté," Loretta said. "Who will you choose?"

TWENTY-SIX

LO

From the moment Lo fell into El Espejo's trap, the thick darkness inside her lifted, leaving behind a sobering clarity. She knew Mayté. Maybe even better than she knew herself. And she saw it all over her face. Mayté didn't want to choose her . . .

And you know why, the tiniest of voices rasped in her ear.

The reflection in her glass prison shifted into images of Mayté. Mayté screaming. Mayté sobbing. Her face red with scarlet humiliation as she answered Lo's question during El Cotorro. Mayté hunched over Alejandro's dead body. Mayté devastated when she wasn't allowed to choose Alejandro to save.

Lo's stomach ached. She reached out toward the mirror again, hands shaky and desperate. "Mayté . . ."

Just outside the glass, Mayté placed her hand on top of Lo's. "La Sirena was right. My heart is broken. You broke it, Lorena."

Lo's own heart shattered into millions of pieces. "That wasn't . . . what I wanted."

Mayté pounded the glass. The thud reverberated through Lo's chest. "You should have trusted me! I would have saved us *all!*" She sobbed, pounding again.

Lo's eyes stung. "No," she croaked. "The house considered Alejandro's help cheating. It would have killed you both if you had gone through with it. But Alejandro's death was enough to appease the house. That's why I did it."

Mayté's face twisted, sending more tears down her cheeks. "How can I even trust your word? You kept *secrets* from me. You lied. Lied about just needing to make it to the final round to win."

"I didn't want you to lose hope. And the others lies were because I was scared. I didn't want to lose you. So I hid things. About my father, about myself. And you—never wanted to see them."

Mayté inched closer to the glass.

"I know you can't forgive me," Lo said. "And I understand if you won't, but please believe me when I say that I will *always* choose you over anyone else. Even if it makes you hate me, and even if you wouldn't do the same."

Mayté stared, suspicion and confusion competing in her expression.

Lo's voice broke and she wiped at her eyes before the tears could come. "*You* are the only one I love." She meant every single word. "I wish things hadn't happened this way. But I don't regret saving you. I never will. And it's okay if you don't pick me . . . I d-don't deserve it . . ."

Mayté's lips quivered. She cried out, a horrible, guttural sound Lo had never heard before. It was full of pain. Then silence. Silence for several agonizing moments.

"Let her go," Mayté told El Angelito, her voice soft.

"What?" Lo couldn't hold back her sob. "Mayté—"

"I choose Lo."

But nothing happened.

"I said *I choose Lo.*" Mayté turned toward Loretta, who simply smiled.

The Banker looked away.

"Then go free her," Misterioso taunted.

"But I—"

"I never said that El Angelito would do the rescuing, no, no," Misterioso mocked. "El Angelito gives you the choice of who to save. You have made your choice, now go save her."

Mayté turned to the mirror once again, with furrowed eyebrows.

Lo wiped her face. Something felt wrong. "Mayté, wait. You don't have to do this."

But Mayté ignored her and reached her hand through the glass.

All around her, the glass revealed her own reflection, reaching out to Mayté with a relieved smile. But Lo's own arms dangled weakly at her sides. "Mayté! No!"

Lo's reflection snatched Mayté's hand and yanked her through the mirror.

TWENTY-SEVEN

Mayté

Mayté fell on her hands and knees.

"Mayté!" Carlos slammed his fists against the mirror.

She and Lo sat, surrounded by reflective walls. They showed Mayté's face, eyes bloodshot, hair falling out of its braid, and crusted blood staining her nightgown. Then it flickered into a smirking Lo. But that wasn't the real Lo. No, the real Lo sat at her side, head down.

"Mayté . . . I'm so sorry . . ."

Misterioso put both hands on his hips. "El Angelito granted a chance for María Teresa to rescue anyone she wanted. Unfortunately"—he grinned widely—"it seems she has failed in her attempt."

No. Was it really all over? Mayté slowly stood and looked around. There had to be a way, but all she saw was her own reflection and gaping darkness.

Carlos sank down to his knees in front of the mirror.

Lo curled into herself. "I'm sorry. I'm sorry," she repeated.

A lump formed in Mayté's throat. If her plan with Alejandro truly had guaranteed her death, then Lo really had saved her. She had done that awful thing, knowing it would shatter their friendship into pieces. Knowing that she would suffer for it.

Mayté knelt next to Lo. She hugged her tight, and Lo crumpled into her chest. "If I'm going to lose, I'd rather it be with you than alone."

"I'm sorry," Lo whispered again.

Tears raced down Mayté's cheeks. "You can stop apologizing, because I forgive you."

"Miguel." Loretta's voice brought her back to the game. "We cannot delay this round."

With a frown, the Banker drew the next card and held it up for all to see. Unlike the others, it shimmered in the light as if dusted in starlight and diamonds. The card was mostly black, with golden sparkles in the center. "El Beso de la Fortuna."

·

TWENTY-EIGHT

Lo

Mayté gasped, and Lo's heart raced. This was the card that she had overheard Mayté and Alejandro discussing. The card that the winner needed.

And it was out there, while she and Mayté were still trapped behind the glass.

"Whoa!" Misterioso gasped, but it sounded rehearsed, as if he had done this spiel many times in the past. "El Beso de la Fortuna. The final card of the game. Whoever can claim it will win Fortune's Kiss!"

"I suppose this ending will be a bit anticlimactic, hmm?" Loretta mused. Her gaze flitted to Carlos, who still knelt before the mirror.

The card flew from Miguel's hand and floated to the other side of the room. It spun and winked under the spotlights before it landed near the elevator.

"Well, boy, it's all yours," Misterioso smugly said. "Go on. Claim your prize."

Carlos flashed an uncertain frown.

Mayté placed a hand on the glass. "Carlos—"

"Don't say it!" he snapped, face hardening. "You're still alive talking to me. I'm not winning without you, Mayté."

Behind him, the card glowed brighter as if demanding to be claimed.

The Banker slowly looked to the mirror. The strange expression on his face reminded Lo of when she had unknowingly willed Senora Montoya's death during the first round.

"What if..." Lo's hand found Mayté's. She lowered her voice so only Mayté could hear. "What if we tried one last time?"

Mayté glanced up at her, understanding in her eyes. "You mean, tried influencing the house?"

"Yes. What if we willed it to bring the card to us? No matter the cost, winning the game will undo it."

Mayté nodded with determination.

Bring us the card, Lo thought as she nibbled her bottom lip.

"If no one claims the card, then there will be no winner," Loretta warned. "You will all lose. You will stay here forever, or die!"

No! What if Loretta ended the game before the house brought them the card?

"Ha! Is that really something *you alone* can decide?" Mayté snapped.

Lo couldn't have been any prouder. Mayté was playing on the tension between Loretta and Mysterioso. Using that to buy more time. And it was working.

Misterioso's eyes darkned. He marched to Loretta's throne. "If we're ending the game without a winner, this is a choice we must both agree on."

The two began to argue.

Lo squeezed her eyes shut and prayed as hard as she could. There were legends of humans fervently praying until their sweat became blood. She imagined the desperate agony. *Please. Give us that card. Now!*

When she opened her eyes, the inside of the mirror had changed. Now it reflected the gaming den. The room was exactly the same, but the only people inside it were herself and Mayté.

"Mayté, look." Lo pointed behind them where the card now floated.

Mayté jumped to her feet. She rushed toward the card. Lo followed after her.

"What's your plan?" Lo asked.

Mayté didn't slow down. "I found a book that had records of all the winners and their wishes. There was one wish that kept repeating. Become a Gamemaker and gain limitless power. Your mother said Gamemakers can do anything. I'll wish to become one." Her eyes narrowed. "I'm going to use that power to free us, and destroy the house once and for all."

Lo's mind raced. The wall glowed, showing Loretta, Misterioso, Miguel, *and Mayté* writhing in agony as the house around them crumbled. Just like the house showed her Miguel and Misterioso's origins, it showed her the end results of her best friend's plan. "Mayté, no!" She grabbed her best friend's arm. "The Gamemakers are bound to the house. If you destroy it, you'll die!"

"I . . ." Mayté's eyebrows furrowed. "It's the only way. I'll release you and Carlos first then I can die." She snatched her arm free and ran for the card.

"No! Don't!" Lo raced after Mayté. The entire salon rumbled as a mountain of marigold petals and calaveras—some painted, and others rotting—rose from under the card. Mayté climbed up, but quickly sank into the petals.

Lo stepped onto a calavera and used others to climb ahead of Mayté. The house was on her side. Likely helping her out of self-preservation, but Lo could care less about the house or what it wanted.

No matter what, she refused to let the most important person in her life sacrifice herself.

TWENTY-NINE

Mayté

Mayté sank deeper into the marigold petals. She could barely keep her head above them. She spat out a mouthful and looked up toward the golden card above. Its glittering lights illuminated the nearby petals and calaveras.

No matter how much she struggled, the coveted card wasn't any closer. In fact, it felt as if she were sinking farther and farther away. An overwhelming musky scent washed over her. Decay and burning.

Nearby petals rustled as Lo's inky black form moved past her. Somehow, Lo was able to climb up the pile with ease. Not only would she ruin her chance to destroy this place, but—

If someone with a pure heart claims the card, something miraculous will happen. But if anyone else claims the card, it will further corrupt their heart.

Alejandro's words echoed through her mind. Lo had murdered two people. Despite her reasons, the fact remained. If she got ahold of the card, there would be no hope for her. She would never again go back to being the Lo that Mayté loved.

"Stop!" Mayté snatched Lo's ankle. "You can't go through with this! I won't let you!"

Lo struggled against her, shaking her leg. Mayté clung tighter, grabbing her other ankle with her other hand as well.

"If you grab the card, you'll be like this forever. This isn't you, Lo!"

The struggling slowed. "But you'll die!" Lo said.

"I'd rather die than let this continue! Lo, my *father* came to Fortune's Kiss. That's why I'm here in the first place. I can't keep letting this place destroy lives and dreams. Please!"

Lo stopped struggling. "Maybe this is the price for getting the card in here. There's no way for all of us to get out alive," she croaked.

"I know . . . but I'm okay with that. It's okay, Lo, I promise."

"No!" Lo snapped.

"Only someone with the power of a Gamemaker can get us out of this." Mayté's voice cracked as reality further sank in. "And I would rather die than stay here forever continuing this cursed cycle."

Lo made a strange face. "What if I told you didn't have to do that?" She held out her hand to Mayté.

"I wouldn't know how that would be possible." Yet despite everything, she took Lo's hand.

"It is. I promise."

As they climbed, she whispered her plan.

THIRTY

Lo

They reached the top of the pile. Together.

There was the card, bright, beautiful, and golden. From up here, the rest of the gambling salon looked small, unthreatening. As planned, Mayté snatched the card and held it up.

"I did it, Alejandro . . . ," she whispered.

An even brighter light shot out from the card. Glittering and miraculous, it washed over their glass prison, creating a spiderweb of cracks. Bigger and bigger, until it completely shattered and lit up the entire salon, It filled Lo with warmth and clarity. She still didn't regret killing Alejandro to save her best friend, but everything else leading up to that . . . it was a terrible mistake. Even though she had thought of herself in control, the house had given the darkness inside her full control. And now she was free thanks to the miracle of El Beso de la Fortuna. "Mayté . . ." She fell onto Mayté's lap. "Thank you."

Mayté held her. "Everything's going to be okay now."

The mountain of petals shrank as the two girls slid to the bottom. Carlos met them there, holding Mayté's Lotería board in one hand and a bean in the other. "Mayté, look."

Her board had every space filled except for the one of the middle squares which contained a picture of El Beso de la

Fortuna. With trembling fingers, she took the bean and placed it on the space. "Lotería!" she cried out.

Trumpets blared and golden confetti rained down from above.

"And we have a winner," Misterioso said in disbelief. "Congratulations, María Teresa! We will now grant your wish. What is it that you most desire? Fortune? Power?" His eyes cut to Lo. "Revenge?"

Mayté squeezed Lo's hand. She took a deep breath. "I wish for Lorena de León to replace Loretta de León as supreme Gamemaker for all time."

Loretta stiffened, and Misterioso's jaw went slack.

Lo flashed them a wicked smile. Her earlier dreams may have shattered . . .

Loretta wasn't the Mamá she knew.

But Sera and Sofia were free of her father, and they would have his fortune.

What good would it do if Lo returned?

Frankly, she didn't want to return. Not anymore.

Loretta's folded hands tightened. "Is that so? But would that not make you the same as me?" She tried to sound calm, but Lo had become quite good at reading people. It helped her perform. *Survive.* She could sense her mother's calm facade unraveling like the threads off a beautiful but cheaply made gown. "Do this, and you'll become exactly what you despise."

"I disagree," Lo said, truly at peace. "I understand now what drove you to this, but that doesn't excuse the terrible things you've allowed to take place. I won't use my pain to destroy the innocent." She nodded at Mayté, who grinned back at her.

Loretta stood. Her bronze face twisted with fury and panic. "You can't do this!"

"Actually. She can." Miguel walked over. He pulled off his tie, tossing it aside. "Mayté's wish is earned. That trumps all."

"I have told you my wish," Mayté said, voice firm. "Now make it come true."

Loretta stiffened, before dropping to her knees and writhing in pain. Orange lights raced from her chest and floated toward her daughter.

Lo closed her eyes as a powerful heat flowed through her veins. It felt good. *Felt right.* Now the world almost felt new. The house looked even more splendorous. Glittering dust wafted down sparkling under the candlelight. Marigold petals were sprinkled among the golden rubble. Lorena de León felt more alive than ever before. This was truly who she was, and where she belonged.

Loretta already looked more her age, an accordion of creases across her forehead. A few strands of shiny gray mingled with her curls like spider silk. Her nostrils flared and her face turned red. "What will become of me?"

Lo smiled. "Sera and Sofia need you, you'll remember how to love them."

There was a power in Lo's words as she spoke them. Simply saying it, she could feel a pulsating shift in the air. This was what Gamemakers were capable of. As Loretta said, they could do anything.

Loretta jolted, then blinked as if seeing the world for the first time. The warmth returned to her eyes, the warmth Lo had desperately craved for so long. "L-Lorena?" Even her voice regained that comforting softness Lo had yearned for.

Lo quickly turned away before she could change her mind about staying in the house.

"Lorena, I—"

"Miguel." Lo swallowed hard. "Escort Loretta out, please."

"Very well." With a nod, Miguel stepped out of sight. Lo didn't dare look back. She didn't do well with goodbyes.

Mamá would become the head of the de León family. And she would be her true self. Sera and Sofia would be okay.

"I'm not done," Lo declared. "As Gamemaker I decree that all the innocent souls in the house will be released to the afterlife. Every last one of them. Mayté will be free to leave with Carlos. She will receive a fortune *and* her dreams will come true. *Every last wish and desire.*"

It wasn't a part of the plan they had discussed. But now, as Gamemaker, she could do anything, and she would give her dearest friend in the world all of her dreams come true.

"L-Lo!" Mayté whirled around to face her, but before she could say more, the entire room rumbled. Hundreds of marigolds bloomed on the walls and ceiling. One by one, each flower opened, revealing golden orbs of light. The souls. They floated up. A dreamy, beautiful display. They fluttered around like butterflies, soon vanishing through the ceiling. One lingered around Mayté. She held out her hands to it, fingers trembling, and watched as it floated away. Her eyes glittered with tears.

Lo's own eyes stung, but she smiled. She only wished she could be there to witness Mayté's wishes coming true. Once again, everything was about to change. She turned away to pull herself together.

Mayté suddenly yelped.

"Lo!" Carlos gasped.

Lo's back slammed into the wall. Misterioso crushed her upper arms in a viselike grip.

"Let her go!" Carlos yelled.

"Don't move!" Misterioso grabbed Lo's neck. "I won't let you destroy everything I've worked for!"

She should have been terrified.

And yet . . .

She burst out laughing. "What are you doing? Have you for-gotten—" Her hand shot out, gripping the edge of his mask. "I know how to destroy you, Misterioso."

He gritted his teeth.

"What are you talking about?" Mayté's voice wavered.

"He's hiding his face and name from the house. From the moment he set foot in this place, the house wanted to destroy him."

"What? But why?" Mayté's asked.

When Lo thought back to it, she could picture every contes-tant who walked through the doors. Each of them was viewed as neutral in the eyes of the house. It wasn't until some of them let their emotions get the best of them or figured out the house's magic that things shifted.

Except for one group of people.

Miguel stepped forward. "I think I understand now. He is one of the suitors, isn't he," he said. "The house despises him, but he is trapped here. So, to survive, he hid in plain sight, like a festering wound pumping poison into the house itself."

"Hmm." Mayté rubbed her chin in thought. "No wonder you were always bent on keeping the rules. If the house sniffed out cheaters, it would have found the biggest one of all—you."

"We should get rid of him," Lo said.

Misterioso released her and backed away. "That's absurd. We can't allow a Gamemaker who will turn on the others."

"Why not?" Miguel grabbed him from behind. "I think some new management here would be quite"—he grunted when Mis-terioso tried to break free—"refreshing."

"As Gamemaker, it's my duty to keep the house's best inter-est at heart." Lo strode over to Misterioso. "And you're not it." She tore off his mask and tossed it aside. It landed with a loud clatter.

Shunk.

Lo didn't get much of a chance to take in Misterioso's face, because a blue spike jutted through his chest, impaling him. An alebrije. A cross between a porcupine and peacock with colorful spiked feathers now stained with blood stood proud. The life instantly left Misterioso's brown eyes, and his mouth jutted open.

Miguel released him, grumbling about another ruined suit as he dabbed at the spatters of blood on his lapel. Misterioso crumpled to the floor, and the creature dragged him away. Even though the original Gamemaker was long gone, the house hadn't forgotten her pain and rage.

Retribution. Maybe now this place could be at peace.

"How did Misterioso make his announcements to the entire house?" Lo asked Miguel, who in turn led her to a wooden phone box on the wall. In the center was a small clock and rotary dial. With a slick smile, he handed the receiver to her.

"Attention, everyone." Her voice rang throughout the house. She twirled the long cord with her finger. "As of now, you are free to terminate your employment." No use in having unwilling workers here. She hung up the receiver and sighed. Without any souls bound to the house, she could already feel the weakening magic. It would have to be rebuilt from scratch. Not to mention that she would need new employees. She caught Miguel staring.

"I think you'll be surprised to see quite a few stay," he said, leaning against the wall. "I'm sure many have nothing left to return to."

"And you?"

"I think I'll stay as well." He stuffed his hands in his pockets and pushed off the wall. "You see . . . you were right about Ana Lùcia."

Lo's eyes widened.

"I came here in hopes of rescuing her, but I was too late. She had already become a Gamemaker. She wasn't the woman I loved anymore."

Just like what happened with her mother . . .

"Like most Gamemakers, she lost herself and was killed." His gaze drifted off. "I had nothing left, I vowed to destroy the house. That's why I stayed here, waiting for the perfect opportunity. Loretta wanted me to keep tabs on you, but I soon realized you—"

"—wanted the same thing," Lo whispered. From the moment she had wanted to destroy the house, her dynamic with Miguel had shifted. *He knew.* "Well, now we finally have the chance to work together." She folded her arms. "Or do you still want to destroy the place?"

He shook his head. "I think the house will be much better off now, and what can I say? I've grown fond of you."

"Ohh? Have I finally seduced you?" Lo teased, even though she knew his feelings for her were platonic. It was mutual.

"I wouldn't go that far, cariño." He flashed a devilish smirk.

"I suppose I'll keep you around so long as you behave." Lo turned away only to see Mayté staring at her in shock.

"So, you . . . you're really staying?" Tears filled her best friend's eyes. "You don't have to—"

"I want to," Lo whispered, lest her voice betray her. She closed the gap between them and took Mayté's hands. Her fingers were cold. "And let's face it. I don't belong in Milagro, but here . . . I think I can make it work. I'm sorry I hid my true self from you, but this is who I am," Lo said. "And the fact that you work endlessly to see the good in people. The good in *me*," her voice cracked. "That's what I love about you, and no matter what, you'll always be my sister."

"S-same here, Lo." Mayté's mouth quivered. Seeing her like that made Lo's throat tighten. "I'll always love you."

"I hate myself for everything I've put you through," Lo said.

Mayté let out the tiniest of sobs, and Lo couldn't hold it back any longer.

"B-but wonderful things are awaiting you outside of here. I made sure of it. I know your life is going to be amazing." Tears soaked Lo's eyelashes. "As for me, I want to make this place a sanctuary for people like us with impossible wishes. A place that punishes the wicked and redeems the good." She turned to Carlos and fought to maintain her composure.

"I'm sure if you ask nicely, Mayté will share some of her fortune with you. That will make you an appealing bachelor. Find yourself a pretty girl from a good family to marry. Live happily ever after."

Carlos shook his head. "Lo . . ." He trailed off. He didn't have to say it.

"I know." It was bittersweet. Like biting into chocolates laced with potion. "But I belong here, and you belong in Milagro."

Carlos's eyebrows furrowed. He always made that face when trying to think of a solution. But there was no solution. Not this time.

"Come, now." Miguel motioned for them to follow him to the elevator. "It's time to say your farewells."

THIRTY-ONE

Mayté

Mayté, Lo, and Carlos stepped back into the entrance lobby. Where all of this had begun. That felt like an eternity ago. Mayté ran her hand over the carved alebrije on the wall. The same peacock that had killed Misterioso. "Good boy," she whispered. She and Carlos lugged around sacks filled with golden coins and precious gems. It was more than enough to last a lifetime.

"You're both free to go," Miguel told them.

Up ahead was the exit. Rays of light flitted through the cracks of the door. Milagro was out there. Mayté could have run, but she allowed herself one look back.

Her best friend stood next to the Banker, Miguel. Mayté held up her hand with the scar from their childhood pact.

With a soft smile, Lo held up her own scarred palm. Their blood was forever entwined. She whispered in Miguel's ear. He snapped his fingers, and, in a flash of amber lights and glitter, a book appeared in his hands. He handed it to Mayté. "Take this," Lo said. "Inside you'll find the contents of my soul. That way, you'll always have a part of me with you."

Mayté took the book and studied it. The cover was glittering gold with pearlescent flowers blooming. The pages were also trimmed gold. Now wasn't the time to look inside.

"Your soul book is here and I'll treasure it," Lo said. "And maybe, just maybe, we'll happen to glance at each other's books at the same time."

Carlos cleared his throat, holding back tears. Mayté hooked her arm under his and tugged him forward. "Come on. Let's go." They stepped outside into the most gorgeous sunrise she had ever seen. The kind that made her want to drop everything to capture it in a painting. It was a new day. A new life.

Milagro was almost exactly how they had left it. The trees were green and flourishing, and the warm air promised to grow hot and humid in a matter of hours. It was still summer. It had only been two days, even though it felt like they'd been inside Fortune's Kiss for much longer.

She nodded at Carlos's coin sack. There was more than enough to spare. "This should be enough to get rid of father's debts *and* to secure a new life for our family."

"Mayté . . . thank you." Carlos squeezed the bag tight as if it would up and fly away.

"Be gentle with father. We know now what he's been through, but that doesn't mean you should let him take advantage of you either." She wagged her finger in his face. "*You're* the head of this family, so you'd better start acting like it."

"All right. All right." Carlos headed down the street. It was a straight shot to their shack of a house, but Mayté didn't follow him. He turned back to her, a look of confusion on his brown face. "You're not—"

She shook her head. "I need some time . . . for myself."

"When . . ." Carlos frowned. "When will you be back?"

"I'm not sure," she admitted. "But not for a long while."

The two siblings stood for several moments in silence. Before Fortune's Kiss, this would have caused a big fight, but not this time. This time, Carlos came back and hugged her tight. "Do what you need to do. I'll miss you."

"I'll miss you too. Tell Ma and them not to worry. I'll be fine." This time she meant it.

Mayté's pulse drummed as she stepped out of the inn. A carriage awaited her. *Her.* How long had it been since she rode in a carriage on her own? She climbed inside and told the driver her desired destination.

"And what is the señorita's name?" The driver tipped his hat with a grin.

Mayté sat back in her seat, trying to let herself relax. Her body was still stiff, which wasn't a shock given all she had been through. "Mayté." She smiled. "Just Mayté."

"A lovely name." The driver flicked the reins and the horses began to trot. They were off. It didn't take long to leave Milagro's city limits. A small part of her was tempted to look back, but she resisted the urge. A wave of emotions washed over her, devastating and bittersweet. *But this was right.* Or at least it was the most right of all the wrongs.

She pulled Lo's book out of her bag. It had been two weeks since Mayté returned from Fortune's Kiss, and she hadn't had the courage to look inside until now.

With trembling fingers, she opened the beautiful golden book. The pages inside didn't reflect the same opulence as the outside. The brittle yellowing pages were filled with angry images. Blood. Bruises. Tears. Words scribbled and scrawled out of pain. It was disturbing, but Mayté wouldn't stop looking. She had to know everything about her best friend.

Interspaced between the macabre images were heartbreaking ones. Pictures that were clearly supposed to be of Lo and her mother, but Loretta's image had been torn away. Quivering lips. Little eyes wide with terror. Some pages were empty. They felt so lonely. It broke her heart.

"Oh, Lo . . . ," she whispered. It finally sank in. She'd never truly known her best friend like she'd thought she did. Yet she didn't love her any less. Mayté flipped through the pages until she landed on a picture of herself, Carlos, and Lo. The only joyous page in the book.

That's what I love about you, and no matter what, you'll always be my sister.

A wet drop stained the page. Mayté quickly wiped her eyes and dabbed the water with her rebozo.

She flipped to the end, where the pages were blank but tinged with gold and glitter. Her untold future at Fortune's Kiss. "Lo, thank you for everything. Please be happy too," she whispered. She could only pray that those pages would soon fill up with wondrous images of splendor.

The carriage stopped, and the driver opened the door for her. An older gentleman with warm eyes and a crisp suit helped her out.

"Mayté, welcome. The auction is beginning soon. Are you ready?"

"Yes." She closed the book then followed him through a crowd of eager faces.

The hot sun beat down on her, but she couldn't have been any more joyful.

The bidding began. She proudly admired the canvas. A portrait of Dominic crouched down, surrounded by his beloved dogs. She had started it as soon as she returned from Fortune's

Kiss and couldn't have been more pleased with how it turned out. It was leagues better than the original commission.

"Sold!" The auctioneer pounded his gavel. "To Don Sanchez for twenty thousand gold coins."

Mayté bit her lip to keep from squealing. She had been hoping that Don Sanchez would purchase this painting. He was known for his stunning art collection and was quite generous with showing off the artwork to others.

Now Dominic would be remembered forever.

Soon it was time to go. Mayté walked through the crowd of people. Many complimented her art and wished her well, kissing her cheek as she walked by.

"What will you work on next?" several people asked.

She had been waiting for such a question. "I want to take some time to study charcoal art. I've grown quite interested in it."

With a smile, she continued through the crowd.

"Excuse me, señorita?" a young man called to her.

She almost didn't stop. After all, if she paused to speak to every person, she would be here all day. But something about the voice slowed her steps.

"You said charcoal art?"

"Yes. Someone very dear to me was fond of that medium." She turned to the young man. The breath left her lungs.

A familiar face grinned at her. His hazel eyes were the most beautiful she had ever seen.

"A-Alejandro—"

Mayté pictured her dearest friend's knowing smile and her eyes aglow with mischief.

A Gamemaker, Lo had said, *can do anything.*

EPILOGUE

The group entered the lustrous salon and found themselves shrouded in darkness. It was nothing like they had imagined, but no one complained. How could they? They had finally made it to Fortune's Kiss.

"Welcome to El Beso de la Fortuna!" a honeyed voice boomed. "Fortune's Kiss."

A spotlight beamed, and a beautiful young woman sashayed out from the shadows. Orange marigolds bloomed in her brown curls. She wore a shimmering golden gown with a black top hat. A lacy black veil that looked more like a spider's web hung in front of her face, but it did nothing to obscure her beauty.

"Could she be a Gamemaker?" someone whispered. Legend had it that one of the Gamemakers was the most captivating young woman in all the land. People who claimed to come from the salon recounted their encounters with her. The stories were always the most exciting and incredibly tantalizing.

A young man stood at her side. While the beautiful girl glowed with an irresistible warmth, the man had an alluring coolness to him with his pale face, blue eyes, and crisp white suit. With a smile, smooth as velvet, he kissed her hand.

"Are they lovers?"

"I'm not sure."

"Listen closely," the beauty said. "In order to gamble, you have to wager. Your possessions, your dreams, maybe even your life. It's a big risk, but the reward is even grander." She threw out her hands in excitement. Her playful giggles sounded like tinkling bells. "You'll have to keep your wits about you if you want even a chance to win, but if you do, your deepest wish will be granted." She beckoned to the crowd. "This place is for those with impossible wishes, but beware, the house will bring your darkest secrets to light. Secrets you may not even be aware of. The wicked shall be punished while the deserving will be rewarded. Do you have a wish that's worth the risk?"

Some people squirmed, clearly uncomfortable at the prospect, while others were clearly intrigued.

Whispers floated around as people pointed at members of las grandes familias in the crowd. Another rumor raced around about the Montoya siblings, who suddenly and most tragically had lost their inheritance, being in the room.

"I'm not scared," one of the heirs to las grandes familias declared. A handsome young man who dressed the part of someone who didn't need the magic of Fortune's Kiss. Rumor had it that the young lady he intended to wed ran off and never returned. "I'll beat the game."

"You think so, señor?" The beauty's face lit up with amusement. Could she read his heart from where she stood?

Perhaps looks were deceiving and his intentions were noble.

Or maybe he would soon be in a world of pain.

The beauty twirled. Her gown billowed around, sending out a gust of wind and smoke. One by one, candles lit up, revealing a row of doors.

Her lips, bloodred, curved into a catlike grin. "Who's ready to gamble?"

ACKNOWLEDGMENTS

It is very surreal to be writing this. The journey to my first published novel has been very long. There were many times I thought I would never get to write acknowledgments for any book. When I first began the pursuit of this dream, I never realized how many people would have a hand in helping me. First and foremost, I thank God for putting all of these amazing people into my life.

Dhonielle Clayton, thank you for believing in my writing when it felt like no one else would. Thank you for trusting me with Mayté, Lo, and the world of Fortune's Kiss. Shelly Romero, you're a superstar, and I'm so grateful for the opportunity to develop this story together. Thank you for pushing me to be a better writer and helping me with my Spanish!

Debuting for the first time can be really scary, which is why I'm incredibly grateful for the rest of the team at Electric Postcard Entertainment, Inc. Clay Morrell, Carlyn Greenwald, Haneen Oriqat, and Eve Peña, I truly appreciate all of your encouragement. Thank you for guiding me through this journey. Thank you, Kristen Pettit, for your keen editorial eye. Thank you, Patrice Caldwell, for getting this story into the perfect hands, and another thank-you to Suzie Townsend and Joanna Volpe. I want to especially thank Trinica Sampson-Vera for answering my endless questions! A big thank-you to the Subrights/Foreign

Team: Sarah Gerton, Tracy Williams, and Keifer Ludwig, along with the Contracts Team: Joe Volpe and Gabrielle Benjamin.

Laura Schreiber, from the bottom of my heart, thank you for believing in this story and helping make it better than I could have ever imagined. It truly is an honor to debut with Union Square. Stefanie Chin, Grace House, Renee Yewdaev, Marcie Lawrence, Jenny Lu, Daniel Denning, and Chris Vaccari, thank you for your help in bringing Fortune's Kiss to life. A special thanks to my copyeditors Phil Gaskill and Diane João and proofreader Marinda Valenti. Jorge Mascarenhas, you did a perfect job at capturing the dark decadence of Fortune's Kiss in the cover. Thank you! A big thanks to Daniel Ryan Starke for the stellar author photos. Melissa Vera and Paola Mancera, thank you for your care and thoughtful comments in sensitivity reads.

A thank you to the agents who represented me at different stages of this journey. Veronica Park and Bethany Weaver, I am grateful for your encouragement and cheering me on behind the scenes.

Mom, Dad, and Mattie, thank you for all of your love and support over the years. Thank you for putting up with all my angst and drama that came with rejections and tight deadlines. Brad, I appreciate your enthusiasm and endless marketing wisdom. Grandma, thank you for giving me your Lotería set. I will treasure the memories of playing with you forever. I love you all so much.

Sami, you're both the Lo to my Mayté and the Mayté to my Lo. Thank you for being the best friend a girl could have and sticking by me even during the times I would disappear into my writing cave. Morgan, KK, and Emily, thank you for your friendship and encouragement. CJ, here's to more writing sessions!

Thanks to my coworkers for all of your interest and excitement for this book, a special shout-out to Cameron, Zach, and Deima. I wouldn't be here today if not for Bill Allegrezza. I'll forever be thankful I took your class. Thank you for being the coolest professor ever and reading through all of my cringey stories back in the early days. You saw potential that I would have never noticed otherwise.

Shout-outs to the gamers in the Smash Bros. and Splatoon Club both past and present. Thank you for cracking me up and making my days brighter. You all are dunktastic!

And lastly I have my fellow writers to thank. It would take many many pages to name everyone who has helped and encouraged me throughout this journey. To name a few, thank you Sandra Proudman, Gigi Griffis, Bethany Baptiste, Tatiana Schlote-Bonne, Esme Symes-Smith, and Isi Hendrix. I'm also so incredibly grateful for everyone in The Forge, Avengers of Colour 2020, 2024-ever, Query Warriors, and of course my agent sibs at Weaver Literary.

ABOUT
THE AUTHOR

Amber Clement is a dreamer, gamer, and office assistant. She lives in Northwest Indiana with two naughty cats and a Pomchi who loves to sploot. When she's not writing, she may be spotted exploring the city in search of new inspiration. Her favorite stories are full of glitter, determined girls, and captivating villains.